Garrett qu̲ [barcode] raised the
rifle to his sh̲ ̲ ̲ers slowly
kicked their h̲ [D1648243] ̲rds away,
getting closer.

"Throw up ̲ ̲ ̲ shouted.

They answered with their guns.

His Winchester kicked, and through the smoke he saw the
man in the sombrero bend over the saddle. He heard him say,
"I'm kilt, Billy, I'm kilt," and Garrett realized his mistake.

When the moon reappeared, the riders, all except one,
were gone, and he cursed the Kid's luck.

Praise for the novels
of Johnny D. Boggs

"Boggs is a master. Every page brings surprises; every chap-
ter crackles with action."
—Bruce H. Thorstad, Author of *Deadwood Dick and the Code of the West*

"An entertaining Western in the classic mold . . . with interesting stuff on the weaponry of the times."   —*Booklist*

"A rib-tickling story filled with traditional Western action."
—*Roundup*

"Action from the first page to the last. . . . The reader has to
decide which is the best: the action, the characters, or the set-
ting. This combination is so winning that to make a choice is
impossible. Just enjoy it all."   —*Rendezvous*

LAW OF THE LAND

A GUNS AND GAVEL NOVEL

JOHNNY D. BOGGS

A SIGNET BOOK

SIGNET
Published by New American Library, a division of
Penguin Group (USA) Inc., 375 Hudson Street,
New York, New York 10014, U.S.A.
Penguin Books Ltd, 80 Strand,
London WC2R 0RL, England
Penguin Books Australia Ltd, 250 Camberwell Road,
Camberwell, Victoria 3124, Australia
Penguin Books Canada Ltd, 10 Alcorn Avenue,
Toronto, Ontario, Canada M4V 3B2
Penguin Books (N.Z.) Ltd, Cnr Rosedale and Airborne Roads,
Albany, Auckland 1310, New Zealand

Penguin Books Ltd, Registered Offices:
80 Strand, London WC2R 0RL, England

First published by Signet, an imprint of New American Library,
a division of Penguin Group (USA) Inc.

First Printing, January 2004
10 9 8 7 6 5 4 3 2 1

For the Hogans—
Dennis, Lydia, and Alyvia

"There is no little enemy."
—Benjamin Franklin

Prologue

> *"The Kid now sought a companion bold enough to brave the danger before him, and found one in a young fellow who was known as Tom O'Keefe. He was about The Kid's age, with nerve for almost any adventure."*
>
> —Pat F. Garrett, *The Authentic Life of Billy, the Kid, the Noted Desperado of the Southwest,* 1882

September 16, 1877
La Mesilla, New Mexico Territory

She sang to her lover in Spanish, a haunting melody, the two of them sitting underneath a cottonwood tree, her long, raven black hair dancing in the breeze, his arms around her waist. Old Mesilla looked practically deserted on this Sunday afternoon, and the wind carried her soprano voice across the plaza. Although the singer was strikingly beautiful, the Kid found more interest in her song than in her copper face and aquiline nose. He stood beside the hitching post where he had tethered the gray mare, not really spying on the couple, just listening to her ballad.

"Wisht I could savvy what she was sayin'."

The molasses-slow drawl interrupted the Kid's concentration, and he found a pockmarked lad in a towering, black Texas-style hat and blue twill shirt trimmed with white piping standing behind the *cantina*'s batwing doors, a half-empty mug of more suds than beer in one hand. "She shore sounds perty," the talker went on, and the Kid turned back to the singer. As she began her chorus, he closed his eyes, and translated:

> *I went up El Pico Etéreo*
> *To see if I could catch sight*
> *Of her in the distance.*
> *Only the dust I saw,*
> *Only the dust I saw*
> *Of the man taking her away.*

By the time he finished, her song had ended, and she was leaning forward, kissing her lover. The Kid stepped onto the boardwalk, and the talker backed away from the saloon's doors to let him enter.

"You speak that Mex lingo perty good," the talker said, drained the beer, and offered his hand. "I'm Tom O'Keefe. Lemme stand you to a beer."

He took the proffered hand hesitantly, trying to think of an alias, but couldn't, so he introduced himself honestly: "I'm Henry Antrim, but most folks call me Kid." Although he did not want O'Keefe's company—he had stopped at Mesilla to get drunk, alone—he didn't want to insult the Texican's hospitality, maybe start a fight, and O'Keefe seemed affable, even reminded the Kid of himself, except for the pitted scars on his face and that god-awful twang. Both had wavy hair, blue eyes, and stood about five-foot-seven; thin as a cedar fence post, but as solid as one, too.

Each hooked a boot on the brass foot rail and leaned against the cherry bar, waiting for the dark-mustached bartender to fill two more mugs with draught beer. O'Keefe kept chatting away, even after the drinks arrived, and the Kid hefted the mug and sipped the lukewarm beverage, making a face he used to get when his mother forced him to drink milk. Having never gotten drunk before, he certainly didn't think he could consume enough of this bitter stuff to get the job done.

"It grows on you," O'Keefe said with a chuckle, wiping the foam off his fuzzy mustache. "Where you bound, Kid?"

He didn't know the answer to that. He had been wandering for an eternity, even before his mother died. Frowning at her memory, he took another sip. She had been dead three years to the day, which was why he had ridden to the nearest saloon. He made himself finish the beer, then motioned to the barkeep and said, *"Tequila, por favor."* He had seen enough soldiers and ne'er-do-wells waylaid by that liquor to know it would leave him roostered.

He was born William Henry McCarty, about eighteen years ago, and he never knew his father nor anything of New York City, where he entered the world. His first clear memories were of Indiana, playing war with Joe until his little brother started bawling about always having to play the Rebel, and be killed, while the Kid—he went by Billy back then—got to be the victorious Yankee, which would bring out their mother, a frail woman with a wicked cough, who'd scold her boys to find a better game than re-enacting what she called "the recent unpleasantness." He also remembered William H. Antrim, no matter how often he tried to block out the image of that slick-haired scoundrel who had started courting Ma when Henry was seven, even followed the family all the way to Wichita, Kansas, three years later.

That's when Ma started calling him Henry, saying it got too confusing having two William Henrys under her feet. "My name's Billy, damn it, so call him Henry!" he had snapped back, to his quick regret. Ma might have been frail, looked fifteen years older than forty, but consumption had not weakened her backhand.

When Antrim left for Denver to try his hand in the gold mines, the Kid was overjoyed, even though Ma's beau took young Joe with him. A few months later, Ma, her cough worsening, sold her place in Wichita and took the newly christened Henry to bustling Santa Fe, where he felt downright giddy. Why, he thought, ol' Antrim would never be able to find them in the massive New Mexico Territory. But he did: came down from Colorado, broke as usual, with Joe, and, to William Henry McCarty's bitter resentment, Ma was expecting him. They exchanged vows in the First Presbyterian Church and took off down the Rio Grande, newlyweds, first to Georgetown and soon thereafter to Silver City, to start a new life together. He hated it when Ma introduced him as Henry Antrim, not McCarty.

Antrim didn't spend much time with his new family—fine for young Henry—and Ma started taking in boarders and selling pies to pay the rent and keep her boys in clothes. Henry quickly grew to love Silver City, even when Antrim showed up dirty, busted, and drunk. Why Ma put up with that cad, he never understood, and he couldn't accept that she really believed his promises of striking the mother lode.

When Dr. Webster started teaching school around the first day of January, 1874, Henry liked it. He had always enjoyed reading and grew to love playacting even more. Dr. Webster told him he'd make a fine thespian, and Henry grew quite fond of the theatrical performances and all the attention the girls laid on him after a show. No one made fun of his protruding front teeth when he sang, danced, or recited Shakespeare or poetry on the Morrill's Opera House stage. He kissed his first girl behind the crumbling adobe schoolhouse on Main Street after one performance and enjoyed that, too. His mother never saw him act or sing, though, but promised she would as soon as she could get out of bed, beaming when she said how proud her oldest boy made her.

Ma died, however, and everything changed. Folks said she was just worn out, a scullery maid and a lunger to boot, spent most of her last four months confined to bed, that no-account husband of hers nowhere to be found. Antrim did show up for the funeral, settled Catherine McCarty Antrim's estate, and headed back to Chloride Flat, promising the boys he'd send for them when he struck it rich.

Good riddance, Henry thought, and go to hell.

He stopped going to school, just moped around that fall and winter, hanging around Grover Frederick's billiard hall with some older boys, including quick-with-a-smile Sombrero Jack, who started teaching Henry Spanish, mumblety-peg, poker, and how to roll a smoke, though Henry didn't like the taste tobacco left in his mouth. What he really liked was taking target practice on empty beer bottles at an abandoned adobe house on the south end of town. On the anniversary of his mother's death, Henry and a drunk Sombrero Jack stole clothes from the Chinese laundry run by Charley Sun and Sam Chung. The bandits laughed as they made off with their plunder, hiding shirts and trousers in Henry and Joe's room at Mrs. Brown's place, where Henry paid rent from his part-time work at the butcher shop. He didn't know what he would do with the bounty and couldn't find Sombrero Jack to ask him about it. A little more than a week later, the landlady discovered the clothes and told the county sheriff. Henry was arrested, handcuffed, and locked up in the Silver City jail, and the sheriff went after Sombrero Jack, who stole a horse and lit a shuck for the Arizona Territory.

Looking back on it now, with one beer and two shots of tequila dancing in his belly, the Kid realized he should have stayed in jail. By jingo, he wasn't even sixteen at the time, and Sheriff Harvey Whitehill probably had no intention of sending him to the territorial prison at Santa Fe for robbing a couple of Chinamen, more prank than felony. Yet spending the night in jail had scared him, so he'd slipped off the manacles—a trick he'd learned from Sombrero Jack, who also had large wrists but small hands—shimmied up the chimney and took the ankle express out of Silver City, walking to Arizona Territory, branding himself a criminal, stealing a horse now and then, and throwing a wide loop on some cattle, although he found occasional honest employment as a cowboy and teamster. He liked that country, especially the Mexican *bailes* around Camp Grant, and maybe he would have stayed there if burly blacksmith Windy Cahill hadn't riled him so.

Henry had just stepped out of Adkins' Dance Hall with a pretty little girl named Maria on his arm when Cahill walked up behind them, threw him headfirst onto the ground, then started groping Maria. Henry shot to his feet, pulled Cahill off Maria, and shoved him against the wall.

"What's the matter?" Cahill slurred his words. "You this whore's pimp?"

"You son of a bitch," Henry said, and the next thing he

knew he was on the ground again, only this time Cahill was straddling him, crushing the life out of him with his fat stomach and thighs, slapping him over and over . . . *laughing*.

Freeing his right arm, Henry found the old Navy Colt stuck in his waistband. Cahill's eyes widened when the hammer clicked. He released his hold and started to say something when Henry shot him in the stomach.

So Henry stole another horse and fled Arizona, riding back East, not knowing if the blacksmith had lived or died but guessing the latter since he had been gut-shot and cried "The Kid's kilt me! Gawd A'mighty, the Kid's kilt me certain!" as Henry galloped out of Camp Grant.

That had been in August. Now Kid Antrim figured he was a clothes stealer, escaped convict, horse thief, cattle rustler and, most likely, a murderer.

"I been thinkin' . . . ," Tom O'Keefe was saying.

They sat at a table, although the Kid couldn't remember leaving the bar. The bottle of tequila, with only three fingers left, and several empty mugs of beer littered the tabletop. Whenever the Kid closed his eyes, he felt dizzy. Yes sir, he had met his goal. He was roostered.

"What you been thinking?" Henry laughed at the sound of his voice.

"Ain't no jobs to be had in this part of the ter'tory," O'Keefe said. "So let's you an' me ride out to Lincoln County. Man, I hear tell that place is so big a fella can lose hisself forty or fifty times. We could get us some jobs punchin' cattle over by Seven Rivers or up north near Fort Stanton. Wouldn't that suit you right down to the ground, pal?"

He could work cattle, even his own, but losing himself forty or fifty times in the biggest county in America sounded even better.

"You'd want me to ride with you?" He sounded skeptical.

"Hell yeah," Tom O'Keefe said, slapping the Kid's shoulder so hard it hurt and splitting the remains of the tequila between them. "We're pals, ain't we?"

September 19, 1877
Guadalupe Mountains, New Mexico Territory

Actually, he did consider Tom O'Keefe a friend. A body couldn't help but like the young Texican, despite his ceaseless banter and out-of-tune singing of old Confederate songs, usually *The Bonnie Blue Flag.* They had stumbled out of the Mesilla saloon, throwing up much of the beer and tequila on the dusty plaza streets, and spent the night in a wagon yard in neighboring Las Cruces, then rode out for Lincoln County, crossing the Organ Mountains to Tularosa, where a slim Irishman named Pat Coghlan told them there were jobs to be found in the Pecos Valley. Coghlan warned the cowboys to take the longer route through the Hondo—Apaches were acting up again—but O'Keefe talked the Kid into trying the shortcut straight over the Guadalupes.

After making camp, O'Keefe carved up his bacon and dropped thick slices into the skillet. Although his mouth watered at the aroma, the Kid asked: "You reckon this is smart, Tom: a fire that big, frying up bacon like that? I mean, with Indians around?"

O'Keefe laughed. "I ain't seen no injuns, pard. The way I figger it, that Coghlan fella was a-lyin' to us, didn't want us to get to the Pecos Valley an' get them good jobs. My pa always tol' me, don't you never trust no Irishman. Damned mick." He looked up from the sizzling skillet. "Antrim ain't Irish, is it?"

He honestly didn't know, didn't care about that name anymore, but McCarty was an Irish name, and his mother talked with a thick brogue until the galloping consumption took her to glory. He started to say that when he realized . . . "Tom . . . O'Keefe's an Irish name."

"Like hell it is," his partner fired back. "O'Keefe is a Texas name, by gawd. I was born in Red River County, my pa was born in Red River County, an' his pa was born in Red River County." With a wink, he broke out into song:

> *We are a band of brothers,*
> *And native to the soil,*

Fighting for our liberty
With treasure, blood, and toil.
And when our rights were threatened,
The cry rose near and far,
Hurrah for the Bonnie Blue Flag
That bears a single star.

He stopped long enough to tell the Kid that even if Coghlan hadn't been lying, he felt safe in Apache country as long as he had a good friend and partner, then suggested the Kid climb down to the natural spring a couple hundred yards below to fill their canteens.

Once he reached the spring, the water looked inviting, so the Kid pulled off his boots and socks and soaked his feet after filling both canteens. Shaking his head as O'Keefe's chorus echoed across the mountains, he tried to remember when he had felt this happy. Probably not since singing and dancing with his classmates at the Silver City opera house. He had a friend in Tom O'Keefe and a new life to begin in Lincoln County. Above, on the ridge, O'Keefe kept singing:

Hurrah! Hurrah!
For Southern rights hurrah!
Hurrah for the Bonnie Blue Flag
That bears a single star.

The scream jerked the Kid's eyes open, and he stood in the pool, slipping on the wet rocks and landing with a splash, starting to shout out his partner's name but stopping himself. What he heard sounded like a catamount's cry, but a gunshot boomed from camp, another, another, echoes making the shots sound like a Civil War battle. He saw them at that moment, a dozen Apaches brandishing carbines, black hair and buckskins, colorful silk headbands. A horse screamed—the Kid's gray—and he grimaced. O'Keefe kept shouting, but the Kid couldn't move. He had no gun, just a pocketknife, his Navy Colt holstered by his bedroll, Winchester in the scabbard of his saddle. What chance did he have, charging up that ridge?

More gunshots cannonaded, and he started running, splashing out of the water, scurrying up the rocks—away from camp—and diving behind the skeletal, rust-colored remains of a piñon killed by pesky bark beetles. Some animal had started burrowing underneath the trunk, and the Kid turned into a badger himself, digging with his hands, sweating despite the chill of the gloaming, crawling into the pit as far as he could go, as if he were doing a shimmy-shake up a chimney. His brother always said he was part snake.

The Apaches could have found him, of course, killed him easily, but no one came that night, and shortly after dawn he backed out of his hole. Cautiously, he returned to the spring, finding his socks but not his boots, and neither canteen. He climbed up the ridge, slipping twice on loose rocks, cringing at the sound of the tumbling stones, half-expecting the noise to bring the Apaches back to finish him off.

He didn't find Tom O'Keefe, and only a trace of camp: ash from the fire and large red ants scurrying around the remains of bacon grease poured onto a stone. The horses were gone, his saddle, everything. *An Indian joke.* They left him out here alive, no food, no water, no weapon, not even boots to protect his feet from sharp stones and cactus spines.

The Kid summoned up enough courage to call out O'Keefe's name, but the only answer was the ghostly echo of his voice. His friend was dead by now, and he'd soon be joining him. He returned to the spring and drank his fill before walking up the trail over the mountains, *The Bonnie Blue Flag* blaring in his mind.

September 22, 1877
Seven Rivers, New Mexico Territory

When Ma'am Jones heard the racket out by the chicken coop, she figured it was one of her brood, likely the youngest—that boy had no sense—tormenting her good layers, so she removed her apron, stepped out of the kitchen, and picked up a solid piece of kindling. Cracked knuckles would learn that boy some manners.

Ma'am dropped the stick when she saw him, though, crossed herself and thought she was staring at a haunt. The apparition turned, just as startled as she was, and said something Ma'am couldn't understand. But she read his filthy, sunburned face and those sad blue eyes. Her motherly instincts—she and her man Heiskell had already sired ten kids—took over as she ran to the boy, scooping him into her arms as he stumbled. His eyes fluttered before rolling into the back of his head.

"Heiskell!" she screamed, running back to the house. "Heiskell, get some water to boilin'!"

She laid the boy on the kitchen table and unwrapped his swollen, bloody feet. His lips were blistered, bleeding, his face almost raw beneath the dirt, fingers caked with mud, dried blood, and grime. Ma'am dipped a rag into a wash basin her oldest daughter brought over and held it over the boy's mouth, squeezing gently as water trickled onto his lips. His mouth quivered, his swollen tongue went to work, and his eyes opened.

"He's got teeth like a beaver," said Heiskell, who had walked over while the water boiled.

"Hush up," Ma'am told her husband.

Her eyes misted over as the stranger focused on her. "How you feel, son?" she asked. When he didn't respond, Ma'am said, "I'm gonna wash your feet, then put you in a hot bath. You likely got sunstroke. How long you been out there?"

He shook his head, uncomprehending.

"That's all right, son," Ma'am said, scooping him into her arms again. "You just rest."

"What's that?" the Kid asked.

"Hot milk," Ma'am Jones told him.

He made a face. "I don't like milk."

She forced the glass into his hand. "Drink it. It's good

for you. Later, we'll try a little food, but you need to rest first."

When he just stared at the cup, she changed her tone: "You want me to hold your nose, pour it down your throat?"

The Kid drank the milk.

Two days later, the Kid could stand, wearing a pair of old boots that belonged to Ma'am and Heiskell's oldest boy, John. The Kid told them what had happened in the Guadalupes, although he omitted what he considered his cowardice by not running to help Tom O'Keefe, and thanked them for their kindness. He built his strength on rest and Ma'am Jones's cooking, and within a week started helping around the ranch, taking target practice with John Jones on evenings, finding a new friend and his old, confident self. He cracked jokes with the youngest, flirted with the oldest girl, even let John win one shooting match.

"Where you bound, son?" Ma'am Jones asked him over supper one night.

"Lincoln County," he said. "Was looking for ranch work maybe."

The woman frowned. "You're already in Lincoln County, only it ain't the safest place to be a cowboy." She looked up at him, waiting, and the Kid realized she wanted his name but was too polite to ask. He didn't want to use Henry Antrim—he had always hated that name—and Kid didn't seem to fit right now, either. He started to say McCarty, but Tom O'Keefe's melody banged through his memories again, and he answered: "My name's Bonney. William H. Bonney." He recalled his childhood, the years before Antrim, and added: "Folks call me Billy."

She nodded. "Well, Billy Bonney, my name's Barbara, and like I was sayin', times are hard in this county. John Chisum's full up, no jobs yonder, and he's got his hands full anyway what with rustlers tryin' to run roughshod over him and his brothers. You got that rapscallion Lawrence G. Murphy with an iron grip on the reservation and most of Lincoln, you got newcomers flockin' in here with blind ambition and no brains, and you got those banditti rustlin' cattle, burnin' homesteads, killin' and plunderin' . . ."

"Jessie Evans!" snapped Heiskell, filling his pipe with tobacco. "Damned scoundrel. An' Jimmy Dolan's worser than Murphy, mark my words, Ma'am."

John Jones nodded his agreement. "You can't get a job lessen you can shoot a gun."

"I can shoot," the Kid answered, and John winked. Sombrero Jack often told the Kid he was a natural, as good a pistoleer as he had ever seen, and the Kid figured he was a better rifle shot. John Jones could attest to both after their shooting matches.

"Well," Ma'am was saying, shaking her head, "if you was my youngun, I'd tell you to ride back from whence you came, boy. Lincoln County ain't nothin' but rotten these days."

He shook his head sadly. "I got nowheres to go, Ma'am."

"You can borrow my horse, Billy," John Jones blurted out. "Send her back when you get a job."

The next morning, Ma'am loaded the Kid down with a potato sack full of biscuits, ham, jerky, and airtights of tomatoes. He almost cried when he threw a stiff leg over the saddle on John Jones's bay mare and leaned forward to take Ma'am's hand in his own. He wished he could stay, but Ma'am and Heiskell had ten children to take care of, and they didn't need another mouth to feed.

"Can't thank y'all enough," he told her. "You been like family."

"You just take care of yourself, Billy," Ma'am said and hurried back into the kitchen, dabbing her eyes with an apron.

He thanked John next, for the loan of the horse, the boots, the target practice. John offered his Winchester, but the Kid shook his head, saying he would buy one at Lincoln.

"You'd do better buyin' a rifle and six-shooter somewhere other'n Lincoln!" Heiskell Jones shouted from the corral. "Murphy an' that scalawag Dolan'll rob you blind at their store!"

The Kid smiled at the old man's tirade, shook hands with John, and thanked him once again.

"We're pals," John told him, and the Kid tried not to think of Tom O'Keefe. "A body ain't much of a man if he don't look after his pals."

"Yeah," he said tiredly and kicked the mare into a walk, reining up when Heiskell Jones called his name. The Kid looked back at the hardscrabble ranch.

"I don't know if he's hirin', Billy," Heiskell said, "but if you get to Lincoln, you might ask for John Tunstall. He's new to these parts, a foreigner, but Dick Brewer speaks highly of him, an' he's got a ranch. Might find work there."

The Kid repeated the name. "John Tunstall. Thanks."

Part I

Part 1

Chapter 1

"The Hindu here drew a long sigh, as he said: 'The enemy of man is man, my brother.'"
—Lew Wallace, *Ben-Hur: A Tale of the Christ,* 1880

September 26, 1878
Las Vegas, New Mexico Territory

The last thing Ira Leonard remembered with any certainty from the night before was blowing the whore a kiss as he left her crib. He seemed to recall thinking about trying to buck the tiger at Doc Holliday's faro layout but opting for a bottle of forty-rod at the Bloated Coyote and staggering back to the one-story house he rented from Old Lady Valdez. He knew he had made it to the bed, and recollected a dream in which he had thrown up on his pillow. When he rolled over, trying to block out the pounding in his head, he realized *that* had not been a dream.

Muttering an oath, he retreated the other way and swung his legs over the bed. The pounding continued until he at last understood it wasn't his head—well, not *only* his head—but somebody beating the hell out of his front door. He stood, almost crashing onto the chest of drawers, and cursed a little louder, wondering what kind of fool would come knocking this early on a Sunday morning. Then he looked at the Regulator clock on the wall. One-thirty. And he remembered: *Today is Thursday.*

"I'm coming!" he shouted, and splashed water from the basin over his face, drying himself with a towel and combing the vomit from his hair. He had gone to bed with his clothes on, even his boots, but he changed shirts so he would look at least partially presentable, killed the last bit of rotgut he found in the bottle underneath his quilt, threw on a morning coat, and made for the front door.

The couple standing on the porch in front of him didn't quash his hangover, but they did startle him so much that Susan Wallace's face turned ashen, as if she thought Leonard was suffering another one of his asthma attacks, while her husband merely put a strong hand on Leonard's shoulder and said amiably, "We are no apparitions, Judge, just travelers paying a visit to a dear friend on our journey to Santa Fe."

Leonard recovered enough to say: "I'm no judge, Governor. Not in the territory."

"And I am no governor, Ira," Lew Wallace said, "until I am qualified and sworn in." A smile appeared between Wallace's thick mustache and beard. "It is bully good to see you."

He considered inviting them inside, thought better of it, and suggested they take a stroll to a café on the plaza. Lew Wallace agreed; he wanted to discuss affairs after his wife caught up on old times.

At forty-six, Ira Leonard felt ten years older, mainly because of the whiskey he drank, chasing it with petticoats and cigars. Born in Connecticut, he had been reared in Batavia, New York, and moved to Wisconsin, where he was admitted to the bar shortly before the War for the Suppression of the Rebellion. He had met Wallace during the hostilities, and the two men, although polar opposites, struck up a friendship. Both had practiced law before the war, yet Wallace's interest lay in politics, the gospel, his own writing career, and salvation for his fellow man. Ira Leonard loved the law but had no interest in politics, hated to write, and didn't know if he believed in God, although he figured he would learn soon enough if the Good Book was indeed the gospel; asthma was bound to kill him shortly.

He had been a judge in Jefferson City, Missouri, from 1870 to 1874 but could barely breathe in that humid, stifling town, and doctors had suggested he head west for his health.

He hung his shingle in Boulder, Colorado, for four years, but late in the spring he turned south to New Mexico Territory: drier, prettier, and so violent it had need of another lawyer.

President Rutherford B. Hayes had appointed Wallace territorial governor to replace the scandal-plagued, incompetent Sam Axtell, or at least that was the word going around Santa Fe, Las Vegas, and Cimarron. Lew Wallace's appearance at Leonard's front door confirmed that rumor, and he had even admitted that he would become the territory's leader as soon as he was sworn in. When Leonard had first read the article speculating that Axtell was being removed and replaced by "gallant Civil War hero Lewis Wallace" in the *Optic*, he had been astounded. He could picture Susan soaking up the culture, the Spanish, the Indians, the natural beauty . . . but not Lew Wallace. The last he had heard, Wallace had been on the lecture circuit after his novel, *The Fair God,* had been published in 1873.

"I read your book, General," Leonard said as they sipped coffee, calling Wallace by his rank during the late war.

"That makes three." Wallace winked at his wife.

"Balderdash. I found it a fine historical romance," he exaggerated if not outright lied, "so may I offer my belated congratulations?"

Wallace bowed, trying not to look pompous but failing. "I am working on a new one, Ira." Wallace could hardly contain himself. "For Harper and Brothers. My missionary tome, if you will. Perhaps it could even lead you, sir, to Jesus Christ and the Kingdom of God."

"I'll buy a copy as soon as it is published," Leonard said.

"Nonsense," Susan spoke. "We shall send you one."

Wallace cleared his throat, set his glass of water on the table, and checked his timepiece. "We have not much time, Ira, before we must be on our way to Santa Fe. I was wondering if I might impose on you." Susan patted Ira's hand and excused herself.

"By all means." Ira Leonard was a drunk, agnostic, and ne'er-do-well, but he was not without ambition or pride. He was a good lawyer, had been an excellent judge back in Missouri, and would like to be a judge in New Mexico. General

Wallace, his friend—and within days to become *Governor* Wallace—could help him reach that goal.

"I have inherited a cauldron," Wallace said. Leaning forward, he lowered his voice to a whisper. "I will not speak ill of my predecessor, but nor will I follow in his footsteps and be run out of the territory, shamed, listening to gossipmongers and liars. I had my fill of those after Pittsburg Landing. I still read accounts where they say I acted too slow. But we won the battle, and I was promoted to major general . . ." He sank back, exhaled, and shook his head. "I need an adviser, Ira. I know you have not been in the territory long, but could you give me your impressions of the situation in Colfax and Lincoln counties?"

Leonard was eager to help. "Axtell was a horse's ass, General, and the people up in Cimarron and E-Town loathed him. I think that situation can be repaired, sir, with a man of your persuasive power. There have been a number of murders; the people are scared, but I think once Axtell has left the territory, those people will settle down if you just show them some support, listen to them, and overturn that insane act Axtell railroaded through the legislature that transferred the judicial powers of Colfax to Taos County."

Wallace beamed and withdrew a silver-plated cigar case from his coat pocket. "You are on top of this matter, as I expected, Ira. Not bad for a man who has only been in the territory for a few months. I spent a night in Cimarron on our way down from Trinidad, met with the editor of the *News and Press,* Frank Springer, and with William Lee and other leaders of the county."

"You're on top of this matter, too, General," Leonard said and took a proffered cigar, allowing his friend to clip and light it.

As Leonard puffed on the cigar to get the tip glowing, Wallace asked: "What of Lincoln?"

Leonard removed the cigar. "That's a much harder rock, General," he replied, shaking his head, and began to explain the complicated situation as best he understood it.

Greed had ignited the Lincoln County War, and then a bunch of lawyers really muddied things up. Lawrence G.

Murphy had been running a ranch in the county and a store known as The House, charging exorbitant prices and, many said, engaging in extortion, embezzlement, and fraud. Then came John Tunstall, an Englishman seeking business ventures, who started not only a ranch, but also a store to compete against Murphy's, now run by another Irishman named James Dolan. Tunstall had been backed publicly by lawyer Alexander McSween and privately by cattle baron John Chisum.

Back in February, Lincoln County Sheriff William Brady had sent a posse to Tunstall's ranch to attach the Englishman's property in some frivolous lawsuit, and the so-called lawmen had met Tunstall on the road, killing him while he was resisting arrest, if you believed the official report, or murdering him in cold blood, if you believed the McSween faction. In retaliation, a bunch of Tunstall's cowboys and friends formed a group they called the "Regulators," with legal authority meted out by a justice of the peace, and went after Tunstall's murderers. Two deputies were arrested and, again, shot while trying to escape, if you believed the Regulators, or murdered in cold blood, if you sided with the Murphy-Dolan camp.

There was no denying the fact that on the first of April, Sheriff Brady and a deputy were murdered on the streets of Lincoln by the Regulators, who were led by a young cowboy called William H. Bonney, alias the Kid. The leader of the Regulators, an affable chap called Dick Brewer, was killed a few days later at Blazer's Mill on the Mescalero Reservation when the Regulators gunned down Murphy-Dolan man Buckshot Roberts. After that, there were other incidents, shootings, rumored murders, and attacks, until the matter reached its climax in July at the house of Alexander McSween in Lincoln.

After a five-day battle, the Murphy-Dolan scoundrels set the house on fire, shooting down as many men as they could when they raced out of the inferno. Among the dead was Alexander McSween. Among those who escaped was William H. Bonney.

"What was the army doing during all this time?" Wallace demanded.

"Watching," Leonard replied. "The commander at Fort Stanton is a Murphy man, or I should rather say, a Ring man."

"Ring?"

"The Santa Fe Ring, General. Businessmen and political leaders—Irish most of them, all false Republicans. Murphy was definitely one of them. You remember how you used to tell me, during the war, that the quartermaster corps and sutlers were the most corrupt and powerful force in the world?" When Wallace nodded, Leonard went on. "They can't hold a candle to the Ring."

"Who is the judge for that district?"

"Bristol. I don't recall his first name, but if he isn't part of the Ring, he's controlled by it."

A long silence filled the room, broken when Wallace sighed and asked: "So, how do we go about restoring civilization, law, and order to Lincoln County?"

Leonard felt his hangover returning. "I'm not sure we can, General."

September 28, 1878
South Spring River Ranch, New Mexico Territory

"Billy!"

Sallie Chisum felt, as her mother used to say, *her heart catch in her throat*. She hadn't seen Billy Bonney since he rode out with the Regulators in March, taking prisoners Bill Morton and Frank Baker to Lincoln to stand trial for the murder of Billy Bonney's boss—and her father's and uncles' good friend—John Tunstall. Morton and Baker never made it to Lincoln, at least, not alive. Neither her father nor Uncles Pitzer and John discussed the shooting, like they avoided the mention of Sheriff Brady's assassination or the killing of Buckshot Roberts, whenever Sallie was present. She didn't want to see Billy now, but here he came, smiling that smile that made girls overlook his squirrel teeth.

"Miss me, Sallie?" he asked, and she tightened her grip on the reins. She had gone for her morning ride, stopping on the creek to let the gelding drink while she leaned against a cottonwood, but she straightened, peering down the trail, worry etched in her face.

Billy Bonney stopped. "I won't hurt you, Sallie," he said.

She faced him again, saw his hurt, and shook her head, her long blond locks catching on the cottonwood bark and pulling tightly. "Ouch!" She brought a hand to the back of her head, telling Bonney that she wasn't worried he'd hurt her, but that one of the Jinglebob riders would hurt him. He stood in front of her then, lifted his own hand, and rubbed her head.

"That tree tried to scalp you, Sallie," he said, jovial again. "Must be an Apache cottonwood."

"Apaches don't scalp, Billy, and you know that. You shouldn't be here. Judge Bristol's got the sheriff looking for you, and so does Jimmy Dolan."

"What about your Uncle John?" He spoke through clenched teeth.

"You know him better than that, Billy."

"Thought I did, but he has done nothing but . . ." He shook his head, took her hand, and brought it toward him, turning her palm up and grinning again. Holding her hand in his own with his right, he reached with his left into his vest pocket and pulled out two candy hearts, which he dropped in her hand.

"Brought you a present," he said, and frowned in jest. "Providing you haven't been dancing with anyone else while I've been gone."

She couldn't help but smile. "No one dances better than you, Billy," she said, and let him steal a kiss, a short one, before pushing him away.

"Your Uncle John around here?" he asked.

Sallie shook her head. "He's in Las Vegas, meeting with lawyers. He's being sued again, his stock's being rustled, plus there's the whole . . ." She couldn't finish, and dropped her head.

"Yeah," she heard Bonney say.

She walked around him and let him help her into the sidesaddle. When she looked back down at him, she saw the boy who had charmed her so while working for John Tunstall, not the cold-blooded killer people said he had become.

"You should give yourself up, Billy," she told him.

He snorted. "Yeah, and get shot down like . . ."

"Morton and Baker?" Her face flushed; so did his.

"I was going to say John Tunstall, Sallie. He was my friend. He was real good to me. He didn't deserve to die like that."

"No one deserves it, Billy," she said. "Why did you come here?"

"To see my gal." The smile had returned.

"Right! You have girls all over Lincoln County, Billy. I'm not deaf, nor blind."

"But you're the only one I bring candy hearts to."

She reached for his hand. "Why did you come here?" she asked again.

"Business," he answered, and she shook her head again, felt a tear roll down one cheek. "Billy, the war's over. Mr. McSween's dead, Mr. Tunstall's dead, and so are Morton, Baker, and Sheriff Brady. You need to get out of the territory. Or maybe . . ." She paused, wet her lips, and looked back at him. "There's a new governor coming to Santa Fe, Billy. At least, that's what the papers say. They're kicking Axtell out. He might do something. He might understand before . . ."

He patted her leg. "I'm not going to die, Sallie. Not yet. You better ride back to the ranch before your pa gets worried. Don't fret over me, and tell your Uncle John that I'll be paying him a visit sometime soon. To settle our account."

She didn't know what he meant by that and didn't want to push him. She nudged the gelding into a walk, hearing Billy Bonney call out to her as she left the creek bed and picked up the trail to the Chisum ranch. *"Vaya con Dios!"*

September 29, 1878
Las Vegas, New Mexico Territory

When he heard Huston Chapman's voice just before he entered the stagecoach station, Ira Leonard cringed. He liked Chapman well enough, even considered him a friend, but that big, one-armed, self-righteous lawyer could be an insufferable son of a bitch when in one of his holier-than-thou moods, and from his tone, Chapman was sounding the bugles against injustice.

Leonard painted on his best smile and turned at the sound of Chapman's pounding footsteps, sticking out his right hand and hailing the lawyer while staring at the woman trying to keep up with Chapman.

A burly man in his early thirties with a well-groomed beard, penetrating gray eyes, and left coat sleeve pinned up just below the shoulder, Chapman had been in Las Vegas less than a month, entering a law partnership with a cad named Quinton after working a few years for the Atchison, Topeka & Santa Fe Railroad in Colorado and Kansas. In a matter of weeks, he had managed to offend most of the legal establishment in Northern New Mexico. Yet Leonard liked the man and envied Chapman's energy.

The woman commanded more of Leonard's attention. She looked tired, perhaps from trying to keep up with Chapman, with a round face, dark eyes, curly brown hair pulled into a tight bun, and thin lips that showed no intention of ever turning into a smile.

"Leonard," Chapman said while pumping his arm. "I've been looking all over town for you. Your office is closed, and the sign on the door said you wouldn't be back for a week."

"I'm bound for Santa Fe," Leonard said. He hadn't had much business in Las Vegas to speak of anyway.

"Damnation, I was hoping I could persuade you to handle a couple of affidavits while I'm gone."

"What about Quinton?" Remembering his manners, he tipped his hat, wishing Chapman would remember his and introduce the lady. The woman offered a barely perceptible nod in return.

Chapman rolled his eyes at the mention of his partner's name and thundered: "I'm off to Lincoln to see justice—"

"Lincoln?" Leonard was incredulous. No one went to Lincoln these days, not without an armed escort or thoughts of suicide.

"That's right, Leonard. This is my client, Susan McSween, and I plan on bringing that coward Colonel Dudley, that wretched James Dolan, and Jessie Evans and his gang to their knees . . ."

He was going on, bantering incessantly, but Leonard ignored him, removed his hat, and offered his hand to Susan McSween, who took it after overcoming her shock. "My sincere condolences, Mrs. McSween," he said, which shut up Chapman. "I only met your late husband in passing, but he seemed a fine man, passionate about his clients, and few men, lawyers in particular, had his sense of decency."

"Thank you," she said meekly and let him hold her hand just a tad longer than most ladies would call acceptable. Right then and there, he liked Susan McSween.

Chapman was at it again, railing against the Santa Fe Ring and the Murphy-Dolan cabal, the military, everyone involved in the Lincoln County War who had sided against McSween and Tunstall—who had murdered them, and many others—but he shut his trap when Leonard pulled on his hat and demanded, "Surely you're not taking this lady back to Lincoln after all she has been put through!"

The reply came from Susan McSween. "I am not scared, Mr. Leonard. What more can they do to me?"

They can plant you alongside your dead husband, he thought. They likely had no qualms over killing women. He held his tongue, though, and nodded his respect to the widow. Before Chapman could start up again, Leonard held out his hand.

"I'm not trying to tell you your business, Huston," he said, "but if I were you, I would stop in Santa Fe before continuing on to Lincoln. Just for a day or two. I'd be honored if you would accompany me to the capital." He smiled. "There's a man I would like Mrs. McSween to meet."

Chapter 2

"God damn that ring. It's the worst God damn outfit of them all."

—John Henry Tunstall

September 30, 1878
Santa Fe, New Mexico Territory

Samuel C. Parks, associate justice of the New Mexico Territory Supreme Court, shook Lew Wallace's hand after swearing him in as the new governor. The ceremonies had been quiet, just a handful of newspaper editors, dignitaries, and Wallace's friends, which seemed fitting considering Wallace's new home. For all he had heard about the end of the Santa Fe Trail, the bustling capital rich with history and culture, a touch of Europe in the far West, the town—he dared not call it a city—was unassuming. His wife found Santa Fe charming, but Wallace would have chosen another adjective. The fireplaces were too small, considering how cold it got at night, and the rooms of his so-called Palace were cramped, dusty, ill-lit. Centipedes dropped from the ceilings, the chiles poured over every meal scorched the roof of his mouth, and more than half the residents spoke Spanish or some Indian language, and little or no English. Back in Washington, D.C., Wallace had told President Hayes he would accept the governorship on the condition that he be offered a more suitable position soon.

He prayed that old Rutherford, good Republican and army veteran that he was, would not forget him in his hour of need.

Still, New Mexico had its positives. The territory was chock-full of mining properties, so if he made the right investment, he might leave the territory a wealthy man, or at least better his paltry two-thousand-four-hundred-dollar annual salary as governor, and quiet Santa Fe turned even quieter at night, almost a graveyard, so he could write without interruption and finish his novel-in-progress. He felt confident he could assuage the people, or at least the political leaders, of Colfax County.

Lincoln, however, troubled him.

Before his inauguration, he had listened to the widow of a Lincoln County counselor, a Mrs. McSween, relate the events of the past spring and summer. He found her to be one tough woman, with a formidable if irksome lawyer as her champion, and she shed nary a tear when recounting the siege that ended with her home burned to the ground and her husband and others killed.

"So many lives lost," he had said, shaking his head somberly.

"It would have been more if the Kid had not taken charge," she had replied. "He kept the Regulators together."

That had not been the first time he had heard of this Kid, alias William H. Bonney, alias Kid Antrim. He desired to learn more of this young ruffian, who was starting to remind Wallace of the fictional hero he had created, Judah Ben-Hur. Susan McSween and her attorney, Huston Chapman, blamed James Dolan for her husband's death, but as an old army general, Lew Wallace felt the commander of Fort Stanton, a blowhard named Nathan Dudley, should be held accountable. He made a mental note to try to have the colonel removed as soon as possible. He would discuss the matter at supper tonight with Ira Leonard.

As he stepped inside the Palace, a reporter asked him about the troubles down in Lincoln County.

"If peace and quiet are not restored in Lincoln County in the next sixty days," he said in a firm voice, "I will feel ashamed of myself."

Now he just had to figure out how he could live up to his boast.

October 15, 1878
Las Vegas, New Mexico Territory

The smart play, Ira Leonard knew, would be to fold. He held a pair of aces, but the betting around the table climbed rapidly, and he felt insecure. Tobacco smoke covered the room like a shroud, stung his eyes and made every breath difficult, yet he added to the fog by puffing on a cigar, washing down the smoke with Gilbert Muir whiskey.

Huston Chapman had suggested they drop in at Big Bill Bozeman's Gambling Parlor—commonly called BBB's—in town, and Leonard had been enough in his cups to agree, so here he sat playing five-card draw with Chapman, two Las Vegas merchants, cattle king John Simpson Chisum, and gambler Doc Holliday, dealing poker tonight instead of faro.

Chapman had tossed his cards onto the deadwood and kept hammering Chisum, who likewise folded, about the state of affairs in Lincoln County. No one else at the table seemed interested, although Leonard half-listened to the conversation; after all, he was Governor Wallace's legal adviser.

"It's a hundred and fifty to you, sir," Doc Holliday said in a pleasant Georgia accent. Leonard blinked. He had been focused on Chisum's rustling problems. He called the bet. *Hell, no one folds a pair of aces.*

"What about the Bonney boy?" Chapman asked Chisum. "Couldn't he help you?"

The cattle baron laughed while lighting his pipe. "Billy Bonney is my biggest problem, Mr. Chapman. I'd bet a thousand dollars he's rustling most of my stock."

Leonard focused on Chisum, a thin man with graying hair and a long handlebar mustache. The elements had weathered his face, aged him considerably, but he appeared to be in excellent health except for a nasty-looking boil on his neck. No, not a boil, but a growth of some kind. He stopped staring but listened intently. Governor Wallace had expressed an interest in learning all he could about William Bonney, and Chisum knew the lad.

"But I thought Bonney was on your side," Chapman said. "That's what Sue tells me."

So, Chapman was now on a first-name basis with his client. *Was this jealousy?* Leonard wondered. *Criminy, Mrs. McSween's husband is hardly even cold.*

"Bonney's on his own side," Chisum sang out in a Texas twang. "He likely hates me as much as he hates Jessie Evans and Jimmy Dolan. Blames me for his troubles."

"Why?"

"Because he's a kid. He has to blame someone. Anybody but himself."

Leonard looked at his cards. He had not improved his hand. Holliday opened for another hundred dollars, the two merchants folded, and the second gambler called and raised fifty. Another hundred and fifty to Leonard, who tossed in his hand with a sigh. A pair wouldn't win this hand, not with that kind of betting. Holliday raised another hundred, and the gambler called. After suppressing a cough, Holliday turned over a pair of queens. The other gambler shook his head and said, "All I had was jacks, Doc," and reached for his whiskey.

Leonard watched dumbly as Holliday raked in the mound of chips, silver, and greenbacks. He had folded the winning hand, a pair of aces to boot. A hell of a gambler he was.

"Gentlemen," Leonard said in a friendly voice, tossing the cigar stub into a spittoon. "You've practically busted me. I'm calling it a night."

He shook hands around the table and walked into the cool night, Huston Chapman and John Chisum right behind him. Chisum headed for a hotel on the plaza, while Chapman and Leonard walked toward Leonard's home.

"What do you feel like?" Chapman asked. The man had more energy than a mustang colt.

"Stomach bitters," he answered, and Chapman laughed heartily.

"I thought you and I were going to tree this town before I leave for Lincoln." Chapman checked his pocket watch. "It's only two-thirty, Leonard."

He felt an asthma attack coming on and wanted to get home soon. "You're really off to Lincoln again?" he asked.

"I am. I've waited almost a month for your friend the gov-

ernor to do something about the state of anarchy. He's as gutless as Axtell." Chapman had Lew Wallace all wrong, but
Leonard held his tongue and instead warned the counselor
about the dangers of Lincoln County.

"I can't prepare my case up here," Chapman said. "I've
sent word to Colonel Dudley, asking him to guarantee Sue's
safety. He won't act, of course, because the damned Ring
pulls his strings, but that's all right. I'll sue his worthless
hide, too. Sue needs to see justice carried out, and I'm the
man to do it." Chapman's voice softened. "I was hoping you
would come with me, Leonard. I'd make it worth your while.
Rob Widenmann's already collected a hundred pounds sterling from Tunstall's daddy in England, and Widenmann gave
the money—that's five hundred dollars, my friend—to Sue."

Leonard shook his head. He knew Robert Widenmann
only by reputation. One of Tunstall's friends, Widenmann
had managed an appointment as a deputy marshal and had
been one of the leaders of the Regulators after Tunstall was
murdered. Some people called Widenmann honest, others
said he was shadowy and a coward. Of course, every story in
Lincoln County had two widely opposite sides. That's why
he had been surprised to hear John Chisum call Bonney a cattle rustler. Chisum had always supported Susan McSween,
and she spoke of Bonney with high favor. Suddenly, Bonney
appeared to be making enemies on both sides of Lincoln
County's proverbial fence.

Chapman mentioned the money again, and Leonard
sighed. While Robert Widenmann likely had Susan Mc-
Sween's best interests at heart, Leonard could not say the
same about Huston Chapman.

"Is that why you're representing her, Huston? To take her
money? Or John Tunstall's daddy's?"

"I'm representing her because no one else in this whole
damned territory has the guts to do it. I know you do not
show yellow. Come with me."

"You have a partner, Huston. Why are you always asking
me to assist you?"

"Because you, sir, are a friend. Quinton is no honey-
cooler. You'd watch my back, and, hell, Sue McSween's a

handsome woman, and I think she fancies you." He shot a glance down the boardwalk, grinning, and lowered his voice. "After all, you got her in to see the governor, and I hear that chastity and faithfulness aren't her strongest suits. Some say she and Chisum went at it whenever her late husband wasn't around, and she'd let Widenmann and some of those Regulators dip their wicks when Chisum wasn't there. I doubt if she even charges, unlike those Mexican doves you fancy."

Leonard stopped, gripped a wooden column for support, and caught his breath. Chapman was the horse's ass, talking about a lady like that, repeating childish gossip behind her back. He felt like punching him, but couldn't. He could barely stand, and Chapman was so drunk he didn't notice. Just kept on talking, making his case.

"You heard Chisum. Sue's got no one. I can bring suits against Dudley, Dolan, even Murphy, if he hasn't kicked the bucket by then. By God, Leonard, I'll bring the entire Santa Fe Ring down. I'll expose Judge Bristol, everyone. Justice will be served. We'll be heroes. This will make you a judge, I guarantee it. Come with me."

What he wanted to say was that Huston Chapman couldn't guarantee anything but a bullet in his head. He didn't need another attorney to help him in Lincoln County; he needed a battalion of mercenaries. Chapman finally fell silent and began rolling a cigarette with his one hand, still unaware of Leonard's breathing difficulties. His lungs started working again, but he felt weak.

"What'll it be?" Chapman asked after sticking the cigarette in his mouth and striking a match on a hitching rail.

"I'm not going with you, Huston," Leonard said and hurried home. Behind him, Chapman bellowed:

"Then I'll go it alone, damn you! I don't need anyone."

October 21, 1878
Santa Fe, New Mexico Territory

Thomas B. Catron scooped up a handful of wet dirt, dropped the clods on the coffin, crossed himself, and thanked the

priest for the fine eulogy he had delivered at the funeral of
Lawrence G. Murphy. A Masonic symbol had been engraved
on Murphy's casket, and most of the Montezuma and Par-
adise lodges had attended the funeral despite the persistent
cold drizzle, rare for Santa Fe. The Montezuma lodge announced that it would be in mourning for thirty days in
recognition of the fine Mason's passing.

Catron—Confederate veteran, Mason, and controlling
partner of the First National Bank of Santa Fe, who had just
tendered his resignation as United States attorney—walked
to a crowd of mourners huddling underneath a pine. William
Rynerson, attorney for the Third Judicial District and the
tallest man Catron had ever known, was the first to offer his
hand.

"I just got to town yesterday," Rynerson said. "I'm sorry
to hear about Major Murphy."

"Don't be. I visited him a month ago. If our Lord were
merciful, he would have been dead then."

"Carcinoma," Jimmy Dolan said. "Hell, I didn't even recognize him when I saw him two weeks ago."

A younger man Catron didn't know, but who appeared to
be on a friendly basis with Rynerson, started to say something, but Catron silenced him by lifting his head. Others in
the crowd he didn't trust, didn't know, and damned if he
would stand around in the rain, maybe catch his death, when
he could be warm and dry. He coughed slightly, turned back
to Rynerson, and flashed the Masonic distress signal. Rynerson gave a slight nod—he would know to meet him at the
New Era Chop House and Restaurant—and Catron headed
for his surrey, where his driver stood waiting.

When they had finished the plates of oysters and two
glasses each of Jameson, Catron withdrew from his grip a
folded copy of the *Santa Fe Weekly New Mexican* and began
reading: "The democratic press continues to howl about the
'Santa Fe ring.' The same words are a favorite phrase with
the democratic candidate and campaign orators, and all alike
howl and shout ring, ring, ring." He let the snickers die
down and cast a complimentary nod at newspapermen

William Manderfield and Thomas Tucker before resuming his recital.

"So far, no facts, no evidence, no information has been furnished. Now we say that the people cannot fail to regard the talk about a Santa Fe ring, and the charges against it, as false and invented only to mislead and deceive. And those who charge the existence of such a combination must necessarily be regarded as liars and slanderers. Now, Democrats, put up or shut up. Furnish some facts, some evidence to justify it, or stop your ridiculous cry of ring and your senseless and unfounded assertions that a ring exists at Santa Fe which is in any manner unfriendly to the interests of the people. If you cannot get up any better material for campaign uses than a howl about an imaginary ring, you will be regarded by the people as being very feebleminded, as well as exceedingly malicious and mendacious."

He soothed his dry throat with whiskey and faced Manderfield: "Your hand, sir?"

"Actually," the journalist replied, "it was Thomas's."

"My compliments to you both."

"So what is it that troubles you?" Rynerson asked. He didn't take the secret distress signal lightly. Nor did Catron.

"Gentlemen," he told the newspapermen, "if you will excuse us . . ." He liked Manderfield and Tucker. After all, they gave him good press. But they were journalists, and as such could not be trusted completely. They bowed graciously, thanked him for the meal and drinks, and left.

Rynerson had introduced his much shorter friend as attorney Simon Newcomb, an aspiring Mason and lawyer, a man who could go far with the proper guidance and the Ring's backing. If long, tall Rynerson vouched for him, that was good enough for Catron. The remaining men at the table he had known for years: John D. Bail, another lawyer from the southern part of the territory; Jimmy Dolan, Murphy's right-hand man; and John Henry Riley, Murphy's former business associate. These were friends and colleagues, men he valued, albeit to various degrees. He lowered his voice.

"Where's Jessie Evans?" Catron asked Dolan.

"I don't keep track of him."

"You should."

Thirty years old, if that, Dolan owed the late Lawrence G. Murphy everything. Both had been born in Ireland, their brogues thicker than adobe walls, and both could drink a drunkard into oblivion. Murphy had taken Dolan under his wing at his store in Lincoln, and the boy worked his way up from hired help to partner and, now, owner. Dolan was ruthless, ten times harsher than Murphy, but Dolan lacked Murphy's tact and tempered diplomacy. Men like Dolan, like Jessie Evans, came in handy at times, but if not held on a tight rein could bring scandal and ruin.

"Our new governor may be a Republican, but he is not our friend," Catron continued, "and he would like to rid the territory of our friends."

"Jessie Evans is not a friend, Thomas," Rynerson said sharply.

"But he is handy." Catron never lifted his eyes off Dolan, who couldn't hold the attorney's stare.

"The last I heard, Jessie was in Texas, Mr. Catron," Dolan said, his voice more respectful now. "Around Fort Davis, his old stamping grounds."

"Can you get word to Jessie to keep quiet but stay handy? We might need his guns again."

Dolan nodded and started to say something else, but Riley interrupted him. "I thought we agreed to lay low—"

"A precautionary move, John," said Catron, who never took his eyes off Dolan. "That's all. Tell Jessie to keep his Colt in its holster. And, Dolan, you keep yours holstered, as well. The McSween woman has hired a lawyer—"

"A one-armed, loudmouthed piece of dung," Dolan shot out.

Catron glared. He didn't like being interrupted. Dolan mumbled an apology and stared at his empty glass.

"The lawyer is bedeviling the good colonel at Fort Stanton, and word is that this lawyer in Las Vegas . . ." Catron paused, trying to think of the man's name.

"Leonard," Riley said.

"Right. Leonard. He apparently has Governor Wallace's ear. They're old friends, from the late war. Damnyankees." A ripple of nervous laughter rounded the table. Catron smiled, pleased that they had enjoyed his joke.

"From what I hear, Wallace is more concerned with this book he's writing," Riley said, "than anything else."

"Lew Wallace is a politician, gentlemen," Catron said. "And he's not a friend of ours like Sam Axtell. Wallace needs Lincoln County to simmer down. Then he'll get another appointment from President Hayes and be out of our affairs. Until he is gone, however, we need to keep Lincoln County quiet. That's you, Mr. Dolan. No guns. No murders."

"What if the Kid shows back up?" Dolan asked petulantly.

"Then Mr. Rynerson and I, with help from Judge Bristol, will see that he hangs. But the Kid isn't coming back, because he knows he's dead if he does." He scanned the table, meeting everyone's eyes, nodding as he spoke. "Gentlemen, the Lincoln County War almost ruined us all. It probably sent Major Murphy to his grave, but I will not be brought down by scandal. I backed Murphy, and I backed you, Riley, and I will continue to back you, Dolan. There is a fortune to be made, a fortune for all of us. Tunstall is dead. McSween is dead. Most of the Regulators have fled the territory. We won. Let us not lose everything now." He stared again at Dolan. "No gunplay. Let Mrs. McSween and her lawyer stew until they get tired. Let the new governor think his mere presence has brought tranquility to our territory. Don't piss on me, gentlemen."

He refilled the glasses with the last of the Jameson, and lifted his in toast. "To Lawrence G. Murphy. Here's hoping he was in heaven thirty minutes before the devil knew he was dead."

Chapter 3

*"The thanks of the people of New Mexico are due
Governor Wallace for the firm stand and the effective
measures taken by him in this matter, his action
being worth thousands of dollars to the people at
large in quelling the lawlessness that so lately
existed in Lincoln County. Peace is ours again, and
Governor Wallace has cause to congratulate himself
for having brought it about within sixty days as he
said he hoped to do when he first came to New
Mexico."*

—*Rocky Mountain Sentinel*, November 14, 1878

November 13, 1878
Santa Fe, New Mexico Territory

For the information of the people of the United
States, and of the citizens of the Territory of New Mexico in especial, the undersigned announces that the disorders lately prevalent in Lincoln County in said
Territory have been happily brought to an end. Persons
having business and property interests therein and who
are themselves peaceably disposed may go to and from
the County without hindrance or molestation. Individ-
uals resident there but who have been driven away, or
who from choice sought safety elsewhere, are invited
to return, under assurance that ample measures have
been taken and are now and will be continued in force
to make them secure in person and property. And that

the people of Lincoln County may be helped more
speedily to the management of their civil affairs, as
contemplated by law, and to induce them to lay aside
forever the divisions and feuds which, by national no-
toriety, have been so prejudicial to their locality and
the whole Territory, the undersigned, by virtue of authority in him vested, further proclaims a general pardon for misdemeanors and offenses committed in the
said County of Lincoln against the laws of the said Territory in connection with the aforesaid disorders, between the first day of February, 1878, and the date of
this proclamation.

And it is expressly understood that the foregoing
pardon is upon the conditions and limitations following:

It shall not apply except to officers of the United
States Army stationed in the said County during the
said disorders, and to persons who, at the time of the
commission of the offense or misdemeanor of which
they may be accused, were with good intent resident
citizens of the said Territory, and who shall have here-
after kept the peace and conducted themselves in all re-
spects as becomes good citizens.

Neither shall it be pleaded by any person in bar of
conviction under indictment now found and returned
for any such crimes or misdemeanors, nor operate the
release of any party undergoing pains and penalties
consequent upon sentence heretofore had for any
crime or misdemeanor.

Lew Wallace

Governor, Territory of New Mexico

"I'm having this printed in Spanish and English in the
Sentinel tomorrow, along with the *Independent, New Mexican,* and other papers in the territory," Governor Wallace
said. "Any feedback now will be most kindly received."

Thomas Catron kept his rage in check and slid the paper
across the governor's desk. He had not read all of the proclamation, just enough to make him grind his teeth, and now he

waited for William Rynerson, Ira Leonard, and Justice Parks to finish placating that vainglorious dullard. Catron had been invited because, until his replacement, Sidney Barnes, arrived, he was still the U.S. attorney for the territory.

"There has been no violence to speak of in Lincoln County since I took office," Wallace went on, as if his mere presence had silenced the six-shooters down south. "I find this measure not only acceptable, but needed to keep the peace. Are there any objections, gentlemen? Any questions?"

"Amnesty?" William Rynerson asked incredulously. Lincoln County fell in the prosecuting attorney's district, which was why he had been invited to witness Wallace's pruning and prattling. A fifty-year-old Kentuckian with a long, scruffy beard and dead blue eyes, Rynerson had first arrived in New Mexico during the Rebellion, when he had marched with the California Column. He wasn't a bad sort for a Yankee, but he sported a mean temper, and Catron wondered if that six-foot-nine giant would shoot the pompous jackass. It wouldn't be the first time for Rynerson. Back in '67, Rynerson had shot the territory's chief justice dead in the lobby of the Exchange Hotel because the dunce had insulted Rynerson's reputation. Claiming self-defense, Rynerson had been acquitted of the murder charge the following March.

"What this says, Your Excellency," Rynerson continued, his voice laced with sarcasm, "if I read it correctly, is that those murdering sons of whores that cut down deputies Morton and Baker get off scot-free. We should indict the whole damned lot of those Regulators and hang them from the nearest tree."

When Wallace leaned forward in his chair, his eyes blazed with anger, which surprised Catron. He had never seen the governor show any emotion. "What this also says, sir, is that the posse that killed John Henry Tunstall is also eligible for amnesty, within the conditions I have prescribed. That means those who have not already been indicted for any foul crime. And if you ever speak with disrespect in this office, sir, I will personally see that you rue the rest of your life. You do not have to respect me, Mr. Rynerson, but you will respect my office."

What surprised Catron even more was that Rynerson mumbled an apology and sank back in his chair.

"Sheriff Brady and Deputy Sheriff Hindman were not killed by a legal posse, Governor," Catron said, with plenty of respect, although he had none for Wallace.

"And thus does not meet the conditions I have set forth."

Catron nodded. At least Wallace hadn't freed the Kid . . . yet.

Justice Parks recrossed his legs, cleared his throat, and adjusted his spectacles. "I don't know, Lewis," he said softly. "One reason Lincoln County has been quiet of late might be that these border ruffians, Jessie Evans and his banditti, the Kid and his gang, most of those men have fled the territory. Aren't you inviting them back with this amnesty?"

"I think not, Samuel," Wallace replied. "As I told Mr. Catron, amnesty does not include William H. Bonney, because of his indictment against Sheriff Brady, or this Jessie Evans character, because of the myriad charges against him. What I pray this proclamation does is give the good citizens of that county hope, allows them to return to peaceable pursuits with confidence in the law, and because of my stipulations of conditions, it shall not entice men like Bonney and Evans to return. Anything else, gentlemen?"

No one spoke, and Wallace congratulated himself by handing out cigars before Rynerson, Justice Parks, and Catron left the office. Parks headed for the courthouse, while Catron invited Rynerson to the New Era for a drink. Ira Leonard stayed behind with Wallace. "Likely to wipe the governor's arse," Catron told Rynerson as they crossed the plaza.

"I got a letter yesterday from Huston Chapman," Leonard said after the servant closed the door.

"As did I." Wallace lit his cigar.

"He says Lincoln is still a hell town," Leonard said.

"I have no doubt. One of these days, I shall have to visit Lincoln myself. You will accompany me when the time comes, I pray?"

Leonard sucked on his cigar. He had turned down Chapman's request to travel to Lincoln, but he knew he could not say no to Lew Wallace. He didn't answer the question, though, merely put on a smile, then withdrew his cigar and pointed to a line in Wallace's amnesty proclamation. "This 'It shall not apply except to officers of the United States Army' and so forth . . . Why bring the army into the matter, sir?"

"You do not think it will placate Colonel Dudley, Ira?"

"With all due respect, Governor, I think it will touch him off."

Wallace answered with a gleam in his eye, and Leonard shook his head. He had underestimated his friend.

"Two things I want, Ira," Wallace said at last. "I want Nathan Dudley cashiered. He did not just watch those cut-throats murder Mrs. McSween's husband and burn her house to ashes: He had a cannon pointed at that house. Huston Chapman wants to indict our good colonel for arson, and I am behind him. Chapman is a good man. Dudley is a disgrace to the uniform you and I wore to put down the South's insurrection. That I will not abide."

"And the second thing?"

"The Santa Fe Ring. I want it exposed and broken. Now, if you will excuse me, Ira, I must get back to my manuscript."

Leonard bowed slightly, found his hat and coat, and headed for the door. He wanted to believe Wallace's quest for justice, needed to believe in something besides whores and Taos lightning. He liked the amnesty proclamation but had to side with Justice Parks on one point. Despite Wallace's conditions, the pardon could blow up in the governor's face. As he put his hand on the doorknob, he turned around and said, "Governor, I fear Justice Parks might be right. A lot of those men, the Kid especially, have nothing to lose. They could ride back to Lincoln in hopes that you'll pardon them, too."

The governor answered with another gleam and wry grin.

November 23, 1878
Tascosa, Texas

The worst thing about the Texas Panhandle, the Kid thought, had to be the country's utter lack of trees. The wind swept down from Wyoming, maybe even Montana or Canada, and by the time it hit Tascosa, with not a thing to block its path for a thousand miles, maybe, it slammed into a man like a poleaxe. A blue norther was blowing in, dropping the temperature thirty degrees in a matter of hours, and sleet would soon carpet the ground. He pulled his dark sugarloaf sombrero tighter as he waited outside the corral, wondering if that wool-headed butcher would make an offer for his cattle before his lips froze.

"What happened to these beeves' ears?" the butcher shouted over the howling wind.

The ears were jinglebobs, Mr. By-God-John S. Chisum's idea of identifying his cattle. A good rustler with a running iron could alter Chisum's Long Rail brand, so the self-proclaimed King of the Pecos had his cowboys notch his cattle's ears. The butcher had to know this—he had bought stolen livestock before, from the Kid even—so the Kid made himself smile, though the very act hurt his crackling lips, and quipped: "Every damned one of 'em got caught in a Mc-Cormick's Reaper. I tell you, Sid, sodbusters are ruining the open range."

The butcher let out a horse-laugh and patted an old mossy horn's back as he walked out of the corral. "Come on, Sid!" the Kid shouted. "Before this wind notches my ears, and yours, and we all wind up looking like jinglebobs!"

The butcher laughed again, tossed the Kid a rawhide purse jingling with coin, and said he would draw up a bill of sale while they wet their whistles at Slick Slater's whiskey mill across the street.

Inside the saloon, the Kid found his partners—Tom O'Folliard, Doc Scurlock, Charlie Bowdre, and Jim French—playing poker with a tall drink of water in a green bib-front shirt, red print bandana, fancy stitched boots, and high-crown black hat. A Sharps rifle rested across the stranger's lap, not the most comfortable position for a heavy buffalo gun like that. The Kid pulled up a chair from the neighboring table and squeezed in between O'Folliard and Bowdre, tossing the pouch on the green felt and wrapping an arm around each man's neck.

"Payday, boys. Sid's making out the bill of sale." He pushed back his sombrero and stared at the tall fellow, grinned, and asked, "You mind if I join this game?"

"It would be a pleasure," the man drawled and held out his hand. "Name's Garrett. Pat Garrett."

"I'm Billy Bonney."

Sid Overstreet brought over the paper and a shot of rye, patting the Kid's back. After signing the bill of sale, the Kid slid his whiskey across the table to Garrett. "On me, pal. I'm not much of a whiskey drinker."

Garrett lifted the glass in salute and shot it down. "I am," he said pleasantly, and passed the cards he had shuffled to Scurlock for a cut.

Thirty-two hours later, the card game was over, the norther had blown through, and the Kid had busted Garrett, taking him for just about everything except that Sharps Big Fifty, his long-barreled Colt revolver, and those fancy boots. Garrett took his losses in stride and accepted the Kid's generosity of standing him to a whiskey and breakfast.

"You're mighty kind, Little Casino," Garrett said.

The Kid snickered and came back: "You're all right, too, Juan Largo." Garrett towered a good nine inches over the Kid.

Garrett killed his rye while the Kid sipped black coffee. The rest of the boys gathered at the bar and drank beer.

"Where you bound, Garrett?" asked Doc Scurlock, who, like Garrett, hailed from Alabama.

"New Mexico," Garrett answered. "Figured I'd try to land a job around Fort Sumner."

"Ain't no . . . no . . . b-buffler in Fort . . . Sumner . . . no more," stumbled Charlie Bowdre, nodding at Garrett's Sharps.

"Other ways to make a livin'," Garrett said.

"By jingo, Pat," the Kid said. "Charlie and I have plenty of friends in Fort Sumner. We'd be honored to ride with you, if you're of a mind. We were thinking about going on down to Lincoln."

Garrett nodded. "I'd enjoy the company. Maybe I could win some of my money back."

None of the Kid's friends could hide their shock, which is why they had not won at poker. "Let me talk things over with my pals, Pat. Give me a minute, and I'll meet you over at the café for breakfast."

"I t-t-th-thought we was . . . th-th-through rustlin', Billy," Charlie Bowdre said in his Mississippi stutter after Garrett left the saloon. "I . . . th-thought we weren't . . . goin' back t-t-to . . . New . . . Mexico."

A prematurely balding man with big ears, brown mustache, and Van Dyke, Bowdre wore a gray hat at a rakish angle and a bib-front shirt stained with tobacco juice. He was about thirty years old, short, bowlegged and dumber than a fencepost, but he held a grudge like no one the Kid had ever known, turned into a demon during a fight, and killed without blinking an eye.

"Don't you want to see Manuela, Charlie?" the Kid asked jovially. Manuela was Bowdre's wife, and a mighty fine dancer. Hell's bells, the Kid wouldn't mind seeing her again himself, providing Charlie didn't find out about it.

Bowdre looked at his beer as if expecting to find the answer beneath the foam.

The Kid pulled out a folded, ripped copy of the *Rocky Mountain Sentinel,* one of the Santa Fe newspapers that didn't print what the damned Ring ordered published. "This new governor has issued amnesty."

"What's . . . th-tha-that?" Bowdre asked.

"A pardon. Means we're guilty of nothing from the time Mr. Tunstall was killed to the date this was published, about a month ago. It means we can go back and live in peace."

Doc Scurlock shook his head. "It doesn't apply to us, Billy, and you know it."

Scurlock had lost his front teeth in a fight some time back, dressed like a farmer, didn't talk much, and looked dumber than Charlie Bowdre, but had to be one of the smartest men to ride with the Kid. In his cups, he would overcome his reticence and recite poetry, some he had written himself. Scurlock never admitted it, but the way he patched up bullet wounds and knife cuts, the Kid figured he had at least studied to be a doctor, hence his nickname. In fact, the Kid had to think hard to recall Scurlock's first name: Joseph, Joshua, Josiah . . . something like that. The Kid didn't know Scurlock had even read Wallace's amnesty proclamation until now.

"Maybe it doesn't, Doc," he said, "but Sallie Chisum says she thinks this Wallace fellow would listen to us. I don't think he'd hang us without a trial. Truth is, I think we'd get pardoned."

"And then what?" Scurlock said. "Dolan's still running Lincoln County. And the Ring is running everything else. We'd be murdered within a month."

The Kid turned to French and O'Folliard. Frenchy's face remained a blank. He never made a decision, never would, and always followed the will of the majority. Big Tom, however, would side with the Kid. He always had, so the Kid had to persuade Scurlock or Bowdre to ride to Lincoln.

"Doc," he began, "you have a wife, too."

"I'll send for her. Thought I might try teaching school in Texas somewhere."

"You can always leave if things don't work out."

Scurlock shook his head. "It would be like crossing the Rubicon, Billy."

There was that damned Shakespeare again. The Kid swept off his sombrero and slammed it against his thigh. "Hell, I thought we were pals! You boys want to hear the truth? Well, here it is: I'm tired of running. I'm tired of rustling Chisum's beeves. I'm tired of thinking that we left Lincoln with our tails tucked between our legs. I'm going back, boys. Maybe I'll hang, maybe I'll get shot dead, but I'm going back. To be with my friends."

"You mean your *queridas*," O'Folliard said with a smile, and the others snickered.

The Kid winked. Bowdre and Scurlock stared blankly at the back bar, likely thinking about their wives, and the Kid knew he had them won, no matter what they said. Crossing the Rubicon, hell. This wasn't one of the Bard's plays. They could always leave if things got hot again, and Scurlock likely would, but the Kid wouldn't. He had done enough running in his life. He had abandoned Tom O'Keefe, John Tunstall, Alexander McSween. Never again. He would look after his friends, even if they denied him. "Look, if y'all don't want to ride back, I understand, but I don't think Dolan's men will come after you boys. It's me they want. So if you want to split up, no hard feelings. If you want to ride with Garrett and me, I'll treat y'all to breakfast."

O'Folliard followed him out the door. Bowdre stepped into the cold a few seconds later, and Scurlock and French joined them at the restaurant table before the waitress brought over coffee.

Chapter 4

"On account of an accident in his early youth, our son lost one arm and he was always an object of our most anxious solicitation. We preferred that he should remain nearer home, but his energy and enterprise knew no bounds. He spurned the idea that he could not accomplish with one hand anything that others could do with two."

—William W. Chapman

January 22, 1879
Santa Fe, New Mexico Territory

Judge Warren Henry Bristol tested Lew Wallace's faith in the Constitution and laws of the United States and its territories. The fifty-five-year-old jurist's files overflowed with complaints and condemnations ranging from malfeasance to gross manipulation of the law. *He shouldn't be disbarred,* Wallace thought. *He should be hanged.*

A thin man with a balding head, big green eyes, and a graying beard whose right corner was permanently browned by tobacco juice, Bristol took a seat beside District Attorney William Rynerson and crossed his legs. "That will be all," Wallace told the deputy marshals who had escorted the judge to the Palace of the Governors. When the governor had learned Bristol was staying at the Palace Hotel, he had sent three notes requesting a meeting. Each had been ignored, so Wallace summoned the territorial marshal and demanded Bristol's presence, even if he had to be arrested.

"Bristol," Wallace began after the officers had left, "I have been looking at the records of Lincoln County—your district, sir—and I am dismayed to see that you have canceled the past two terms of court."

"It was too dangerous, Governor," Bristol responded. "A grand jury did convene during the April term, but I felt the situation too precarious to proceed with trials, considering the bloodshed, Sheriff Brady's murder, and so forth, and things remained unsettled in November."

That might have been partially true. Ira Leonard had reported that the grand jury had billed Jessie Evans, George Davis, Miguel Seguro, and Frank Rivers for the murder of John Henry Tunstall, and also returned accessory indictments against James Dolan and Deputy Sheriff J. B. Mathews. William Bonney, John Middleton, Fred Waite, and Henry Brown were indicted for the murders of Brady and Deputy Hindman, and Dolan and John Riley were indicted for rustling. Alexander McSween, Rob Widenmann, and others had been no-billed on various charges, but none of those indicted had ever been brought to trial. In fact, Wallace had seen Dolan and Riley walking the streets of Santa Fe bold as brass, and as far as he knew, the only person ever arrested was Jessie Evans, who conveniently escaped from the Lincoln jail.

"I was governor in November and asked you to call a grand jury. You did not even respond to my letters, sir, much as you failed to respond to my notes desiring your presence here. As I have told Mr. Rynerson, I will not tolerate disrespect for this office. I have managed to bring about a Court of Inquiry for Colonel Dudley. That takes care of the military end of this debacle. Now a grand jury must be impaneled in the name of civilian justice."

"I never got your notes, Governor." The smirk told Wallace that Bristol was lying and didn't care if he knew it.

"A grand jury will convene in April in Lincoln, Bristol. You and Mr. Rynerson shall see to it."

"Begging Your Excellency's pardon," Bristol began, "but that's not too smart. Dudley's Court of Inquiry and the grand jury will be meeting around the same time, and maybe you don't know it, but the Kid's back in Lincoln County. So is Jessie Evans. In the interest of safety for the citizens, I don't think court should convene this term, either."

Wallace lost his temper, rare for him, and slammed his fist on the table, almost knocking a humidor to the floor. "Confound it, man, in the interest of justice, court must be held! And why have not the Kid and Evans been arrested?"

That question had been directed at Rynerson, who stopped twisting the ends of his mustache. "It's not easy keeping a lawman in the town of Lincoln, Governor. The last one never got paid, so he quit. George Kimbrell's filling in. We need a good sheriff down there, Governor. Someone who can kill or capture the Kid."

Kill or capture, Wallace noted, *not capture or kill.* And Rynerson hadn't even mentioned Jessie Evans.

"I understand you recently purchased some land in Lincoln County," Wallace said calmly and enjoyed the shock on Rynerson's face. Huston Chapman had been doing a most thorough job investigating the situation in Lincoln County.

"Yes, sir," Rynerson replied at last. "A man must look to the future. My salary as district attorney doesn't pay that well, as you know, Governor, and Lincoln County is prime ranch land."

Wallace nodded. "I am sure that is what John Tunstall had in mind when he claimed that land. And now you own it."

Rynerson twisted his mustache again, nervously this time, and Bristol's eyes got even bigger. Leonard and Chapman had been right. The Santa Fe Ring threw a wide loop. Rynerson and Bristol were either puppets or puppeteers of the Ring.

"A grand jury will convene in April in Lincoln," Wallace said, "and the term of court will be held as well. I will travel to Lincoln in March to assess the situation, to give the law-abiding people of that community hope, and I fully expect the lawless element to be arrested, tried, and convicted. Good day, gentlemen."

February 10, 1879
Las Vegas, New Mexico Territory

"Nice rig," Ira Leonard said as Huston Chapman set the brake to the phaeton he had parked in front of Leonard's office.

"It's Sue's." Chapman struggled with his one arm to climb down from the buggy and shed his linen duster, which he tossed onto the seat.

The two men exchanged handshakes, forgetting their tiff back in October.

"Where is . . . ?"

"She's still in Lincoln." He touched the side of his mouth, partly swollen, with a handkerchief. "Bum tooth. Don't worry, Sue's safe. I drove up to file a few papers, write some letters, and"—he winked—"to see an old friend. Staying busy with the governor?"

"Not as busy as you."

In a matter of months, Huston Chapman had managed to uncover that District Attorney William Rynerson was moving onto the late John Tunstall's land, had gotten Susan McSween appointed administratrix of the estates of her husband, Tunstall, and Dick Brewer, and had irritated the officer corps at Fort Stanton. His ceaseless lambasting had caused Colonel Dudley to request a Court of Inquiry to investigate his handling of military matters during the five-day siege that ended with the McSween house being torched and McSween gunned down. He was making headway, while Leonard and Wallace, fighting the army's current of channels to have Dudley removed, had made little advancement.

"There was a rumor that William Bonney surrendered to the interim sheriff," Leonard said.

"'Tis only rumor, although Sue says he's back in the territory, probably hiding out at Fort Sumner, where he has more Mexican girls chasing him than you do, Leonard. And I hear Sallie Chisum's as chaste as Sue. The Kid might be trying to get inside her chemise."

Leonard shook his head. One of these days, Chapman would get his head shot off talking about a woman.

"Anyway," Chapman continued, "I haven't seen the Kid. Haven't had the pleasure of meeting Dolan or Evans, either, but I will. Word is that they are back in the county, too."

"Well, you did fine work, Huston. The governor's proud of you. He's going to Lincoln next month. I'm sure he'll want you to ride with us."

"Can't wait. I'll be back in Lincoln within the week. You and your general can look me up then."

Leonard's face hardened. "Huston, that's a fool's play. You've risked your life enough. You've done enough."

"I'm just starting, Leonard," Chapman said. "And I didn't stop by your office to listen to you mother me. I came here for a drink, to kill a toothache, and I am dying of thirst."

February 15, 1879
Fort Sumner, New Mexico Territory

The tumbler of rye slid across the bar and stopped in front of the sombrero the Kid had just laid on the top. He looked at it curiously, then turned his neck slightly and caught sight of the bartender. Immediately recognizing the long-legged, lanky rapscallion, he broke out in a henlike cackle, although the bartender couldn't hear him above the music, voices, and dancing.

"*Buenos noches,* Juan Largo!" the Kid shouted at Pat Garrett, and slid the whiskey back across the slick bar top. As Garrett scooped up the glass, the Kid added, "You know I don't drink."

"I do, Little Casino," Garrett said, although the Kid couldn't hear him, and killed the whiskey.

He put the sombrero back on his head, wrapped his arms around the two raven-headed ladies standing next to him, and approached Garrett, introducing him to the slim Paulita and corpulent Deluvina Maxwell, two of the prettiest *señoritas* in the entire territory, and the best dancers.

"We've met," said Garrett, tipping his hat at the girls before shaking the Kid's hand. "It's been a spell," Garrett said. He excused himself to pour a *vaquero* a shot of mescal, but the Kid didn't wait for him. The band had started another song, so he escorted Paulita to the floor. Two dances later, he was back, asking Garrett for a cup of coffee and telling Deluvina, Paulita's adopted sister, he would dance with her in a minute or two, after he caught up on old times with his *amigo*.

"When I left you with Pete Maxwell," the Kid said, "I didn't think he'd hire you to pour rotgut."

"It's a livin'," Garrett said.

The Kid's head bobbed, and he leaned against the bar, his back to Garrett, smiling at the sight of the dancing, the sound of the music. He spotted Charlie Bowdre stumbling through the number, and he pitied his poor wife's feet. Even Doc Scurlock was cutting the rug. "I love these *bailes*," he said. "Makes a man forget all of his troubles."

"Where have you been, Billy?" Garrett asked.

"Here and there."

"Sellin' anymore cattle with deformed ears in Tascosa?"

His smile vanished, and he turned toward Garrett. "Now, Pat," he said, "have you been listening to some of John Chisum's riders?"

Garrett shook his head. "No, Billy, I heard it from John Chisum himself."

The frown hardened, but he couldn't hold it. He hit Garrett's shoulder lightly, shook his head, and grinned. "Chisum owes me, Pat. He promised me five hundred dollars a month during the Lincoln County War and never paid me a dime, so I've just been collecting what's rightfully mine and the Regulators'. Now lose that long face, Juan Largo. I'm here to celebrate."

"What's the occasion, Billy?" He topped off the Kid's coffee and refilled three more glasses down the bar.

"Amnesty," the Kid answered when Garrett returned. "A truce."

"I hear the governor's amnesty doesn't apply to you, Little Casino."

"Not with the governor, Juan Largo." As he led Deluvina Maxwell to the dance floor, he yelled back at Garrett: "With Jessie Evans!"

February 18, 1879
Lincoln, New Mexico Territory

He wished he were drunk.

Jessie Evans had murdered John Henry Tunstall a year ago to the day, and now the Kid had initiated a parley with the bandit. He had joked about it with Pat Garrett, with Bowdre, O'Folliard, Scurlock, and French, but he couldn't smile now, not with his stomach rumbling so. Bowdre and O'Folliard had offered to ride to Lincoln with him, Scurlock had simply called him a fool, and French had, typically, said nothing, but the Kid wouldn't risk their lives. He knew better than to trust Jessie Evans, but something had to change. He couldn't run forever. It was time to face the truth.

Jessie Evans and Jimmy Dolan had won. Now it was time for a truce, time to end the bloodshed, time to go on with their lives. He might be able to surrender to the new governor, get a fair trial, get a piece of this amnesty. Wallace, Sallie Chisum said, was a fair man with a keen sense of justice. He would understand that the killings had not been murder, but war.

He rode past the two-story Dolan store known as The House, once the L. G. Murphy & Co. headquarters, past the Wortley Hotel, half-expecting a bullet in his back, and held his breath as he passed the empty lot where once had stood Alexander McSween's lovely home. The Tunstall store remained dark, and the buckskin gelding snorted and shied away from something. A ghost? The horse recovered, and he rode on, reining up in front of Ike Stockton's saloon.

Jessie Evans leaned against the adobe structure, puffing on a cheroot, flanked by Jimmy Dolan and Billy Mathews. He felt the urge to draw his pistol, cut down those sons of bitches, but he caught the shadows in a window and then spotted Edgar Walz leaning in the doorway, a double-barreled shotgun in his arms.

"Light down, Billy," Evans called out. "But first toss down your weapons. Nobody comes to a peace parley heeled."

He kept his hand near the butt of his Colt. "Unbuckle yours first, Jessie."

"Hell, Kid, you're impossible to treat with."

When Walz lifted the shotgun, the Kid yelled: "I don't care to open negotiations with a fight, but if you bastards come at me four at a time, I'll whip the whole damned bunch of you!"

He waited. The shotgun never raised any farther, and finally Evans tossed his smoke into the street and hooked his fingers in his gunbelt. "All right, Kid, we all keep our guns. Now, why don't we step inside and talk things over peaceably?"

They were drunk, the whole lot of them, and celebrating, shooting at mice behind Stockton's saloon. The Kid breathed easier now but kept his hand close to his revolver. Evans and Dolan had agreed that no one would be killed unless Evans or the Kid were notified that the truce was being terminated. If anyone broke the peace, the transgressor's throat would be cut.

Laughing, Evans and his men wandered onto the road that cut through Lincoln. Spotting his horse still hobbled in front of Stockton's saloon, the Kid said, "I'm calling it a night, boys. I'll see y'all later."

"No sirree." Jessie Evans slurred his words. "It ain't even ten o'clock yet, Billy. We got a lot of drinkin' and funnin' to do."

When he started to protest, Dolan pointed his revolver toward Juan Patrón's house. "Hey, Jessie, look at what the wind blew our way." The Kid grimaced. Walking down the street was Mrs. McSween's one-armed attorney, back from Santa Fe, looking like hell. He held a white handkerchief, rolled into a ball, against his mouth.

"Like I said . . ." Evans ejected the spent shells of his .45 and replaced them with live rounds. He slapped the cylinder gate shut, lowered the hammer, and holstered the Colt. "We got a lot of funnin' to do." Evans, Dolan, and Billy Campbell, another man the Kid wished he had killed months ago, stepped into the street. Mathews and Walz soon followed.

"Who are ya, an' what are ya doin'?" Campbell demanded.

Huston Chapman looked up at the line of men blocking his path. The wind picked up, and the Kid, chilled to the bone, retreated into the shadows.

"My name is Chapman," the lawyer shot back at Campbell, "and I am attending to my business!"

Campbell pulled his pistol and shoved the barrel into Chapman's broad chest. "Then you dance," Campbell said, and Evans and Dolan cackled. Billy Mathews suddenly looked sober and stepped off the street underneath the saloon's awning.

"Damned if I will dance for a drunken mob," Chapman said. "Now, I'm freezing and have a damned toothache, so—"

Campbell cocked his Remington. "Don't you cuss me, you damned cripple."

Huston Chapman laughed, and the Kid had to give the man guts. "You don't scare me, boys. You've tried to scare me, and it's no use. Am I talking to Mr. Dolan?"

Evans pushed Campbell aside, and for a moment the Kid thought Evans was breaking up the tomfoolery, but the gunman said with a sneer, "No, but you're talking to a damned good friend of his!"

Nothing happened. Maybe it was over. As the Kid let out his breath, a gunshot ripped through the night, ringing his ears. The muzzle flash almost blinded him, and when the spots faded away, he saw Dolan holding a short-barreled Colt while Huston Chapman staggered back, beating his smoldering coat with his one hand, then dropping to his knees. "My God," he said, gasped, and fell onto his back. "I am killed."

Fueled by the wind, the smoking coat began to burn furiously, and when small flames erupted, Evans stood over the lawyer's body, emptying a bottle of forty-rod onto the fire. Campbell and Mathews took off down the street, yelling something, and Walz hurried into Stockton's saloon.

"Is he dead?" Dolan asked.

Evans tossed the empty bottle on the ground and, laughing, staggered into the saloon. "Come on, Kid!" he shouted.

Dolan holstered the gun and sniggered. The Kid stared at the burning body until he became aware of the stench of burning flesh.

"Sweet Jesus Christ in heaven," he whispered. Dolan stumbled through, back into the street, pulled out his pistol, and tossed it beside the corpse.

"Looks like he shot himself." Dolan winked before pushing through the saloon doors.

The Kid wet his lips and, quietly, removed the hobbles on his gelding's forefeet, swung into the saddle, and rode back through town. No one opened a door, no one peered through a window, not even at the sheriff's office. Lincoln being Lincoln, nobody would venture into the streets until after sunrise.

Suddenly he laughed as everything became clear. He had ridden to Lincoln to set up a tenuous truce with Jessie Evans, but he left with something even better. He had witnessed a murder, the murder of a prominent man, an attorney who had been communicating with the governor. He had not been able to convince himself that if he surrendered, he would be pardoned, but now he had a good hole card. He could bargain with Governor Wallace and have his revenge on Dolan and Evans after all.

Chapter 5

*"You have no idea how pleasant it is to have one
hearty assistant and sympathizer in my work. To
work hard trying to do a little good, but with all the
world against you, requires the will of a martyr."*
　　　　　　　　　　　　　　—Lew Wallace to Ira Leonard

March 5, 1879
Fort Sumner, New Mexico Territory

The lanky gent with the big hat and Southern drawl boarded
the stagecoach at Fort Sumner, mentioning in passing that he
hoped to find work better suited to his skills in Lincoln. He
was supposed to meet John Chisum at Sam Wortley's hotel.

"Are you a cowboy?" Lew Wallace asked.

"I've cowboyed, I've run buffalo, I've poured drinks, I've
kept the peace," Pat Garrett replied with a laugh. "Done just
about ever'thing 'cept raced chariots."

Ira Leonard turned his attention from the passing dust outside to Garrett. The governor had leaned forward, saying "Really?"—suddenly interested in the passenger whose long legs
hogged most of the Concord. Leonard became suspicious of
the mustached stranger. Why would he mention chariots unless he knew the governor's novel-in-progress included
Roman chariot races, and how could he know that? Wallace
had described his action sequences only in the privacy of the
Palace and in their room at Pete Maxwell's house the previous night. Garrett had not been privy to that conversation, or
had he? It wouldn't have been hard to spy on Wallace or over-

hear his baritone voice despite the thick walls of Maxwell's house.

"I doubt if Mr. Chisum has chariot racing in mind, young man." Wallace offered Garrett a cigar.

"You're likely right, Governor. Imagine he wants me to end his plague of rustlers."

"It is interesting you should mention chariots, sir." Wallace began recounting his idea for *Ben-Hur,* and Garrett pretended to be interested while smoking the cigar. Leonard decided Garrett was harmless. If he had spied on Wallace to find an entrance into conversation, that just made him a politician on par with the governor. Leonard looked out the window again, his mind occupied by various conversations with Huston Chapman, images of the strapping attorney. The stagecoach eventually left the windswept prairie of the Río Pecos and begun climbing into the mountains, the juniper and cholla making way for piñon and chamisa. He didn't look back until Garrett mentioned Billy Bonney.

"You know the Kid?" Wallace asked.

"In passin'." Garrett shifted his legs uncomfortably, whether from the subject or lack of legroom, Leonard couldn't be certain.

"Do you trust him?"

"Bonney's not a bad sort. Now, I don't know the long and short of his affairs durin' all those killin's, but he's well-respected at Fort Sumner. Girls take to him like flies to a gut wagon, and I ain't figured that out right yet, buck-toothed as he is. But, yeah, I reckon I'd trust him, as long as I ain't riled him none."

March 6, 1879
Lincoln, New Mexico Territory

Nestled in a verdant valley with an omnipresent piñon-scented breeze, the village of Lincoln seemed utterly peaceful—but then, Ira Leonard had felt the same about the dogwoods surrounding Shiloh Meeting House until he saw the elephant for the first time in April of '62. He had walked away from that brutal battle stunned, wounded, and, for the first time in his life, doubting God's existence.

Lincoln had not been the site of a bloody Civil War engagement, but the people of the territory, even newspaper editors back East, had called this, rightfully so, a war. He found the population, mostly Mexican, to be reticent and untrusting, much as his troops had been after the first day of battle at Pittsburg Landing.

Only one road cut through the town, which featured a handful of adobe buildings and a few farms, buttressed against the mountains and the peaceful Río Bonito. The stagecoach had stopped at the Wortley Hotel, catty-corner from the Dolan Store, the only two-story structure in town, and after registering, Leonard and Wallace left Garrett to await John Chisum's arrival and walked to the courthouse on the other side of town. After Wallace buried his head in the papers and got Juan Patrón to translate from Spanish, Leonard went to the cemetery between the ruins of the McSween house and the former Tunstall store.

The wind picked up, and removing his hat would leave him cold and a hypocrite. He stopped briefly at the white cross with Alexander McSween's name carved in it, then found Tunstall's marker and walked past several other mounds, many of them unmarked, before reaching the freshest grave, a simple plank serving as the tombstone, no epitaph, not even flowers, and the name, painted with whitewash instead of carved, misspelled.

Houston Chapman
Killed 18 Feb. 1879

"I don't know why I feel responsible," he started, shook his head, and kicked a dirt clod. "Damned if I'll stand here talking like a fool." *Who could hear him? God?* He laughed. *Huston?*

Yet Leonard did feel responsible. Maybe if he had traveled to Lincoln with Chapman. . . . Well, what did it matter? Chapman had been shot dead, and no one had lifted a finger to stop it. No one had even pulled his body out of the street until the next morning, and, from the reports from Green Wilson, Lincoln's justice of the peace, the Reverend Taylor Ealy, and Sheriff George Kimbrell, the body had been badly burned, almost beyond recognition, but the missing arm made the victim obvious, and Juan Patrón, who had ridden with Chapman from Santa Fe, positively identified the corpse from the clothes that hadn't burned and a handkerchief with his initials.

By all rights, Chapman's lout of a partner should be down here demanding justice, seeing to the affairs of Susan McSween, but Quinton remained a gutless marvel. Leonard decided he would pay Mrs. McSween a visit. He'd also make sure he carried on Huston Chapman's fight. He owed his friend that much.

Some people said the Lincoln County War was over, but neither Wallace nor Leonard believed that. Yes, McSween, Tunstall, and Murphy were dead. Yes, the Dolan store was closed, and Dolan was facing indictments. But the winds of war still blew hard. William Bonney and Jessie Evans remained free, as did Dolan. Leonard could do something about that, and not just for the sake of Susan McSween, and not just for the sake of Huston Chapman's memory. Leonard had come to New Mexico Territory because of better prospects for a lawyer, and he hoped Lew Wallace would help him receive a judge's appointment.

Chapman had been right, though. Wallace and Leonard had accomplished little in Santa Fe. You couldn't carry on a fight two hundred miles away from the front lines, so he would stay here. He would start interviewing the people of Lincoln tomorrow morning. He would start preparing a case . . . against whom—Dolan, Dudley, Evans, the Kid, the Ring—he wasn't sure. Above all, he would stop being a drunk and gambler and start being a lawyer again.

March 7, 1879
Las Cruces, New Mexico Territory

As The Worshipful Master of the Lodge, 32nd-degree Mason William Rynerson took his seat on the eastern side of the adobe temple. Turnout tonight was low, mainly because Rynerson did not trust the apprentices, deacons, and stewards in Aztec Lodge Number 3 and so had not told them about the assembly. He didn't completely trust Albert J. Fountain and John D. Bail, but they were lawyers—Fountain even published a newspaper—and he might have need of them soon. You could learn a lot about Freemasons during meetings. Five other men finished their chats before pulling up chairs: 3rd-degree Mason Judge Warren Bristol, a Scottish Rite leader from Las Cruces, two ranchers in Doña Ana County, and a hotel owner from Old Mesilla.

They talked about the latest murder in Lincoln County, idle gossip mostly, and Senior Warden Albert J. Fountain suggested the Lodge donate—anonymously, of course—food and money to Lloyd Little's widow, seeing how she had taken his death hard.

"Killed by rustlers," one of the ranchers, a gray-bearded catamount named McGarrity, snapped. "Lincoln ain't the only place full of crime. I wish someone would tell Governor Wallace that."

"Amen," commented John D. Bail.

The Freemasons unanimously agreed with Fountain's proposal, and, before the meeting broke up, talk ranged to politics, news from the States, and the prospects of the approaching railroad. As he sipped his Scotch, Rynerson shook hands with Judge Bristol, who looked over his shoulder before saying in a hoarse whisper: "Jimmy Dolan has certainly botched everything in Lincoln."

"I knew it was a mistake when Catron brought Evans back from Texas," Rynerson agreed.

"Well, what am I to do? The Kid saw Dolan kill that lawyer."

"The Kid won't testify, Warren. If he did, he would be arrested, tried, convicted, and hanged. And there were no other witnesses, except Jessie Evans and his boys, and they won't talk."

"I don't know about Billy Mathews."

"He won't talk, either."

"Even so, there will likely be enough evidence for a grand jury to indict. People saw Evans and Dolan on the streets, for God's sake, including Juan Patrón, and he has mighty high standing in Lincoln. Wallace will make sure of those indictments. I . . ." He stopped, smiled, and stepped aside as Albert J. Fountain interrupted them, refilled Rynerson's tumbler, and cracked a joke about his most recent appearance in court with Judge Bristol. He thanked both men for backing his plan to aid Mrs. Little before excusing himself and hurrying to thank Jack McGarrity before the rancher left the lodge.

Rynerson nodded at the lawyer's back. "What do you think of Fountain?"

Bristol shrugged. "As a newspaper editor or a lawyer?"

"As one of us."

"He's a staunch Republican, a good Freemason. Has an interest in politics, too. Married some greaser back during the War, got a brood of halfbreeds. He's honest. Pretty good lawyer, and the ranchers like him. He has no tolerance for rustlers."

"And Bail?"

"Bail follows orders. He's got more ambition than balls. I'd rather have Fountain defending me."

Rynerson laughed. "By the grace of God, Warren, it won't come to that." He enjoyed the fact that Bristol found no humor in his joke. "What were we discussing?"

"The grand jury, and court next month. Wallace is in Lincoln by now, with his shadow, Ira Leonard. He's rallying support."

"McSween and Tunstall rallied support, Warren, and look what it got them. Don't fret over the governor or Mr. Leonard. Catron can handle them. If Dolan is indicted—and you're right, he most likely will be—have him surrender to Sheriff Kimbrell. That's safer than having the Kid aiming at him. Set his bail high. That son of a bitch needs to be taught a lesson. Give him a long court date and tell him to marry that Mexican he's been wooing and take a long honeymoon. By the time he comes back, Wallace will have forgotten all about the Lincoln County War and Huston Chapman's murder."

Chapter 6

"He was the center of interest everywhere he went, and though heavily armed, he seemed as gentlemanly as a college-bred youth. He quickly became acquainted with everybody, and because of his humorous and pleasing personality grew to be a community favorite."

—George Coe, on Billy the Kid

March 12, 1879
Lincoln, New Mexico Territory

At least, Lew Wallace thought, the cook staff at the Wortley Hotel did not lace every dish with green or red chiles. Sam Wortley himself brought over plates of mashed potatoes, roast beef, and biscuits, and the aroma caused Wallace's mouth to water. The meat was so tender, he didn't need a knife, and the gravy poured over the potatoes tasted heavenly.

"You are quiet this evening, Ira," he said after dabbing his lips with a napkin.

"Preoccupied, General," the attorney replied with a false smile. "I'm sorry."

"As long as you are not worrying. I think we have made substantial progress in bringing a lasting peace to this backward community." Instead of waiting for Leonard's response, Wallace tore into his supper, nodding with enthusiasm when Sam Wortley asked if the governor would care to sample a piece of apple pie for dessert.

They had made progress, too, at least in the matter of the violence and anarchy. What disappointed Wallace was the absence of any mining ventures in Lincoln; no investment opportunities were to be had here. On the other, official, hand, Wallace felt certain he could obtain indictments against Dolan and Evans for Chapman's murder. Juan Patrón, a well-liked former schoolteacher, county clerk, and judge who had served as speaker of the house in the territorial legislature, had seen Dolan, Evans, and a handful of other men taking target practice near Ike Stockton's saloon as he and Chapman rode in from Santa Fe. No one else was on the streets, and everyone knew the bad blood between Chapman and Dolan's men. It wouldn't be enough for a conviction, but an indict-ment—anyone, he had learned during his years on the bar, could be indicted—would be a great start. Other witnesses might follow Patrón's example. Surely someone else had witnessed the foul murder.

Less than a week ago, he had spoken to a crowd in front of the Torreón, a strange-looking structure of rocks, wood, and mud that, he had been told, was built as a fort for pro-tection against Apaches back when Lincoln was known as La Placita del Río Bonito. The peasants had applauded when he asked for witnesses to come forward—none had—and cheered when he told them, with Squire Green Wilson trans-lating into Spanish, that he was asking that Colonel Dudley be removed as commanding officer of Fort Stanton.

In the morning, he would return to the Torreón to an-nounce that Juan Patrón would command the newly formed Lincoln County Mounted Rifles, a posse of citizens respon-sible for law and order in the area. Patrón's group would as-sist the county sheriff or act in his stead. That should lead to more applause. *Too bad most of them cannot read English.* He smiled at the thought. *They would likely all buy copies of my novel upon its publication.*

He kept his smile as Green Wilson walked into the hotel's small dining room. Wilson lived in a little adobe hut far off the road, across from the old Tunstall store. The locals either called him Green (if they were American) or Juan Batista (if they were Mexican), although John B. "Green" Wilson was as Mexican as Lew Wallace. An elderly gentleman with a white mane, brilliant green eyes, and a cedar walking cane, Wilson had mentioned that he originally hailed from Illinois, but he spoke Spanish, which he said he had picked up during the Mexican War, like a *vaquero*.

"Join us for supper, Squire." Wallace started to rise, but the kind justice of the peace told him to keep his seat.

"I don't eat supper anymore, Governor," Wilson said. "My teeth and stomach can't handle it. I have coffee and a tortilla for breakfast and a full meal at noon. That's enough for an old bag of bones like me, sir."

Sam Wortley brought over the slices of pie.

"How about dessert, Squire?"

"No, sir. That hurts my teeth." He lifted his trembling right hand into his coat pocket and withdrew a crumpled envelope. "This is for you, Governor. It arrived moments ago."

He examined the paper: no return address, no postage, and a sloppy scrawl he did not recognize. Suspicious, he looked up at the justice of the peace for an explanation, but Wilson was gone. Ira Leonard asked something, but Wallace didn't hear, and he used a butter knife to break the seal and pulled out the letter. He read with interest, wet his lips, and passed the paper to Leonard while he began his dessert.

> *I have heard that you will give one thousand dollars for my body, which as I understand it, means alive as a witness against those that murdered Mr. Chapman. If it was so I could appear at court, I could give the desired information, but I have indictments against me for things that happened in the late Lincoln County War and am afraid to give myself up because my enemies would kill me.*
>
> *The day Mr. Chapman was murdered I was in Lincoln at the request of good citizens to meet Mr. J. J. Dolan, to meet as a friend so as to be able to lay aside our arms and go to work. I was present when Mr. Chapman was murdered and know who did it, and if it were not for those indictments I would have made it clear before now. If it is in your power to*

annul those indictments, I hope you will do so, so as
to give me a chance to explain.

 Please send me an answer telling me what you can
do. You can send answer by bearer. I have no wish to
fight any more. Indeed, I have not raised an arm
since your proclamation. As to my character, I refer
to any of the citizens, for the majority of them are my
friends and have been helping me all they could. I am
called Kid Antrim, but Antrim is my stepfather's
name. Waiting for an answer, I remain,

> *Your obedient servant,*
> *W. H. Bonney*

Leonard passed the letter back to Wallace. "How many
times does he mention the word *indictment*?" asked his
friend, grinning.

 "I think his terms can be met." Wallace stirred sugar in his
coffee.

 "Well, it's what you wanted, but you should consider this:
Bonney has been indicted for the murders of Brady, Hindman, Morton, and Baker—all peace officers, although I
admit I use that term with reservation. If you grant him
amnesty, the Ring will make sure you are crucified in the papers. And it will draw the wrath of Rynerson and Catron."

 "Devil's advocate, Ira?"

 Leonard's eyes brightened. "It's your dance, General."

 "Indeed, sir. This pie is delicious. Try yours, my friend,
before it grows cold." He took another bite, washed it down
with coffee, and said, without looking at Leonard, "I dare say
Mr. Bonney shall be in need of a good attorney. Mayhap you
know where he can find one."

March 16, 1879
Río Hondo, New Mexico Territory

When Charlie Bowdre took the letter from Yginio Salazar,
the Kid asked the Mexican to rest his horse and join the boys

around the campfire for some friendly poker, but Salazar just shook his head, wouldn't even meet the Kid's eyes. He had been like that since being shot and left for dead trying to escape the burning McSween house. It was his own damned fault, though. The Kid had told Salazar not to dally, to make his break with him and the boys. He had turned yellow that night and since then wouldn't accept the Kid's olive branches, and the Kid was getting mighty sick of offering them. Yet he still liked Salazar.

"*Wilson te dio esa recado, Yginio?*" the Kid asked.

"*Sí.*"

"*Y es del gobernador?*"

"*Eso dijo Señor Wilson.*"

"*Nadian te perseguio?*"

"*No.*"

"*Estas seguro?*"

"*Sí.*"

"*Estas seguro que no quieres jugar cartas, Yginio?*" He switched to English. "You know how sorry Charlie and Tom are at poker. It would be free money."

Salazar shook his head, still staring at his horse's neck, and the Kid gave up. "All right. *Mil gracias, Yginio. Vaya con Dios.*"

"*Gracias, Billito.*"

As Salazar rode out of camp, the Kid added in a whisper: "Go to hell."

Charlie Bowdre opened the letter and started to read, but Doc Scurlock snatched it from him after the stutters began and passed it to the Kid.

> *Come to the house of old Squire Wilson at 9 o'clock next Monday night alone. I don't mean his office, but his residence. Follow along the foot of the mountains south of the town, come in on that side, and knock at the east door. I have authority to exempt you from prosecution if you will testify to what you say you know.*
>
> *The object of the meeting at Squire Wilson's is to arrange the matter in a way to make your life safe. To*

*do that, the utmost secrecy is to be used. So come
alone. Don't tell anybody—not a living soul—where
you are coming or the object. If you could trust Jessie
Evans, you can trust me.*

Lew Wallace

"Well?" O'Folliard asked.

The Kid stuck the note in his vest pocket, looked at his cards, and tossed his hand onto the deadwood. "You boys meet me at San Patricio in a few days. If I'm not there for the *baile,* I'll be dancing with the pretty *señoritas* up in heaven."

March 17, 1879
Lincoln, New Mexico Territory

He could pass for a Mexican in the dark, sometimes in the daylight if he pulled the sombrero down low over his eyes, but once he knocked on Green Wilson's door, no one would mistake him for some poor *granjero.*

His heart pounded as he jerked the Winchester carbine from the saddle boot, nervously keeping his eyes trained on the back of the Dolan store. He waited, checked his pocket watch, and considered turning back, riding out of Lincoln and returning to San Patricio. Better yet, he would go up to Fort Sumner and see Paulita Maxwell. She had bigger breasts than Sallie Chisum and would let him feel them after a few dances. Sallie was prettier, smarter, too, but not as free with her kisses or as good a dancer. He shook away the images. That kind of thinking would get him killed. Time was running out, and he had to make a choice.

"Hell." The Kid left his horse hobbled beside a wall of juniper, then waited for the moon to disappear behind a cloud before he took off in a crouch, diving into a depression.

An icy wind picked up, almost freezing the sweat to his skin and shirt.

An owl hooted, and a pig grunted from the stinking pen behind Old Man Stanley's *jacale.* Nothing else. Another minute passed before he scrambled to his feet and zigzagged through the brush, slowing as he neared the Aguayo home and walking, waiting for his breathing to return to normal, toward Green Wilson's home.

He drew the Colt with his left hand, keeping the more familiar Winchester in his right, and walked through the squire's garden, approached the east door, and waited. He listened, but heard only the wind. He could see the shadows through the window but heard no conversation, no footsteps. The aroma of coffee and a piñon fire made him desire warmth, and he tapped the Winchester's barrel against the door, aware of his clammy hands.

"Come in," came a voice that wasn't Green Wilson's.

The Kid pushed the door open, covering the inside with the Winchester. Green Wilson stood beside a table, stirring a cup of coffee, looking as old as Methuselah, and the Kid dismissed him and concentrated on the second man, a gent in a fine broadcloth suit and silk cravat, neatly trimmed mustache and beard, long fingers . . . unarmed. He couldn't see anyone else, but the house remained dark, lighted by only one lantern, and it had been turned down low. Squire Wilson was as miserly as they came, and coal oil wasn't cheap this far from civilization.

Keeping the Winchester trained on the stranger, the Kid spoke: "I was sent for to meet the governor at nine o'clock. Is he here?"

The man at the table rose, smiling warmly, and extended his hand. "I am Governor Wallace."

The Kid didn't lower the carbine. "Your note gave promise of absolute protection."

To the Kid's surprise, the governor's smile never faded, even with the .44-40 barrel pressing against the man's coat button. He could blow Wallace in half if he wanted to. "I have been true to my promise," Wallace said. He jutted his chin toward Wilson, who held his coffee cup in a trembling hand. "This man, whom of course you know, and I are the only persons in the house."

He walked around the table, finally satisfied, and shoved the Colt into its holster. When Wallace gestured at the table, the Kid pulled up a chair, lowering the Winchester's hammer but keeping the carbine cradled on his lap. Wallace sat across from him.

"What I desire of you, William, is your sworn true testimony," Wallace began, and the Kid liked the man's voice, a soothing bass, the way he always thought his father must have sounded. "In less than a month, court will be held, and I want to bring those responsible for the nefarious and callous murder of Huston Chapman to the gallows. You say you saw this act. Well, all I ask of you is to tell the truth, under oath, before a jury."

"That would be my death warrant, Governor."

"You will be safe, lad." *Lad.* John Tunstall had often called him lad, though he looked barely older than the Kid. He had admired Tunstall, too, although that foreign accent of his could make a body's skin crawl. "You should know that troopers from the Ninth Cavalry, acting on my orders, tracked down and arrested Jessie Evans and Billy Campbell last week. Both are being held in the stockade at Fort Stanton, again on my orders, along with various other fiends. You are safe."

He hadn't heard about Evans, which made him relax a tad. "And my indictments?" he asked.

Wallace's smile widened. The man had the whitest teeth the Kid had ever seen. "If you uphold your end of the bargain, William, you will be well rewarded. In return for your testimony, I will let you go scot-free, with a pardon in your pockets for all your misdeeds."

Too simple. There had to be more to this. He wanted to trust Wallace, and did trust Green Wilson, but the governor had no idea how powerful Dolan was in these parts. If he surrendered, Dolan would kill him, sure as shooting. He'd see to that, he or the Santa Fe Ring.

"How do we go about this, Governor?" he asked.

Wallace almost laughed. "The first thing that must happen, William, is you are arrested, beaten up, and thrown into that dungeon the local constabulary dares call a jail."

Chapter 7

"There is nothing to be looked or hoped for from the tribunal. It is a farce of judicial investigation and ought to be called and designated 'The Mutual Admiration Inquiry.'"

—Ira Leonard

March 21, 1879
Lincoln, New Mexico Territory

"I can't believe he actually went through with this," Ira Leonard said.

Yet down the dusty street rode William H. Bonney, flanked on his right by a big fellow in a farmer's slouch hat. Neither man acknowledged Governor Wallace, who sat on the Wortley Hotel's front porch smoking a cigar and looking quite contented. The two riders dismounted in front of the Tunstall store and disappeared around the far side of the building.

"Who is the big man with Bonney?" Wallace asked Green Wilson, rocking in a chair next to the governor.

"Tom O'Folliard," the justice of the peace answered. "Billy's shadow."

Wallace crossed his legs and pitched his cigar into a brass cuspidor. "Ira," he said, still smirking, "were I you, I would introduce myself to Mr. Bonney and make sure the sheriff and his posse do not rough up the lad too much. Or kill him."

Leonard took a deep breath and left the covered porch. By the time he pushed open the whitewashed gate and stepped onto what passed for a sidewalk, Sheriff Kimbrell and a group of deputies were marching from the courthouse. Leonard's lungs seemed to shrink, and he loosened the cravat, sweating, knowing, with his asthma, that he would never reach Bonney and O'Folliard before Kimbrell's group.

He figured the Kid and O'Folliard were at the graves of Tunstall and McSween, and when he heard one of the deputies say, "They done us a favor. We won't have to take 'em to the cemetery," he picked up the pace. Too late. The posse disappeared around the corner, and moments later came the shouts.

"Hands up, Kid!"

"You son of a bitch! What's he doing here?"

"You're under arrest. Hand over your gun!"

"You want to start the ball, Kimbrell, make your play!"

"We ain't surrenderin' to the likes of him!"

"Billy! Damn it, Billy, put down that gun. I said hold it Billy! Jesus—"

Leonard stumbled while rounding the corner, righted himself, and shouted, vaguely aware of guns swinging in his direction. *What a fool's play! I could easily get shot.* He thought Bonney had been pulling his gun, about to botch the whole affair Wallace had arranged, but understood now that Kimbrell had been yelling at one of his deputies, J. B. "Billy" Mathews, who pivoted and trained his Smith & Wesson on Leonard. Another deputy shouldered a shotgun, keeping Bonney and O'Folliard covered.

"Put the gun down, Billy!" Kimbrell shouted at his deputy.

Leonard found his breath. He had to lean against the store's adobe wall, but he could talk. "These men are surrendering to the law. If anyone fires his weapon, he will answer to Governor Wallace."

"This bastard tried to murder me," Billy Mathews said. "I was there when he shot Sheriff Brady and George Hindman down . . . right over yonder." He pointed the revolver's barrel down the street, then grudgingly rammed the .45 into its holster.

"He deserves his day in court," Leonard said.

"So did Morton and Baker," another deputy said, "and he murdered them, too."

"So did John Tunstall, Alexander McSween, and Huston Chapman." Leonard pushed himself from the wall and stood as straight as possible. He nodded at Bonney and O'Folliard, who pitched their weapons beside Tunstall's grave.

"They're your prisoners, Sheriff," Leonard told Kimbrell. "But if something happens to them while in your custody, you'll be indicted and convicted."

He watched as the deputies searched the two prisoners roughly, clenching his teeth while they tossed them onto the ground and clamped manacles on their wrists and ankles. O'Folliard swore as the iron bit into his flesh, and one of the deputies kicked him in the ribs. Leonard let this pass, staring at Bonney, a kid, just like he was called, yet a man who didn't utter a sound, even when Mathews gave him a solid boot in the side.

"Take 'em to the pit," Kimbrell ordered. "An' chain 'em to the wall. These boys ain't goin' nowhere till we hang 'em."

March 19, 1879
Lincoln, New Mexico Territory

"The key to authoring a novel that captivates the reader," Lew Wallace explained to Leonard, Sam Wortley, Green Wilson, and Susan McSween in the hotel dining room at breakfast, "is having your hero take one step backward for every two steps forward. In the novel I have almost completed, for example, my protagonist, Judah Ben-Hur, is made a galley slave . . ."

Ira Leonard lost interest in Wallace's grandiloquence and began focusing on William H. Bonney, the forthcoming Court of Inquiry for Colonel Nathan Dudley, and the grand jury. More than twenty men had been arrested and were being held at the Fort Stanton stockade, and another dozen or so were chained to the walls in the town jail, which, indeed, was a covered pit. Prisoners climbed down a ladder into the cavern to be chained to the walls or given free reign to walk about the cramped quarters. The ladder was removed whenever the prisoners were not guarded. Buckets were lowered with food and water, and others, full of dung and urine, were hauled out by rope. Poles lashed together, resembling a coyote fence more than a ceiling, served as the roof.

The place reeked, and after a day or two, the prisoners looked half-dead. Two of the Kid's cohorts, Doc Scurlock and Jim French, had been arrested and confined in the pit. About the only member of the Regulators still wanted was Charlie Bowdre, and the Lincoln County Mounted Rifles were on his trail. Most of the Murphy-Dolan men, including Dolan and Evans, could be found under heavy guard at Fort Stanton.

Things were falling into place.

Bonney and O'Folliard had been removed from the pit after only one night. The Kid had given his word to Kimbrell and Wallace that he would not escape and so had been transferred to Juan Patrón's *casa* at the edge of town. There, Bonney played poker, ate fine meals prepared by Mrs. Patrón, and found royal treatment. At night, from his hotel room at the other end of Lincoln, Leonard heard the strumming of guitars and the sweet Spanish voices of men and women serenading the Kid. Leonard couldn't understand the words—his Spanish was limited to *gracias, por favor, tequila, cerveza,* and a few impolite phrases Mexican prostitutes had taught him—but he didn't have to. They worshiped William H. Bonney. So the prosecution's first move would be a change of venue. How could he win that argument? He couldn't. So what would be the next step?

He shook his head. It didn't matter. Bonney would never come to trial, not if he testified against Dolan and Evans. He'd be pardoned, and Leonard—though he had been hired by Bonney, and Susan McSween as well—had plenty of cases and clients to keep him busy.

A man cleared his throat, and Leonard noticed a black trooper from Fort Stanton standing behind the screen door, not daring to step inside this white establishment. No one made a move, still listening to the vainglorious Wallace, so Leonard excused himself and walked outside.

"Mr. Leonard, sir," the sergeant said uncomfortably. "Capt'n Carroll sends his compliments, sir, an' his regrets as to this matter." He handed Leonard a folded slip of paper. Leonard sighed after the first sentence.

"How did it happen, Sergeant?"

"Don't know, sir. Wasn't on duty last night. Capt'n Carroll, he just ordered me to deliver this to you an' the gov'nor. Will that be all, sir?"

"Yeah." The trooper turned on his heel and walked to his horse. Leonard stepped forward and leaned against a column for support. The screen door squeaked open, slammed shut, and he knew Lew Wallace had come outside.

"Bad news, Ira?" Wallace asked.

He nodded, turned, and passed the note to the governor. He thought about saying *one step backward* but knew better than to act smart or show Wallace the slightest disrespect, even though Wallace's politicking and trips to mining properties had started to weigh upon him. "Jessie Evans and Billy Campbell escaped last night."

April 13, 1879
Fort Stanton, New Mexico Territory

James Dolan grinned as he walked out of the guardhouse. He tipped his bowler at Lew Wallace and Ira Leonard and said, "God loves the Irish, me friend," and mounted his horse. No one stopped him as he rode out of the compound and took the road leading to Lincoln. No one could stop him. Judge Warren Bristol had seen to that.

"All of our work . . ." Wallace shook his head.

Leonard said nothing, simply stared, wondering who had saddled Dolan's horse, who had known the judge would grant a *habeus corpus* petition and release Dolan and fourteen other scoundrels. None of the others was brazen enough to smirk at Wallace as he left the post; none of the others was powerful enough to have his horse saddled and waiting for him.

"We'll get Dolan," Leonard said. "He'll be back in jail after the grand jury convenes."

"Maybe." For the first time since he had taken office, Wallace sounded defeated. "But what of Jessie Evans, the fiend?"

"We'll get him, too. We still have Bonney."

Wallace's head bobbed slightly, and Leonard turned to face the boisterous party leaving the post adjutant's office, which had served as a makeshift courtroom to hear the lawyer for *Dolan et al.* argue his case.

I should have anticipated this, Leonard thought, *after Evans and Campbell escaped.* That still hadn't been convincingly explained to him.

Prosecuting attorney William Rynerson patted Wallace's shoulder and said, "Give me a stronger case, Governor. Give me a stronger case, and I'll see that these felons are imprisoned or executed."

The bastard was mocking Wallace, mocking Leonard, and blood rushed to Leonard's head. Rynerson didn't care about justice, didn't believe in it unless it helped his personal or political causes. The attorney and judge stepped off the porch and headed for the commanding officer's quarters, likely to celebrate in private. The defense attorney stopped and extended his hand.

"You made a strong case, Mr. Leonard," he said in an Irish brogue. "I look forward to sparring with you again in court."

"Thank you, Mr. . . ." Leonard shook his head. "I'm sorry, I can't recall your name."

The lawyer's smile slipped just a bit. "Simon Newcomb," he said. Leonard knew that. He never forgot a name, especially that of a prig who had beaten him in a courtroom. He studied the attorney's pockmarked face, exchanging small talk, though he cared for nothing Newcomb had to say. What interested him was the gold pin on the lapel of Newcomb's vest, a pin just like the tie tack he had seen worn by Rynerson and Bristol, a pin just like the one he had seen on Thomas Catron's coat in Santa Fe.

The pin of a Mason.

April 18, 1879
Lincoln, New Mexico Territory

Lew Wallace gripped Leonard's hand firmly, then pulled the lawyer into an embrace. "I leave this fight to you, Ira," he whispered. "I know you will do your best."

The governor still sounded whipped, but Leonard smiled when released from the stranglehold. "It's not over, General." The two men stepped away from the hotel's door to let a couple of Mexicans through with Wallace's luggage, which they tossed into the rear boot of the waiting stagecoach. "We'll whip 'em, just like we whupped the secesh at Pittsburg Landing," he said, thickening his accent deliberately. "Them Rebs thought they had us on the run after the first day."

"Well," Wallace said, "carry the fight to them, but be careful. You have made enemies, and remember what happened . . ."

He couldn't finish, didn't have to. Leonard would never forget Huston Chapman, shot dead just down the street, and the site of the McSween house stood vacant. Sometimes, at night, he thought he smelled smoke as he walked past the eerie lot. He was Susan McSween's lawyer, and William H. Bonney's, Tom O'Folliard's, Doc Scurlock's, and Jim French's. He was leading the charge against Colonel Nathan Dudley in the Court of Inquiry and had helped bring two hundred indictments against many Murphy-Dolan men.

Nathan Dudley and former Sheriff George Peppin were charged with arson for the burning of Mrs. McSween's home, and Jessie Evans had been named an accessory. Dolan and Evans had been indicted for the murder of Huston Chapman.

The defense attorneys, Las Cruces and Mesilla men Albert Fountain, John Bail, Sidney Wilson, and Simon Newcomb, had pleaded with Judge Bristol for changes of venue in all of the cases, and Bristol had granted all of the motions. That hadn't surprised Leonard.

"It is up to you and Mr. Rynerson," Wallace said.

"Rynerson's no friend," Leonard said. "He's bent on going after the Kid. He's a Dolan man."

"Keep Bonney safe, Ira. He is the one who can bring down the Santa Fe Ring and Colonel Dudley."

"I'll do my best, General."

They shook hands again, and Leonard watched the governor climb into the stagecoach. Ten minutes later, it had disappeared, leaving behind a thick trail of dust that drifted toward the mountains. Sam Wortley stepped outside to fire up his pipe and canonized Lew Wallace, said he was the true definition of a gentleman and had captured the hearts of the citizens of Lincoln by coming to this town, by fighting the powerful House and that rapscallion Nathan Dudley.

"But . . ." Wortley let out a sigh. "I guess Governor Wallace had to get back to Santa Fe."

"Yeah." Leonard's shoulders sagged. He wanted a drink. He was alone, fighting an enemy he knew he couldn't defeat, and Wallace wasn't going back to Santa Fe, not yet. He was heading west, to Silver City, to look at a mine he hoped to purchase.

April 25, 1879
Lincoln, New Mexico Territory

He was in his cups and glad to be. Ira Leonard hadn't been drunk since he arrived in Lincoln, and figured he deserved one night to forget about his plight. He had not heard from Lew Wallace, who might be in the capital by now, but hadn't expected to. Leonard's clients, Susan McSween and William Bonney, were the ones being crucified in the Court of Inquiry, not Colonel Nathan Dudley. And now, just yesterday, district attorney William Rynerson had informed him that he would not honor the governor's pardon of Bonney for the murders of Brady, Hindman, Morton, Baker, and Buckshot Roberts.

"Damn it," Leonard had said, "the Kid testified in the grand jury that he saw Dolan murder Huston Chapman. Wallace promised him amnesty."

"It's not the governor's job to make those promises. If he wants to pardon Bonney, let him—after I convict him. I'll be

damned if I will free a man who has murdered five peace officers, including a county sheriff."

"Buckshot Roberts was no peace officer, and the others
were nothing more than squat assassins."

"Go to hell, Leonard. I'm doing my job."

Another step backward. He shook his head as he fumbled
with the lock, finally heard the click and pushed open the
door to his room. He had managed to get Tom O'Folliard
freed on Wallace's amnesty proclamation, but Billy Mathews
and the other Dolan gunmen had also met the requirements.
Wallace's saying was skewed out here; it was more like five
steps backward for every half-step forward.

He turned up the lantern and opened the window. The
wind carried the strains of a fiddle and a woman singing,
most likely to the Kid over at Juan Patrón's place. It sounded
like a Spanish version of *Lorena.*

Tomorrow, he'd have to tell the Kid that the governor's
word was no good, not when facing the Santa Fe Ring. If he
wanted to roam the territory free, he'd have to beat Rynerson
in a court of law, be acquitted in a murder trial. Maybe
Leonard could swing that in Lincoln, but Judge Bristol
would grant a change of venue, move the trial to La Mesilla,
perhaps Las Vegas. No, Mesilla for sure. Las Vegas was out
of Bristol's jurisdiction.

He muttered an oath and slammed his hat against the wall.

That's when the bullet shattered the glass, and he was
falling, crashing against the bed, bouncing off the mattress,
pitching to the floor. The roar of gunfire deafened him, show-
ering him with glass and chunks of adobe.

There must be an army out there, he thought, and felt
blood in his mouth.

Just like that, the shots ceased, and he heard shouting, the
pounding of horse's hooves, footsteps down the hall. The
woman had stopped her serenade, or maybe he just couldn't
hear her. He tried to stand but couldn't breathe. Someone had
dropped an anvil on his chest.

"Mr. Leonard!" Sam Wortley pounded on the door. "Mr.
Leonard, are you all right?"

His vision blurred. He tried desperately to loosen his tie,

but blood trickled from the corners of his mouth, and his lungs refused to work. He couldn't move.

God, I'm dying, he thought, and the room spun into black oblivion, and he felt himself floating toward the vigas, looking down at the dead.

Chapter 8

*"The war in Lincoln County has done that section
infinite harm. Such wholesale slaughter creates
terror in the minds of good, law-abiding people, and
those who contemplated emigrating hither will
hesitate long before venturing their lives and
property in so reckless a community. Bad men, on the
other hand, will seek it as an asylum and hiding
place from crime."*
—Las Vegas Gazette, June 15, 1878

June 17, 1879
Lincoln, New Mexico Territory

The Kid slipped the gambler's ring over his pinky before
dealing five cards each to Juan Patrón's two daughters and
himself.

"What you got?" he asked, and the five-year-old, spitting
image of her mother, showed him the hand. He pursed his
lips, nodding, and looked at the seven-year-old's cards.

"All right," he said, laying his cards faceup on the dirt
floor. "Mercedes, you have two pair, kings and threes, a pretty
good hand. So you'd discard the nine and draw one card." He
tousled her dark locks, and she grinned. "Amparo, you're old
enough. What would you do?"

She answered in Spanish, saying that as she held three
fives, she would keep them and throw away the ten of clubs
and ace of spades.

"Some people might keep the ace as a kicker," he said.

"Make us think you have two pair, and on the other hand, if you draw another ace, you have a full house."

"No, *El Chivato,* it means death."

"Naw. This is poker."

She shook her head and crossed herself, and he sighed. "Well, I got two small pairs, sixes and threes. I'd toss the jack and draw one. Now, since we're just playing for fun, not money, I'm gonna turn over your cards. Mercedes, you get a jack. Doesn't help you any, so you can't beat your sister. Oh, don't pout. You'll beat her the next time. Amparo, you get a six and a queen. Doesn't improve your hand, but you're still winning. Three of a kind's really good in this game. And the only way I can beat you is with a full house, and since Mercedes has my threes, I'll need another six, which isn't going to happen since the other sixes are already out. But if we were playing for real, I wouldn't know that." He turned over a card and blinked.

Amparo crossed herself again.

"Son of a gun," he said. "There are two aces of spades in this deck. That would likely get somebody, me since I'm dealing, shot." He gathered the cards and scolded the seven-year-old. "I told you, girl, this is poker. These aren't tarot cards, and the death card there means change, not necessarily death." The girl stood, gathered her skirt, and ran away, and the Kid sighed. "Mercedes, now I'm in big trouble."

"Por qué, El Chivato?"

El Chivato. He liked his Spanish nickname. It sounded better than the Kid.

"Well, Amparo will most likely tell your mother, and she'll tell Juan, and he'll skin me alive for teaching you a naughty adult game. And . . ." He saw the deputy standing in the doorway. "You best run along. Looks like I got a visitor."

The deputy disappeared behind Amparo, and the Kid smiled at the two people who walked inside. Big Tom O'Folliard removed his hat and squatted on the floor beside the Kid. Sallie Chisum remained standing, looking prim and proper— and quite beautiful.

"You look right pretty today, Sallie," he said. Her face remained solemn, so he hit O'Folliard on the arm and grinned wider. "How does it feel to be a free man, Tom? Pardoned by the governor. Can't wait till I'm with you, pal."

"Billy . . ."

He looked back at Sallie, and his face hardened. Another glance at O'Folliard told him something was wrong.

"What is it?"

"Ever'thing," O'Folliard said.

The Kid kept his eyes on Sallie, who brushed away a tear. "There isn't going to be a pardon, Billy," she said. "Not for you."

"But Governor Wallace promised—"

"Rynerson won't agree to the terms."

"But he's the governor, damn it."

"What does your lawyer say?"

The Kid snorted without answering, stood up, walked to the wall, and looked out the window. "Who told you this, Sallie?"

"I heard it from Uncle John."

That returned the smile, and he looked back at her, pushing his hat up. "Spying for me, eh? That's my girl."

"Don't joke, Billy. This is serious. Uncle John says the U.S. marshal's on his way from Santa Fe. He's going to arrest you, Billy, take you to Old Mesilla to stand trial for the murder of Buckshot Roberts."

"I didn't kill Buckshot Roberts, Sallie. Tom, you know that as well as anybody."

"It doesn't matter," Sallie said. "If they don't convict you for that, you'll be tried for the murder of Sheriff Brady."

O'Folliard added: "That's if you make it to La Mesilla, Billy. You know how them lawdogs are. They'd shoot you for spite."

"I gave my word to Governor Wallace."

O'Folliard again: "He ain't livin' up to his."

Sallie came to him, embraced him, and whispered, "You have to get out of here, Billy. I don't want to see you die." She kissed him softly on the forehead before hurrying outside.

The Kid looked at O'Folliard, who pulled himself to his feet. "You seen Doc Scurlock?"

O'Folliard shook his head. "He lit a shuck for Texas after

Mr. Leonard got him out on bail. Jim French rode out with him."

"Charlie?"

"He's up at Fort Sumner with his wife, dodgin' the law."

"You ought to have followed Doc and Frenchy, Tom. Ain't nothing stopping you. You're a free man." The next words were bitter, but directed at Governor Wallace and not his friend. "Got a pardon in your pockets for all your misdeeds."

"Figured I'd stick with you, *amigo*." The guard poked his head in the doorway again. "There's a dance at Fort Sumner," O'Folliard said. "Thought I might try to cut the rug with Paulita or Deluvina tomorrow night."

The Kid understood—he would meet O'Folliard at Pete Maxwell's place, if he managed to escape—and began shuffling the cards as O'Folliard left. He was still dealing solitaire when Sheriff Kimbrell returned at dusk and clamped the handcuffs on his wrists. "See ya in the mornin', Kid," he said and left, locking the door behind him.

"Idiots." The Kid clenched his teeth, folded his thumb, squeezed his fingers together, and tugged on the iron cuffs until he had freed his small hands, tearing off just a few pieces of skin. "You'd think they'd learn." He waited an hour before knocking on the door, which swung open as soon as one of the Lincoln County Mounted Rifles keyed the lock. The Kid handed the handcuffs to the grinning Mexican and crossed the yard to the tack room, where he pulled out his saddle, blanket, and bridle. One of the Mounted Rifles brought him his horse, even helped him saddle the gelding.

As he swung into the saddle, he tipped his big sombrero at the guards, all friends of his, or Mexicans who knew of him, and respected him. "Boys," he said in Spanish, "I'm tired of this. Tell the governor I got tired of waiting."

June 27, 1879
La Mesilla, New Mexico Territory

Judge Warren Bristol's gavel snapped. "Bail is set at three thousand dollars," he said and adjourned the court.

He met William Rynerson in his chambers. The tall district attorney had helped himself to Bristol's Tennessee whiskey and had propped his boot heels on the judge's desk. Bristol hung his robe on a hook and squeezed past the grinning Rynerson to get to his chair. Seated, he hooked out the plug of tobacco in his left cheek, pitched it into a cuspidor, and rinsed out his mouth with the liquor.

"You've been busy." Rynerson finally removed his feet from Bristol's desk.

He spat out the whiskey into the cuspidor and filled an empty glass on his desk. "Two hundred indictments were handed down in Lincoln County alone." He took a drink. "We'll both be busy thanks to our governor. And even busier if the Lincoln County Mounted Rifles round up some more banditti."

Rynerson snorted. "Mounted Rifles, my arse. You mean the governor's heel flies." He drained the whiskey, slid the glass across the table, and straightened. "Don't you think three thousand dollars was a bit—"

"Jimmy Dolan can afford it, Will. And you told me to teach him a lesson."

"I was going to say a bit low. After all, he is charged with murder. Did he orchestrate that Leonard deal?"

"He says it was Jessie Evans's doing. Evans fled the coop, went back to Texas. He'll be back, Will. He always comes back, that son of a bitch."

"Not this time, Warren. The Texas Rangers arrested him in Fort Davis, Fort Stockton, somewhere down there. Speaking for the district attorney's office, I don't think the Territory of New Mexico will ask for extradition. Let him rot in Huntsville."

Bristol sipped his whiskey. It was a good thing, letting Texas have that scalawag. If Evans was brought back to New Mexico, he might start talking. Maybe Texas would hang him. They hanged just about everybody over there. "Did you hear the Kid escaped?" he asked.

Rynerson laughed. "Lincoln is not Yuma or Alcatraz, Warren. The easiest thing to do in New Mexico is escape from jail. Tell Dolan that, in case he finds himself locked up after he returns from his honeymoon. And we'll get the Kid, mark my word. Now, I have to travel to Fort Stanton to see how our friend Nathan Dudley fares."

July 6, 1879
Lincoln, New Mexico Territory

He fingered the tumbler of tequila absently, finally shrugged and opened the desk drawer, from which he removed pen and paper. He stared at the blank stationery as if waiting for divine intervention and at last dropped the pen and reached for the liquor.

The tequila burned his tongue, and he grimaced.

Ira Leonard had bitten his tongue when Jessie Evans and his gang tried to kill him on the night of April twenty-fifth. He had almost bitten the damned thing off, and for the next several weeks had sounded like a simpleton when he tried to talk, which didn't help him in the courtroom. He was alive, though. No bullets had struck him, and his only scars were his tongue, which was healing, a few cuts and bruises, already healed, and his hair, which had turned stark white. And there was that nightmare, that vision he could not forget, staring down at a body . . .

He polished off the whiskey and picked up the pen. No sentiments. No heaping on the praise or lambasting others with blame. Just the facts.

   General Wallace:

     I regret to inform you that the Court of Inquiry exonerated Colonel Dudley yesterday afternoon at Fort Stanton. Another strike against us, but, as Susan McSween's attorney, I am bringing Dudley to court to face charges of arson and libel.

     I will not surrender, or run.

                             Your obt. servant,
                             Ira E. Leonard

He reread the note before folding it and sticking it in an envelope. He would post it the morning and wait on the stagecoach. Likely he would see Governor Wallace before the letter arrived in Santa Fe. He wasn't running, but he had to leave Lincoln. There was nothing for him to do now, nothing he could do until Dudley was brought to trial in La Mesilla in November. He needed to return to Las Vegas to handle his caseload there and earn some money. So far, the only client paying his bills in Lincoln was Susan McSween. William Bonney had escaped, breaking his word to Leonard and Wallace, and Doc Scurlock and Jim French had jumped bail. Leonard had had to forfeit the bond he put up for those two.

He smiled at the light tapping on his door, popped a peppermint in his mouth, and pulled on his coat. Susan McSween stood in the hallway, looking ebullient in her Sunday best.

"I'm Presbyterian," she said, "but I was hoping you would accompany me to the Catholic church this morning, Ira."

"I'd be delighted, Sue."

That was another change from April twenty-fifth. He had been going to Mass every week since, listening, though he still couldn't grasp much Spanish. Today, however, he thought he would head to the confessional and had been practicing his statement, running it through his mind, though he knew it by heart, like he would an opening or closing summation.

Bless me, Father, for I have sinned. It has been seventeen years since my last confession.

September 15, 1879
Cerrillos, New Mexico Territory

The mining superintendent named Manlio Douglas picked up a small stone from the pile of rubble and placed it in Susan Wallace's hand. "As you see, *señora*," he said in an accent of Scottish and Mexican blended like forty-rod whiskey, "you find gemstones in the trash. This was probably mined during the time of the *conquistadores*."

"Amazing," she said and showed her husband the fingernail-sized turquoise embedded into a small piece of rhyolite. "It's very beautiful."

"*Sí, señora.* Come, perhaps you would like to see the view from the top of the hills."

"Go ahead, dear." Lew Wallace gestured toward his ambulance, where a man was tying his horse to the left rear wheel. "As you see, business has tracked me down from Santa Fe."

He watched her go before picking his way along the loose rock toward the road. He liked the town of Cerrillos, and Susan loved the turquoise being mined here, but he couldn't see himself investing in this operation. Gold or silver, maybe copper. But turquoise? The price was good, and he had read about the gemstone in the magazines, but turquoise didn't have the prestige of silver or gold. He would pass. When he got back to the Palace, he would begin making plans for another trip to Silver City.

"General." Ira Leonard held out his hand.

"I didn't know you were the cavalryman, Ira," Wallace said beaming. "It's a long ride from Santa Fe in a saddle, sir."

"Not that far, General. And enjoyable."

Wallace caught a glimpse of the crucifix hanging on a rawhide thong around the lawyer's neck, but said nothing of it. "I trust you have important news."

"Bonney was arrested in San Miguel County, sir. A gambling charge. He paid a fine and was released but is still there."

"Ira, Ira, Ira . . ." Wallace shook his head. "You did not ride all this way to tell me that."

In the miserable town of Shakespeare near the Arizona border, Wallace had seen a gila monster bite a dog in some senseless sport the locals enjoyed. A peasant had shot the hideous lizard in the head with a revolver, but the gila monster refused to let go, even after it had died, and the Mexican was forced to kill the dog as well to put her out of her misery. Ira Leonard reminded Wallace of that gila monster. Once he sunk his teeth into something, he wouldn't quit.

"I'd like to find Bonney, General. With your permission . . ."

Wallace stopped him by raising his hand. "Ira, the jury ac-

quitted Nathan Dudley of arson. Judge Bristol dismissed the
indictment against him for libeling Mrs. McSween. We lost
that fight, sir, and there is no shame, for we have tasted a
measure of success. Dudley has been transferred from Fort
Stanton. That is something, at least. Maybe he shall rot at Fort
Bascom. Bonney is out of Lincoln County. Jessie Evans is in
jail, soon to be imprisoned in Texas. The railroad is being laid
at a fast clip, and people feel comfortable again, even in Lincoln and Colfax counties. What is more, they feel safe. James
Dolan is out of business, too. All right, the case against him
for Huston Chapman's murder has been quashed, but face it,
without the Kid, we had no witnesses, no hope of a conviction."

"I'd still like to go after the Santa Fe Ring, General. I
thought you did, too."

"If I had the time, Ira. But I must complete my book, and
these mining speculations are consuming more time than I realized. I am off to White Oaks next month." He laughed,
shaking his head. When he had last visited Lincoln County,
there had been no such place as White Oaks, but gold had
been discovered there in August, and the place—less than a
day's ride from Lincoln—was booming. He should have in-
vestigated the mining opportunities in Lincoln County more
thoroughly last spring.

"I'd still like to find Bonney."

"Confound it, man!" He removed his hat and slapped it
against his thigh, startling the horse tethered to his ambulance.
"William Bonney stabbed us in the back, Ira. Cannot you see
that? I would like to find the Kid, sir, and see him hanged."

"He was scared, General. That's all."

"We would have protected him."

Leonard started to argue, thought better of it, and shook his
head. Wallace took a deep breath, held it a moment, and
slowly exhaled. "I apologize, Ira, for losing my temper. Bonney betrayed us, though. Betrayed me. If you want to risk
your life again, feel free to pursue him. But as for me, I wash
my hands of him."

November 20, 1879
La Junta, Colorado

The Kid pulled up a chair beside Charlie Bowdre and Tom O'Folliard in the little bucket of blood across from the cattle pens. "Payday, boys," he said, tossing a wad of greenbacks onto the table and wrapping an arm around each man's neck.

"S-s-son of a g-g-gun, B-Billy," Bowdre said. "You . . . did it."

"I told him that John Chisum hired us to settle up his business," the Kid said and let out an uproarious laugh. "Damn fool believed it, too." Bowdre reached for the roll of bills, but the Kid snatched the money first, grinning, telling Bowdre he couldn't be trusted. While asking the bartender for a cup of coffee, he peeled off ten dollars for O'Folliard. "I'm also gonna buy you a new outfit, pal," he said. "You don't look fit to be riding with a noted desperado like me."

"W-wh-what a-bout m-me, B-B-B . . . ?" Bowdre couldn't finish.

"You get thirty bucks, my friend, 'cause you're a family man."

He started to stuff the rest of the money—more than seven hundred dollars—into the deep mule-ear pockets of his trousers when a greenhorn-looking gent in shiny brogans walked over with a whiskey in his hand.

"Pardon me, suh," the fellow said in an exaggerated Texas drawl, "but I was wonderin' if ya could break this hunnert-dollar bill fer me. I'd like a room at Ma Coyne's Boardin' House, but she can't change this. I'll buy ya a drink for ya troubles."

He slid the note to the Kid, who picked it up, nodded, and reached below the table. Only instead of bringing out a handful of twenties, he stuck a .41-caliber revolver in the man's face.

Chapter 9

"Billy was one of the kindest and best boys I ever knew. He was not bloodthirsty; he was forced into killing in defense of his own life. In all his career he never killed a native citizen of New Mexico, which was one of the reasons we were all so fond of him."
— Martín Chávez

January 10, 1880
Fort Sumner, New Mexico Territory

Felipe Benigno, who sawed a fiddle like he was born with the instrument, asked Pat Garrett—calling him Juan Largo, the handle the Kid had bestowed upon him—to spell him behind the bar, and Garrett readily agreed. Hell, it meant at least three or four whiskeys he wouldn't have to pay for. He was pouring himself three fingers of rye when the Kid entered the saloon.

He almost didn't recognize him with that black sombrero, peach-fuzz whiskers, and dirt hiding his sunburned face. The Kid, however, instantly recognized Garrett, screaming, "Juan Largo! By God man, it's good to see you again."

Garrett glanced at a drunk Texan sitting alone at a table, but the hellbender, who called himself Joe Grant, neither noticed nor cared. *"Café, por favor,"* said the Kid, tossing a nickel on the bar.

"Where you been, Little Casino?" Garrett asked but kept

his eyes on Joe Grant. The Kid lifted the tin cup Garrett had filled and clinked it against Garrett's shot glass.

"I been around, Pat. Dropped by to see Paulita."

"Uh-huh." He couldn't blame the Kid for that. Paulita was one handsome woman, although Garrett wondered if the Kid knew that Paulita's brother wouldn't be happy to see him courting his sister. Pete Maxwell, though, was the least of the Kid's concerns. Garrett lowered his voice and looked at the Kid. "You might want to lay low, Billy. Folks are huntin' you."

The Kid never stopped smiling. "Folks like you, Juan Largo?"

"I'm chasin' rustlers, Billy. That's all. And so far, I ain't been lookin' too hard for certain men Mr. Chisum has posted."

"That's good, Pat. 'Cause I hear that you've tossed a wide loop from time to time. You might have to string yourself up." He laughed.

Joe Grant stumbled to the bar next to the Kid, demanding a clean glass and new bottle. Garrett stood downwind of the gunman and grimaced. He had raised hogs that smelled better than the Texan. The Kid must have also gotten a whiff of Grant, for he slid down the bar a couple of paces and shook his head.

Grant whirled, noticing the Kid for the first time but not recognizing him. "Who's this greaser?"

Still smiling, the Kid shrugged. "*Yo soy Juan Chiz-zum.*"

"The hell you say. You ain't John Chisum. I know Chisum. Don't you lie to me ever again, greaser." He pushed his coattail behind his back and lowered his hand near the butt of a Schofield .45. "Or I'll bury you next to the Kid after I kill him."

Garrett refilled Grant's glass and left the bottle. "On the house," he said, but Grant kept staring the Kid, and the Kid suddenly became interested in the reeking gunman.

"You gonna kill Billy Bonney?" The Kid thickened his Mexican accent.

"Hell, yeah. I'm gonna stomp that little quim to the

ground. Then I'm gonna blow out his brains, cut off his head, and take it to Chisum."

"No fooling. With that?" Wide-eyed, he pointed to the Schofield. Grant fumbled with the gun before bringing it out of the holster and pointing it at the Kid's stomach. Just then, Charlie Bowdre, Tom O'Folliard, and a third man Garrett didn't recognize walked in and froze.

"Boys," the Kid said pleasantly, knowing who had just entered the saloon without taking his eyes off Grant. "This *gringo* is going to kill Billy Bonney when he finds him. With this gun. Can I touch it, mister . . . ?"

"You ain't touchin' my gun, you boot-licker."

"Aw, come on. You can hold mine. With his left hand, he slowly pulled the nickel-plated Colt Thunderer and slid it down the bar. Grant eyed the double-action revolver with suspicion.

"What's a greaser like you doin' with a fancy gun like this?"

"*Quién sabe? Por favor, amigo,* let me see your gun. Why, to touch the pistol that killed Billy Bonney will be something I will tell my grandchildren. You can shoot me with my own pistol if you don't trust me, *señor.*"

Joe Grant picked up the Thunderer with his left hand, using it to cover the Kid as he handed him the Schofield. Garrett downed his rye. He couldn't believe the fool. Come to think of it, he didn't know who was the bigger fool, Joe Grant or the Kid. Merrily, the Kid scampered across the saloon, showing off the weapon to his pals, who stood perplexed. The Kid started squealing in Spanish, his back to Grant and Garrett, and the pistol disappeared. Grant lost interest and reached for the bottle. Two drinks later, he suddenly whirled back at the Kid, demanding: "You damned *cabrón,* I want my gun back."

"*Sí.*" The Kid raced back like an idiot, slowly pushing the Schofield in its holster, pretending to polish the walnut butt before stepping back to his coffee cup. "*Con permisso, señor, mi pistola?*"

Grant roughly slid the Thunderer to the Kid, who picked it up admiringly while dropping his left hand into the deep pocket of his Mackinaw. "So, John Chisum hired you to kill Billy Bonney?"

"I ain't talkin' to you no more, greaser," Grant muttered.

After snickering, the Kid shucked his Mexican accent. "Juan Largo, this fool is dumber than he stinks." He pushed back the sombrero with the Thunderer's barrel and stared at Grant. "How can you kill somebody when you can't even recognize him?"

"You little piss proud." Grant drunkenly drew the Schofield.

The Kid didn't move.

Garrett held his breath.

Grant thumbed back the Schofield's hammer, waiting, but the Kid just kept grinning. "Prick," Grant said before pulling the trigger. Garrett jumped back, expecting a gunshot but hearing only a loud metallic click. Grant stared at the revolver as if it were foreign to him, cocked the big .45, and jerked the trigger again. Only then, after another click, did the Kid move.

His left hand flew out of the coat pocket, and his fingers opened. Garrett and Grant watched the bullets from Grant's pistol fly toward the cottonwood vigas.

"They don't work too good without these," the Kid was saying. He had emptied the Thunderer into Grant's chest before the bullets hit the floor.

March 27, 1880
Fort Sumner, New Mexico Territory

Sallie Chisum held her breath when Billy Bonney walked into the room, some Mexican girl on his arm. She didn't feel jealous, just fear for her uncle, who stood at the bar ordering a whiskey from thin-lipped Pat Garrett. The Chisums had come to Fort Sumner for the dance, but Felipe Benigno stopped fiddling when Bonney, leaving the pretty girl in the doorway, made a beeline for John Chisum. Sallie stepped away from the punch bowl and started to say something.

Bonney pulled his pistol and shoved it in her uncle's face.

"The way I figure it, Chisum," he said, "you owe me five hundred dollars. More, most likely more, but I'll settle on five hundred."

She had often heard it said among the Jinglebob cowhands that John Chisum could talk his way out of his own funeral. If he was scared, he didn't show it. He simply finished his drink, paying no attention to the shiny barrel inches from his nose. "Let me get a smoke, Billy, for then I can talk better."

He found his pipe and began stuffing it with tobacco while Billy just stood there. Sallie looked at the Mexican girl—Pete Maxwell's sister, she thought—who stared at the floor while fingering her rosary. She was really pretty, and now Sallie did feel a twinge of jealousy. She had refused to believe all of the stories about the Kid—a cold-blooded killer with a *querida* in every village—until now. Her uncle was talking again, and she looked at him.

"That's better." John Chisum struck a match on his thumbnail and lit the pipe. "Now, Billy, listen. If you talked about that money until your hair was as white as mine, you could not convince me that I owed it to you." He puffed on the pipe, smiling, and gently pushed the barrel of Billy's gun away. For the first time in her life, Sallie saw a Billy Bonney who looked confused, beaten. "Billy, you couldn't shoot an honest man, could you, while he was lookin' you square in the eye?"

The pistol began to shake in his hand.

"You have killed several men, I know, but they needed killin'."

"Like Joe Grant," he said, defiance in his voice and eyes again, and the pistol started to rise.

"You know me better'n that, Billy. I don't hire drunks, and I don't hire fools. The war's over, Billy, and I'm an old man. You shoot me, you wouldn't be takin' that many years off my life. Now, did you come here to dance with that fine-lookin' *señorita*, son, and maybe with my niece?" His head tilted in Sallie's direction. "You're on center stage, Billy." The pipe returned to her uncle's lips, and he stood waiting.

Billy looked at Sallie briefly, then stared at the girl in the doorway. Finally, with a smile, he holstered the revolver. "Aw, you're not worth killing. Come on, Felipe. This is a dance, isn't it? I'm in the mood to dance all night."

He wasn't, though. She knew that. He was embarrassed, and Sallie felt sorry for him, sorry that . . . maybe . . . she had ever led him on. He stayed for only two dances, both with the Maxwell girl, before sneaking out like a whimpering puppy. That's all he was, Sallie knew. All he had ever been.

April 23, 1880
Santa Fe, New Mexico Territory

The piece of currency made its way down the line in the Palace of the Governors office, from U.S. Marshal John Sherman to Lew Wallace to U.S. Attorney Sidney Barnes to William Rynerson to Justice Samuel Parks, each holding the bill to the light, and finally to Ira Leonard. The paper was good, with only minor smudging in the left corner; otherwise no one would be able to tell it was counterfeit. Leonard wondered how many of these one hundred dollar duds were being passed.

Azariah F. Wild, the Treasury Department agent who had brought the bill to the governor's office, answered the question before Leonard said it aloud. Wild was a thin man with a balding head, mild-looking except for a nose that apparently had been busted more than once, and a scar underneath his chin.

He spoke with surprising authority. "We don't know how many of these are in circulation, but this one came from a merchant named James Dolan, whom some of you know. A cowhand called Billie Wilson passed it to him. Or should I say, this Billie Wilson was *pretending* to be a Texas cowhand. My informants say Wilson is the leader of this counterfeit ring, and he's from Ohio. His partners are Tom Cooper, W. W. West, and Sam Dedrick. He also may be running with an bandit called Kid Antrim, alias William H. Bonney."

"Bonney." Leonard hadn't meant to say the name aloud, and felt the heat rush to his head as the other men stared at him.

"Lincoln County again," Barnes said in disgust.

Wild's small head bobbed. "We've found bogus money in Lincoln and White Oaks. Now, if Marshal Sherman will issue warrants for the arrest of these men, I think we can solve this matter quickly."

"I prefer not to do so," Sherman said.

"What?" Wild was flabbergasted, and Leonard couldn't blame him.

"It's Lincoln County, sir," Sherman said.

"I'm well aware of that, Marshal, but—"

Rynerson interrupted him. "You don't know Lincoln County very well, Agent Wild."

"I've read the newspaper stories. But from the reports in Washington, sir, Governor Wallace has cleaned up the lawless element."

Wallace sank into his chair.

"Not all of it," Rynerson said. "Rustling is rampant, and as you have pointed out, the Kid is still free. It's no surprise to me that he is an associate of this counterfeiter."

"They must be stopped," Wild said.

"If I could get some help down there," said Sherman, trying to cover his retreat. "But the county sheriff there is worthless, and, with all due respect, Governor, the Lincoln County Mounted Rifles, a vigilante group, is not upholding the law. Too biased. But it's not Governor Wallace's fault. Your intentions were good, sir."

Wallace nodded at the halfhearted compliment.

"We need a solution," Barnes said. "We need someone who can make a difference in Lincoln County."

For the first time, Wallace spoke. "Gentlemen," he said, "I think I might have that solution. John Chisum has recommended a man who can clean up Lincoln County, and I believe he is right."

October 6, 1880
White Oaks, New Mexico Territory

The letter must have been slipped underneath the front door of Susan McSween's new house sometime after they left for the Wednesday night prayer meeting in the ever-growing gold town. She picked it up, recognized the handwriting, and handed it to Ira Leonard.

"It's from Billy," she said.

He ripped it open excitedly as he moved closer to the lantern. "No one would blame you if you dropped him, Ira," she said softly, "like a hot rock, which is what he is. He's almost gotten you killed once already."

"That was a blessing," he said absently.

With a mirthless chuckle, she shook her head. "You are quite the bibleback for a man who still drinks tequila and enjoys frequent dalliances with a certain widow."

He didn't appear to hear her, and she sighed while reading over his shoulder.

6 Oct. 80
Judge Leonard:
  I'm tired of running and am willing to face a jury of my peers. If you can talk to Governor Wallace about upholding his end of the bargain, I have new information that might prove helpful to the man chasing the counterfeiters. If Pat Garrett is elected county sheriff, I will feel more confident. Pat's a good man, and a friend. Just make sure Governor Wallace keeps his promises.

                              Your pal,
                              W. H. Bonney

"Poor kid." Leonard folded the letter.

"Poor?" she said acidly. "He's running around with a confidence man passing around false hundred dollar notes, he's rustling John's cattle, he's got a dozen Mexican wenches who think he's Romeo, and he's got you for a lawyer, and you won't even charge him a dime."

"Poor kid," Leonard repeated. "John Chisum is backing Pat Garrett for sheriff, and Garrett's first order of business will be to track him down. If the Santa Fe Ring can't kill him, Garrett and Chisum will. Billy thinks Garrett's his friend, but he's being played for a fool."

Exasperated, she muttered an oath and headed for the bedroom. "I've known the Kid longer than you. I've seen him at his best and at his worst. You're the fool, Ira, and it's the Kid who's playing you. You'll learn that soon enough. See yourself out, will you?"

Chapter 10

*"Emigrants are coming in, and we only need peace
to become a prosperous and happy people."*
                                    —*Mesilla News,* March 1, 1879

November 3, 1880
Las Cruces, New Mexico Territory

In front of a boisterous crowd at the Aztec Lodge Number 3,
a beaming William Rynerson lifted his glass of whiskey. "It is
a pleasure to introduce my friend, my colleague, and the new
attorney for the Third Judicial District of the Territory of New
Mexico, the honorable Simon B. Newcomb."

From the back of the adobe temple, Newcomb bowed
slightly and maneuvered through the crowd, smiling, shaking
hands as glasses clinked and a few men clapped politely. He
gripped Rynerson's hand, feeling like a dwarf standing next to
this living, bearded telegraph pole. "Come shake hands with
this fine Freemason," Rynerson said.

"It's high time you retired, Will!" a voice shouted, and
Rynerson joined the laughter.

Newcomb's facial muscles hurt from his permanent smile
as he stood there listening to the well wishes of men like Al-
bert J. Fountain, Warren Bristol, Numa Reymond, and John
Lemon, the latter two partners of Rynerson, along with James
Dolan, in the Feliz Land & Cattle Company in Lincoln
County.

"What made you decide to give up your powerful job to

this young runt?" asked rancher Wesley Sutton, who winked his amusement while crushing Newcomb's hand.

"Fifty-two is too old to be preaching to jurors who don't even speak English, Wes," Rynerson answered. "But I'll be keeping my eyes on this young man, making sure he has the best interests of the territory foremost in mind when he stands up in court."

Someone else asked about Pat Garrett and his landslide victory yesterday as Lincoln County sheriff.

"John Chisum has favored us by supporting Pat Garrett," said Rynerson, playing the politician again, "as our governor has favored us by appointing Simon here as my successor. Between the two of them, I think the lawless element in our territory will soon be obliterated."

"Including the Kid?" banker Timothy Merriman asked.

"Specifically the Kid."

December 3, 1880
Santa Fe, New Mexico Territory

Ira Leonard lifted the book, bound in beautiful morocco leather, from the brown paper and read the title: *Ben-Hur: A Tale of the Christ.*

"It is one of only ten copies bound in leather like that," Lew Wallace said, "and I have inscribed a sentiment for you."

Leonard opened the volume carefully.

> *To Judge Ira E. Leonard, who found true salvation through His love and without my help.*
>
> > *Yours in Christ,*
> > *Lew Wallace*
> > *30 November 1880*

"It's beautiful, General," Leonard said. "I will read it before my trip back south. When was it published?"

"A few weeks ago. I am already receiving grand reviews, and I am confident President Garfield will appoint me to a position worthy of my status after his inauguration."

Wallace clipped a cigar and leaned back in his chair while Leonard walked to the window and stared at the falling snow blanketing the deserted plaza with a white carpet. He lit the cigar. "But of course, you did not travel all the way from White Oaks in this weather for me to repeat accolades. I have heard about Bonney's latest depredations."

Not quite a week earlier, William Bonney and his *compadres* had been caught by Sheriff Garrett's posse at the Greathouse & Kuch ranch. One of the deputies, named James Carlyle, had been shot dead, and in the confusion, Bonney and his gang had escaped.

"Your client is always murdering peace officers, Ira. It does not bode well for his future."

"With all due respect, Bonney did not kill Carlyle. The deputy was shot by one of his own men. A terrible accident, but not premeditated murder on the part of my client."

Wallace stared at a blue stream of smoke snaking toward the cottonwood vigas. "You were there?"

"No, sir. Bonney told me this in a letter."

The governor shook his head sadly. "I cannot help you with Bonney, Ira. Frankly, Mr. Barnes, Agent Wild, and Attorney Newcomb are urging me to post a reward for the young fiend's delivery to justice. He is a murderer. You have heard how he shot down that gentleman—Grant, I believe he was called—in Fort Sumner less than a year ago. And he is riding with a wanted counterfeiter. I pray he does not pay you with Wilson's hundred-dollar notes."

"I would expect better from you, General, than low sarcasm," Leonard said.

Wallace, looking hurt, apologized before Leonard left the office.

December 15, 1880
Anton Chico, New Mexico Territory

The Kid swept off his sombrero when Elodia Rosendo brought him a sackful of warm tortillas on her way to confession. She had likely planned to give the food to the priest, but the Kid always knew she liked him better. He had danced with her two daughters on numerous occasions, had always dropped a handful of coins at the church door, and a tad more at her front gate, whenever he rode by. Doc Scurlock used to joke that the Kid was playing Robin Hood, but the Kid—and an educated man like Scurlock—knew better. The money left behind at a bump in the road like Anton Chico was a good investment for hard times like these days.

After he thanked and praised her, Elodia Rosendo promised to remember the Kid's name in Mass and said she would not give the long-legged, thin-lipped peace officer any tortillas or let him and his ill lot water their horses from her cistern even if that *pendejo*—the Kid's eyebrows arched at her use of such a word—had gotten married in that very church where they stood.

The Kid tossed the sack to Charlie Bowdre and stared at the twin-steepled, white-washed adobe. "You mean to tell me that Juan Largo got hitched . . . there?" He turned back to her and repeated the question in Spanish.

"Sí."

"Con quien se caso el?"

"Apolonaria Gutierrez."

"Son of a gun." He had often danced with her, too.

He thanked Elodia Rosendo again for her generosity and help and watched her until she disappeared inside the church, then cursed Billie Wilson to stop hogging the food. The counterfeiter smiled and tossed him a corn tortilla.

O'Folliard and Bowdre had never understood why the Kid had invited Billie Wilson to join them. After all, when they first met up in Colorado, Wilson had tried to pass them a shise bill, and the Kid had drawn his Thunderer, pulling the trigger slowly, watching the hammer self-cock and the blood drain from Wilson's face before lowering the hammer and laughing out loud after Wilson drenched the front of his striped breeches.

For that matter, the Kid never understood why Billie Wilson had elected to ride with them after embarrassing himself so. Months later, though, they had grown to like each other. Billie Wilson was a Yankee, quick with a joke and smarter than anyone who had ever saddled up with the Kid except Doc Scurlock, and Doc had lit a shuck for Texas. He could talk to Wilson about anything from Shakespeare to Milton, from guns and money to women and fashion.

"We're branching out," the Kid had told O'Folliard and Bowdre. "You two boys always said we needed to get out of the rustling business. Billie here can pass his bad money, I can gamble, and we'll hurt the Ring where they'll miss it the most."

Big Tom O'Folliard had tried to make a joke: "You can call yourselves the two Billies!"

"B-b-b-branchin' . . . out." Bowdre had nodded with a smile.

He was still branching out, he thought as he swallowed the last bit of tortilla before tightening the cinch on his bay mare and pulling himself into the saddle. Murderous Dave Rudabaugh, a friend of Bowdre's, had joined the riders at White Oaks back in November. Rudabaugh had been robbing trains and stagecoaches across the West for a few years. The gang was changing. Gone were the Regulators, seeking revenge for John Tunstall's murder, although O'Folliard and Bowdre remained from those times. These days, they rode together to stay alive. The Kid didn't like Rudabaugh one whit, but with Pat Garrett on his trail, he might need Rudabaugh's guns.

"Garrett," the Kid whispered tightly. He thought he might have a friend in the newly elected Lincoln County sheriff, but old Juan Largo had been hounding the Kid for a month now, riding him harder than anyone since William Brady. He looked down the road, hoping he wouldn't detect any more dust. Their horses needed a rest.

No luck. He cursed Garrett again, although the dust could have come from some civilian teamster or Mexican family. He couldn't take that chance, though.

"Did you post your letter to your sweet wife, Charlie?"

"Yeah."

"Then let's ride, pals." He smiled his old Billy smile to cheer up his friends. "I hear there's a dance at Fort Sumner tomorrow night."

Chapter 11

"I saw the two Billies the other day, & they say they are going to leave this country. That was my advice to them, for I believe it is the best thing they can do."

—Charlie Bowdre

December 15, 1880
Las Vegas, New Mexico Territory

After settling into his office chair, Ira Leonard unfolded the *Gazette* and let out a sigh when he came to the advertisement on the front page. Wallace had wasted little time. He couldn't blame the governor's methods, knowing how Wallace felt betrayed by the Kid, but William Bonney was Leonard's client, and this announcement, although small and with Bonney's name misspelled, was grim. The governor had likely placed similar advertisements in newspapers throughout the territory.

"This will bring out every piker in New Mexico," he said to himself and dropped the paper on his lap.

BILLY, THE KID.

———

$500 REWARD.

———

I WILL PAY $500 REWARD TO ANY PERSON OR
PERSONS WHO WILL CAPTURE WILLIAM BONNY, ALIAS
THE KID, AND DELIVER HIM TO ANY SHERIFF OF NEW

MEXICO. SATISFACTORY PROOFS OF IDENTITY WILL
BE REQUIRED.

LEW WALLACE
GOVERNOR OF NEW MEXICO

He longed for a drink but had not taken a sip of nose paint since Susan McSween had ended their relationship, though she retained him as her attorney. She had been right, too. Instead of acting like a Christian, he had been nothing more than a creeping Jesus, one of those religious hypocrites he had scoffed at before Jessie Evans had tried to kill him and he had realized just how much the fires of Hell scared him. No more John Barleycorn, no more cigars, and no more horizontal refreshments with women of the tenderloin or buxomly widows.

Leonard felt better, too. He hadn't suffered an asthma attack in weeks, had lost a few pounds, so that he needed his suspenders to keep his pants up, and his brain didn't seem so addled. He leaned back in his chair, glanced at the *Gazette* again, and ran his fingers through his beard. The notice did not say "dead or alive," but *capture*. The Santa Fe Ring, Thomas Catron, Sidney Barnes, William Rynerson, and his cynical replacement, Simon Newcomb, would likely prefer the law bring the Kid in as a corpse, but Sheriff Pat Garrett was a *me* politician. The rumor going around Las Vegas and Santa Fe had it that Garrett had hired Ash Upson, a Lincoln County journalist and postmaster—but mostly a drunkard— to ride with the posse and ghostwrite Garrett's account of his pursuit of the Kid. Bonney's outlawry had started garnering notice in papers back East, and Garrett must have figured that a book might earn him a tidy profit. The governor's reward would appeal to Garrett, and he might try his best to bring Bonney in alive. On the other hand, the Ring would likely pay Garrett extra if he killed the Kid.

Still, Leonard decided he would begin working on the assumption that Bonney would be captured alive and stand trial. He would begin preparing his case. He'd head back to Santa Fe in the morning. He hoped the Kid had enough sense to know that his best chance of staying alive was in a courtroom, not in a gun battle against Pat Garrett.

December 16, 1880
Puerto de Luna, New Mexico Territory

He bit into the apple, the first solid food he had eaten since leaving White Oaks two days ago, and devoured the fruit in front of Alexander Grzelachowski's store while the twenty or so members of his posse sampled the contents of the Pole's whiskey selection.

Pat Garrett stared at the dust until he could just make out the horseman, gave the apple core to his buckskin gelding, and washed down his breakfast with tepid water from his canteen. By the time he had replaced the stopper and secured the canteen to the saddle horn, the rider had dismounted. Garrett stepped away from his horse and waited for the newcomer, whom he recognized, to finish beating the dust off his chaps and hat. Joseph Lea looked at the men gathered closest to the store and shifted his feet uncomfortably.

"Capt'n," Garrett called out, and Lea turned, breathing easier as he covered the distance quickly. They shook hands.

"Long way from home," Garrett commented.

"Lookin' for you, Sheriff," Lea said in an easy Tennessee accent. Lea had been a colonel in the Confederacy. Why everyone demoted him to captain, Garrett could not guess. Lea unbuttoned his coat, reached inside with his right hand, but stopped. One of Garrett's men had backhanded another deputy to the ground and stood over him, cursing him, pointing a double-barrel shotgun at the man's groin.

"Bob," Garrett said, annoyed, and the man whirled, his eyes violent, but stopped when he recognized Garrett. "If you don't cork that temper, I'll take that shotgun from you and send you home. Now help Jim up, and you boys stop actin' like a bunch of flat-noggins." Garrett shrugged an apology at Lea.

"That's Bob Olinger?" Lea sounded incredulous.

"I got some good men with me, Capt'n," he said defensively. "Admit I got my share of sheezicks, too, but a body can't be that particular when he's chasin' the Kid. In case you ain't heard, Dave Rudabaugh's ridin' with him, not just that flimflam Billie Wilson."

With a slight nod, Lea withdrew a crumpled envelope. "I heard," he said. "Got this yesterday. Rode all night to bring it to you."

Garrett pulled out the letter and struggled to make sense out of the chicken-scratch scrawl and lack of punctuation. He gave up briefly, turned to the third and final page, and squinted to read the signature: *Respt. Chas Bowdre.*

"Charlie Bowdre." He whistled and read the letter carefully while Captain Lea explained.

"Bowdre wants to quit the gang, Pat," Lea said. "He says the Kid and that counterfeiter want to leave New Mexico Territory. All Bowdre wants is to live in peace with his wife. I know him, Pat. He trusts me. That's why he wrote me that letter. He knows the Lincoln County War's over, and ridin' with the Kid today ain't like it was when they was Regulators, avengin' Tunstall's murder." He stopped long enough to let Garrett finish the letter. When Garrett folded the papers and handed them back to Lea, the captain said, "I think Bowdre can help you catch the Kid."

"He trusts you," Garrett said. "Do you trust him?"

"He never done me no wrong."

"I hear he's a killer. I hear he shot Buckshot Roberts without cause. There's enough indictments on him to keep the district attorney busy for the next ten terms."

"Billy Bonney's the big snag in this territory, though. You know that, Pat. I think if I write him back—the Kid thinks he's writin' his wife, Manuela, and I'm supposed to reply to her over at Fort Sumner—he can lead you to Bonney."

"All right, Capt'n, you write your letter. Tell Bowdre I'll put in a good word for him with the governor and Newcomb, but you tell him he'd best quit the Kid *muy pronto,* because when I catch Little Casino—and I will—we won't be choosin' our targets real careful." He nodded at Olinger and the other drunken posse members, now laughing, drinking, and playing monte on the Pole's front porch. "I ain't ridin' with twenty Pinkerton agents, Capt'n. You tell Bowdre that."

Garrett watched Lea hurry back to his horse, mount up, and ride away, and he shook his head. Lea was so aghast at Garrett's posse, he didn't even bother to feed or water his horse, though he'd likely do that at some nearby greaser's jacal or a friendly ranch. Garrett tugged on his mustache, thinking. He had never been much of a letter writer, but Bowdre and Lea had given him something to study on. He pivoted toward the store and yelled, "Cal!"

Cal Polk, one of the few deputies he trusted, lowered his horse's right forefoot, slid a hoof pick into his back pocket, and walked over.

"You need me, Sheriff?" Polk asked.

"What was the name of that Mexican you questioned earlier this mornin'?"

"José Valdéz. He said he hadn't seen the Kid, though."

"Yeah. Well, I want you to ride back to his place, take Olinger and Juan Roibal with you. Tell him to write a letter to Bonney. Tell him to say that we've rode back to Roswell with Capt'n Lea and that it's safe at Sumner."

Polk shook his head. "Pat, he won't do that. Bonney's like a brother—"

"You're smarter than that, Cal," he snapped. "That's why you're takin' Olinger with you. Send the letter in care of Manuela Bowdre at Fort Sumner." He looked skyward. The clouds were getting grayer, and the wind was picking up, turning colder. It would snow before nightfall. "We'll meet you at the Gayheart ranch. Make sure that letter gets delivered to Mrs. Bowdre tonight." He walked back to his horse, gathered the buckskin's reins, and yelled: "Mount up, boys!"

December 19, 1880
Fort Sumner, New Mexico Territory

Garrett's boots disappeared in the snow, and he wondered if even Little Casino would travel in such weather. He pushed open the door to the old army hospital with the stock of his

Winchester, kicked the snow off his boots, and felt refreshed by the warmth from the fireplace, the smell of Arbuckles', hot whiskey, tortillas and beans. Deputy Jim East handed him a steaming cup of coffee, and Garrett smiled.

The Kid would come tonight. The note from José Valdéz would bring him, and the promise of hot food, warm beds, and maybe those two petticoats he fancied at Pete Maxwell's house, Deluvina and Paulita. It was just a matter of time. He tossed the rifle on a table and checked his watch—eight o'clock—and heard someone stumbling through foot-deep snow. The door slammed open, and Deputy Lon Chambers cried out: "Somebody's comin' in from the east, Sheriff."

"Boys, get your guns." Garrett shoved his watch into his vest pocket and grabbed the Winchester. "None but the men we're after would be ridin' on a night like this." Of the five men in the hospital, four followed him into the frozen night; the fifth, Ash Upson, was passed out on the floor, curled up with a bottle of rye.

Garrett had stationed his men throughout the town, which wasn't much of a town, really—nothing more than an abandoned fort now occupied by Pete Maxwell's family and hired hands, plus a bunch of strumpets and out-of-work saddle tramps—like it had been when he had first ridden into New Mexico with Little Casino, Charlie Bowdre, and the others.

Keeping to the shadows, Garrett moved through the snow and nodded at Juan Roibal. Roibal wet his lips and shouted, *"Tequila! Mas tequila, por favor!* My blood is frozen." That was the signal for his scattered posse. A whistle, a coyote's cry, or something else wouldn't have worked. Little Casino was too smart for that.

A freezing fog began thickening, rising off the snow like a graying curtain, and he knew he had to act fast, while they could still see. He could just make out the riders in the moonlight riding down the Blanco Road. His heart quickened, and he used the Winchester's barrel to motion Barney Mason to circle around the building and cut off any escape. A horse snorted, and someone spoke, the voice too muffled to understand. Garrett quietly pulled back the hammer and raised the rifle to his shoulder. The moon disappeared behind a cloud, and he swore softly, although he could still make out the figures. The snow reflected enough light, and he had seen that the man riding out front wore a big Mexican sombrero.

He held his breath as the riders slowly kicked their horses into a walk. Three hundred yards away, getting closer. Fifty . . . finally ten.

"Throw up your hands!" Garrett shouted.

They answered with their guns.

His Winchester kicked, and through the smoke he saw the man in the sombrero bend over the saddle, heard him say, "I'm kilt, Billy, I'm kilt," and Garrett realized his mistake.

He fired again and heard nothing else but a battery of explosions. When the moon reappeared, the riders, all except one, were gone, and he cursed the Kid's luck. Garrett stepped from the shadows and walked toward the dun horse. The slumped rider—he was too big for the Kid, Garrett could see now—lifted his head as Garrett grabbed the reins.

"Don't shoot, Garrett," Tom O'Folliard whispered and fell into the snow. Cal Polk pushed him over with his boot, and O'Folliard groaned. He had been shot in his chest, almost in the heart, dropping beads of frozen blood that sank into the snow.

"Get him inside," Garrett told Barney Mason. He picked up the crushed sombrero, one he had seen the Kid wear often, and hurled it into the darkness.

The boys were playing poker, waiting for Big Tom O'Folliard to die, when Garrett walked inside the old hospital. Garrett had sent Cal Polk and Jim East to follow the Kid's trail. He knew they'd lose it in the fog and darkness, but that didn't concern him. His trap had almost worked, and they had wounded at least one horse. Little Casino's luck was playing out. They'd catch him in a few days.

Manuela Bowdre stood beside the table serving as O'Folliard's bed, holding his hand. Garrett poured a cup of coffee, sweetening it with two fingers of Ash Upson's whiskey. One of the Maxwell girls—Paulita, he saw—barged into the room and gasped, but Manuela shook her head, telling her it wasn't

Billy, and the pretty *puta* crossed herself and left, but not before casting a malevolent glare at Garrett.

After taking a sip from the mug, Garrett walked to the table. Manuela Bowdre would not meet his gaze, but he didn't care what she thought about him anyway.

"Tom," Garrett said.

"God damn . . . you . . . Garrett," the big man stammered. "Hope . . . to see . . . you . . . in hell."

"I wouldn't talk like that, Tom," he said, though he didn't believe in Hell, or God. "You'll be dead in a few minutes."

"Go to . . . hell . . . you . . ." He laughed. "You . . . long-legged . . . son of a bitch."

"Where's Little Casino, Tom?"

No answer.

"He must have thought mighty good of you, Tom, lettin' you wear his greaser hat like that, knowin' we'd be aimin' for you."

"Won it . . . ," he said. "Poker . . . Can I have . . . a drink of . . . water?"

Now Manuela looked up at Garrett, who nodded.

"Weather won't help your pals none, Tom. We'll catch 'em soon. Tell me where to find him."

No answer.

Garrett took another sip. Manuela hurried back with a water-filled gourd, lifted O'Folliard's head, and spoke to him softly in Spanish. Tears rolled down her cheeks, and she pleaded with him to drink.

"Water can't do him no good." Garrett reached over with his left hand and closed O'Folliard's eyes.

Chapter 12

"Every one who has heard of Billy 'the Kid' has heard of his beautiful bay mare, about whos[e] speed some remarkable stories are told. Billy kept the beautiful mare very carefully and always reserves her for an emergency, fully appreciating her good qualities, and knowing full well that no other animal could run her down."
—*Las Vegas Morning Gazette,* January 4, 1881

December 22, 1880
Stinking Springs, New Mexico Territory

Icicles had formed on their beards by the time they reached old Alejandro Perea's miserable forage shack. Dave Rudabaugh, whose horse had been hit during the ambuscade at Fort Sumner and died after running a couple of miles, rode double behind Tom Pickett, a friend of Charlie Bowdre's who had brought them José Valdéz's letter from Bowdre's wife. Billie Wilson's horse had played out; so had Wilson. Counterfeiters weren't used to such hard traveling. He had lost his hat during the row at Sumner and whimpered so much that Bowdre gave him his just to shut him up. Bowdre, riding beside the Kid, dismounted into the deepening snow, drew his Colt, and kicked open the stone building's lone door.

"It's . . . e-emp-ty," Bowdre stuttered, and the riders stiffly swung from the saddles.

"Let's build a fire," Billie Wilson said, "and see if there's something to eat. I'm starved."

"No fire." The Kid led his bay through the door, while the others tied their mounts outside to the ends of the vigas sticking through the stone wall. There wasn't room for any more horses in the cramped little building anyway.

When Rudabaugh struck a match against a stone to look around, Wilson said he wished they had a candle.

"Why don't we just burn some of your shise notes?" Rudabaugh said bitterly, closing the door behind him. "You ain't gonna be able to spend 'em before too long." He shook out the match and struck another one.

The inside smelled of dust and hay, and the Kid could feel the wind sweeping in through cracks between the stones, but it was noticeably warmer inside, and it beat freezing to death on the Llano Estacado. He knocked snow and ice off his sombrero and thought briefly about the hat O'Folliard had been wearing. He decided not to think about Big Tom anymore and kicked a blanket he spotted on the floor. When no rats scampered from underneath it, he picked it up, beat off the dust, and settled down, bracing his back against a hay bale.

Rudabaugh's match flickered and died, leaving the five men and bay horse in total darkness. Outside, the wind wailed. Bowdre fumbled with the knots securing his bedroll behind the saddle's cantle and finally gave up, covering himself with hay to keep warm. Someone, most likely Rudabaugh, uncorked a bottle. Whiskey gurgled.

"How long can we stay here?" Billie Wilson asked.

"Till morning," Tom Pickett answered. "Then I'm parting ways with you boys."

"I-I-I'll . . . be . . . ri-ridin' with . . . you," Bowdre said.

"It's time I left the territory, too," Wilson said.

Hell, the Kid thought, Fort Sumner and this windswept prairie seemed like a thousand miles from the rugged mountains around Lincoln. He always figured he would be safe here. He cursed the Ring, John Chisum, and the others who hated him, or, in Pat Garrett's case, had betrayed him.

"You ready to quit New Mexico?" Rudabaugh asked. "Now?"

He laughed because they expected that from lighthearted William H. Bonney. "Before Christmas? You know they'll be throwing a regular fandango at Pete's, and I haven't gotten my present from Paulita yet."

Someone sniggered. "If you boys want to leave," he added, "I won't stop you." Actually, he'd be glad to be rid of the whole lot, even Charlie Bowdre and his incessant stuttering. Bowdre was worse than Garrett. He thought he was tricking the Kid with his recent interest in correspondence, but the Kid wasn't blind, and no stammering killer could play him for a fool. He'd sell out the Kid for thirty pieces of silver. Let them all go, quit him like Doc Scurlock and Jim French. They weren't his friends, not anymore.

His horse broke wind, and the Kid said: "Criminy, boys, the way you-all fart, it's a wonder I've tolerated you as long as I have."

They laughed at his joke. William Bonney . . . Kid Antrim . . . *El Chivato,* always the jester. Let them think that.

December 23, 1880
Stinking Springs, New Mexico Territory

They heard snores from inside the stone building as the sky began lightening in the east. Only three horses were tied outside, none of them Bonney's bay, but Pat Garrett doubted the gang had split up. Someone climbed out of the arroyo with him, and he smelled Bob Olinger.

"Rush 'em?" Olinger asked.

"No," Garrett said. "We'll wait till full light." He backed down, leaving Olinger with his shotgun and whiskey jug, and found Cal Polk. "Cal," he said, "take six of the boys around back. Juan, you look after the horses, and don't let 'em bolt when the shootin' starts. The rest of us'll wait here."

"Why don't we rush 'em?" Olinger had rejoined the posse. "Sneak up on 'em while they's sleepin'?"

"Because we got 'em bottled up in that shack. Ain't but

one way in. If we go rushin' in now, before we can all see clearly, they'll scamper like they did at Sumner, and the Kid shoots pretty good, Bob. You'd make a pretty target runnin' across the flats. We wait."

"How do we play it when it gets light?" Barney Mason asked.

"We'll announce our intentions when the first gent steps through that door."

"If it's the Kid?"

"Kill him!" Olinger snapped. "You cut the head off a rattler . . ."

"The governor might not pay that reward if he's dead," someone argued.

"Keep your voices down." Garrett wiped his ice-crusted mustache. "We kill the first man out the door."

When the door opened shortly after dawn, one man stepped outside into the snow. He wore a sugarloaf hat with a green hatband and carried a nosebag toward the nearest horse. It might be the Kid, but then Tom O'Folliard had been wearing Bonney's hat at Fort Sumner. It didn't matter one way or the other, Garrett thought, and, after nodding toward the others, thumbed back the Winchester's hammer.

Their guns barked simultaneously, and the man cried out as bullets tore into him. The feed bag disappeared in a snow drift, and the horses cried, tugging hard against the tethers. Lead whined off the rock wall as the man staggered back and fell through the doorway. "Hold your fire!" Garrett yelled, lowering his rifle. Just as soon as the shooting stopped, another man leaped outside, grabbing the reins to one terrified horse and jumping back inside before anyone chanced a shot.

"He's tryin' to get that hoss inside!" Olinger shouted, but Garrett just smiled.

"Let him." He braced the stock against his shoulder and waited.

The dun mare, still spooked from the shooting, had no interest in joining the party inside. Someone inside the shack cursed, tugged harder on the reins. The horse pranced, whinnied, and finally lowered its head. When it was blocking the door, about to go inside, Garrett shot it in the head. The horse dropped in a heap, and Garrett whispered to Jim East, "If Billy's horse is inside, he'll play hell gettin' her over that carcass."

Another curse from inside the cabin, and the door slammed shut.

Minutes passed. Garrett wet his lips, anxious. Finally came a voice he did not recognize: "Bowdre is dying and wants to come out."

"Shit!" Garrett sighed. First O'Folliard, now Bowdre. He told Mason, "We've killed the one man we didn't want to kill."

"Couldn't be helped," the deputy said. "He'll have to take his medicine."

"Send him out!" Garrett shouted and waited.

The door opened, and Charlie Bowdre staggered outside, clutching his stomach.

"He's still carrying his pistols," warned Mason, lifting a Remington Rolling Block.

"I doubt if he could hold one," Garrett said.

After ten yards, Bowdre sank to his knees, and Garrett thought he might topple over there, but he pulled himself up, plowing through the snow, bleeding like a hog at a slaughterhouse, leaving a trail of blood. He stopped briefly, looking left to right, confused.

"Over here!" Garrett yelled, and Bowdre swallowed, coughed, continued. Garrett handed his rifle to Mason and climbed out of the arroyo to meet the dying man.

"You damn fool!" Mason shouted. "You'll get your head blowed off."

Garrett didn't think so. There were no gunports or windows in the stone cabin, and Bowdre, blood seeping from the corners of his mouth, posed no threat. "I w-wish . . . ," he said. "I . . . w-w-wish . . ." He collapsed in Garrett's arms.

He dragged him down the arroyo and laid him on a blanket. Bowdre blinked once and was dead.

Another voice called out from the shack; Garrett recognized this one. "Juan Largo, is that you?"

"You know it is, Billy!" Garrett answered.

Silence.

"Get some coffee boilin'," Garrett ordered Mason. "And fry up bacon. Them boys ain't goin' nowheres."

Two hours later, Garrett decided to begin negotiations.

"How you fixed, Billy?"

"Pretty well," the Kid answered, jovial as always, "but we have no wood for breakfast. Your coffee smells good."

"Come and get some. Be a little sociable."

"Can't do, Juan Largo. Business is too confining. No time to run around."

Garrett laughed and went back to the fire to warm himself. He'd try again after dinner.

"It's no use."

The blood from the dead horse outside spooked the bay, and the Kid knew Rudabaugh was right. No matter how hard he spurred, he couldn't motivate his horse through the door. Cursing underneath his breath, he slid off the bay, careful not to knock his head on the low ceiling.

"They got us, Billy," Pickett said. He had been willing to give up since seeing his pal Bowdre shot to hell.

A few hours ago they had tried to chisel a hole through the rear wall, a long shot to be sure, but the posse must have heard the noise because someone had fired a couple of rounds at the spot, the bullets spanging off stones, and they had given up. The Kid's bay horse was their last chance, unless they wanted to make a break outside afoot, and that wouldn't get them anywhere except dead like Bowdre.

"Got another pot of coffee on, Billy!" Pat Garrett yelled. "And a wagonload of hot chuck for you boys!"

"Go to hell, you cowardly son of a bitch!" He meant it, too. His sense of humor had evaporated.

"Now, Billy, what would your ma say about that language?"

"You leave my mother out of this!" he shrieked until his voice cracked. "You hear me, Garrett? You don't mention my mother!"

"Billy . . . ," Pickett pleaded.

He kicked the wall and sighed.

"The game's over, Billy," Rudabaugh said.

His eyes blazed. "You're facing a rope, Dave, same as me."

"Yeah, and I figure I got a chance escaping any jail they lock me up in. Ain't got no chance here."

"How many jails have you clumb out of?" Billie Wilson asked, and the Kid smiled. He could turn his anger off and on like a spigot on a keg of beer.

"You got a pretty good lawyer, too," Rudabaugh said, "from what you've told me. Besides, if you want to get that present from Paulita Maxwell, I warrant they'll be takin' us through Fort Sumner on the way to Santa Fe."

He knew they were right, especially Billie Wilson. No jail had ever held him for long, so if the posse outside didn't kill them on the spot, he probably could escape. Having never seen the jails in Las Vegas or Santa Fe, he wondered if either had a chimney. He cracked open the door and yelled: "Pat, how many men you got out there?"

"An army, Little Casino. Got enough grub to feed an army, too. You boys must be hungry."

"You give your word you'll treat us fair? Give your word as a pal?"

"You got it, pardner."

He made himself grin his ol' Billy grin as he opened the door and tossed his Thunderer over the dead horse. He took a deep breath and stepped into the light, raising his hands over his head. The wind made him cringe, but the smell of coffee and bacon started his stomach rumbling. He spotted the towering Garrett immediately. A man to Garrett's right raised his rifle, but the Kid never stopped smiling. Garrett told the deputy not to shoot, yet the big buffalo rifle didn't waver.

"Kill the son of a bitch!" the man said. "He's slippery and might get away."

"You kill him," Garrett said, "and I'll bury you." The barrel dropped.

"I thought you had a hundred Texans out here," the Kid said, feeling easier now, covering the distance between the stone shack and the arroyo quickly. "Hell, if I had known there was no more than this, you'd never have gotten me."

Garrett handed him a tin cup.

"That may be, Little Casino," Garrett said, "but I thought it was better for you to come out and get a good square meal. Don't you?"

Chapter 13

*"Judge Leonard passed through here on his way
East in January and promised to come and see me on
his way back, but he did not fulfill his promise. It
looks to me like I am getting left in the cold."*
—Billy the Kid to Governor Lew Wallace, March 4, 1881

December 24, 1880
Santa Fe, New Mexico Territory

Dust-mote-filled rays of light crept into the cold, dark room,
and Ira Leonard thought he might suffer an asthma attack before he finished his work in the territorial archives. After
drawing the curtains to let in much-needed light, he turned
around, sighing at the task before him. He had no idea what
he was looking for, just something that might help him at
trial . . . if Bonney ever came to trial. Even if he had an inclination, or had been struck by divine revelation, he could
not guess where to begin. Files were scattered about like
grapeshot, stacked here and there in unlabeled boxes or simply thrown on top of each other.

On the nearest shelf he found yellowed paper, almost
brown, written in Spanish, and assumed it to be some land
grant. Next to it was a copy of a meaningless order from former Governor Sam Axtell. More than two centuries sepa-
rated the two items, but here they were filed together.

Wearily, he sat down at a table covered with rolled maps,
most of them military, all of them fairly recent. He rolled one
over, picked it up, and held it to the light, reading on the side:

Mescalero Reservation, 1873. Apaches had jumped the federal reserve during the past year, adding to the governor's woes, so some unfortunate servant of the people had likely been sent to this abyss to bring the maps to the governor's office and return them.

The door opened, and he looked up, surprised to find former U.S. Attorney Thomas Catron standing in the hallway, smoking a cigar, smiling that irksome smile. Catron flicked ash and stepped inside, ignoring the sign that prohibited smoking lest three centuries of records, maps, and letters be reduced to cinders.

"I was told I could find you here," Catron said. Though he no longer held public office, Catron wielded much power in the territory with his successful bank, law firm, and contacts. He coughed, probably from the dust and not tobacco smoke, and grinned the grin of knowledge. He had news; could hardly wait to spill his secret.

Leonard busied himself, opening the map of the reservation as if he did not care what Catron had to say. He stared at the map as if it cited legal precedent and said, without looking at the visitor, "You have found me."

"And Pat Garrett has found the Kid."

His head shot up. Catron's grin stretched wider.

"Alive or dead?" Leonard asked.

"Alive, at last correspondence. Tom O'Folliard was killed in ambush at Fort Sumner. A few days later, Garrett's posse caught the Kid's gang at some line shack, storage bin, or farmhouse. It depends on who's telling the story. Bowdre was shot and killed resisting arrest, but the others—Bonney, Wilson, Rudabaugh, and one more—surrendered without a fight. Garrett was taking them to Las Vegas, where they'll catch a train here while we can figure out what to do with them. Of course, by now they could be shot dead trying to escape, and, from what I hear, Dave Rudabaugh won't be welcome in Las Vegas. They might all be lynched."

"What case will come first?"

Catron shrugged. "That's up to Judge Bristol and prosecutor Rynerson—I mean Newcomb. I just thought you would like to know."

He thanked Catron through clenched teeth and looked back at the map. Catron laughed, wished him a merry Christmas, and left him alone with the dust.

Leonard began rolling up the map, but stopped when a small red block drew his attention. He brought the map closer and read the black ink next to the red symbol.

Blazer's Mill.

Divine intervention? Luck? He wasn't sure, but he muttered a prayer of thanks and unrolled the map for closer inspection. "Merry Christmas," he whispered.

January 21, 1881
Santa Fe, New Mexico Territory

The mustached Mexican in his best wool suit guided Warren Bristol to the private room at the New Era Chop House and Restaurant, where the judge found Thomas Catron, William Rynerson, Simon Newcomb, U.S. Attorney Sidney Barnes, James Dolan, and other prominent Masons from the Santa Fe, Las Vegas, and Las Cruces lodges—even politician W. G. Ritch—enjoying Irish whiskey and oysters. The Mexican took Bristol's greatcoat, pulled out a vacant chair, and asked, "Could I interest the judge in a drink before supper?"

"Whiskey," he said, taking a cigar offered by Catron.

The Mexican disappeared, and Newcomb struck a lucifer on the table, brought up the match, and lit the judge's cigar.

"The Kid has been busy writing our governor," Catron said.

Rynerson laughed. "Too bad our governor's too busy traveling east to west."

"Wallace has no interest in Mr. Bonney," Ritch said. "Not with his book a literary masterpiece, and not with a new president about to take office. He shall be gone by summer."

"Maybe before," Rynerson said. "And how was your day, Warren?"

Rynerson knew the answer. You couldn't keep secrets from this crowd. Besides, Newcomb had been in the courtroom earlier that afternoon and had already told that tall gent everything that could have interested him. "I set bail for Billie Wilson at five thousand dollars. He didn't have it, so he's back in jail with the Kid and Rudabaugh."

"I'm surprised," Catron said. "It stands to reason that five thousand would be a small amount for a counterfeiter."

"That leaves the Kid," said Newcomb, ending the banter. Serious frowns began forming around the table.

Dave Rudabaugh had pleaded guilty to mail robbery and had been sentenced to life, although he still faced a murder charge as well. Billie Wilson would be tried and convicted for counterfeiting, if he didn't plead guilty and hope for a lesser sentence. Charlie Bowdre's friend, Tom Pickett, had also entered a guilty plea on lesser charges and had been sentenced to six months and fined five hundred dollars. The rest of the banditti were either in prison, dead, or had fled New Mexico. The only cases waiting to be heard were the score facing William H. Bonney.

"The Kid's slick," said Dolan, already in his cups. "He's escaped I don't know how many times."

"Sheriff Martinez is taking care of that," Catron said. Bristol didn't know what the attorney meant by that, but he didn't ask. The waiter brought him his drink, and he tasted it. Brandy, not whiskey, but he didn't complain. He was too damned tired. "Don't worry," Catron added. "The Kid will stand trial."

"Which trial comes first?" Newcomb asked.

U.S. Attorney Sidney Barnes, a six-foot-tall Kentuckian with flowing red dundreary whiskers, leaned forward with interest, starring at Catron. Newcomb would handle the territorial case, while Barnes would prosecute a federal trial. Bristol, by virtue of his territorial and federal appointments, would be seated on either bench. Everyone looked to Catron for the answer. Bristol set his glass on the table and his cigar in a brass tray already overflowing with ashes.

"The venue has been set for La Mesilla for all capital charges facing Mr. Bonney," Catron said. "He is not well known in Doña Ana County, but I do not believe one can overlook the affinity the Mexican population has for this little rounder. The jury's the key."

"The jury's the key to any case," Barnes said.

"Which is why I think he should be tried in federal court for the murder of Buckshot Roberts." Catron refilled his glass.

"Why?" Newcomb asked.

Bristol answered. "*Voir dire.*" He had expected that. Newcomb still looked puzzled, so, after another sip of brandy, he explained: "In federal court, the judge handles the questioning of the jury panel, not the attorneys." He couldn't help scolding Rynerson's protégé. "I would think the prosecuting attorney for the Third Judicial District would know the law."

"I knew that," Newcomb said defensively.

"I'll seat a jury that will convict the Kid," Bristol said.

"Don't underestimate Mr. Leonard, friends," Catron said.

"Hell, he's only visited the Kid once since he arrived in jail," Dolan said. "I don't think he cares what happens to his client."

Catron glared. "Don't underestimate Leonard the way you and Murphy underestimated the Kid . . . and Tunstall . . . and McSween."

February 10, 1881
Blazer's Mill, New Mexico Territory

The captain at Fort Selden, a crumbling subpost just north of Las Cruces, had insisted on providing Ira Leonard an escort, and Leonard was glad to have the six colored troopers along, even if they had not seen one Apache, even if the soldiers seldom spoke to him and only the sergeant looked him in the eye.

They reined up at the little settlement of scattered buildings in the Tularosa Creek canyon, dominated by the big sawmill on the far side of the creek. The place seemed busier than the gambling dens of Las Vegas. Leonard swung down from the chestnut mare he had rented at Las Cruces, handed the reins to the sergeant, and unfastened his grip, tied behind the saddle with rawhide.

"I won't be long," he said, adding, "I hope."

Leonard glanced at the cemetery on the hillside as he walked toward a two-story adobe, then spotted a man with an armload of firewood walking toward the house. He had a square face, thinning white hair, and a neatly groomed mustache and beard. The man saw him and paused, staring with suspicion. A moment later, he dropped the load of wood and straightened with a grunt, placing his right hand on his back.

"You shouldn't be lifting, Doc," Leonard said. "Not with your back, sir."

Dr. Joseph H. Blazer still didn't recognize him, so Leonard held out his hand and introduced himself.

A smile erupted on Blazer's face, and he swallowed Leonard's hand with two meaty paws. "Gee-whillikens, Ira Leonard, your hair is whiter than mine."

"Lincoln County will do that to a fellow, sir."

"Lord, how I know that. What brings you out here? You still representing Mrs. McSween? How is Susan?"

"She's fine, sir. Living in White Oaks, talking about going into the cattle business. But I'm here as William Bonney's attorney, Doc."

Blazer nodded. "I read in one of the papers that Garrett arrested him. For goodness sakes, where are my manners? Come inside, Ira. I'll pour us both a cup of coffee."

The doctor's home was spartan—his wife had been dead more than ten years, and it showed—but the coffee tasted good.

"Bonney," said Blazer, shaking his head. "I was foreman of the grand jury back two—no, three—well, a few years ago. His name came up more than once."

"I know, sir." He opened his grip. "I expect him to be tried for the murder of Buckshot Roberts. I know you remember that."

"Would to God I could forget." The old man shook his head. "But Bonney didn't kill Buckshot. Bowdre did, only Buckshot was one game rooster, killed Dick Brewer and put the fear of God into those other Regulators before he died."

"But Bonney was here?"

"Yes, he was here all right."

"Then he could be charged with murder even if he didn't

pull the trigger. That's what the prosecution will argue, I expect."

"Well, sir, I never cared much for Bonney. Didn't know him that well, to be honest. But I'll do anything I can to help you, Ira. You don't have to serve me a subpoena. Just tell me when I have to show up, and where. Old Mesilla, I warrant?"

"Yes, sir." He pulled out the Mescalero Reservation map. "I'd like to ask you about the fight here. But first, I was wondering if you could help me with this."

Doc Blazer excused himself to find his spectacles as Leonard unrolled the map.

March 19, 1881
Santa Fe, New Mexico Territory

The light almost blinded the Kid.

He cursed, tried to shield his eyes with his hands, but the iron shackles were bolted to the floor, and the jailers had learned about his small hands and large wrists. For days the Kid had tugged until his wrists turned raw, but he couldn't free himself from the heavy manacles.

The door closed with a solid thud, and blessed darkness returned. He waited for the orange spots to fade away. Only then did he realize he had a visitor.

"Who's there?"

"It's me, Billy," said Ira Leonard.

"Where the hell have you been? You came by in January, and I ain't seen you since! I've been writing Governor Wallace, begging him to come visit, but he won't even answer my letters. I thought you was gone coon or turned Judas like Wallace."

Leonard's voice remained soothing. "I haven't abandoned you, Billy. I've been working on your case for the past few months. I told you that when I last visited. They're going to send you down south in a week or so. How long have they held you in solitary?"

"End of February." He laughed, his spirits lifted by the presence of a friend. "Rudabaugh, Wilson, and me had started a tunnel, hiding dirt and rocks in our mattresses. We had dug our way almost to Bridge Street, but Sheriff Martinez had put a turncoat in our cell. That *hijo de cabrón* told the jailer what we were doing, and he told Martinez, and the sheriff and a deputy marshal paid us a visit. I've been here ever since. Don't know what happened to Wilson and Rudabaugh. What day is it?"

When Leonard told him, the Kid cursed.

"I can't tell you how many times I've written Governor Wallace. Not easy, either, with these bracelets on, and the jailer charges me tobacco, on tic, for pencil and paper. I don't smoke, Ira. You reckon you could give that reprobate a sack?"

"I'll do it, Billy."

"I saved some of the notes Governor Wallace wrote me, and they can hurt him. You tell him that. He can get me out of this fix."

"General Wallace isn't going to help you, Billy, no matter how many times you write him or how often you threaten him."

"I'm not threatening him. How can I threaten him?" He lifted his hands as far as they could go, rattling the chains. "How can I when I'm shackled like a damned nigger?"

"Wallace is no longer governor, Billy. President Garfield accepted his resignation yesterday and has replaced him with Lionel Sheldon of Ohio. After Wallace leaves, if Sheldon is not here, W. G. Ritch will act in his stead, and Ritch is a Ring man. The general hopes for an appointment near the Holy Land."

"Closer to his Jesus country, huh?"

He heard Leonard sigh and decided maybe he shouldn't insult Leonard's newfound religion. "I haven't abandoned you, Billy, and I think I have a strong case for your defense. I'll tell you about it on the train. And I'll see what I can do to get you out of solitary."

Leonard knocked on the cell door, and the Kid screwed his eyes shut against the coming light.

"They going to try me in Old Mesilla?" he asked after the door had slammed shut.

Leonard's voice was muffled. "That's right, Billy."

He grinned. "Well, find out what the jail's like there, will you, Ira? This one, and the one in Las Vegas, haven't been worth a tinker's damn."

March 29, 1881
Las Cruces, New Mexico Territory

He felt better now that he was far from Santa Fe. Santa Fe's police chief, a Mexican named Francisco Chávez, had made sure the Kid's handcuffs were secure before turning him over to deputy marshals Tony Neis and Bob Olinger, and attorney Ira Leonard, for the trip to Doña Ana County. The Kid didn't mind Olinger, as long as the ill-tempered blowhard kept his mouth shut, and Olinger was obliging, although he kept that shotgun trained at the Kid's belly as the stagecoach jostled about on the road from Rincon.

He wondered how much La Mesilla had changed since he rode in that September day in '77, when he had met Tom O'Keefe and his life had been changed forever. He frowned at the memory of O'Keefe, staring out the window at the passing country, mostly dust, and did his best to forget all about that long-dead talkative Texan. Back then, it took forever to travel from Santa Fe to La Mesilla. Now that the rails had been laid, the journey took less than two days—a day by train to Rincon, then nine hours by stagecoach to the county seat—barring bad weather.

Ira Leonard's plan sounded like a good one, although the Kid wasn't sure if the Ring-backed judge or the prosecutor would let it stand. It didn't matter. One way or the other, the Ring would see to it that William H. Bonney faced a death sentence, and that didn't bother him, either. He didn't have any friends in La Mesilla, but he had scores in Lincoln, and they'd have to hang him in the county seat. He understood enough law to realize that.

And he would never hang in Lincoln.

The stage swayed to a stop at the way station, and the driver shouted down for the passengers to stretch their legs.

Olinger prodded the Kid with that scattergun. Leonard helped him up and guided him out of the coach, where thirty or forty people had gathered. All kinds, too. The Kid saw a few sporting girls, businessmen, farmers, Mexicans, a couple of gunmen maybe, lawmen, and a handful of newspaper reporters. He had enjoyed talking to newspaper men in Santa Fe and Las Vegas and hoped he would get a chance down here. A big man with a thick mustache stepped forward. He was no inkslinger, not with a rifle cradled underneath his armpit and an arsenal strapped to his waist.

"Which one's Billy the Kid?" the man said, revealing a star pinned to the lapel of his plaid vest.

This passes for a sheriff in Doña Ana County? Can't he see my handcuffs?

He looked at the sporting girls, winked, and raised his hands, letting the bracelets jingle, and put both hands on Ira Leonard's shoulder.

"This is your man," he told the sheriff, enjoying the explosion of laughter.

Part II

Chapter 14

"We are all aware that partisan feeling has run very high, that it has been very intense and very bitter. . . ."

—Judge Warren Bristol

March 30, 1881
La Mesilla, New Mexico Territory

The courthouse and jail occupied the plaza's southwest corner in what had been a store until after the Civil War, catty-corner from the dram shop where the Kid had met Tom O'Keefe and gotten roostered about three and a half years earlier. It wasn't much of a courthouse, just a block of cracked adobe and weathered vigas that provided a regular turnpike for mice. The Kid had counted sixteen scurrying across the thick pieces of cottonwood last night and this morning. He would have slept despite the rodents but for the noise. If it weren't the bells ringing at the Saint Albino Church on the north end of the plaza, it was shouting from the Corn Exchange Hotel just across the street from the Kid's cell. The jail's walls seemed mighty thin, and he considered tunneling out, but the streets were too busy. So he just stretched out on his cot and counted mice.

He heard the sheriff's spurs when the door separating the jail from the rest of the one-story building opened, and also what sounded like children singing. *Singing?* Maybe he was dreaming.

"I'm gonna escort you to the privy out back, Bonney,"

Sheriff James Southwick said. "Then we're goin' to the courtroom." He patted the butt of a holstered Colt. "Don't try nothin'."

The Kid swung off the bunk and held out his manacled hands, but the lawman shook his head. "The irons stay on. Judge's orders."

"Then who'll wipe my ass?" He grinned at the sheriff's frown. "You?"

Southwick unlocked and opened the jail cell without answering, then nodded toward the back door, where Bob Olinger stood with his shotgun. The Kid's good mood vanished at the sight of the deputy marshal, who drew the bolt and pushed open the door, stepping outside first, cocking the hammers as the Kid walked past him and into the two-seater.

He unbuttoned his fly and urinated, staring at the collection of newspapers, magazines, and corn cobs stacked in piles as necessaries. It was hot down here in the desert, and the outhouse smelled ripe, but the Kid took his time. He didn't need the paper, just had to empty his insides of the pot of coffee he had for breakfast, but the outhouse gave him an idea. He couldn't tunnel his way out of jail, but it would be easy for someone to leave him a revolver underneath the papers. But who? Nobody in Old Mesilla.

Olinger pounded on the door with the stock of his shotgun. "Finish it, Kid, or I'll clean your arse with both barrels."

"I'm coming." After buttoning his trousers, he stepped outside, smiling again. "Is this where you buy your tonic, Bob? Smells just like you."

The deputy pressed the shotgun against the Kid's stomach, but Southwick told him to stop, and Olinger jerked the gun away. Still smiling, the Kid followed the sheriff back through the jail and into the main courthouse, where they were almost trampled by screaming, smiling children, most of them dirty Mexicans in muslin and sandals, as they ran outside into the sunlight, their screams growing louder as they raced to the shade trees and grass on the plaza's park.

"What the hell!" the Kid said.

"School," the sheriff explained. Olinger poked the shotgun into the Kid's back.

"School?" the Kid asked, but Southwick turned mute, nodding at a hardwood bench where Ira Leonard sat. The sheriff and Olinger stopped, and the Kid walked toward his attorney, who shook his cuffed hand and motioned for him to have a seat.

"Why were all those kids in here?" the Kid asked.

"School is held here, too. They're having recess, I guess."

"*School?* In a county courthouse and jail?"

Leonard grinned. "Well, they don't hold class when there's a hanging, Billy."

The lawyer's wit made him grin. "Maybe they should. They'd get a real education." His smile, however, faded as Leonard withdrew a sheet of paper from his coat pocket. The Kid noticed the lawyer's outfit for the first time. He was right smartly attired in a suit of black broadcloth, white shirt and paper collar, and black silk string tie. A big black hat rested, crown down, beside him. The Kid felt like a saddle tramp in his sweat-stained clothes.

"Judge Bristol is about to pass sentence on another case; then you'll be arraigned." He passed the paper to the Kid.

"Who's Bristol trying now?"

"He's sentencing Billie Wilson."

The Kid's frown hardened. He stared at the list of names on the sheet. "What's this?"

"A list of prosecution witnesses that have been subpoenaed."

Bonnie Baca . . . James Dolan . . . Isaac Ellis . . . Billy Mathews . . . He stopped reading to shout: "At least two hundred men have been killed in Lincoln County the past three years, but I didn't kill all of them!"

"Don't worry, Billy. And keep your mouth shut unless I tell you to answer. When you do answer a question, just answer *that* question. Don't expound on anything unless you're prodded by the prosecutor. What I mean by that is if you're asked where you were on the fourth of April, 1877, you say 'Blazer's Mill' or, better yet, 'riding through Lincoln County.' You don't say what you were doing until asked that. Barnes is a pretty good attorney, but I've dueled against better. All that happens today is you'll be arraigned. The judge will ask if you have funds for a lawyer. I'll introduce myself as your representation."

The Kid lifted his manacled wrists, and Leonard stopped to hear his question. "I never actually asked you this, but how much is this going to cost me?"

"We'll work something out, Billy."

"Because I'm broke."

"That's all right. The case will be called. I'll ask for bail, but it'll be denied, and you'll go back to jail. Tomorrow, most likely, you'll enter a formal plea of not guilty, and Bristol will set a trial date, probably sometime next week, and order a *venire facias*—get a panel of potential jurors. Then I'll spring my trap."

"Why wait?"

"Ambuscade. I don't want to give Barnes time to prepare his argument."

The Kid grinned. He knew about ambuscades. They appealed to him.

The door to the courtroom opened, and Deputy Marshal Tony Neis and two other men escorted a sobbing Billie Wilson toward the jail cells.

"Let's go." Leonard stood.

The Kid, eyes locked on the slumping form of the counterfeiter, couldn't move.

March 31, 1881
La Mesilla, New Mexico Territory

The courtroom was long and narrow, about fourteen feet wide and just under thirty feet long. Rough-cut planks, carpeted with sawdust, served as the floor, giving the room the appearance of a saloon, but the county had tried to make it slightly presentable by painting the adobe walls white. A wooden platform had been built at the end of the room, a high-backed chair and flat desk serving as the judge's bench in the rear center, a chair on the left for witnesses, and small tables and rickety chairs on the corners for the prosecution and defense. A barrister's bookcase—the glass long since shattered and removed—had been wedged into the far corner, and beside that stood the American flag. There was also a kiva fireplace in the opposite corner, but there would be no need for it.

It wouldn't be comfortable for anyone, Ira Leonard thought, but spectators needed the toughest hides. Eighteen planks of the thickest Mexican hardwood served as benches, with no backs for the newspaper reporters, witnesses, and the curious to lean against.

Through the walls, Leonard heard children trying to recite the lesson from a *McGuffey's Reader* and the braying of a donkey somewhere on the plaza. The courtroom remained practically empty except for guards, clerks, bailiff, attorneys, and William H. Bonney. Today was another mere formality. The circus wouldn't start until arguments began.

"All rise."

Cause Number 411, The United States of America versus Charles Bowdre, Doc Scurlock, Henry Brown, John Middleton, Stephen Stephens, John Scroggins, Fred Waite, George Coe, and William H. Bonney, alias Henry Antrim, alias Kid Antrim, was called to order after Judge Bristol entered the room and took his seat. The charge: the willful and felonious murder of Andrew Roberts, alias Buckshot Roberts, on April 4, 1878, at Blazer's Mill, Lincoln County, New Mexico Territory, on the federal reserve for the Mescalero Apaches.

"I only see one defendant, Mr. Barnes," Bristol said.

"The others are either dead or cannot be located," Barnes said in a pleasant drawl. "At any rate, the United States is ready to proceed against Mr. Bonney."

"Any objections, Mr. Leonard?"

"No, Your Honor."

"What say the defendant? Guilty or not guilty?"

Leonard prodded the Kid with his elbow. "Not guilty."

"Very well. I'll order the county clerk and sheriff to round up potential jurors. Today's Thursday, and my docket's full. Dozens of murders and one rape." He raised his eyes, which bored into the Kid. "Maybe after this term of court, Lincoln County shall be rid of its lawless element." Then he sighed and found his gavel. "Trial date is set for next Tuesday, the fifth of April. Any objections?"

Neither attorney voiced disapproval, and Bristol's gavel slammed.

"It went just like you said it would!" the Kid exclaimed after being locked in his cell. The sheriff had left a stool in the hallway for Ira Leonard, who pulled pencil and writing tablet from his satchel.

"We have a long row to hoe, Billy," Leonard cautioned. "And I need you to be honest with me. I haven't asked you much about what happened at Blazer's Mill, but now I must. Don't lie to me, but understand this: I am an officer of the court and will not allow you to perjure yourself on the stand. That would lead to my disbarment."

"I thought you said you'd get this case squashed."

"Quashed," Leonard corrected. "That's my intention. That's why I'll file my motion on Tuesday."

"So why do we have to have this particular interview?"

"Because Bristol's a Ring man, Billy. He might toss my motion into the outhouse."

The Kid nodded solemnly.

"Tell me," Leonard said. "Everything."

Chapter 15

"Boys, he's a bad hombre, well-armed, and I ain't going to ask anyone to go and get him, but who will volunteer? Anybody?"

—Dick Brewer

April 4, 1878
Blazer's Mill, New Mexico Territory

We were Regulators by then, duly appointed by Green Wilson. So the first thing you need to know is that everything we did was legal. Mr. McSween said so. We didn't wear any badges—didn't have any. I picked out the name "Regulators." Had read it once in a dime novel and liked the sound of it.

Anyway, Green Wilson had handed Dick Brewer a stack of arrest warrants for the Murphy men responsible for John Tunstall's death, and we had been riding mighty hard looking for those *hombres,* even after we—even after Brady got killed. Dick had heard that a bunch of the men we were after were hiding out on the Mescalero Reservation, so that's where we were looking. I know Jimmy Dolan said we went to Blazer's Mill with murderous intentions because we knew Bristol and Rynerson would be riding through that way, coming from Old Mesilla, but don't hold truck with that lie. We rode there because we were hungry.

Let's see. Dick Brewer was our captain, though I don't know who elected him. He was popular, though, a nice gent, and he had truly admired John Tunstall, and John had thought the world of Dick. Charlie Bowdre and Doc Scurlock were with us. So was Henry Brown, Middleton, Waite, MacNab, John Scroggins, Dirty Steve, George Coe, and Ignacio Gonzales. MacNab got killed on the Fritz ranch later that month, and Ignacio got shot up pretty bad at the McSweens'. And Dick . . . Well, you know what happened to him.

Like I said, we rode down to Doc Blazer's to eat. We had been running cold camps after the Brady killing, and Mrs. Clara—Indian agent Frederick Godfroy's wife—dished up some mighty fine grub at the mill. She was a fiery woman, though, and when we got there, she met us with a rolling pin in her hand, telling us she'd be pleased to serve us dinner as soon as we shucked our arms. That had been her policy since she started taking in boarders and serving meals. She didn't cotton to firearms under her roof. Dick told her we were Regulators, but she said that didn't matter one whit to her.

I was the first one off my horse, the first one to unbuckle my gunbelt and place it on a bench by the door. "I don't know about you boys," I said, grinning, "but my bellybutton's rubbing against my backbone." As soon as I went inside, the other boys dismounted and disarmed—all except John Middleton. Dick told him he'd have to stand guard, keep a lookout for any Murphy men, but would be spelled as soon as one of the others finished eating. Middleton put our horses in the corral and stood there staring up and down the road, most likely cussing us because we got to eat first.

The first person we saw inside was Frank Coe, George's cousin, eating a bowl of green chile stew with mutton, which is what I ordered. Frank wasn't a Regulator. I'd like to settle that matter. He just happened to be there that day. Well, we had just finished eating, and Dick started arguing with Mrs. Clara about the bill. She wanted us to settle up, but Dick told her we were Regulators and didn't have to pay. It's custom, you see, for places like that to provide free meals and bunks for peace officers, and like I said, we were duly appointed. Mrs. Clara argued that she'd go broke if every rascal who claimed to be a lawman in Lincoln County got a free meal.

They were still dickering about it when Middleton almost busted down the door.

"You that hungry?" Henry joked, but Middleton was in no jocular mood.

"Buckshot Roberts just rode in!" he shouted.

Dick turned away from Mrs. Clara. "Roberts?" He looked at us. "I have a warrant for him." He looked back at Middleton and asked if Roberts was armed.

"Mighty well armed, I'd say. Got a pistol and a Winchester. Knife, too."

That's when Frank Coe stood, wiped his mouth, and dropped a coin on the table. He told us that he knew Roberts, was his neighbor, and if it set well with "Capt'n Brewer"—that's what he called Dick—he'd "go out and have a parley"—his words, again—with Roberts. Dick agreed, and Coe stepped outside. So did Middleton, to keep an eye on our guns while the rest of us talked it over. We waited a few minutes, but Charlie started growing restless. He didn't like Roberts at all. I didn't either. He was a Dolan man, and he had been one of those who killed John Tunstall. Dick, ever the peacekeeper, asked for volunteers because Roberts was such a hard rock. We all were game and headed outside, started strapping on our guns.

"Where are they?" Brewer asked Middleton.

"Coe walked him around the corner."

"Is he armed?"

"He was carrying his Winchester. He left his pistol on his mule over yonder." He nodded at the corral.

We heard Coe and Roberts arguing, Coe pleading with that man-killer to hand over his weapon, that he would stand by him, make sure he wasn't murdered by us, and Roberts firing back that he'd never give up to the likes of us. He figured I'd kill him for certain. "No, no, no!" I heard Roberts shout. "Not to the Kid! Never to Bowdre!"

Charlie spit and started walking. "I . . . ain't w-w-w-waitin' . . . no m-more."

He was right, too. Coe and Roberts had been talking for about a half-hour. That man wasn't going to surrender, not peaceably. Henry, MacNab, Middleton, and George Coe were the first to follow Charlie. The rest of us followed, not altogether certain about how to play this and absolutely not in a hurry to start a fight.

"Roberts!" Charlie yelled. "T-throw up . . . y-your h-h-hands." I tell you, it was almost right comical, Charlie stuttering like that, but there weren't no stammering when Charlie pulled his pistol. The rest of us stood behind or beside Charlie, waiting.

Frank Coe stepped away, and Roberts just glared at us.

"Not much, Mary Ann," he said, and swung that Winchester. Guess that was his idea of a joke, trying to be a poet.

He and Charlie must have fired at the same time. Roberts fired from the hip—fastest man with a long gun I ever saw—and his bullet smashed Charlie's belt buckle, doubling him over, and ricocheting, tearing into George Coe's right hand, taking off his trigger finger. Charlie's only shot hit Roberts in the side. I saw the dust and blood pop off his clothes, but he didn't act like he had been wounded, not mortally.

Roberts kept levering that Winchester, firing like he was an army. Middleton fell with a bullet in his chest. Another shot spanged off Doc Scurlock's holster and tore down his pants leg, sending him to the ground, squealing like a stuck pig, though the bullet did nothing more than ruin his trousers and burn his thigh. When a bullet tugged my bandanna and another grazed my side, I dived back around the corner.

"Too hot for me!" I yelled. A bunch of others agreed, because they followed right behind me.

We waited till the smoke cleared, then Dick peered around the corner.

"Where is he?" MacNab asked.

"I think he's fortin' up in Doc Blazer's office. He dropped his rifle and left a trail of blood."

Henry said: "I think you killed him, Charlie."

Charlie was still doubled over, fingering the dent that .44 had put in his brass buckle. "H-he . . . d-d-damn near . . . done me . . . in."

He had also put Middleton and George Coe down, Coe clutching his gun hand and writhing like a snake with its head chopped off, Middleton just lying on the ground, shaking his head as if he couldn't believe he had been shot. Nobody went to move Middleton just yet. Roberts might have dropped his rifle, but Frank Coe told us he was dead certain Doc Blazer had a rifle in his office.

A lot of folks had gathered behind us, and Brewer spotted the justice of the peace in the crowd, a cowardly fellow named Easton.

"Go in there!" Brewer yelled at Easton. "Bring Roberts out!"

"No," Easton fired back. "You and your men leave. There's been enough bloodshed already."

But Dick's blood was boiling. "I'm not goin' nowhere," he said. "I got a warrant for Roberts, and I'm bringin' him out if I have to pull down that house." He spotted Doc Blazer and asked him to bring Roberts out, but Blazer shook his head.

"Let him die in peace," Blazer said. "You shot him."

"You got a gun in your office, Doc?" Henry asked.

Doc Blazer nodded. "A Springfield rifle."

Dick shook his head violently. He asked the Indian agent if he would bring out Roberts, but Godfroy also said no. Well, we were in a fix, with Roberts barricaded in the doc's office, but Dick said he had a duty to bring him in. He figured if we got closer, we could finish him. Dick took off running around the house toward a stack of logs by the sawmill. I shrugged and followed him, Henry right behind me. The rest of the Regulators stayed behind. I'm not calling them cowards, mind you, just telling you what happened.

We made it to the woodpile. Roberts didn't even chance a shot at us.

"Maybe he's dead," Henry said. "Looked like Charlie hit him pretty bad."

"Maybe," Dick said. He eased his head up above the woodpile, dropped back in a hurry. "I see him," he whispered. "By the door." He said a quick prayer, swung up quickly, aimed his rifle, fired, and ducked.

Nothing.

"Did you hit him?" Henry asked.

"I don't know. Don't think so. Rushed my shot."

"You ought to try, Kid," Henry told me. "You're a better shot with a long gun than Dick."

I grinned. "Captain Brewer is doing fine."

Dick wet his lips. Maybe Roberts was dead. There hadn't been a sound from Doc Blazer's office, even after Dick fired. We waited five long minutes. Then Dick decided on another shot. He closed his eyes, lips moving in prayer, then opened his eyes, let out a deep breath, and eased his head up for a better look. Roberts must have been waiting all that time, patient like an oyster. As soon as Dick peeked, we heard the shot, and Dick fell like he had been poleaxed.

"Christ!" Henry shouted.

Blood and brains had splattered across Henry's face, and he turned white as Mrs. Clara's tablecloths, wiping the mess with his bandana. I stared at Dick. The bullet had struck him in the eye and blown out the back of his head. He was dead before he hit the ground.

Well, I'll be the first to admit that I had seen enough, knew we were whipped. "Let's get out of here, Henry!" I ran, keeping my head low, Henry doing the same. We crossed the footbridge and didn't stop till we were back at the chuck house. Some of the boys had gotten up the nerve to drag Middleton into the shade. Doc Scurlock was stuffing John's wound with a silk bandana, and Doc Blazer was wrapping squirming George Coe's mangled hand.

Charlie pulled himself up. "W-wh-what h-happen-ed?"

"Buckshot Roberts just blew Dick's head off!" Henry snapped. "This vein has played out, boys." He tipped his hat at Mrs. Clara and trotted off for the corral.

"Dick Brewer's . . . dead?" Doc Blazer looked up in astonishment.

"Yes, sir," I said. "And, pals, Henry Brown has one fine idea."

There was no point in staying. Besides, MacNab said Agent Godfroy had ridden off to bring back the army while Dick Brewer was getting killed. We left Middleton and George Coe with Doc Blazer—neither could ride—and rode off. I thought Middleton was a goner, but he had more sand than I figured. Last I heard, he married some fifteen-year-old and lit a shuck out of Lincoln County. Don't know where he settled.

Well, you know what happened to Buckshot Roberts. Charlie's bullet was mortal, and that old reprobate died kicking and screaming the next day. They planted him on the hill beside Dick. Kind of fitting, don't you think?

No, I didn't kill Buckshot Roberts. Hell, it was him who almost sent me to Glory. I'm glad he's dead, because he was one bad fellow, but I do admire the man's grit.

Yes, sir, he licked our crowd to a finish.

Chapter 16

*"Is Judge Bristol aware that he is a public servant
and not an autocrat? Has he forgotten that he is paid
a salary to do his duty rather than to neglect it?"*
          —*Grant County Herald*, December 22, 1877

April 5, 1881
La Mesilla, New Mexico Territory

Mexicans—some businessmen, but mostly *vaqueros* and
farmers—made up the jury panel. Less than twenty had taken
seats on the uncomfortable benches at the front of the courtroom, which made Ira Leonard frown in contempt. *A panel
of only seventeen to choose twelve jurors? In a federal murder trial?* A handful of newspaper reporters sat at the rear,
probably to catch a breeze, although Leonard figured that
was a mistake. The banter of the children next door would
make it hard for the reporters to hear what the judge and
lawyers said this morning. Some would sacrifice comfort before long and make their way closer.

"If there are no objections," Judge Bristol said, "I will
begin questioning the jurors. For the record, I have made
Mariano Toribio interpreter since few of these men speak
English." He nodded at the swarthy man with a graying mustache and ill-fitting sack suit sitting at the end of the second
row.

Leonard cleared his throat and rose, resting his right hand
on the small table in front of him and Bonney. "May it please
the court, the defense withdraws its not-guilty plea and

moves that the indictment be thrown out because the United States has no jurisdiction in this matter." He picked up the twenty-two-page motion he had just finished writing an hour earlier and brought it to Bristol.

Sidney Barnes was already on his feet, objecting before Bristol had taken the document from Leonard's hand.

"Your Honor," Barnes said, "the murder was committed on the Mescalero Indian Reservation, which is federal property and thus falls under federal jurisdiction."

"Not quite." Leonard stepped back, confident, and headed back to his table, where he picked up the map of the reservation and returned to hand it to the U.S. attorney.

"As this map, and several affidavits attached to my motion, note, Blazer's Mill is not part of the reservation. Doctor Joseph H. Blazer settled in the Tularosa Canyon in 1869, before the current reservation was established. The map before Mr. Barnes's attention shows Blazer's Mill to be private property, and for the record, the map is a military map. It's federal. Who should know better? Thus, this alleged crime was not committed on federal property, but private property. It is a matter for the Territory of New Mexico, not the U.S. attorney's office. Your Honor will also see affidavits from the commanding officer at Fort Stanton and the Indian Bureau. I respectfully ask the court that the federal indictment be thrown out, the case dismissed with prejudice." He sat down and ran his fingers through his white hair.

Next to him, the Kid, hands still shackled, smiled gleefully.

"Mr. Barnes?" Bristol said, head bent, staring intently as he devoured the contents of Leonard's motion.

"This is ridiculous, Your Honor." Barnes's voice held a razor-sharp edge. "The crime was perpetrated on the Mescalero Reservation, or should I say Indian country. Even if the property is privately held, it still falls under federal jurisdiction. May I point out that after the shooting, the Indian agent, Frederick Godfroy, requested help from the United States Army. Mr. Godfroy, also a representative of the U.S. government, had his office at Blazer's Mill, too.

Jurisdiction over Indian country exclusively belongs to the federal court, sir."

Bristol nodded, and Leonard felt his stomach churn. The judge had a reputation for following his own course, damn the law, damn the people. Citizens of Grant County had petitioned Washington demanding Bristol's removal back in 1877, citing several instances of abuse of power. He had once refused a continuance in a murder trial, denied the defense attorney's motions and exceptions, and sent the defendant, likely an innocent man who had riled the wrong people, to the gallows. He often met with attorneys *ex parte,* negotiating, the stories went, sentences like a sutler bartering with Indian traders. On several occasions, he had changed his rulings in the middle of trial in order to help the defense attorney or prosecutor, then made the clerk expunge the record so that his decisions could not be questioned.

Yet he remained on the bench.

Thomas Catron had made sure of that, arguing that Bristol was in fact honest, a master of federal and territorial law. Warren Bristol owed his job, maybe his soul, to Catron—and the Santa Fe Ring.

Why did I think he would give me a fair deal? Leonard shuddered at the thought.

"I am going to call a recess," Bristol announced, "to give Mr. Barnes time to study your motion, Mr. Leonard. Court will reconvene at two o'clock this afternoon, at which time I will allow the U.S. attorney to make a more informed argument. After that, I will take into consideration both arguments and announce my ruling in the morning. We'll see you at two, gentlemen."

April 6, 1881
La Mesilla, New Mexico Territory

Judge Bristol hooked tobacco from his mouth and tossed the quid into a spittoon before nodding at the bailiff and taking his seat. The Kid studied the judge, trying to read the old man's face, but decided he couldn't. He'd make a mighty fine poker player.

As Bristol settled into his chair, the Kid leaned back. He tried to swallow but couldn't, and he wanted to reach for the pitcher of water on the table in front of him but dared not move. His irons would rattle, and he didn't want to make any noise. The whole courtroom, packed for the first time since his trial began, remained deathly quiet. No noise came from the schoolroom next door, and the Kid fancied those little buttons leaning against the wall, at their teacher's orders, trying to hear the judge's ruling. Criminy, even the plaza sounded deserted, as if the entire two thousand souls who populated Old Mesilla were taking a siesta or had crammed into the courthouse today.

Bristol found his spectacles and slid them up on his nose, coughed slightly, and turned the page of a document he had brought in. Finally, he looked up, scanning the crowd before his eyes met Ira Leonard's.

"The arguments placed before the court yesterday make two key points. Mr. Leonard says the crime of Cause Number Four-Eleven, The United States of America versus Charles Bowdre, Doc Scurlock, Henry Brown, John Middleton, Stephen Stephens, John Scroggins, Fred Waite, George Coe, and William H. Bonney, alias Henry Antrim, alias Kid Antrim, was committed on private property and not specifically on the Mescalero Apache Indian Reservation. Therefore, he says, the United States has no jurisdiction in this matter. This is a technical point, and I, for one, would hate to free a murderer on this matter alone. Murder cases should be decided by twelve honest and true men, not an overworked jurist."

The Kid's heart sank. He could almost feel the hangman's noose being slipped over his head, tightening against his Adam's apple.

"The United States attorney argues that because Blazer's Mill is located on the federal reserve, it is in fact Indian country, and thus his office holds jurisdiction. To plead his case, Mr. Barnes cites the facts that on the day of the Andrew Roberts murder, Indian Agent Frederick Godfroy, a man I have long known, sent for the United States cavalry to help bring peace to the settlement. He also points out that Agent Godfroy's office is located at Blazer's Mill. It's all Indian country, says Mr. Barnes, and thus falls under federal jurisdiction, not the Territory of New Mexico."

Bristol turned another page. The Kid glanced at Leonard, who looked dead, not even blinking, barely breathing.

"It is an argument worthy of consideration, but so is Mr. Leonard's. This is a decision I do not wish to make. If I grant Mr. Leonard's motion, I am possibly freeing a murderer, and I firmly believe that the late Andrew L. Roberts deserves justice. I knew Roberts as well. No better man ever lived. He died performing his duty, died in agony because of the callous, cold-blooded acts of border ruffians who set Lincoln County ablaze with cowardly criminal acts.

"That said, if I grant Mr. Barnes's motion, I am giving the United States jurisdiction that the appeals courts would frown upon. Mr. Barnes says the crime fell in 'Indian country,' but I do not hold with that, for no part of the Territory of New Mexico is designated as such. If I were to side with him, I would in fact be granting the U.S. attorney jurisdiction over any place some redskin had trod."

He turned another page.

"Therefore, it is the reluctant decision of this court to grant the motion for the defense."

The back of the courtroom exploded in shouts, quickly silenced by Bristol's gavel.

"Cause Number Four-Eleven is dismissed. The defendant, however, is to be remanded to Sheriff James Southwick and held until Thursday, when he is to be brought to trial in this courtroom, Third Judicial District, to face a charge of the murder of Lincoln County Sheriff William Brady on the first of April, 1878." He looked at the prosecutor. "Do you wish to make an exception, Mr. Barnes?"

The U.S. attorney slowly shook his head. "I think it best, Your Honor, to let Mr. Bonney be tried and hung by the Territory of New Mexico, and thus save the United States expenses and rid the world of an outlaw."

Bristol slammed the gavel again.

The Kid couldn't rein in his emotions. He slapped Leonard's knee. "Son of a gun!" he shouted. "You did it."

April 6, 1881
Las Cruces, New Mexico Territory

"I would have thought better of you, Warren," William Rynerson told Bristol at the Masonic Lodge that evening.

"Barnes's argument was rubbish," Bristol fired back. "I had to grant Leonard's motion. He was right!"

"Since when did that stop you?" said Simeon B. Newman, an inkslinger and Freemason who had started a newspaper shortly before the Kid arrived in La Mesilla. He had started the paper, *Newman's Semi-Weekly,* for the sole purpose of hanging William H. Bonney. He had started it because Catron and Rynerson had given him money for the enterprise, knowing full well that the newspaper would fold shortly after the Kid's conviction. Bristol spit tobacco juice into a tin can he held and met the journalist's glare. Catron could just as easily order Newman to start a campaign against the Honorable Judge Warren Bristol.

"There's a new governor about to take office in New Mexico," Bristol said evenly. "There's a new president in Washington. I've been hanged in effigy. I've been libeled by newspapers better than yours, Newman. But in these uncertain times, I will not make myself a target, get myself thrown off the bench. Thomas Catron is a powerful man, but he's no longer the U.S. attorney. I don't have many friends in Washington or Santa Fe, and I'm not risking my neck . . . for anyone."

"Sidney Barnes is the U.S. attorney, and I doubt if he'll do you any favors after today's ruling."

"Barnes knew he was licked yesterday. I did the only thing I could."

Rynerson stepped between them, drink in hand. "Gentlemen, the Kid stands trial for Brady's murder. He won't escape the gallows. Judge Bristol acted fairly, Simeon. It takes a brave man to take an unpopular stand, even with the law on his side. Come on, let's relax." He herded both men to the bar, where Albert Fountain and John Bail were playing saloonkeepers, serving drinks, lighting cigars, and making jokes.

Bristol tossed away his tobacco. "Rye all right, Judge?" Bail asked.

"It doesn't matter," he replied softly.

"Catron was right," said Dolan, already in his cups, leaning against the bar to keep from collapsing to the floor. "We didn't give Leonard enough credit."

"He's as irascible as an old bantam," Rynerson agreed. He looked around. "I guess that's why Newcomb isn't here. Must be preparing his case."

"He better be," Dolan said. "No telling what Leonard'll do. Hell, the way he fought for that whore McSween, it's a wonder they didn't hang Nathan Dudley."

"Maybe we should kill him," Newman said.

Bristol seethed. Luckily, neither Bail nor Fountain had heard the newspaperman. Bail and Fountain might be Masons, but Fountain, in addition to his law practice, had published a newspaper, and Bristol had never trusted, nor liked, journalists.

"Who?" Dolan asked. "The Kid?"

"Leonard." He grinned. "That'd give me something to write about!"

"Shut up, the both of you," Rynerson said, and smiled when Bail turned from the back bar and refilled his drink, then slid a shot of whiskey to Bristol.

Bristol downed the liquor in one swallow, set the empty glass on the bar, and started to order another. A thought stopped him.

"Maybe," he said, "we won't have to."

Chapter 17

> *"Well, perhaps some of them will think me half man*
> *now; everyone seems to think I was some kind of*
> *animal."*
>
> —Billy the Kid

April 8, 1881
La Mesilla, New Mexico Territory

The Territory of New Mexico versus John Middleton, Henry Brown, William Bonney, alias Kid, alias William Antrim, had indicted the defendants—of whom only one had been located and arrested—for having "unlawfully, feloniously, and with malice aforethought" shot and killed Lincoln County Sheriff William Brady on April 1, 1878. George Hindman had also been killed, but the prosecutor was trying Bonney for Brady's murder only. Taking no chances, Ira Leonard thought. If Bonney was acquitted, he could still face another trial for Hindman's death, although that case would be greatly weakened by a previous acquittal.

This would be tougher than the Buckshot Roberts case. Leonard had no grounds for a dismissal, no loophole in the law. It would be the Kid's word against the word of several witnesses, but those had long been William H. Bonney's enemies. If he could make the jury see that everyone the prosecution put on the stand had a reason to lie, he could raise reasonable doubt. That would be his plan, after *voir dire*.

"What say the defendant?" Judge Bristol asked. "Guilty or not guilty?"

"Not guilty," the Kid answered.

Leonard looked at the list of possible jurors—nobody he recognized, no one who had been one of the Kid's enemies, no Ring men, no friends of the House. Nor could many of them speak much English, so Judge Bristol would have to appoint another interpreter. Leonard turned in his chair. People had packed into the courtroom again. He had spotted two Indians, shoulders wrapped in colorful blankets despite the warmth, on the back row when he first walked inside, but now he couldn't see them. People flocked inside as if it were a *cantina* serving free beer—a collection of Mexican businessmen and farmers, several cowboys, reporters, even two lawyers from Las Cruces he recognized: John Bail and Albert J. Fountain. He had no idea why they were here.

"Mr. Leonard?"

He looked back at Bristol.

"It has come to this court's attention that you are the attorney of record for Susan McSween, widow of Alexander McSween."

Leonard frowned. Bristol had known he was her lawyer for years. That was no surprise. That old blackheart was up to something.

"I am, Your Honor," he said hesitantly.

"You have represented her in a number of litigations?"

"Yes, sir."

"In fact, she has filed civil suits alleging arson and murder stemming from the loss of her house and husband in Lincoln three years ago."

He still didn't know where Bristol was leading him, so he said nothing, but began tapping a pencil nervously on the desk. Beside him, the Kid just stared blankly.

"This is a murder trial, Mr. Leonard. A man's life is at stake, and that man should be accorded the very best legal representation. Your relationship with Mrs. McSween clouds that appearance, and as you should know, the mere appearance of impropriety cannot be overlooked."

The Kid leaned closer. "What's he getting at?"

He whispered for Bonney to keep quiet.

"Your Honor—" Leonard began, but the judge silenced him.

"If you lose this case, your representation of Mrs. McSween could be grounds for appeal. You could lose the case intentionally, sir, and that conviction could help your other client, Mrs. McSween, sue Mr. Bonney, or whatever his real name is, for causing the death of her husband. She and you, sir, seem to have no qualms when it comes to filing civil suits."

He stood now, protesting, but Bristol shouted him down.

"It is the appearance, sir! I am not suggesting you would do this, but my sole purpose is to make sure the defendant gets a fair trial—without immediate grounds for appeal."

"Your Honor, I will resign as Mrs. McSween's attorney!" he pleaded, but he knew he had lost. He had ambushed Sidney Barnes and Bristol with his motion for dismissal in the federal case. Now Bristol and prosecutor Simon Newcomb were exacting revenge.

"It's too late for that, sir. Therefore, I am removing you as defense counsel and appointing John Bail and Albert Fountain, who I see are here, in your stead. I will grant the attorneys two hours to meet with the defendant. Court will reconvene at ten-thirty."

He fell back in his chair, stunned, fighting for breath as his asthma reappeared. Bristol tapped his gavel, then disappeared into his chambers.

"He can't do that!" the Kid shouted, but Leonard shook his head sadly.

"He just . . . did." He waited, praying, and after a moment could breath again. "He's a judge, Billy. He can do anything he wants, or so he thinks."

This wasn't the first time Bristol had overstepped his authority, but Leonard knew better than to file an appeal. He'd lose. He'd have to fight some other way.

The two court-appointed lawyers were walking toward the defense table, fighting against the tide of exiting spectators. So were Sheriff Southwick, Bob Olinger, and the bailiff, already being cannonaded with questions by reporters, most of them asking for interviews with the Kid, not interrogating them about the judge's ruling. Leonard turned quickly to his client, or rather, his former client.

"Billy, they can't stop me from visiting you in jail. Or keep me out of court. I'll be here. I'll meet with you. Bail and Fountain are good lawyers."

"They're Ring men!"

"I don't know that. I know they're Masons, but so were George Washington and Ben Franklin. So was my uncle. It doesn't make them bad." *They might be puppets, however, toys of Catron and Rynerson.* He spoke quickly. "The prosecutor can't prove you were there, Billy. Remember that. The burden of proof is on him, and all of his witnesses hate you. That's reasonable doubt. That's your defense."

He stood up. "Whatever you do, don't take the stand."

The Kid decided Albert Fountain was a fair man, although a bit stodgy, even standoffish. He appeared to be in his forties, with thinning dark hair and a brushy mustache and a fancy suit that made Ira Leonard's look like some cowboy's threadbare Sunday-go-to-meetings. He had heard that Fountain married a Mexican, had a passel of kids, and the Kid thought he might one day marry a Mexican himself, so that drew him to the attorney, although he didn't ask about the man's wife.

He wasn't certain about John Bail, an older man with a pockmarked face and massive gray beard. Bail didn't say much, appeared inconvenienced by Bristol's appointment, and spent most of the interview in the Kid's jail cell studying a match and cigar he twirled in his fingers.

"If you ain't going to smoke that thing," the Kid finally said, grinning, "pass it through the bars, and I'll set it afire."

Bail stared at the Kid as if he were a cockroach, then returned cigar and match to his vest pocket.

When the Kid shrugged, Fountain continued his questioning.

"Ira Leonard gave me a list of potential character witnesses, Billy," the lawyer said in a nasal Yankee drawl. "The prosecution has scores of witnesses. Are you sure you can't think of anyone else who could testify on your behalf?"

"Sure, Albert." He liked saying Albert. The name made him grin. "John Henry Tunstall . . . Alexander McSween . . . Tom O'Folliard . . ."

"Someone *living,* Billy," said Fountain, unamused.

The Kid's smile vanished. "Well, sir, they're all dead because of the Lincoln County men that'll be testifying against me. That prosecutor doesn't like me, either."

Fountain sighed. "I'll do my best, Billy."

"That's all I'm asking you to do. Well, I do have one more question. How much is this going to cost me?"

"We were appointed by the court, Billy. Doña Ana County will foot the bill. You don't have to pay a dime."

"That's good, because, well, I find myself without funds."

"It's all right, Billy. Now, should we lose the case, and you wish for me, or Mr. Bail, or both of us to continue as your representation and handle appeals, we'll have to talk about payment."

"Well, I reckon we'll play that hand after it's dealt us."

Simon Newcomb's opening argument, though boisterous, bored the Kid. That cock of the walk went about ranting and raving, pointing a bony finger at the Kid, spitting fire and brimstone like a Baptist preacher at a revival meeting, barely giving Mariano Toribio time to translate the prosecutor's downright slander into Spanish. *Hell,* the Kid thought, *some of those words can't be put in Spanish.*

He stared at the jury, not recognizing one face. He glanced at the names Bail had written down. Refugio Bernal, Crescensio Bustillos, Felipe Lopez, Pedro Martinez, Merced Lucero, Benito Montoya, Hilario Moreno, Pedro Onopo, Luis Sedilio, Pedro Serna, Jesus Silva, and Jean Telles had been seated in less than forty-five minutes. Ira Leonard had told him to expect jury selection to take the rest of the day.

He glanced over his shoulder and looked for Leonard, looked for the white hair, but gave up. Leonard was probably far back in the courtroom, and he couldn't see over the hats worn by the cowboys on the fifth row. He wondered why Judge Bristol didn't make them take off their sombreros. It didn't matter, though. He'd talk to Leonard tonight.

"After all of the evidence I will present you," Newcomb demanded, "you will have no choice but to find the defendant guilty and sentence him to death by hanging. Thank you."

He sat down and began mopping his brow with a handkerchief. The Kid yawned. Newcomb seemed to be a passionate fellow, but the Kid had heard his comments a hundred times, and it seemed that a man with Newcomb's reputation—he had been a defense attorney before replacing Rynerson, had once gotten Jessie Evans and John Kinney acquitted—could have thought of something a little more original than William H. Bonney is a monster and must be killed.

Albert Fountain slightly rose from his chair. "Your Honor," he said, "may it please the court, the defense will postpone its opening remarks until the Territory has rested its case."

He arched his eyebrows. *Can he do that?*

"So be it," Judge Bristol said. The Kid shrugged. *I guess he can.* He'd ask Leonard about it later. "Are you ready to proceed, Mr. Newcomb?"

"I am, Your Honor."

"You may call your first witness."

"The Territory calls Deputy Sheriff J. B. 'Billy' Mathews."

Son of a bitch. The Kid clenched both fists. He'd sell his soul for a Winchester right now. He should have finished that job three years back.

Chapter 18

"Killing people in Lincoln is the leading industry at the present time. They kill anybody, native or stranger, with or without cause according to circumstances and inclination."
—*Las Vegas Gazette*, April 13, 1878

April 8, 1881
La Mesilla, New Mexico Territory

Even in his stovepipe boots, Jacob B. "Billy" Mathews stood a couple of inches shorter than the Kid. His skin had remained fair despite several years in southern New Mexico, and he spoke like some Tennessee horse thief while being sworn in. Mathews stared at the Kid all the while, his blue eyes burning with a hate the Kid knew better than most.

"Mr. Mathews," Simon Newcomb began, "where were you employed on the first of April, 1878?"

Mathews broke his stare and turned in his seat toward the prosecutor while Mariano Toribio translated the question for the jury. "I was a deputy sheriff of Lincoln County."

"You were in the town of Lincoln on the date in question?"

"I was."

"Who was the sheriff?"

"Major William Brady."

"What happened that day?"

The Kid shook his head, amused. It struck him funny, the

Spanish translations sounding like an echo to Newcomb's questions and Mathews's answers.

"I got up early that morn and headed over to the Wortley for breakfast. Major Brady, he had a ranch a few miles east, so he rode in and met me at the hotel, 'long with the other deputies."

"What were their names?"

"There was George Hindman, John Long, and George Peppin."

"Go on, sir."

"Well, we finished breakfast right around nine o'clock and walked outside." He paused, wet his lips, and continued. "We walked down the street, mindin' our affairs, and Major Brady stopped to talk with Ham Mills's wife. She had called him over, you see. The rest of us kept on walkin', and I stopped when I heard Brady chuckle. Saw him tip his hat at Missus Mills and trot on toward me to catch up. He told me Missus Mills had just played an April Fool's joke on him. I asked him about it, smilin', and he was about to tell me when they waylaid us."

"Who do you mean by 'they'?"

He was looking at the Kid again. "Him . . . Brown . . . Middleton . . . the whole damned lot of 'em."

Bristol spit out tobacco juice and admonished Mathews for using profanity in his courtroom. The witness muttered an apology while Newcomb asked the record be noted that Mathews had identified the Kid.

"Please continue, Mr. Mathews."

"It was ugly. I fit in the War for the South, but I never seen nothin' like that. Bullets tore into Major Brady, and George—George Hindman, I mean—he cried out and collapsed in the street. I was totin' my rifle with me, cocked it, fired once or twice, but you couldn't hit them assassins: They was hidin' behind an adobe wall. Couldn't even see 'em. Major Brady, he fell into a sitting position, said, 'Oh, Lord,' and they started shootin' again, just a-pepperin' the major's body. I ran as hard as I could for cover, Peppin right behind me. Me and Peppin went to the Cisneros house, Peppin runnin' through the front door, and me divin' behind the house.

John Long, he took off the other way. I heard him cry out, knew he was hit, but he made it to the Torreón."

"By the Torreón you mean the Indian tower up the street from the Tunstall store?"

"That's it."

"Go on."

"Well, sir, for a while the shootin' stopped. I knew Major Brady was dead, shot up like he had been, but Hindman was on his back, moanin', beggin' for water. 'Bout that time, Ike Stockton ran out of his saloon. He was screamin' his head off, sayin', 'Don't shoot, boys, don't shoot! I'm bringin' George inside my place!' He lifted George up by his shoulders, started draggin' him to his saloon, and those sons of . . ." He stopped, biting his lower lip, and stared at his boots. He was shaking.

The courtroom had turned quiet, except for the dull sound of a boy reciting a math equation in the schoolroom. Mathews finally looked up, shot the Kid a menacing glance, and coughed slightly.

"I'm sorry, Judge. Anyway, as Ike pulled George to the saloon, someone fired. I saw the dust pop off George's vest. Ike give a shout and dropped George in the dirt, ran back to the saloon, slammed the door. Then it got quiet again.

"A short time later, two of those squat assassins ran toward Major Brady's body, one firin' at the Torreón and the Cisneros house, the other headin' for the major. I shot my Winchester, hit 'em both—hit one of 'em pretty good in the thigh. Think I nicked the other one in the hip. Anyway, both of 'em were limpin' when they skedaddled. Tried to shoot 'em again, but they made it back behind the Tunstall store and into the corral. 'Bout five minutes later, somebody opened the gate to the corral, and they galloped toward the Río Bonito and headed out of town. All of us—Peppin, me, and Long—shot at 'em but didn't hit none, but I figured they'd left one of those murderers behind. The one I hit in the leg. No way he could sit a saddle, and I found blood leadin' into the Tunstall store but couldn't find the killer. I bet somebody was hidin' him."

"You recognized the assailants? I want you to be absolutely certain."

Mathews's head bobbed. "Yes, sir, I most certainly did. The Kid there, he was the one runnin' for Major Brady's body, the one I think I hit in the hip. I saw John Middleton and Henry Brown when they rode out of the corral. Didn't recognize the fellow that ran out with the Kid, the one coverin' him, but he was a big man. And I'll bet Rob Widenmann was with 'em, but—"

"Objection," Albert Fountain said in a dull voice, head down, busily scratching notes on a pad of paper.

"Sustained." Bristol sounded just as bored.

"How many men would you say committed this act of murder, of cowardly assassination?"

"Five men rode out, but, like I said, one of 'em was hurt too bad to ride. I think he, and maybe another of 'em, stayed behind."

"Six or seven, then?"

"Yes, sir."

"But you are certain that the defendant was one of them?"

"No question about it."

"Thank you, Mr. Mathews. I pass the witness, Your Honor."

As soon as Newcomb sat down and the interpreter finished, Fountain looked up from his notepad and set his pencil aside. "Mr. Mathews, you said when the shooting commenced, you tried to fire back but could not hit any of them, could not even see them. Why was that?"

"They was hidin' behind an adobe wall, a high one, at the Tunstall corral."

"How did they manage to shoot Sheriff Brady and Deputy Hindman?"

"They had poked holes through the wall."

"I see. Then you and Deputy Peppin ran down the street?"

"That's right."

"Toward the Wortley Hotel?"

Mathews tilted his head. "Well, in that direction, I reckon. To the Cisneros house. It's across the street from the other end of the Tunstall store."

"Away from the corral where the men shooting were stationed." It wasn't a question, but Mathews answered anyway, nodding his head and mumbling *yes*.

"But Deputy Long, he ran the other way? Correct?"

"Yeah, he took off down the street, all the way to the Torreón."

"Which, as the prosecutor has said, is on the same side of the street as the Tunstall corral."

"That's right."

"But your view would be blocked by the store because the corral is behind the store. Isn't that so?"

"Well, it . . ."

"Yes or no, Mr. Mathews." The Kid smiled. Maybe Judge Bristol had done him a favor. He wondered if Leonard would have used this strategy.

"Yeah."

Fountain raised his voice. "So you couldn't see any of the shooters."

"Well, John had a better look, but I sure as hell—beg your pardon, Judge—I sure seen the Kid and the other fellow when they ran to Major Brady."

"But you only recognized the defendant?"

"That's right."

"While being shot at?"

"Yeah, but . . ."

"Sir, you'd have this court believe that you were able to recognize a man in those conditions?"

"I hit the both of 'em. I'd say I could see 'em pretty good." Mathews looked proud of his reply, but Fountain only smiled.

"But you identified only one. How could you recognize the other two men indicted, Brown and Middleton?"

"I saw 'em when they lit out."

"You had a clear view by then?"

"Well, no, but . . ."

"Deputy Long had a better view, isn't that so?"

"Yeah."

"Isn't it true, sir, that Deputy Long told you that he recognized Middleton and Brown? You didn't see them. You didn't recognize anyone."

"I saw the Kid. I'm swearin' to that."

"But not to seeing Middleton and Brown."

"Why does that matter?" Mathews snapped. "They ain't even on trial!"

Bristol warned Mathews again.

Mathews sighed before answering. "Well, John Long said it was 'em, and I believe him."

Fountain waited for the translation, his smile widening. "You lied, sir. You perjured yourself." The Kid waited for Newcomb to object, but the uppity prosecutor sat across the aisle staring at the Kid's counsel in disgust, disbelief.

"Look." Mathews sat up. "It happened three years ago. A man forgets some things, but I know I shot the Kid. I know he was there."

"You just said you *thought* you hit him. Now you *know?*"

"I know he was there!" The Kid almost felt sorry for the fool. He wouldn't be surprised if Mathews broke down and started bawling.

Fountain wasn't finished, though, and kept charging, merciless. "Do you know if Mr. Bonney fired the bullets that struck Sheriff Brady?"

"He was there!"

Now Judge Bristol looked annoyed. "Answer the question, sir!"

Mathews leaned back in defeat. "Well, there ain't no way to tell that. It's like I said, they were hidin' behind the high-walled corral."

"It seems to me that John Long would make a better witness, sir, since he had a clear view of the corral. Why isn't Mr. Long testifying?"

This time, Newcomb objected, and Bristol sustained.

"I'll rephrase the question," Fountain said. "Do you know the present whereabouts of Deputy Long?"

Mathews shook his head. "No, sir. He lit out of the county not too long after Major Brady was murdered."

"Where were you going that morning?"

"To the courthouse."

"Why?"

"Well, Major Brady had announced that court would be held that day, but it was actually to be the followin' week. He was goin' to straighten that out."

"It took all four of you?"

Mathews didn't answer until instructed by the judge. "Well, we was just walkin' with him."

"And you just happened to be carrying a Winchester rifle," Fountain stated.

"I like to be prepared." Mathews had grown sullen.

"Isn't it true, sir, that you were in fact preparing to arrest Alexander McSween on some trumped-up charge? Or murder him? You knew he was arriving in town that day!"

"That ain't so."

"And the Regulators behind the corral were merely protecting McSween's life?"

"That ain't right. It ain't so. We was goin' to post a notice on the courthouse. That's all we was doin'. And them Regulators weren't nothin' but murderin' dawgs."

"You dislike William Bonney, don't you?"

"He ain't no friend of mine."

"Indeed. You led the posse to arrest the defendant's former employer, John Tunstall. Isn't that so?"

Newcomb rose. "I don't see where this is leading, Your Honor."

"Credibility, Judge," Fountain replied.

"Proceed," Bristol said. "Answer the question, Mr. Mathews."

"Yeah."

Fountain pulled a letter from the notepad, and the Kid recognized the Lincoln County Sheriff letterhead. His attorney finally stood, walking to the witness chair while introducing the letter into evidence and asking Mathews to read it aloud.

Lincoln, N.M., Feb. 15th, 1878

J. B. Mathews
Deputy Sheriff

   Dear Sir: You must not by any means call on or
allow to travel with your posse any person or persons
who are known to be outlaws. Let your Mexicans
round up the cattle and protect them with the
balance. Be firm and do your duty according to law,
and I will be responsible for your acts. I am, sir,

                              Respectfully yours,
                              William Brady
                              Sheriff, Lincoln County

"These were your orders when you left Lincoln to attach
Alexander McSween's cattle at the Tunstall ranch because of
an ongoing lawsuit?" asked Fountain, handing the letter to
the clerk.

"Yeah."

"But you allowed Jessie Evans, Bill Morton, and Frank
Baker to join the posse?"

"I didn't want Jessie with 'em."

"But he went along. And you ordered Morton to lead the
group."

"Yeah."

"And John Tunstall was murdered by them!"

"He was killed resistin' arrest. That's what they tol' me. I
wasn't there, though."

Fountain laughed. "*Convenient.*"

Newcomb stood again and objected. Bristol told Fountain,
who had walked back to the table but remained standing, to
rein in his emotions.

"You were indicted for Tunstall's murder?" Still, Newcomb did not object.

"Yeah."

"You took advantage of Governor Wallace's amnesty?"

"Yeah. I didn't want to, mind you. I wanted to clear my

name in court, but my lawyer said to take the amnesty deal and be done with it all, so that's what I done."

"You used the amnesty proclamation, but the Kid couldn't?"

"He wasn't no lawman."

"He was a Regulator, duly appointed by Justice of the Peace Green Wilson."

"He's a cold-blooded man-killer."

"And you hate him."

"You're damned right I do!"

Fountain grinned as he sat down. "No more questions, Your Honor." John Bail whispered something about reasonable doubt and patted the Kid's back.

Simon Newcomb stood to request a redirect, which Bristol granted. The Kid eyed the prosecutor curiously.

"John Tunstall was shot and killed by a Lincoln County sheriff's posse?" Newcomb asked.

"Yeah. But I had nothin' to do with it."

"You're not on trial, Mr. Mathews. The defendant had worked for Mr. Tunstall? Isn't that true?"

"Yeah."

"He liked Tunstall."

"They were pals. I seen 'em together many times, real friendly."

"So Bonney wanted to avenge Tunstall's death?"

"Everybody knowed that."

Bristol sustained Fountain's objection and instructed the interpreter to tell the jury to disregard both question and answer.

"Let me rephrase that question," Newcomb said. "If the defendant rode for revenge, would that, in your estimation as a former peace officer, be a reason to gun down Sheriff Brady?"

Fountain fired another objection, but Bristol overruled this one, and Mathews grinned crookedly as he answered, "Yeah."

Newcomb and Fountain then started arguing some point of law. The Kid stopped listening, another scene, one he wished he could forget, flashing through his mind.

Chapter 19

"God that I could in some way that would not pierce and wound your heart tell you that you son John is dead!"
—Alexander McSween to J. P. Tunstall, February 23, 1878

February 18, 1878
Lincoln County, New Mexico Territory

"Billy."

The Kid groaned, pushing aside the hand shaking his shoulder, and tried to burrow into his sugans.

"Billy."

The hand returned, firmer this time, and the Kid cursed and sat up. "Criminy, Dick, it's pitch dark. You said we'd be traveling at first light."

Dick Brewer laughed. "You got a long ways to go before you make top hand, Billy. Come on. John's got a pot of coffee brewin', and it's warmer inside."

He had something there, the Kid granted him, and crawled out of his bedroll, wiped sleep from his eyes, and found his bearings. Brewer was already walking away, heading for the flaring light that told the Kid where to find John Henry Tunstall's ranch house. The Kid had stayed in line shacks cozier than Tunstall's house, a two-hundred—if that—square-foot log house with gun ports recently cut into the timbers, letting in the freezing wind, but it remained a tad warmer inside than camping in the Englishman's front yard. The Kid tripped over a sandbag out front—one Tunstall and the boys had filled over the past two weeks. *Planning a barricade,* the Kid thought. *Preparing for a war.*

Brewer held the door open for him, and the Kid stepped into the light. Tunstall sat in his rocking chair, puffing on a pipe, talking to Rob Widenmann while Henry Brown kept checking the coffee pot on the stove in the corner and Fred Waite stitched a tear in his saddlebags with sinew and a long needle. John Middleton and William McCloskey followed Brewer into the cramped cabin, and Brewer closed the door. They'd wait, sipping coffee, until it was light enough to saddle their horses. That was one habit the Kid never understood about cowboys. *Why not sleep until dawn, then have a cup of coffee and saddle up?*

"Good morning, lad," Tunstall said with a smile. "Sleep well?"

"Didn't get enough of it."

After a hearty laugh, Tunstall tapped his pipe on the rocker's arm. He was a young man, not much older than the Kid, with a mustache the color and texture of peach fuzz and a scraggly beard that could likely be washed off—no need for a razor. The Kid had been working for Tunstall since leaving the Jones ranch at Seven Rivers in the fall of '77. Old Heiskell Jones had offered some good advice, recommending the Kid look up Tunstall for a job. He no longer thought about losing himself in Lincoln County. Instead, he figured he had found a home. Tunstall treated him like a man, not a kid, not some outlaw, and asked nothing of him but an honest day's work, which the Kid gladly gave. Once, back in December, Tunstall had bought the Kid a stack of dime novels he fancied, although he said he would have to introduce him to Dickens and Shakespeare. The Kid had surprised him by reciting a few lines from *Romeo and Juliet,* which he remembered from his playacting days in Silver City.

"Well, you are not the waif I have been led to believe," Tunstall had said. "I think we shall get along marvelously."

Until the last few months, when Murphy's and Dolan's men started tightening their stranglehold, he had never seen Tunstall lose his temper. Times were changing, though, the kettle boiling. First Lawrence G. Murphy, and now James

Dolan, had been feuding with Tunstall over his ranch, over opening his store in Lincoln to compete against The House, and over befriending attorney Alexander McSween, who had persuaded Tunstall to invest his future in Lincoln County.

He didn't understand the legal matters, lawsuits and criminal charges, more lawsuits and more accusations. Those things got so complicated they'd leave an educated man addlebrained, but the situation was starting down a trail that the Kid understood all too well. So did Tunstall. Since the first of the year, he had been carrying a double-action .44-caliber Webley Bulldog. Following a court order, or rather orders from Murphy, Dolan, and the damned Santa Fe Ring, Sheriff William Brady had attached Alexander McSween's property and now had started to attach some of Tunstall's property, citing the fact that Tunstall and McSween were partners.

They knew the sheriff would have a posse here sometime today. Tunstall said Brady could attach anything he wanted—the stove, the shovels, sandbags and anvil—but he wasn't about to get Tunstall's horses. This morning they would herd the livestock to Dutch Martin's place on the Río Peñaso. Dutch Martin could be trusted.

"Coffee's finally boiling," Henry Brown announced and fetched a cup off the table.

Tunstall asked—he never ordered anything, not as long as the Kid had known him—William McCloskey to ride over to Dutch's place and make sure everything was all right, and McCloskey left with a nod, taking a lantern so he could find his saddle and tack—and his roan. The rest drank till first light, then saddled their horses. An hour later, they headed for the trail, Fred Waite driving a buckboard filled with supplies, the rest herding nine Tunstall mares, good horseflesh every one.

Ten miles up the road, Waite turned the buckboard along the La Junta wagon road. "We'll meet you at Dutch's!" Tunstall shouted as he led his horses and men down the Parajito Springs shortcut. Henry Brown made it only a mile farther before his buckskin threw a shoe on its right forefoot. The Kid reined up as Brown swung to the ground and muttered an oath.

"Can you make it to Dutch's?"

"Nah. I'll ease this ol' nag back to the ranch, shoe him, and meet up with y'all later in town."

The Kid frowned. Henry Brown had ridden with John Chisum before joining the Tunstall outfit, and Chisum didn't hire greenhorns. Brown was as game a man as the Kid had ever known, and they'd miss his guns if trouble came.

"Look after yourself, Henry," the Kid told Brown, who mumbled something unintelligible while fishing a sack of chewing tobacco from his vest pocket. The Kid spurred his bay to catch up with the others and tell Tunstall what had happened to Brown's mount.

Later, when he and Brown figured out that the posse followed Brown's tracks to catch up with Tunstall, Brown had cursed the luck. If his horse hadn't lost that shoe, he never would have limped back to the ranch and found Deputy Billy Mathews and his posse waiting. The posse wouldn't have known where to start looking, but now those banditti had only to backtrack Brown's trail. The Kid had shrugged. "It would have happened sometime," he had told his pal. "You're lucky they didn't kill you, too."

Brown had met Billy Mathews and his men back at the ranch, lying that he had not seen Tunstall or the horses the sheriff wanted. The deputy didn't believe a word, and told Bill Morton to go after them. Morton said Jessie Evans wanted to come along.

"I don't care who you take," Mathews had said. More than a dozen men, including Evans, had ridden out while Brown shoed his horse and seethed.

The afternoon sun was sinking behind the foothills as the Kid yipped despite blinding, choking dust, slapping his lariat against his chaps, urging the tired horses along through a canyon, John Middleton riding drag beside him, both men dreaming of coffee at Dick Brewer's place just up the trail. They'd sup there before riding on to Dutch's.

Middleton heard them first. He reined up hard and shot a look down the canyon. The Kid didn't even know Middleton had stopped until he shouted and spurred his bay. Spinning in the saddle, the Kid almost dropped his lariat when the first bullet whistled overhead.

He couldn't recognize any faces, for they were too far away, although within rifle range. Another bullet whined off a rock. By the time the third shot had been fired, the Kid was beating his horse's flanks with the lariat, spurring past the Tunstall livestock, toward his boss and friends, who had stopped at the sound of gunfire.

"For God's sake, follow me!" Middleton yelled as he loped toward the cemetery of boulders lining the top of the ridge.

"What, John?" shouted Tunstall, confused, dazed, his dun gelding dancing nervously. "What?"

More shots dug into the ground, and the horses they had been driving bolted. The Kid echoed Middleton's warning as he loped past, but Tunstall just looked dumbly at the charging posse. Maybe frozen in fear. The Kid had heard of that happening to men in battle, and this was a battle. *No, not a battle. A cowardly ambush and assassination.* Dick Brewer's horse started bucking, hit by a piece of lead or a rock, but, with Widenmann's help, he managed to regain control, and they galloped for the cover atop the ridge.

They left John Henry Tunstall there.

The Kid never looked back until he had dismounted behind a boulder. He jacked a round into the Winchester he had pulled from the scabbard and chanced a look after another eruption of gunfire. He couldn't see anything but dust.

"They've killed Tunstall!" roared Middleton, his face pale.

No one answered. Brewer wet his lips. Widenmann checked the cartridges in his Remington, though the killers were well out of pistol range.

"What do we do?" the Kid asked.

"We can't leave John," Brewer said.

"He's dead!" Middleton snapped.

"You don't know that!" Brewer fired back, but they all knew it. Middleton was the only one who would say it. The Kid felt his stomach churning, his heart sinking, and tears welling.

"Did you recognize anyone?" Widenmann asked no one in particular.

"No," Middleton said. "Listen, we can't stay here. Must be at least twenty of 'em."

Not that many, the Kid thought, although he remained silent, *but more than enough to kill us all.*

Another shot echoed across the ravine.

"Oh, God." Brewer bowed his head.

Widenmann holstered his revolver. "John's right, Dick. We can't hold them off from here. Our best bet is to ride into Lincoln, tell Mr. McSween what's happened."

February 19, 1878
Lincoln, New Mexico Territory

So the four of them left John Tunstall behind, sneaking into Lincoln late that night like scalded dogs. Alexander Mc-Sween called a meeting at his house that lasted well past two o'clock and persuaded Green Wilson to swear out warrants for the arrest of Tunstall's killers. No one had recognized any of the posse members—no one even knew for certain that Tunstall was dead—but the Kid and Brewer named sixteen men anyway. It was as good a guess as any: Evans, Dolan, Hindman, Mathews, Morton, Roberts, Baker . . . Hell, they were all responsible, whether they had been there or not.

Florencio Gonzales and three other men brought in Tunstall's body later that day. "They killed Mr. Tunstall's horse, too," Gonzales told the Kid. "And bashed in Mr. Tunstall's head." He crossed himself. The Kid cursed.

That afternoon, Constable Atanacio Martinez deputized the Kid and Fred Waite to help him arrest Evans and Dolan, who were drinking and laughing in front of the House. Sheriff William Brady was there, too. The laughter softened but didn't stop when Martinez approached them. Waite and the Kid stayed back a few paces, the Winchester clasped tight in the Kid's hands.

"What do you want, greaser?" Evans tossed a bottle to Frank Baker and rested his right hand on the butt of his Colt.

Martinez silently pulled the arrest warrants he had tucked inside his trousers and handed them to Brady. He didn't say a word.

"I see," said Brady, passing the papers to Dolan. "I'll help you make this arrest," he added in his thick Irish brogue and slowly drew his Smith & Wesson. Then he moved quickly, pivoting and lashing out with the revolver, slamming the barrel into the constable's head. The Kid started to raise the Winchester, but Brady had thumbed back the hammer, weapon pointed not at Waite or the Kid, but at the prone, unconscious form of Martinez.

"Come on, you yellow bastards!" Brady shouted. "I'll blow this damned greaser's head off."

The Kid froze. Evans had leveled his Colt, and a dozen more men had stepped outside, weapons drawn. He glanced up and down the street, looking for Brewer, McSween, Widenmann, anyone to help, but the one road through Lincoln had become deserted.

"You call the tune," Evans said with a smirk.

The Kid savagely tossed the Winchester in the dirt. Fred Waite raised his hands over his head.

Brady holstered his pistol and walked toward them. "Well, I said I'd help make an arrest, and that's what I'm bloody well doing. Jessie, Frank, help me escort these *real tough* men to our jail. Mathews, you and Hindman cart our constable along, too. Let's go, Kid."

He was still in jail when Tunstall was buried on the twenty-second of February. For that, he swore, Sheriff William Brady would pay.

Chapter 20

"Ike Stockton, who was for so long a terror in Rio Arriba County, this Territory, and in Southern Colorado, and who was recently killed at Durango, kept a saloon in Lincoln plaza at the time . . . and was supposed to be a secret ally of The Kid and gang."
    —Pat F. Garrett, *The Authentic Life of Billy, the Kid, the Noted Desperado of the Southwest,* 1882

April 8, 1881
La Mesilla, New Mexico Territory

Isaac Ellis had been running a mercantile on the eastern edge of Lincoln, some of the prettiest property in town, and the merchant had always treated the Kid with kindness. The Kid would orchestrate shooting matches against Ellis's sons, Will and Ben, usually betting breakfast or a nickel. He'd even let them win sometimes, but not often. You couldn't find a better breakfast in Lincoln, not even at the Wortley.

He had always considered the Ellises friends, so he felt sick to his stomach when Simon Newcomb called the merchant as the prosecution's next witness.

"How long have you lived in the town of Lincoln?" Newcomb asked after Ellis had been sworn in.

"I came down from Colfax County back in '77, bought Daniel Dow's old place, and started my business, a mercantile. We had been in Cimarron four years before that, Kansas and Missouri before that."

As soon as the translation had been finished for the jury, Newcomb asked, "Do you recognize the defendant?"

"I do. He visited my store many times. His name's Billy Bonney; at least, that's what he called himself most of the time. Some folks called him Kid, and I've heard him called Antrim a few times. But I know him as Billy, short for William H. Bonney."

"He was a customer?"

Ellis nodded. "Customer, yes, and a friend to me and my boys."

"What did he buy?"

Ellis looked at the Kid and smiled. "Penny dreadfuls, mostly. He had an appetite for those silly novels from the Wide Awake Library, Beadle's, fanciful stories. I teased him about it more than once."

"Did he purchase anything else regularly?"

"Well, ammunition." Ellis faced the prosecutor. "He and my sons took a lot of target practice behind the store, over toward the river."

"Was he a good shot?"

"An excellent shot, with revolver or rifle. He favored the .44-40, since the bullets could be used in his Winchester and single-action Colt, at least in the beginning. Later, he bought one of those double-action Colts, the Thunderer, .41 caliber. He said it fit his hand better, didn't kick as hard."

"Did you see him on or about the first of April, 1878?"

"He rode in that evening; I mean the last day of March. Chatted a spell with us and bought a box of .44-40s and a half-dime novel, if I'm not mistaken."

"Was he alone?"

"No, sir. Several Regulators rode in with him. Henry Brown bought a pickaxe and two boxes of ammunition."

Newcomb's head bobbed. "A pickaxe? One that could be used to knock gun ports into an adobe wall?"

Fountain shouted an objection, arguing that the witness had no idea what the pickaxe was to be used for, that it could have been bought for mining purposes, ranch work, anything.

"I did not ask if he knew why Mr. Brown bought the

hardware," Newcomb told Judge Bristol. "I merely asked if it could be used for a particular chore. He runs a mercantile, Your Honor. He would be an expert in that matter."

"He's implying . . . ," Fountain started, but Bristol waved his hand and spit out tobacco juice.

"The jury can consider what he's implying, Mr. Fountain, or not consider it. Go on, Mr. Newcomb."

Smiling, Newcomb walked back toward his table. "Did you see the defendant the following day?"

"No, sir. I heard shooting down the street that morning while I was unloading an ox cart with my sons. Will, my oldest, asked if he should go investigate, but I told him to stay close. A little while later, we saw several riders loping down the riverbed. Couldn't get a clear view of them, but one of them wore a big Mexican sombrero. Ben said he thought it was Bonney."

"Did you learn what the shooting was about?"

"I did. After seeing the riders, Will begged me into letting him see what the commotion had been about. He's a man, full grown, so I relented. He came back and told me that Sheriff Brady had been killed, along with George Hindman."

"Did any other Regulators visit you that day?"

"Yes, sir. Alexander McSween rode in with Dick Brewer and some others around noon. George Peppin tried to arrest McSween, but McSween wouldn't let him. He said Peppin had no authority. His position as deputy sheriff expired with Sheriff Brady's death. I reckon that was true. Anyway, Peppin didn't lock McSween up."

"Did McSween appear shocked at the news of Brady's murder?"

"He just sighed. Dick Brewer, he muttered an oath and said, 'Billy!'"

Newcomb thanked the merchant before he sat down. Fountain remained in his chair beside the Kid. "You did not witness the shootings of Brady and Hindman?" he asked.

"No, sir."

"You did not recognize Mr. Bonney as one of the riders loping down the Río Bonito?"

"No, it's like I said. Ben thought it was Billy because of the sombrero."

"But it could have been a Mexican? It could have been anyone?"

"I can't swear that it was Billy, no, sir. Nor could Ben."

"You said he and Henry Brown bought ammunition the day before. Did anyone else buy ammunition?"

Ellis chuckled. "Mr. Fountain, you know as well as I do that selling guns and bullets was a right profitable business in Lincoln County in 1878."

That prompted a hearty laugh across the courtroom. Even Judge Bristol smiled, and as soon as Mariano Toribio finished his translation, the twelve jurors started snickering, like simpletons late getting a joke. That caused the rest of the court to laugh again, and the chortles continued until Bristol, still smiling, tapped his gavel. Albert Fountain hadn't laughed once, however. Hadn't even grinned.

"Yes or no, Mr. Ellis?" Fountain demanded.

"Sure. I sold plenty of bullets, even some weapons, that day, and the day after."

"Sell any other picks?"

"Probably. I'd have to check my ledger, though."

"You said Dick Brewer said, 'Billy,' after hearing of the sheriff's death. Is the defendant the only Billy you know?"

"No, sir. I know a whole slew of them."

"Did Dick Brewer say he had witnessed the shooting?"

"No, sir. He hadn't. He had just ridden in."

"So Dick Brewer had no idea who had shot Sheriff Brady."

"He couldn't have."

Fountain nodded. "No more questions."

Everyone, including the Kid, called Bonifacio Juan Baca—old Saturnino Baca's oldest son—Bonnie. After being called by Newcomb, Bonnie Baca strolled down the aisle in a black suit that probably cost more than most of the jurors earned in three months. His black mane was slicked back, not a hair out of place, and the Kid caught a whiff of tonic as he walked past. Evidently, Baca had stopped at the tonsorial parlor before coming to the courthouse. That was like him.

"If Your Honor does not object," Baca said after being sworn in, "I would prefer to translate my own answers—and the questions from the attorneys, of course—for the jury." He spoke without a trace of an accent. "I am fluent in Spanish. I am not casting aspersions on *Señor* Toribio, but I like to translate my own words."

That was like Bonnie Baca, too.

"Objections?" Bristol asked.

Simon Newcomb rose with a slight bow. "None, Your Honor. Mr. Baca served as translator for Colonel Nathan Dudley's Court of Inquiry at Fort Stanton two years ago. His reputation is sterling. We would have suggested he be hired as court interpreter for this trial were he not a witness for the Territory."

Bristol turned, bored. "Mr. Fountain?"

"He may speak, Your Honor, providing *Señor* Toribio is allowed to correct any mistakes or challenge anything he says. Toribio is the interpreter of record, sir."

With the judge's approval, Newcomb began his questioning. He was Bonnie Baca, born and reared in Lincoln County, and had lived there all his life, except when he was attending college at the University of Notre Dame from 1872 to 1874. Baca smiled when he told the court, first in English, then in Spanish, that he had been an honor student at Notre Dame.

"Really?" Newcomb sounded impressed. "But you would have been only fifteen years old when you started there?"

"Yes," he said, and turned to the jurors, translated Newcomb's question, and answered again, "*Sí.*"

"Upon your return to Lincoln, where did you go to work?"

"I was employed by the Lawrence G. Murphy Company. I worked for Major Murphy as a clerk and later served James J. Dolan in the same capacity."

"Do you know the defendant?"

"Yes, sir. He is William H. Bonney. Some people called

him Billy. I always called him Kid, *El Chivato*. I saw him at several dances in Lincoln County. We joked with each other, cutting in on each other's dances. I remember once when he was dancing with Miss Sallie Chisum. I'd cut in, and he'd bow graciously, and just a few bars later, he would tap my shoulder and ask for the pleasure. I went on like that for the entire waltz. Miss Sallie, I think she enjoyed the humor much more than Billy or myself."

The Kid smiled, remembering the scene exactly as Baca had described it.

"Were you working at the store on the first of April, 1878?"

"Yes, I was."

"What happened on that day?"

Baca sighed, more to the jury, the Kid thought, and began recalling how he had been inside the store shortly after breakfast when he heard shooting. He rose from his desk and walked cautiously to the door, peering outside to find George Peppin and Billy Mathews running down the street to the sound of gunfire and startled, barking dogs. Both men took cover inside or behind the Cisneros house.

"Did you see Sheriff Brady?"

"Yes. He was dead in the street." He shook his head while translating for the jury.

"Go on."

"Well, I turned back to tell the customers what was happening. I heard more shots and took another look. I saw two men running toward Sheriff Brady's body. Deputy Mathews began firing at them, and I believe he wounded both men, for they retreated, both of them limping. After another few minutes, I heard horses. Deputy Mathews, Deputy Peppin, and, I believe, Deputy Long opened fire, but the men escaped."

As the translation began, the Kid turned to Fountain, but the lawyer seemed preoccupied, rapidly taking notes, so he whispered his concerns about Baca's testimony to John Bail. Bail nodded, wrote a note himself, and told the Kid not to fret.

"Did you recognize either of the men that ran toward the sheriff's body?" Newcomb asked Baca.

"I could not answer with absolute certainty, but one of the men looked like the defendant."

"Thank you. I pass the witness, Your Honor."

Albert Fountain leaned back in his chair, twirling a pencil in his fingers. "'*Looked like.*' You mean it could have been anyone?"

"Anyone who looked like Billy Bonney," said Baca, shrugging.

"The Dolan store is not next door to the Tunstall store, though, is it?"

"No, sir. It is down the road, on the other side of the street. I have never measured, so cannot accurately answer as to the exact distance."

"Farther than fifty yards?"

Newcomb quickly argued that the witness had already testified that he did not know the exact distance. Bristol sustained the objection and noted Fountain's exception.

"There was much shooting?"

"*Habia mucho tirotero?* Yes. *Sí.*"

"You were scared?"

"*Tenias miedo?* Yes. *Sí.*"

"Yet you're positive the man you saw *looked like* the defendant. Could you identify the other person?"

He again translated for the jury before answering, "No."

"The only person you *thought* you saw was William Bonney! Did you see this man shoot Sheriff Brady?"

Baca, frowning harder, said he did not, that Brady was dead by the time he looked out the door.

"Thank you," Fountain said and leaned forward, waiting until Baca started to rise, then asking: "You say you attended the University of Notre Dame?"

He sank back in his chair, repeated Fountain's question in Spanish, and answered with a nod.

"That costs money. Who paid your tuition, for your books, your transportation to Indiana and home?"

Baca said it had been Major Lawrence G. Murphy.

Fountain arched his eyebrows. "You must owe the late Major Murphy a great deal."

Newcomb objected, Bristol sustained, but Fountain merely smiled. So did the Kid.

His stomach was growling, and, sitting in the back row next to two Indians, Ira Leonard wondered when Judge Bristol would call a recess. He wanted to talk to Bonney, give him some ideas to pass on to Albert Fountain, who was doing a fine job on Bonney's behalf. Leonard had been prepared to take plenty of notes illustrating Fountain's bias, but the attorney had shown none. Among the legal circuits, Fountain was considered a righteous man, a zealous lawyer, a man whose reputation was above reproach. So far, Leonard reluctantly admitted, Fountain was living up to that.

Ike Stockton was sworn in, and Mariano Toribio returned to his interpretation duties. Stockton, an uncouth, bearded man with a nose that had been broken more than once, settled into the chair and crossed his legs.

After the preliminary questions, Newcomb asked Stockton to tell the court what had happened on the day William Brady was shot dead in the street.

"I was in the back of me place," Stockton said, "waterin' down me whiskey when the shootin' commenced. I headed for the front door, seen that Brady was bleedin' and plumb full of holes. George Hindman was on the ground a few feet from the sheriff, moanin' somethin' fierce, beggin' for water. I saw them rifle barrels pointin' out of holes knocked into Tunstall's corral, then I hollered at 'em that I was bringin' George inside. So I run out there, grabbed George, started draggin' him. Then one of them cowardly sons of bitches fired again."

Bristol warned Stockton not to use profanity in his testimony, and Stockton whispered an apology and continued.

"I dropped George—he was dead; last shot had hit 'im right in the heart—and jumped back into my place, bolted the door, and yelled at them sorry cusses that had done the shootin', called 'em low-down murderin' cowards. That was about it. They rode off later, and I come outside, helped Mathews and Peppin take the bodies into the shade. Then I rode out to Fort Stanton to fetch their doc for the coroner's inquest."

"Do you know the defendant?"

"That's the Kid. Bonney. He's been in my saloon many a time. He was there when Chapman got kilt—"

"Yes or no will suffice, sir. He was a frequent customer?"

"Well, I never sold him no liquor. Don't think he drunk John Barleycorn. But he'd come by with his pals and, sometimes, his enemies."

"Did you ever hear him threaten Sheriff Brady?"

"He wanted him dead, that's for certain."

Fountain leaped from his chair with an objection, and Bristol reminded Stockton to answer the question he had been asked and not salt it with his opinion.

"Not him. But I did hear Henry Brown say Brady would pay. Said he and the Kid would see to that."

Newcomb sat down, satisfied, and Fountain rose, tugging on his mustache as he approached the saloon keeper.

"Let me get this straight," Fountain began. "You *water down* your whiskey?"

Everyone—including Leonard—broke out laughing. The humor was so out of character for a pious man like Fountain. Leonard was still shaking his head when Bristol silenced the uproar with his gavel. After that, Fountain turned serious.

"Did you see the defendant fire his weapon at Sheriff Brady or Deputy Hindman?"

"Nope."

"Did you even see Mr. Bonney on that day?"

"Can't recollect that I did."

"And you only heard Henry Brown's threatening remarks. How many people have you heard threatened in your saloon, sir?"

Stockton snorted. "A right smart, I reckon."

"Have all of them been murdered?"

"Nope." Stockton grinned. "Just John Tunstall, Alexander McSween, Buckshot Roberts, Major Brady, George Hindman, that lawyer Chapman, Charlie Bowdre . . ."

Bristol silenced him with his gavel.

Fountain headed back to his chair, and Bristol adjourned court until two-thirty. Leonard was the first man out of the courtroom, heading straight for the sheriff's office and jail cells.

Chapter 21

"Dangerous diseases require heroic treatment. That's what is needed now."

—Ira Leonard

April 8, 1881
La Mesilla, New Mexico Territory

As soon as he hung his robe in his chambers, Judge Warren Bristol donned his Stetson and meandered through the cramped courthouse and across the crowded plaza until he reached the Head Quarters. It looked as if half the people in town had chosen the *cantina* to slake their thirsts, and not because of the free pickles and sandwiches offered between noon and two o'clock. James Dolan, drink in hand, met him just inside the door and guided him to the private room in the back.

Members of Aztec Lodge Number 3 in Las Cruces jokingly called the back room Rynerson's Private Suite because the former district attorney often held high-stakes poker games here after court was adjourned. Rynerson sat there now, but the table held no chips or cards, just two jars of pickles and a tray of cold sandwiches. Simon Newcomb arrived after Bristol lit his cigar, bringing three glasses and a bottle of Bushmills. At least the label said Bushmills. For all Bristol knew, the owner of this grog shop filled expensive bottles with the throat-blistering popskull Ike Stockton served in Lincoln.

"I think we might've been better off letting Leonard try this case," Dolan said. "That Fountain's one hard rock."

"He wasn't my choice." Bristol pulled out a pickle and bit into it. He swallowed, staring at Rynerson, and added, "I merely removed Leonard and followed Mr. Rynerson's suggestion."

"Albert's doing his job," Rynerson said. "The case has a long way to go."

Newcomb reached for a sandwich. "I think we're doing fine on the prosecution side. Bonnie Baca did a magnificent job, and old man Ellis's testimony was particularly damning. Besides, I have several more witnesses to call. Stockton's testimony might not wash, but it didn't hurt us, and those damned Mes'cans are impressed by authority. Billy Mathews was a deputy sheriff, by God. And so was George Peppin, who I'll call this afternoon or tomorrow." He crammed the small sandwich into his mouth, ate it hurriedly, and washed it down with whiskey. After wiping his mouth, he added, "I've seen men hanged with less evidence."

Bristol answered with a volley: "And I have seen men acquitted with more."

He ate another pickle and tested the whiskey. The latter wasn't that raw.

"Who's your next witness?" Rynerson asked. "Remind me."

"Bonnie's father, Saturnino. Then I'll call John Chisum, and close with George Peppin and the *Reverend* Taylor Ealy. Baca's testimony will just back up what everyone has said so far. Chisum wants the Kid hanged more than anyone. Peppin was there, and Ealy nursed one of those assassins. I'll put him on trial."

"The jury might not like that," Bristol said. "He's a man of God."

"Presbyterian, or so he claims. The Mes'cans are all Catholics. I bet they shall enjoy it."

Dolan shook his head. "I'd like it better if we got Bob Olinger to blow the Kid's brains out, say he was trying to escape. And why ain't Green Wilson testifying, or his boy?

Wilson got shot in the arse by a stray bullet when Brady got murdered."

"Green has always been an enemy to us," Rynerson said. "He backed McSween's play, he backed Tunstall's play, and he made the Kid a damned Regulator. He's not a witness for us. And if anything happens to the Kid in Mesilla, I'll personally see that you rot in hell, Dolan. This isn't Lincoln. You don't shoot people in the streets."

Dolan topped his glass. "I still don't like the way Fountain's handling this. He's a Mason. One of us. You bloody well ought to talk to him, Will."

Rynerson rose, although he had to duck to keep from hitting his head on the ceiling. "You just do your jobs," he told Newcomb and Bristol. "And you . . ." He shook his head at Dolan. "You lock yourself up in the Texas Pacific Hotel and don't set foot in the courtroom." He opened the door, letting in a cacophony of voices, fiddle music, and the smell of tobacco.

"You'll talk to Fountain, though, won't you?" Newcomb said in a whine.

"No," Rynerson said. "Not Albert."

He had never seen Bonney lose his temper, not this way. The Kid paced back and forth in his cell, kicking the walls, his cot, slamming his right fist into the palm of his left hand, cursing so vilely, so loudly, that Sheriff Southwick finally rushed in and threatened to douse the Kid with a bucket of water if he didn't shut up. The sheriff turned to Bob Olinger, standing guard with his shotgun by the back door, and shouted, "You see to it, Bob, you hear me?"

Olinger's nod was barely perceptible, and then the sheriff whirled to face Leonard, sitting on a stool in the hallway. "And you make sure he stays quiet, sir. He's your client, and there's a bunch of kids just across the buildin'. They don't need to hear that kind of language." Southwick stormed out, and Leonard shook his head.

"I guess he hasn't heard that Judge Bristol replaced me and that you are no longer my client," Leonard said softly.

"Yeah. Well, what brings you here anyway?" the Kid asked.

Leonard reached into his grip and pulled out a sweet roll, which he held up for Olinger's inspection before tossing it through the iron bars.

"I picked this up at Dorn's bakery," he said. "Thought you might be hungry."

He grinned as the Kid tore into the cinnamon roll, knowing his sweet tooth. With his mouth full, the Kid said, "It sure beats the hog and hominy they give me here." His smile returned, and he fell back on his cot, swinging his legs up and resting his head in his hands on his pillow.

"I'm thinking Judge Bristol done me a favor," he said, staring at the ceiling. "I think Mr. Fountain's likely a better lawyer than you are, Ira." He turned his head, his smile growing.

"Fountain's done all right," Leonard agreed. "There are a few things I wouldn't have done, but he has been strong on cross. Now that you've got something in your stomach, and you realize your attempts to rile me are futile, why don't you tell me what ignited your temper?"

The Kid sat up quickly, his eyes wild. "I treated Isaac Ellis like I would an uncle," he snapped, "and he bushwhacks me like that. Saying how his boy Ben said it might have been me ridin' down the Río Bonito. That shouldn't have been allowed, should it? I mean, isn't that what you call heresy?"

Leonard couldn't help but grin. "Hearsay," he corrected. Bonney was an intelligent boy, and it amused him whenever he made a mistake. "Fountain could have objected, but I don't think Bristol would have sustained it. Is it grounds for appeal? No."

"Well, that hurt, but Baca's testimony really galled me. Bonnie and I were pals. At least, I thought we were, even though he worked for Murphy and Dolan. We had fun at the *bailes,* courting the same girls. He had no reason to lie like that."

Leonard raised his eyebrows. "How did he lie?"

The Kid stood, started pacing, his temper boiling. "Just keep your voice down," Leonard cautioned.

"Southwick doesn't scare me." The Kid didn't stop pacing. "He won't leave me soaking wet. He keeps begging me to say something nice about his jail whenever he lets one of them inkslingers in here." A mouse raced across one of the vigas, and the Kid shook his head. "Say something nice about this pigsty?"

"It's not Sheriff Southwick that concerns me, Billy." Leonard tilted his head slightly down the hallway.

The Kid understood. *Bob Olinger.* He sat down again. Besides Olinger, the cells currently housed other criminals, and Leonard didn't trust them, either. Billie Wilson occupied the first cell, waiting to be shipped back to the territorial prison outside Santa Fe. Two convicted murderers, waiting for their execution next month, bunked next door.

"How did Baca lie?" Leonard whispered.

"There's no way he could have seen Brady's body or anyone running toward it from the corral behind Tunstall's store. Not from the door to Dolan's store."

Leonard opened his notepad and scribbled a note. "How about upstairs?"

"He said he looked out the front door, remember? Even upstairs, I don't think he could have seen much. It has to be two hundred, two-fifty yards from Dolan's to Tunstall's store. That street isn't straight, and, despite his college education, Bonnie can't see through trees and adobe walls."

Leonard's suspicion mounted. Fountain had been to Lincoln many times. He had to know that. On the other hand, Fountain had tried to introduce the distance into evidence, and the jury might consider that despite Bristol sustaining Newcomb's objection. Fountain had even asked for an exception. Still, it could have been handled better.

"I told Bail," the Kid said. "He wrote it down."

Bail. Leonard pursed his lips, considering that lawyer. He didn't know much about him, just that he was a Mason and had powerful allies in Santa Fe. "It doesn't matter," Leonard said. "Fountain can call a rebuttal witness after the defense testimony ends. Ask him to do that. Someone can take the stand and swear that Baca could not have seen the events he described."

The door opened, and Bail and Fountain stepped inside, surprised to see the Kid's visitor. Leonard stuffed his pad into his bag, stood, and said he would check in after supper. "Remember," he whispered, "stay off the witness stand. Have Fountain discredit all prosecution witnesses. That's your defense."

He smiled as he walked past the lawyers, but Bail stopped him.

"What are you doing, Leonard? Bonney's not your client anymore."

"No," Leonard said, "but visitation has not been restricted, considering how many newspaper reporters have been interviewing him since his arrival. Besides, I can visit a friend, can't I?"

Chapter 22

"*A six-shooter will get you into more trouble than it will get you out of.*"

—John Chisum

April 8, 1881
La Mesilla, New Mexico Territory

Saturnino Baca looked older than his fifty years, his graying beard longer than it was the last time the Kid had seen him, perhaps to offset his receding hairline. He had been a schoolteacher back when this was part of Mexico, and, since it had become a United States territory, a surveyor, Union Army volunteer, freighter, stock raiser, and member of the territorial legislature. Unlike his oldest son, however, he had never once been one of the Kid's friends.

His English was broken, and as Simon Newcomb led him through the preliminary questions, Mariano Toribio struggled to make sense of his answers and translate them for the jury.

"Describe the events of the first of April, 1878," Newcomb began.

Baca sat stooped in the witness chair. He blinked once, emptied his mouth of snuff, and said, "Carlota in Torreón. Play dolls."

"You mean, that Carlota, your youngest daughter, was in the old Indian fort playing with her dolls?"

"*Sí.*"

"On the top floor?"

"*Sí.*"

"What happened?"

"Shots. *Muy*. She run home. Tell *mi* Juanita."

"She ran home, you mean, and told your wife?"

"*Sí.*"

"What did she tell her?"

"Man dead. Juanita fear me. Beg Carlota see."

"Let me get this right, sir. Your wife feared that you might be the man your daughter had seen lying dead in the street? She asked her to find you, to make sure you had not been killed?"

"*Sí.*"

"Did Carlota see the actual shooting?"

Albert Fountain rose to object, saying that what Carlota Baca might or might not have seen was not a question for her father. That would constitute hearsay. If the prosecution so desired, it should call Carlota as a witness.

"Surely, Your Honor," Newcomb argued, "the court will grant some leniency in this matter. I am certain that my distinguished opponents do not want to force a nine-year-old girl to recall a terrible, despicably violent murder she witnessed three years ago. A gentleman as honored as *Señor* Baca would have a much better memory of his daughter's words than she would. After all, three years have passed since the brutal slayings of . . ."

"Your point is well taken." Bristol motioned Fountain to sit down. "But Mr. Fountain's objection is sustained. The witness may answer questions about what he saw, not what his daughter may have witnessed."

Too bad, the Kid thought with a smile. Carlota spoke better English than anyone in the Baca family except Bonnie. And the Kid had always doted on her. Likely she had been on the Torreón playing with a doll he had bought her at Tunstall's or Ellis's store.

"Obviously," Newcomb said after bowing to the judge, "you were not one of the men murdered in the street that morning." He grinned, but no one else found his attempt at humor amusing. "What were you doing at the time of the assassination?"

Fountain objected to the word *assassination,* but Bristol, suddenly surly, told him to shut up.

"Visit *Señor* Aguayo. Come home."

"Did you see anyone while returning home?"

"*Sí. Señor* Wilson. I hear guns. He scream. Fall patch."

"Justice J. B. Wilson, or Green Wilson? He was shot? Fell into his onion patch?"

"*Sí.*"

"Did you assist him?"

"*Sí.*"

"Was he badly hurt?"

He shook his head, and a toothless grin appeared beneath his unkempt facial hair. "Shot in ass."

The courtroom erupted in laughter. Newcomb waited until the outburst died down, then asked, "From Justice Wilson's garden, you must have had a good view of the corral where the assassins were hiding?"

Fountain objected again. "I've been lenient because of the language barrier, Your Honor, but he's leading the witness a bit too far this time."

"Sustained. Ask a better question, Mr. Newcomb."

The prosecutor rephrased the question, and the old man nodded and tapped his forehead over both eyes. "See everything. See him run major."

"You saw the defendant? Running toward Major Brady?"

"*Sí.* It him. More shots. They run. Corral. Ride away."

"You saw William H. Bonney running toward the dead body of the county sheriff, then retreat after Deputy Mathews returned fire? You are positive?"

"*Sí. Billito. El Chivato.*"

Newcomb thanked the witness and took his seat.

"How long have you known the defendant?" Albert Fountain asked without looking up.

Baca shrugged. "*Tres. Quatro.*"

"Three or four years?"

Another nod, followed by a *sí.*

"You dislike him?"

Newcomb stood to object, but even before he had finished, Fountain was arguing about credibility, and Bristol overruled the prosecutor.

Answered Baca: "Threaten me."

"You thought he had threatened you?" Fountain gave the old man a cold stare.

"Scare me. Regulators."

"You were scared by the Regulators after John Tunstall's death. In fact, during the siege of Alexander McSween's house later that year, it was you who begged the army to come to town, which likely resulted in the murder of—"

"Objection!"

"Sustained."

Fountain leaned back in his chair. "Lawrence G. Murphy sent your oldest son to the University of Notre Dame. He employed your son for years. You disliked the Regulators. You dislike the defendant. Wouldn't you lie to see him on the gallows?"

Baca didn't respond. Fountain didn't push him, firing another question: "You claim to have seen Mr. Bonney run toward Sheriff Brady's body. You saw only him?"

"Him." Baca pointed his chin at the Kid.

"Green Wilson had been hit by a stray bullet, and you had the grit to remain in the open during all this musketry?"

Another nod at the Kid. "Him."

"Isn't it true, sir, that you were busy—bravely, I might add—pulling Green Wilson behind his adobe home? You could not have seen the defendant! Don't perjure yourself, sir. I can bring Justice Wilson's son to the stand. Gregorio will swear that he saw you bringing his father out of harm's way."

Newcomb was on his feet again. "He's badgering the witness, Your Honor."

"Answer the question," Bristol said.

"Him." Baca nodded at Bonney again.

"Him. You saw him, only the defendant. While other witnesses claim that two men rushed to the street. You saw only Billy Bonney because you hate him, you fear him. Please sit down, Mr. Newcomb, and hold your objection. I am finished with this witness."

*   *   *

Her uncle looked tuckered out as he sank into the witness chair to the sounds of his groans and cracking joints. Four years ago, Sallie Chisum remembered, Uncle John had been a robust man, quick with a joke or challenge, a man who stood his ground no matter the consequences. But Lincoln County and pettifogging shysters had not been kind to him. He had spent the dwindling remains of his fortune fighting lawsuits and rustlers. He told her he moved to New Mexico in 1867 to "make his pile," although he had earned what most people would consider a fortune before ever leaving Texas. Now, he sometimes told her, he said he'd likely make his grave along the Río Pecos.

Even before he was sworn in, attorney Albert Fountain objected. "The witness was not in Lincoln on the day of the shooting, Your Honor," he said. "Any testimony would be hearsay, inadmissible. He has nothing pertinent to offer."

"Except motive," Simon Newcomb said smugly.

Bristol nodded and spit. "I'll hear what he has to say."

With great sadness, she listened to her uncle. She had long admired and respected her uncles, as well as her father, how they had managed to carve an empire with nothing but guts—and guns, she often lamented, although Uncle John never even carried a pistol. She regretted having lied to him as he told the jury about establishing his ranches, about fighting rustlers, and Lawrence G. Murphy's monopoly. She had argued that he needed someone to care for him, to look after him on the journey from the Chisum ranch to Old Mesilla, someone to keep him company, and he had relented. He'd learn the real reason she made the journey soon enough.

"Do you know the defendant?" Newcomb asked.

"Billy Bonney? Sure. Most folks who ever hung their hat in Lincoln County knowed Billy, some to their eternal regret."

"How's that?"

"Lincoln's a dangersome place, and Billy can be a dangersome individual."

Albert Fountain rose from his seat. "I thought this witness was here to testify as to an alleged motive, not slander."

"Let's move things along, Mr. Newcomb," Bristol said.

The prosecutor did, too, with rapid acceleration.

"You backed the enterprises of John Tunstall and Alexander McSween?"

"I did, sir. I was what you might call a silent partner, but everybody knew it was my money."

"William Bonney worked for John Tunstall? And later served as a Regulator under Alexander McSween?"

"He did. He was an *amigo* to both men. So was I."

"During the late Lincoln County War, did the Regulators ever stop at your ranch?"

"Oftentimes. I give 'em credit at my store on the ranch. Billy, he—"

"I'm still waiting for motive," Fountain interjected. "Not this chin-music."

Newcomb bowed toward Bristol. "With the court's patience, Your Honor . . . ," he began, and Bristol waved down Fountain's objection.

"Did you ever hear the Kid threaten the late Sheriff William Brady?"

Uncle John nodded. "Several times, but not just him. Henry Brown did the most jawin'. McSween was fearful that Brady would try to arrest him, shoot him down like that posse had done John Tunstall. They were in a fix by then, on the run, hidin' in the hills. I told 'em not to be so jo-fired to get 'emselves kilt, or get somebody else kilt. Told 'em that the fire would burn itself out soon, and Evans—even Dolan—they'd answer to the law, real law, or God soon enough."

"Like deputies Morton and Baker answered, shot dead after leaving your ranch that March?"

"They was shot tryin' to escape."

Newcomb stifled a laugh. "When did you last see the Regulators before the murder of Sheriff Brady?"

Uncle John shifted in the chair. "They rode out around the twenty-ninth of March, 1878."

"All of them?"

"Them that was there. Brown, Billy, Widenmann. A handful of others. Alex McSween and Dick Brewer come by a few days later with Billy, Brown, and some of the other boys. That's when I first heard that Brady and Hindman had been kilt."

"What were their moods when they returned to your ranch?"

"Alex was scared. Brewer wasn't with 'em. He was lyin' dead over at Blazer's Mill by then. But Billy and Henry Brown, I reckon I'd say they was as happy as pigs in clover."

Newcomb returned to his chair with a smug countenance. Albert Fountain did not bother to stand.

"What was your mood?" the attorney asked.

"I wasn't sorry to see Brady buried. Wasn't sorry about Hindman, either."

"And Morton? Baker?"

"They deserved what they got, iffen you ask me." He smiled. "Which you just did."

"So, you were just as happy as—how did you put it—a pig in clover. A lot of your riders were just as unmoved at the death of Brady?"

"I reckon so."

"They had just as much motive to kill Brady as did my client?"

"They're no strangers to guns, if that's what you're gettin' at. But they aren't foolish enough to kill a sheriff without my . . . I don't think any of my boys shot Brady, Mr. Fountain."

"But you did not witness the shootings? You have no idea if Bonney was in Lincoln on that day?"

He shook his head. "Couldn't swear to it, no."

Fountain nodded. "No more questions." Uncle John pulled himself up with pain and hobbled back to the firm bench to take his seat beside Sallie Chisum.

His friends called him "Dad," but George Peppin was no friend of the Kid. A smile appeared chiseled underneath the old brick mason's prematurely graying, bushy mustache, yet that was a facade. Peppin would kill a man without hesitation—he was like Charlie Bowdre in that regard—and never frown. He had laughed when the Regulators tried to arrest

him for Tunstall's murder, and he had laughed after Ira
Leonard had persuaded a grand jury to indict him for arson.
All during the siege that led to the burning of the McSween
home and the big killing, the Kid had heard Dad Peppin's
laughter.

A wide grin cracked his weathered face as he swore to tell
the whole truth and sat down.

Peppin's testimony reiterated what Billy Mathews had
said earlier. He had met Brady, Mathews, Hindman, and
Long for breakfast at the hotel, then walked toward the courthouse. He was behind Long and in front of Hindman when
they passed the Tunstall store, only a few yards from the
courthouse. That's when men hidden behind the corral walls
started firing.

"John was closer to the Torreón, so he ran that way," Peppin said. "He took a bullet, but it was only a flesh wound. I
cocked my carbine, saw Major Brady sitting in the street. He
said something, but I couldn't hear the words, my ears was
ringing so, and then the shooting started again. That's when
I started running, following Billy Mathews. I didn't even see
George till I tripped over his body. Don't see how I made it
through that scrape alive."

"Where did you find cover?"

"At the Cisneros place. Juanita started to open the door, to
see what was going on, I guess, but I hollered at her to get
back, and ran inside. I kept the door open, told her to stay in
her bed chambers. Billy Mathews, he took shelter behind the
place."

He repeated how Ike Stockton had charged out of his saloon, tried to drag the wounded Hindman inside, but when a
bullet struck the deputy, Stockton retreated into his place. A
few minutes later, two men charged toward Brady's body.

"Did you fire at them?"

"Started to, but one of them was doing a pretty good job
emptying his Winchester. Two bullets sent splinters from the
door frame into my hand. I let out a little laugh and a curse,
and Billy—Mathews, that is—returned fire. He's a better
shot than me, anyhow."

"Go on," Newcomb coaxed.

"He hit them both. One grabbed his thigh, hobbled back with the other, who was also limping after Billy's shooting. Then they rode out. We kept an eye out for them, but they didn't return. I went over to Major Brady and saw he was dead. George Hindman was dead, too. Then Billy, Deputy Mathews, that is, started following the trail of blood from one of them man-killers he had wounded. I asked Ike Stockton to ride over to the fort, tell Colonel Dudley what had just took place and ask if he'd send his surgeon over for a coroner's inquest. Then I followed Deputy Mathews on the trail of blood. It led to Tunstall's store, but we didn't find the man Billy had shot. Doc Ealy was in the store—living there, he was, with his wife and two girls—and we asked him about it. Figured he had seen that *hombre,* but he said nothing. Deputy Mathews was right mad, but I told him we'd catch the killer sooner or later, and we'd best get a posse together."

"You took charge?"

"Well, I was a deputy, and we didn't have no sheriff. Somebody had to do it."

"You later served in the official capacity as sheriff, didn't you?"

"Yeah. John Copeland took over right afterwards. It seems, by law, we had no authority because Major Brady had hired us, and he was dead. Anyway, I served after they took Copeland's badge away and gave it to me. Then I quit. Wasn't getting paid." He snorted. "I'm not getting my head shot off for nothing."

"Did you recognize any of the two men running toward Major Brady's body?"

"Not clearly." He wasn't going to be called a liar, the Kid figured, not going to be threatened with perjury the way Mathews had been. "One of them looked a lot like the Kid, though. He was wearing a Mes'can's sugarloaf."

"By the Kid, you mean the defendant? Do you know of any reason he had to kill Sheriff Brady?"

"Billy Bonney, the Kid, we called him. *El Chivato,* a bunch of the Mes'cans called him. Yeah, he blamed us all for John Tunstall's death. He didn't want just Major Brady and George Hindman dead. He wanted Dolan dead; me and Jack

Long; Billy Mathews for sure; Frank Baker; Bill Morton; Jessie Evans; Mr. Rynerson, the former attorney." He looked up at Bristol. "He even wanted you dead, Judge."

Fountain objected, but Bristol overruled him, and the attorney began scratching furiously in his notepad. He was still writing several seconds after Newcomb sat down, and had to be prodded by Bristol if the defense wanted to cross-examine Peppin.

"I bet Your Honor's pardon," Fountain said, still writing. He finally put his pencil aside and looked up. "Mr. Peppin, have you ever faced criminal indictments?"

"Objection."

"It goes to credibility, Your Honor."

Bristol pursed his lips. "I'll allow it," he finally said.

Peppin shook his head with another chuckle. "Well, I've had a few."

"You were the sheriff during the big fight in Lincoln that resulted in the deaths of Alexander McSween and several other Regulators?"

"I was there, trying to keep the peace."

"You never cared for the Regulators, did you?"

"I don't like getting shot at, if that's what you mean."

"And you dislike William H. Bonney. In fact, you hate him."

"He's not gonna be invited to sup with me. Not unless I'm heeled."

"Could you see anyone behind the wall during the shooting?"

"Nope."

"So you have no idea who shot Sheriff Brady."

"Well, more than one man shot him. He was full of holes like one of my shirts after the moths got it."

"You don't know for a fact if the defendant even fired his weapon at Sheriff Brady, do you?"

"He fired it at me and Billy Mathews."

"You think he fired it. You can't positively say it was him."

"Well, he bore a striking resemblance to the Kid."

Now Fountain laughed, although his laughter held no

mirth. "Yes," he said, shaking his head. "You saw a man you strongly disliked, while being shot at, the bullets striking so close they filled your hand with splinters. Remarkable."

Newcomb objected again, and Bristol told Fountain to ask questions and not make editorials.

"Who suggested that you take Sheriff Brady's place?" Fountain asked.

"James Dolan."

"Another man who hated the defendant and the Regulators. No more questions."

Chapter 23

"Soldiers and citizens armed. Great danger of being shot."

—The Rev. Dr. Taylor Filmore Ealy

April 8, 1881
La Mesilla, New Mexico Territory

"What is your trade, sir?" Simon Newcomb asked the next witness.

"I am a medical missionary." Taylor Ealy spoke in a mild voice, which Ira Leonard expected. Nothing ever riled the man. He never lost his temper, never swore, never doubted his faith in God or medicine, and, before leaving for Zuni Pueblo, he had lived in Lincoln from 1878 to '79. That certainly tested men of the cloth as well as men of medicine.

The first person he saw after Jessie Evans had tried to murder him two years ago, Leonard recalled, had been the Reverend Dr. Taylor Ealy. He was the first person Leonard asked about salvation, and Ealy had understood him, despite Leonard's mangled tongue. Leonard always believed that to have been a sign from God, proof of the Almighty's existence.

Ealy was fair-skinned, with green eyes, wavy dark hair, and a beard few men would brag about. To the stand he had carried a carpetbag, its gaudy colors a striking contrast to the somber gray suit, black tie, and boiled white shirt worn by the "medical missionary," resting it on his thighs during Newcomb's direct examination.

Newcomb arched his eyebrows. "So you mend souls as well as bullet holes?" This did cause some polite laughter. Ealy bowed as he answered.

"Do you know the defendant?" Newcomb asked.

"William Bonney. He was a friend of Alexander Mc-Sween, and the McSweens allowed my family and myself to stay with them upon my arrival in Lincoln. Later, they allowed us to stay in the Tunstall store."

"Why did you come to Lincoln?"

"To establish a mission and school."

"Did you know John Tunstall?"

"No. I arrived the day after his death. I helped with his embalming, then conducted his funeral."

"That must have been a shock for you and your family, sir. To see such brutality on your first day in town."

Ealy smiled. "As Alexander McSween once said to me, 'You are likely to find this what the Bible calls stony ground.' "

Newcomb waited for the translation before nodding thoughtfully. "Stony ground indeed. Where were you on the day Sheriff Brady was murdered?"

"I was at the Tunstall store, in the living quarters."

"Did you hear the shots?"

"I did."

"Did you see what happened?"

Ealy sighed. "I cannot answer that, sir, as I have told you and your assistants on several occasions."

Leonard leaned forward. He had not expected this, but evidently Newcomb had anticipated it. He immediately asked permission to treat the witness as hostile. Fountain immediately objected.

"It's his witness, Your Honor," Fountain said. "And he's a doctor and a minister."

Newcomb pivoted to face Bristol, barely able to rein in his anger. "The Territory believes that this witness not only saw the murders, but he treated one of the men wounded by Deputy Mathews. This man was a friend of the Kid, a friend of Alexander McSween, scores of Lincoln County ruffians. Blood led to the Tunstall store, and Deputy Peppin testified that when he asked Ealy about the matter, this *medical missionary* turned deaf and dumb. We ask the court's latitude."

"Even if that were the case," Fountain said, "Mr. Newcomb understands the sanctity between a patient and his doctor and the sanctity between a reverend and his flock."

"Flock!" Newcomb shook his head in disgust. "I submit to you that this man is no doctor, and he is no ordained minister. He calls himself a 'medical missionary.' I say he has no proof of either."

Ealy did not appear ruffled. He simply reached into his carpetbag and withdrew two framed diplomas. Apparently, he also had anticipated a fight with the prosecutor.

"Your Honor," he told Bristol, "I am a graduate of Washington and Jefferson College and the Western Theological Seminary in Allegheny, Pennsylvania. I also was graduated from the University of Pennsylvania's medical school in Philadelphia in 1874." He passed the diplomas to the judge while Simon Newcomb stammered.

Leonard laughed softly. The prosecutor had committed the biggest error a lawyer can make. *Never ask a question, never make a challenge, unless you already know the answer, the truth.* As Toribio translated the exchange, Bristol returned the diplomas to Ealy.

"These don't look bogus," Bristol said. "However, the question before the witness was—" He beckoned for the transcripts, examined the page, and read: " 'Did you see what happened?' " He returned the papers to the stenographer. "I think that can be answered without injury to your honor as a doctor or your soul as a preacher."

With a frown, Ealy replied, "The sheriff and deputy were already dead by the time I looked out the window. I'm not a fool, Your Honor. I didn't risk a bullet between my eyes until the shooting stopped."

"Did you see two men run toward the sheriff's body?" Newcomb asked.

Ealy looked at Bristol, who told him he must answer.

"I did."

"Did you recognize them?"

He straightened. "This I will not answer."

"One of the men was badly wounded, sir," Newcomb said. "Deputies followed a trail of blood to the Tunstall store. Isn't it a fact, sir, that you treated this man?"

"Nor can I answer that."

"Even if the judge instructs you to?" Newcomb shouted. He had lost hold of his emotions, another egregious error for an attorney. "You would denounce his authority?"

"I answer to a higher authority, Mr. Newcomb."

Bristol interrupted the dialogue, but his wrath—to Leonard's surprise—was not directed at Taylor Ealy. "And this judge, Mr. Newcomb, has not instructed the witness to do anything. Watch yourself, sir. You are not on the bench."

Newcomb whispered an apology as he backtracked to his chair. "You treated a killer. You—"

"Objection!" Fountain shouted.

"Sustained. Mr. Newcomb, you are courting a contempt fine, sir, and are through examining this witness. Mr. Fountain, do you have any questions on cross?"

Fountain rose, pressing his hands on the table. "Just a few, Your Honor. Reverend Ealy, how well do you know the defendant?"

"I saw him fairly often." His smile widened. "He would come to our meetings when he was in town and sing in our choir. Mary, my wife, loved his voice. He sang tenor. Quite well, I might add."

"Thank you. I just want to make this clear. Sheriff Brady was already dead when you looked out the window. Therefore, you have no idea who shot him. Even if you were a layman, not a doctor, not a minister, could you in all honesty say who killed the sheriff?"

"No, sir, I could not."

Fountain bowed and returned to his seat. Leonard tugged on his beard, while Judge Bristol glanced at his watch. It was growing late, and he would likely adjourn court until tomorrow morning. That was fine. Bonney would end the day on the plus side of the ledger, thanks to Newcomb's bumbling, but Leonard didn't like Fountain's constant questioning on one item. No one could say who killed Brady, who fired the fatal shot or shots, and that, unless it was some kind of feint, appeared to be his defense. That could be a mistake. If Fountain argued in his closing argument that because no one saw who pulled the trigger, the verdict must be not guilty, Newcomb would respond that it did not matter, that if Bonney participated, he was just as guilty.

Maybe it didn't matter. The defense would get its chance sometime tomorrow. Bristol announced that court would reconvene at 8:30 A.M. Saturday, and Leonard bolted out the door. He'd have supper first, then visit Bonney.

The sheriff had moved Billie Wilson to the cell across the hall from the Kid. That made the Kid even happier, having a pal to talk to. They dragged their bunks to the iron-barred doors and ate the mush Sheriff Southwick called supper. Mostly, they just talked.

"Your trial seems to be going better than mine went, Billy," Wilson said softly.

"Oh, don't be glum. Breaking out of jail is about as easy as getting arrested. My bet is you won't be in the penitentiary five weeks, let alone five years."

Wilson shook his head. "Twenty years. That's what Bristol give me."

The Kid stopped chewing. "Twenty?" he said incredulously after swallowing. "For passing bogus money?" When Wilson nodded, the Kid slowly exhaled. "I knew that old man was hard, but . . ." He whistled, then smiled. "Don't fret, Billie. I'll tell you how you can get out of prison."

"My wrists ain't big like yours, Billy." Wilson set his bowl and cup on the floor.

"There's more ways to get free than slipping iron bracelets over your hands." He rattled his chains. "Besides, sometimes even I can't get free of irons, but it doesn't sour my mood. You'll get out of prison, will be staying in the best hotels, eating the best meals, all across the territory. Spending your shise notes, of course." With a wink, he stood, peered down the hall, and shouted: "Ain't that right, Bob? You know damn well I won't hang. And you know damn well Billie Wilson'll be free in less than two months."

Olinger shifted his shotgun and spit on the floor. "Maybe

you won't hang, Kid. Maybe I'll get the pleasure of sendin' you to hell."

While the Kid laughed, the door opened, and Sheriff Southwick walked to his cell. "Got a bunch of newspapermen who want to interview you, Kid. Want me to send 'em in?"

"Yeah. I'm in the mood for some jawing."

Southwick stepped back. "Maybe," he said, "you'll say something nice 'bout this jail. 'Bout me."

"Maybe," the Kid lied. He would never shovel praise on this piss pot.

The bells had started ringing at the Saint Albino Church as Ira Leonard stepped out of the Corn Exchange Hotel restaurant and into the street. He thought, if he could keep his meeting with Billy Bonney brief, he might make it over to the church for confession.

The Plaza was far from deserted. A redheaded urchin cried out the headlines—all condemning Billy Bonney—in the *Newman's Semi-Weekly* he was selling. Locals made their way to the church while cowboys and journalists filled the saloons. Leonard crossed the street, entered the unlocked courthouse door, and made his way to the sheriff's office. Southwick wasn't there. Instead, Bob Olinger looked up from the desk with a scowl.

"You're not guarding Billy?" Leonard said.

"Been spelled. Man's gotta eat."

Only Olinger was no longer eating, his plate covered by *Newman's Semi-Weekly* and a bottle of mescal. He held a pocketknife in one hand, carving up dimes, which took a sharp knife and a strong, determined hand. Leonard watched with curiosity as Olinger returned to his task, cutting the coins and dropping the bits into an opened shotgun shell. He had heard of people using rock salt instead of pellets, and, during the War, many Johnny Rebs had filled their scatterguns, even cannon, with anything they could find. But dimes?

Olinger looked up with a grin. "My bank," he said. "Someday the Kid's gonna be makin' a withdrawal." He folded the knife and leaned back. "What can I do for you, counselor?"

"I'd like to see Bonney."

The deputy's head shook. "No visitors for the Kid. Sheriff's orders."

"But I'm—" He had to stop himself. Bonney was no longer his client. Suspicion suddenly clouded his face. "Sheriff's orders?" he asked. "Or the Santa Fe Ring's?"

"I ain't never heard of no Ring, counselor. The Kid's been too busy. Been hounded too much. No visitors, exceptin' his lawyers, which don't include you no more. You can file your complaint with Sheriff Southwick in the morn, but it won't do you no good." He tapped his badge. "I'm a deputy U.S. marshal. I gots authority."

"And I know the U.S. marshal for this territory."

"Send him a wire. Time you get an answer, the trial'll be over."

The door to the jail swung open, and a half-dozen newspaper reporters meandered out, escorted by a deputy Leonard didn't recognize. The journalists, busy talking and lighting cigars, walked outside, heading for, Leonard guessed, the nearest beer mill. The deputy asked Olinger in a nasal voice if he had finished his supper.

Olinger picked up his shotgun and the dime-filled shell. "Yeah, Homer, you can eat. I'll watch the Kid. Got somethin' to show him anyway." He grinned at Leonard. "Anything else, counselor?"

Leonard nodded toward the retreating newspapermen. "No visitors, eh?"

Olinger's laughter grew louder as he walked toward the cells without replying.

Chapter 24

"Everything is quiet here now, like the calm before a storm which is certainly brewing. We are prepared for it, and will meet it firmly."

—Robert Widenmann to J. P. Tunstall

April 9, 1881
La Mesilla, New Mexico Territory

William Rynerson made it a point to get to the courthouse early Saturday morning. After sitting down on the front bench, he stretched out his long legs, crossing them at the ankles, and waited for Simon Newcomb to arrive. The district attorney came in five minutes later, his facial muscles tightening when he spotted his mentor.

Newcomb set his alligator satchel on the prosecution table, swallowed, and walked toward Rynerson. He looked like a man desperately in need of a full case of Hostetter's Celebrated Stomach Bitters.

"I'm sorry about Ealy," Newcomb said timidly. "I didn't think he'd have the sheepskins to prove he was a graduate of—"

"That's something an amateur would try when he's losing the case, Simon," Rynerson said, bringing in his legs and straightening his posture. "Ealy said he helped with *embalming*. Listen to your witness. You should know better. And you're not losing this case. Your prosecution was strong, is still strong, despite botching your examination yesterday."

Newcomb hung his head without responding.

"You have any more witnesses?"

"No, sir. I'll rest."

"Then crush Fountain and Bonney. Their defense appears to be aimed at the fact no one can say whether Bonney killed Brady. If that's the case, the Kid is practically hanged already. Concentrate on motive, Simon, and forget about the Ealy testimony."

Newcomb looked up. "It would be nice," he said, "if the Kid would testify."

"It would be nice," Rynerson countered, "if Garrett had killed the son of a bitch at Stinking Springs." He stood up, gripped Newcomb's shoulder, and smiled. "I'll see what else I can do about Bonney. I've left Leonard foundering and will speak with Bail again, but don't expect any help. This is your case to win, Simon. Or lose."

He headed outside, nodding a *good morning* at Ira Leonard as the attorney found a seat on the first row behind the defense table. Leonard was persistent. Rynerson had always thought that about him, but so was William Rynerson. He found the bailiff in the sheriff's office and suggested that he reserve the first row for witnesses and the next three rows for members of the press.

"Politely escort anyone who does not have those qualifications from those seats," he said, and headed to his room at the Texas Pacific Hotel, unable to conceal his amusement. He wished he could be at the courthouse to see the look on Leonard's face when the bailiff asked him to find another seat, one farther from the Kid.

As soon as the prosecution rested its case, Albert Fountain stood to face Judge Bristol. "Your Honor," he said, "the defense moves for a directed verdict of acquittal. The prosecution has not met its burden. It has not shown that the defendant shot and killed Sheriff Brady. Its witnesses are biased against Mr. Bonney, and no one has testified that they saw the defendant even fire his weapon at the deceased."

Ira Leonard's head bobbed slightly in approval. He would have made the same motion, but he wasn't surprised when Bristol rejected the argument. In fact, if Leonard had been on the bench, he also would have denied the defense motion. He sat on the back row, after being asked to move by the bailiff, between a blanket-wearing Indian and a cigar-chewing merchant with bad teeth and worse breath.

The courtroom wasn't as crowded as it had been previously, perhaps because it was a Saturday, and Leonard could have sat closer but decided the back row would met his needs. He'd be among the first to leave when Bristol called a recess. Maybe he could get in to see Bonney if Bob Olinger was not a guard. If not, he might slip a note through the Kid's barred window . . . if Rynerson hadn't had Bonney moved to another cell.

John Bail rose to make the defense's opening statement, but Leonard didn't listen. Opening statements didn't mean much; closings were what mattered, oftentimes more important than testimony—despite what a judge might decree. Besides, his mind was preoccupied by the sight of Susan McSween being escorted by a deputy sheriff to the front of the courtroom. She sat beside Robert Widenmann and the other witnesses for the defense.

Why would she be called to testify? And what is Dr. Ealy's wife doing sitting on the other side of Widenmann?

Mary Ealy was a petite woman, shy, plain-looking, with a brilliant alto voice. Now she looked tired, almost worn out. The Kid leaned forward, his eyes smiling at her, as she was sworn in, and John Bail began the questioning. While Fountain had handled the cross-examination of the territory's witnesses, Bail had asked to lead the defense's direct examinations, and Fountain had agreed. So had the Kid. He liked the idea of having two lawyers for free. It was like having an extra gun.

"Ma'am," Bail said, "yesterday we heard your husband testify as to the events of the first of April, three years ago, when Sheriff Brady met his death on the streets of Lincoln. I wonder if you could relate to the court your remembrances of that day."

Bail sat down during the translation and began picking at his thumbnail. On the other side of him, Fountain thumbed through his tablet, making notes with his pencil as Mary talked.

She had been busy baking a Sally Lunn bread in the kitchen when she heard the shots. Immediately, she gathered her daughters, three-year-old Anna and infant Ruth, and took shelter away from the windows.

"Where was your husband at this time?" Bail asked.

"In the Tunstall store, reading his Bible." She sighed, found a handkerchief, and dabbed her eyes. "He was in the store, while we—my daughters and myself—were in the living quarters, in the winter kitchen."

"Did you see anything?"

"No, sir. I stayed huddled with my girls till the doctor came in. He told me what had happened, told me that Sheriff Brady and Deputy Hindman were dead, and suggested that I take the girls to see Mrs. Shields over at the McSweens' house. I did." After another dab, she sniffed and apologized. "I am not as strong as the doctor, sir. I'm afraid that is why we left for Zuni Pueblo, to preach the word, two years ago. The doctor thought it would be less stressful than Lincoln. Only . . . we lost a son there. Oh, how I wish to return to Pennsylvania! This frontier is too barbaric."

The Kid's happiness had faded. He wondered what Mary Ealy was doing on the stand. He had not suggested to either Fountain or Bail that they call her.

"Do you know the defendant?" Bail asked.

"Yes. He's William Bonney. He sang often at Sunday School, or whenever the doctor could manage to hold services while we were in Lincoln. He's a sweet lad. He has such a pretty voice and isn't shy about singing." She put her handkerchief away and offered the Kid a smile, which he tried to return.

"Did you see him on the day Sheriff Brady died?"

"No, sir."

"Have you seen him since that day?"

"Oh, yes, sir. At our services, at the McSween home, several times in Lincoln. I used to play the piano or organ for him and the Regulators, though I certainly missed a few notes. All those guns made me quite nervous."

"Did your husband mention anything about that day? After you returned home?"

Albert Fountain stopped his doodling and looked at his fellow counselor, his face a mask of puzzlement.

"He . . ." Mary Ealy searched the room for her husband but couldn't find him. Bristol mildly asked her to answer the question, and she found her handkerchief again, squeezing it with frail hands. "He . . . the doctor said he had treated a man with a serious injury. He drew a silk handkerchief through a bullet hole in the man's thigh."

Fountain leaned closer and whispered: "What are you doing, John?"

"Trust me." Bail stood, rounded the table, and walked to the witness chair. "Did he say who he had treated?"

She shook her head. "No, sir."

"Are you sure?"

"Yes."

"Did you ever hear the defendant threaten the sheriff?"

"No, sir."

"Did you ever hear Alexander McSween threaten the sheriff?"

"Yes, sir. Well, it wasn't really a threat. Mr. McSween did not care for all of the suffering he had been forced to endure."

"And did you see Alexander McSween on the day of Sheriff Brady's murder?"

"Yes, sir. I did. Later that evening, the doctor and I again visited his house." She smiled politely at Susan McSween. "The McSweens were most gracious friends during our stay in Lincoln."

"Is it true, ma'am, that one of the deputies tried to arrest Mr. McSween, but he refused to recognize the man's authority?"

"That is what I was told."

"Couldn't it be, ma'am, that Alexander McSween ambushed the sheriff, then rode away and came back to town to give himself an alibi?" Newcomb started to object, then shrugged and sank back in his chair. "Isn't it true, ma'am, that the defendant could have been a hundred miles from Lincoln on that day?"

"I . . . I . . . suppose . . . maybe. But I don't think Mr. Mc-Sween would have shot anyone, especially from ambush. He was not that kind of man. He was a devout Presbyterian. He was just tired . . . as am I."

As he returned to his chair, Bail said, "Tired men often do things out of character. No more questions."

He sat down with a grin, but Albert Fountain didn't appear happy. Newcomb said he had no questions for the witness, and Mrs. Ealy quickly exited the courthouse. "You were supposed to ask her about Billy's character, John," Fountain said in a sharp whisper. "You managed to get it into the record that her husband treated one of the wounded men. You gave credence to the testimony that two men rushed Brady's body, and one of those was him." He nodded at the Kid.

Bristol cleared his throat. "Do you have more witnesses, gentlemen?" he asked.

"One moment, Your Honor," said Fountain, his eyes burning. "I—"

The Kid shot out of his chair, his chains rattling. "Y'all think it was me?" he shouted. "Hell, I'll drop my pants. See if there's a bullet scar!" He quickly switched to Spanish and repeated his statement for the jury, raising his voice to make sure they heard over Bristol's pounding gavel and shouts.

Fountain pulled the Kid, who was fumbling with the buttons on his trousers, to the chair, almost toppling the two of them over, while Bail began apologizing to the court. "That was stupid, Billy," Fountain said. "The previous testimony said you weren't the one shot in the thigh. Now sit down and stay quiet." The Kid smiled again, staring at the Mexican jury, reading their faces.

"One more outburst," Bristol said through a tight jaw, "and the defendant will find himself held in contempt of court."

"Yes, Your Honor," Bail said. "It will not happen again. May it please the court, the defense now calls Robert Widenmann."

Bail kept his examination of nervous, lazy Robert Widenmann brief. The Kid didn't grin at him. Oh, he liked Widenmann well enough, most of the time, but the big German had
always been looking after himself, begging Tunstall's pa
over in England for money. He had never been a pal and
hadn't been much of a Regulator, backing down to Jessie
Evans, hiding out after the Brady deal. Widenmann testified
he had been in Lincoln on the day of the shooting but had
not seen anything, too busy feeding Tunstall's bulldog. He
knew the defendant well, liked him for the most part, although he had not seen him much over the past three years.

"You served as a deputy United States marshal during the
Lincoln County War, did you not?" Bail asked.

"I did. The Ring got my appointment reversed, though."
Newcomb objected. Bristol sustained. Bail went on.

"You also served as a Regulator, duly appointed by Justice Green Wilson to uphold the law after the murder of John
Henry Tunstall?"

"I did."

"Did the defendant serve with you?"

"Yes, sir."

"So he was a peace officer?"

"We all were."

"No further questions."

Simon Newcomb leaped to his feet before Bail sat down,
making a beeline for the squirming witness, firing out his
first question: "Before you became this self-proclaimed
peace officer, did you ride with John Tunstall?"

"I did."

"You were one of his escorts on the day he was killed,
isn't that the truth?"

"I was with him, if that's what you mean. But I didn't see
him get killed."

Newcomb laughed. "Like you didn't see Brady and Hindman riddled with bullets—when you admit you were at the
Tunstall corral."

Widenmann sat upright. "I said I'd been at the corral earlier. I said I fed his bulldog. He'd left him with the Mc-
Sweens a while back, and—"

"Dog indeed!"

Fountain objected, and Bristol sustained.

"Was the defendant with you on the day Tunstall died?"

Fountain objected again, but Newcomb argued: "It goes to motive, Your Honor."

"I'll allow it," the judge said. "The witness will answer the question."

"He rode with us."

"I see. And it was after John Tunstall's death that you all became Regulators?"

"Yes."

"To apprehend the murderers of John Tunstall?"

"Yes."

"Did you have arrest warrants for Bill Morton and Frank Baker, two members of the posse that killed Tunstall?"

"Yes."

"Did you apprehend them?"

"We did."

"By we, does that mean the defendant was with you?"

"He was there."

"What happened to Morton and Baker?"

"They were shot trying to escape."

Newcomb laughed without humor and returned to his chair. "Yes, each man was shot nine times." He shook his head. "William McCloskey was also a Regulator, wasn't he?"

"Yes."

"He was killed, too. What was he trying to do . . . escape?"

"McCloskey was killed by Morton. He snatched McCloskey's gun."

"Come now, don't play this jury for a bunch of fools. Isn't it true, sir, that Morton and Baker were murdered, and McCloskey died trying to protect them?" Fountain fired another objection, but Newcomb continued his assault: "I submit to you that McCloskey was the only Regulator interested in justice. He paid for his beliefs with his life."

Said Fountain: "There is an objection, Your Honor."

Bristol tapped his gavel. "Ask a question, Mr. Newcomb,

or sit down. The jury will disregard the prosecutor's poetic argument until he can repeat it, without objection, in his closing summation."

Newcomb smiled. "I have nothing else for this witness."

The last time Susan McSween had sat in this courtroom, she had listened to scoundrels such as that impertinent Nathan Dudley slander her good name. Now she swore to tell the truth in hopes that it might get Billy Bonney off the gallows, although the judge staring at her was the same lout who had guffawed when Dudley testified that she was a woman without virtue. She kept her testimony short, remembering what Ira Leonard had told her before her trial against Dudley: *Answer only what you are asked.*

Billy Bonney was a fine man, she said, although Dick Brewer would likely have remained the leader had he had not been killed by that Roberts rowdy shortly after Brady's death. Bonney had served as a Regulator, and contrary to what Mr. Newcomb or James Dolan would have you believe, the Regulators were the only real law in Lincoln County.

"Did your late husband ever mention the attack on Sheriff Brady?" John Bail asked.

"Not often," she said.

"Did he ever say who had killed the sheriff and deputy?"

"No."

"Was he with you on that day?"

"Not that morning. He arrived that afternoon, after Brady was dead. I saw him that evening at our home."

"So he could have killed the sheriff, for all you know?"

She couldn't hold her laughter, and shook her head. "Alex?" she said incredulously.

"*For all you know,* Mrs. McSween?"

She rolled her eyes. "I suppose," she said in a bored voice, and Bail thanked her for her testimony.

Simon Newcomb leaned back in his chair, playing with a pencil. "You did not witness Sheriff Brady's murder, but you were in town when your husband perished. Isn't that so?"

She stiffened and dismissed Leonard's rule of testimony. "I was at my home when those blackhearts burned it down, murdered my husband and other good men. I was there, and the memory is chiseled in my mind." She pressed her temples with her fingers, feeling a headache fast approaching.

"Tell us about that day, ma'am."

Fountain shouted an objection.

"It goes to motive," Newcomb said.

"Motive?" Fountain stood. "How can it be used to show motive, when her husband died in July? My client is on trial for an alleged murder committed in April."

"We ask the court's latitude, Your Honor," Newcomb said.

"I'll hear you out, Mr. Newcomb, and make my ruling after her testimony."

Fountain shook his head. "Exception," he said.

"Noted. Go on, Mr. Newcomb."

The prosecutor smiled. "Please, Mrs. McSween. I know it will bring back horrible memories. I know it will be difficult for you, but tell the court what happened in July a few months after Sheriff Brady was killed."

Chapter 25

*"I am tired of being a refugee. I want to die in my
own home."*

—Alexander McSween

July 19, 1878
Lincoln, New Mexico Territory

We had been barricaded in our own home since that Monday,
the fifteenth. My dear Alex, I fear, was resigned to his fate,
and that is why he rode into Lincoln with Billy and the other
Regulators. Those dear men—boys, really—would have
given their lives for Alex and myself.

So many of them did.

As I recall, Billy was there, at our home, along with Tom
O'Folliard and young Yginio Salazar. José Chávez y
Chávez . . . Francisco Zamora . . . Ignacio Gonzales . . . Vicente Romero. Who else? Jim French. Oh, how could I forget Jim French? Tom Cullins, whom I did not know very
well, and a gentleman named Smith whose Christian name I
disremember. Harvey Morris, of course; he was in our house,
too, but he was not a Regulator. No, I dare say Harvey never
even held a gun in his hand. He was simply a clerk in my late
husband's firm. A lunger, he came west for his health, and
Alex, always generous, gave him a position.

Our house had two wings, as you may or may not remember, and we lived in the west wing. The Shieldses, my
sweet sister Elizabeth and her family, were living in the east
wing.

There were other Regulators in town. If memory serves, Henry Brown, a dear, sweet boy, took his position with a few other men in John's store. And Charlie Bowdre and a bunch of others stayed at Isaac Ellis's place on the far end of town.

Anyway, since my husband returned home, we had been shot at. That cowardly sheriff, George Peppin, sent one of his man-killers to our house to arrest my husband, as well as Billy, so the Regulators were forced to fire at him, and he ran back to that low-down sheriff hiding at the Wortley Hotel. They all were hiding—till that Dudley—oh, forgive me. I will get to that point in a short while.

Other assassins climbed to the top of the Torreón where they fired at us. Thankfully, Billy, as soon as he arrived, had made the boys pile sacks, barrels, even move furniture in front of the windows. We thought we could stay there for months. We thought that maybe the army would come to our rescue, but . . .

Anyway, that's how things had gone for the first few days. And then that despicable *Señor* Baca, he brought Colonel Dudley and his troops into town. They brought a cannon with them, aimed it at my house! How I fumed! That Dudley, he will tell you the cannon was not aimed at my house, but I say it was. I know it was. Plus, whenever Peppin, Dolan, or those monsters walked or rode past our house, they did so under the escort of soldiers of the United States. Once, someone—I believe it was Jessie Evans—fired: The shot went through a windowpane and struck my piano, which let out a mournful dirge. They could shoot at us, yet we could not fire back without endangering the lives of those soldiers—thanks to Colonel Dudley. One trooper, I hear, was wounded, and they said we shot him, but we did not. They blamed us—blamed my husband, that is, blamed him and Billy—for all sorts of crimes.

You can imagine how fraught we were when Billy saw that cannon. For four days, we had suffered because of the mercenary designs of James Dolan and, now, Colonel Nathan Dudley. A short while later, those fiends tried to set fire to our house. They lacked the courage to send their own arsonists. No, those treacherous devils made our servants do the bloody deed. Alex had sent Sebrian, Joe, and George away after arriving Monday, for he did not want them in harm's way. That was his nature, but Sheriff Peppin would not allow them to leave town. Then he made them try to burn us out. But by God's grace, we had a strong home, secure, mostly adobe and hard to burn, and Sebrian and Joe—God bless their souls—did a poor job. Peppin and Dolan tried to make George go with them, too, but he refused, said that would break his parole, and Peppin conceded. Anyway, the fire did not catch. Yet our nerves were raw, so I decided I must take matters into my own hands. Billy opened the back door for me, and I crawled out, slithered like some snake for a hundred yards until I felt safe. Then I went down the arroyo and climbed out near the Wortley. The first man I saw was George Peppin.

"Why are you trying to burn down my house?" I screamed at him.

"If you don't want your house burned down," he said with a horse-laugh, "make the men in there get out of it. I am bound to have the men inside there today—dead or alive."

To argue with him was pointless, so I walked right down the street, kept my head high, walked past my home, John's store. I heard some of Dolan's men laughing at me, making vile, crude jokes, but I ignored them. The army had set up camp near Isaac Ellis's store, and a decent man, a young, sandy-haired lieutenant, escorted me to Dudley's tent. I tried to be civil with him, told him that Alex and I held him in high respect. Yet when I asked him why he was here, he became indignant.

"I don't have to report my movements to you," he said. "However, people have been begging for protection for the past month, so I am here today to help women and children, anyone who requests protection."

Therefore, I asked for protection for my sister Elizabeth and for poor Mary Ealy, who had suffered so much at John's store during the past four days. She had two little girls, and had witnessed such unholy acts since her arrival in February. Elizabeth had children, too. My dear niece Minnie, only ten

years old, had been crying for the past four days. I begged
Colonel Dudley to protect them.

He scoffed. "Your sister has no business there," he told
me. "I will not, indeed cannot, give you protection while you
allow such men as the Kid, French, and others of bad character to be in your house."

How I wanted to slap him. I demanded to know why his
men rode as escorts for Dolan's men and Peppin's so-called
deputies.

"It's none of your damned business," he shot back at me.
"I will send my soldiers where I damn well please." He even
ordered one of his soldiers to shoot me if I struck at him, and
I was tempted, even with the threat of death hanging over
me.

I begged him once again to protect us, but he shook his
head and had one of his troopers escort me from his camp-
ground. He did say that if Alex surrendered to him, he would
protect him, but that promise was false. James Dolan would
have had Alex killed before he ever reached Fort Stanton—
most likely with Colonel Dudley's blessing.

So I went home. Walked through the front door. No one
tried to stop me. No one dared. Alex rushed to me, and I collapsed in his arms. I told him what Colonel Dudley had told
me, and he sank to the floor, shaking his head.

"Then we are doomed," he said softly.

Billy spoke up then. "Doomed? We're not dead yet, Mr.
McSween."

I think Billy became a man that day.

Before, you see, he had been the carefree wanderer, more
interested in singing or dancing, perhaps gambling, spending
his money on those dreadful romances or candy. Since poor
Dick Brewer had been called to Glory in April, though, Billy
had been forced to grow up, to lead the Regulators.

That afternoon, Peppin's men tried to start another fire, in
the northwest corner of our house. Alas, this one caught and
began to burn, slowly at first. Then it began leaping from
room to room, spreading like a grass fire in Kansas. The heat
became unbearable, the smoke blackened our faces, singed
our lungs. Yet Billy remained brave.

"We can stick this out," he said, though his eyes welled with tears from the foul smoke. "For a while, till it's dark. We'll run. Make for the river. It's only a couple hundred yards. Some of us'll get hit, but most of us'll make it. We can run fast. Shoot fast."

Ignacio Gonzales—he had been wounded in the arm during one of those barbaric attacks on our home—started crying. He begged, in Spanish, that we surrender. Billy slapped him.

"Brace up!" he shouted. "Be a man!"

A moment later, Billy crawled toward me, smiling again. "I expect, ma'am," he said pleasantly, then coughed from the smoke. "I expect you had better leave now. A dress isn't good to run in."

I told him no, that I would run in my unmentionables but would not desert my husband, would not abandon his true friends. But Alex took my hand. "Please," he said. "Remember me. Remember us. Remember better times."

I kissed him. I bit my lower lip to keep from trembling, and Billy helped me to my feet, escorted me to the front door, cracked it open, and yelled: "Peppin! You hear me?"

"I hear you, Kid."

"Mrs. McSween's coming out! You boys harm her, and I'll track down every mother's son of you, and you know I'll do it, too."

The sheriff chuckled. "How you gonna do that, Kid? You'll be burnt as bacon in an hour."

"She's coming out, Peppin! No tricks."

After another chortle, the sheriff relented. "Send her out, Kid. We'll be gentle with the *lady*!"

I put my hand on Billy's blackened cheek. "God bless you," I said.

"I'll be seeing you, ma'am," he said softly. "So will Mr. McSween."

That was the last I ever saw my dear husband alive.

Billy later told me what happened. And young Salazar. And Jim French. At nine o'clock, they had no choice but to run for the Río Bonito or die a horrible death in flames. Poor Alex was uncertain, but Billy told him they would make it.

Two groups would try first, and Billy promised to draw Peppin's fire. "When they start firing at us, run for the river," Billy told Alex. "Run like you've never run before. We'll meet back at Mr. Chisum's."

Ignacio, Cullins, and Smith were the first to leave. They took off their boots and sandals and crept through a window, made their way for the gate to the north. They didn't run. I don't know why, don't know how, but they made it. Billy never heard any shooting. That surprised all of them inside.

"Maybe they're asleep," Tom O'Folliard said hopefully.

"Or drunk at Ike's saloon," added José.

"I doubt that," Billy said and stood. "Remember what I said, Mr. McSween. Run. Tom, you want to stay, lead Mr. McSween to the Chisum ranch?"

O'Folliard shook his head. "I'm stickin' with you, pal. If you get killed, we'll get killed together."

With a smile, Billy cracked open the door, and they ran, O'Folliard right behind him, then Harvey Morris, Jim French, and José. They were not as lucky, for the murderers surrounding our house saw them—I guess from the flames consuming our beautiful home—and the enfilade began. Poor Harvey fell dead. He wasn't even armed. The rest of those gallant Regulators emptied their guns as they ran. The first three men who had left also fired, from the river, to cover their retreat, as I believe did Henry Brown and those men who now fled the granary at John's store.

They did this mainly to allow Alex and the others to make their escape, but my husband waited too long. Finally, he ran outside with the remaining men: Francisco, Vicente, and young Salazar, maybe fifteen years old that horrible night.

Only, Peppin's scoundrels were waiting for them. Gunfire forced them to take shelter behind our chicken coop—our good layers and rooster already dead from fright or bullets. Ten minutes later, Robert Beckwith, a no-account gunman, asked Alex to surrender, and my husband reluctantly agreed. They promised to treat Alex and the others fairly, and I believe Alex would never have surrendered if not for those dear boys with him. Beckwith walked toward the coop, and Alex handed him his revolver. That's when Jessie Evans and others opened fire. Alex was killed. So were Beckwith, Francisco, and Vicente. Those demons sacrificed their own, Beckwith, to kill my poor husband. But that was not all. They lacked the human decency to leave, to let the good people of Lincoln care for the dead. No, they performed unspeakable vile acts on Alex's lifeless body as fire consumed our home. They made my servant Sebrian bring his fiddle to the carnage and play while Dolan, Peppin, Evans, and those other cowards drank whiskey and danced.

One of them started to put a bullet in young Salazar's head, but a drunken lout told him not to waste lead on "a dead greaser." That was the one miracle of the night, for young Salazar was still alive, and after those murderers had left my home in ashes, finally departed to continue their celebration at Dolan's store, he managed to drag his bloody body to the Oteroses' place—a half-mile from my home.

Young Salazar lived, but my husband . . .

We buried him next to his dear friend, John Tunstall, the following day.

Chapter 26

*"Chisum got me into all this trouble and then
wouldn't help me out."*

—Billy the Kid

April 9, 1881
La Mesilla, New Mexico Territory

A heavy silence fell over the courtroom after Susan Mc-
Sween left. Ira Leonard scratched his head, Judge Bristol
blinked rapidly, and Simon Newcomb licked his lips, while
John Bail and Albert Fountain stared at each other. As an attorney, Leonard understood everyone's dilemma. Sue's testimony had not amounted to much for either side: pointless to
the case at hand and inadmissible as such. Yet she had managed to paint William Bonney as a leader of men. That could
be used for his character. On the other hand, he had been
shooting at peace officers, and that could be argued for the
prosecution.

The correct move, if Leonard had been presiding judge,
would have been to disallow her testimony, but that, too, was
pointless. The jury had already heard what she had to say,
and no matter how strongly a judge instructed any twelve
men to disregard what had been said under oath, it often
proved impossible. Bristol should have removed the jury
first, listened to her testimony, then made his ruling.

Now neither side appeared willing to make any motion,
and perhaps, Leonard decided, that was the smart play. Just

ride on, call another witness, and the jury would likely forget
what Sue had said by the time they retired to deliberate.

In the end, that's what happened.

Bristol cleared his throat, began carving his plug of tobacco with a pocketknife, and asked the defense to call its
next witness.

"The defense," John Bail said, "calls Miss Sallie
Chisum."

Uncle John had wondered why she wanted to stay in Old
Mesilla after he had finished his testimony. He was in a
hurry to get back to the ranch, only he had never mastered
telling his niece no. "I would like to do some shopping," she
had told him as they dined at the Mesilla Hotel last night.
"Neither your ranch store, nor the mercantiles in Lincoln or
Fort Sumner, are appropriate for a soon-to-be-married girl to
buy good hats, pretty dresses, and other items."

He had laughed while biting the end off his after-supper
cigar. "A horse with good bottom and one of Pitzer's old
slouch hats once filled those bills," he had said, "but I guess
we can wait another day." He knew, of course, that she really
wanted to stay until the jury reached its verdict. Truthfully, so
did he. He didn't know—at least, she didn't think he knew—
that she planned to testify on Bonney's behalf, had planned
to do so since Ira Leonard had asked her to serve as a character witness back in March.

That morning over breakfast, she told him she was going
shopping and would meet him for dinner at the hotel. He had
nodded, said he was feeling poorly and would likely take a
siesta.

Now she took a deep breath after being sworn in, and the
bailiff pulled out the chair for her as she sat down. *Such gentlemen*; but she was used to that. Since her thirteenth birth-
day, men had been wooing her, commenting on her beauty,
her riding skills, asking her, sometimes begging her, for a
dance. Now that she was twenty-three, she had perfected the
method of turning away those advances, unless they were not
unwanted. She stared at Billy Bonney as John Bail walked
toward her.

"First, Miss Chisum," he said with a smile, "allow me to speak on behalf of the entire court in offering our congratulations on your upcoming nuptials. William Robert is a fine man, a good cattleman. We wish you much happiness."

She quickly looked away from Billy, whose cheerful face had fallen melancholy. "Thank you," she said. She hadn't told Billy about her engagement, hadn't spoken or written to him since seeing him at the *baile* in Fort Sumner back in '79 when he had threatened Uncle John. She had always been fond of Billy, yet she knew she could never marry him, no matter how well he danced, no matter how well he kissed. Besides, she never thought he really loved her—until she saw the hurt on his face. Now she feared she had made a mistake coming here.

"Do you know the defendant?" Bail asked.

"I do. He's Billy Bonney. He used to work for Mr. Tunstall and would often stop by the ranch."

"A ranch owned by your uncle, John Chisum?"

"Yes, sir. And my father, and his other brother, Pitzer."

"What kind of character would you say Mr. Bonney possesses?"

"He is of great character." She looked at the jury as she spoke, the interpreter's translations sounding like an echo whenever she paused. "You should have seen him with the children in Lincoln or Fort Sumner. He would buy them toys." She laughed. "I remember once, in Lincoln, I saw him sitting on the banks of the Río Bonito with maybe a dozen little girls and boys, all of them Mexican, reading them some penny dreadful while eating a peach. He would read in English, then Spanish. It warmed my heart." She made himself look at him. "He always warmed my heart."

He smiled again, his eyes again boyish and alive.

"How was he with men?"

"I think most men, my father and uncles included, did not think much of him until after Mr. Tunstall was murdered. By that, I mean they thought of him only as a cowboy, a drifter. But when he became a Regulator, he grew up. Men followed him. Mr. McSween once told me he knew in his heart that Billy would give his life for him, and I am certain that many

Regulators, especially the Mexicans, would have given their lives for Billy. He always considered the Mexicans first. They called him *El Chivato*. It means he-goat, a kid, just a friendly nickname. They admired him, worshiped him."

Especially the ladies, she thought, feeling jealousy's bite when the image of Paulita Maxwell flashed through her mind.

"It has been suggested, ma'am, that after the deaths of Tunstall and McSween, the defendant turned to rustling. He stole cattle belonging to your father and uncles, sold them in Texas and Colorado."

"I never believed those stories," she said. "Billy was a friend to us. He would not steal from us."

"He faces an indictment for rustling in San Miguel County."

"He is on trial here for murder, and I do not believe him guilty of either. Not the Billy I know."

"How do you explain the indictments?"

"A man is innocent until proved guilty, even in a lawless place such as New Mexico Territory, Mr. Bail." She jutted her chin toward Simon Newcomb. "Ask him." Next she easily found William Rynerson in the back of the room, towering over the Mexicans sitting around him, and pointed at him. "Or him."

Newcomb coughed and objected, and Judge Bristol spit out tobacco juice and said softly, "Please, Miss Chisum."

"He has been accused of other murders," John Bail continued.

"Any man Billy killed was in self-defense or to protect his friends," she said. "I even once heard Uncle John tell him that the men Billy had killed 'needed killing.' That was in Fort Sumner, and there were other witnesses."

"Your word is good enough, Miss Chisum. Do you believe he murdered Sheriff Brady?"

"I do not," she said. And she didn't. *Murdered.* That was a strong word. He might have killed Brady and Hindman, but only to protect Mr. McSween. Bail thanked her and returned to his seat.

"But you weren't in Lincoln on April 1, 1878?" Simon Newcomb asked.

"No, sir. I was at the ranch."

"So you did not witness the murders?"

Stupid questions irked her. "Of course not."

"You liked the defendant very much. Isn't that true?"

"I have already testified so."

"He bought you presents, didn't he?"

She shook her head. "If you consider candy hearts and an old Indian pouch presents, yes."

"Was there reciprocation?"

"I bought him small things, those nickel and dime novels he loved, a turquoise crucifix, sweets. He had a sweet tooth. We were not engaged . . ." She regretted the choice immediately, but recovered. "I am not lying to protect him. Candy is not often used as a bribe, sir."

Newcomb had been sitting during this exchange, but now he pushed back his chair and stood. "Did you know Bill Morton and Frank Baker?" he asked.

Bail objected, but Newcomb argued that it showed motive and the defendant's reckless attitude toward violence and revenge. Bristol overruled and instructed Sallie to answer the question.

"I did not know them but in passing."

"When did you last see them . . . alive?"

"It was early March, 1878. I cannot recall the exact date without examining my diary."

"The two men had been arrested by the Regulators, who brought them to the Chisum ranch. They were prisoners. Isn't that a fact?"

"Yes, sir."

"And the defendant was one of those Regulators?"

"He was there. He wasn't the leader, though, not then. That would have been Richard Brewer."

"Where were the Regulators taking those two prisoners when they left the ranch?"

"To Lincoln."

"Were the prisoners securely bound?"

"Their hands were tied . . . in the front, so they could hold horn or reins. I cannot attest to how secure the ropes were."

"Did Frank Baker speak to you before they left for Lincoln?"

She tried not to sigh, but failed. "He did," she replied after a long pause.

"What did he say?"

"He gave me his watch and a letter to his sweetheart. He also had a horsehair bridle. He plaited the bridle himself. He asked me to send those items to his sweetheart at the address on the envelope."

"Thank you, Miss Chisum, but you did not answer my question. What did he say to you? Why did he give you his belongings?"

"He feared for his life."

"Come now, Miss Chisum, what did he say? His exact words! Do not make me subpoena you to bring your diary and read from it. I know you remember—" Fountain yelled his objection, and she looked at Judge Bristol for mercy but found none in the old man's face as Newcomb's assault continued. "Employees of your father and uncle also heard Mr. Baker's remarks. What did he say?"

The judge whispered, "Answer the question, ma'am."

She bit her lip, shot a fretful glance at Billy, and finally relented. "He said, 'I will never live to get to Lincoln.' "

"Thank you. And did he also say he had two friends in that posse?"

"He did."

"Whom did he name?"

"William McCloskey and John Middleton."

"What happened to deputies Morton and Baker after the Regulators led them away?"

"They were killed."

"Mr. McCloskey was also killed, wasn't he?"

"Yes."

"Thank you, Miss Chisum. No more questions."

She felt exhausted, wanted to run to her hotel room and cry, but Albert Fountain rose, asking in a polite voice, "Redirect, Your Honor?"

Bristol silently gave his consent.

"John Middleton was not killed, though, was he?" Fountain said. "Even though Frank Baker called him a friend?"

"He was not."

"You did not witness the deaths of Morton, Baker, and McCloskey?"

"No, sir."

"Did you ever learn why they were killed?"

"I was told they were shot trying to escape. One of them grabbed Mr. McCloskey's pistol, killed him, then the two fled. The Regulators fired at them, killing them both."

"Why did the Regulators arrest Morton and Baker?"

"They killed John Tunstall."

Newcomb objected, saying that no one knew who had killed Tunstall, but Fountain put the question another way. "Did they have warrants for those two men for Mr. Tunstall's murder?"

"Yes, issued by Justice Wilson in Lincoln."

Fountain returned to his chair. "Thank you," he said.

She rushed out of the courtroom, unable to stop a flood of tears, drew a handkerchief from her purse, and leaned against a wooden column in front of the building. She didn't know if she had helped Billy or doomed him to a hangman's noose. The church bells began to chime. It was already noon. She had to find a shop, buy a few things to fool Uncle John, only she did not feel like it.

A hand gripped her shoulder, startling her, and she whirled, dropping the handkerchief.

John Chisum smiled his sad smile and stooped to pick it up.

"Finish your shoppin'?" he asked when he straightened and returned the piece of cotton.

Sallie could only nod.

"Let's go home, Sallie," he said. She bit her lip. You couldn't fool a man like Uncle John. He had seen through her deception, probably even before they left the ranch. They didn't need to wait in Mesilla, and now she realized she didn't want to be in town to learn Billy Bonney's fate. That would make it more painful. They'd find out at the ranch soon enough. News like that did not need a telegraph wire to spread.

Added Uncle John: "Ain't nothin' for us here."

"You're my lawyers," said the Kid, wiping crumbs of stale bread off his fuzzy chin whiskers. "You tell me what to do."

Shaking his head, Albert Fountain began twisting one end of his mustache. He hadn't said much since Judge Bristol called a recess for dinner. John Bail had done most of the talking, repeating how things looked mighty glum, that they had no choice but to put the Kid on the witness stand.

"I can talk real fancy." The Kid took a sip of water. "Just tell me what I'm supposed to say, Albert."

Fountain released his mustache, his face even graver than before. "I will not suborn perjury, young man," he began, and the Kid laughed.

"You're too easy to rile, Albert. I know I can't fib. I swear to tell the whole truth and nothing but the truth, so help me God."

Fountain sighed. "We should have rested after Newcomb, not called any witnesses."

Bail continued his assault. "That would have done nothing for our case, either. I just don't think we've convinced the jurors. And, Albert, you know as well as I do that even though a jury cannot take into consideration that a defendant doesn't take the stand, you know they will consider it—especially a bunch of Mexicans."

Fountain's eyes blazed with anger as he turned suddenly at his colleague, and Bail muttered an apology. Fountain's wife was a Mexican.

"No one can say who fired the fatal bullets," Fountain began, looking at the Kid once more. "That has been our defense. Billy, I haven't asked you until now, but I must: Did you murder William Brady?"

He shook his head. His voice turned respectful. "And I'll say that under oath, sir."

"You'll be butchered by Newcomb," Fountain said.

He shrugged.

"I still would advise you not to testify," Fountain said, "despite Mr. Bail's arguments. If the jury brings in a guilty verdict, you will hang. Make no mistake about that. Judge Bristol is neither a lenient nor forgiving man."

His smile returned, his voice filled with humor. "Albert, I'll bet my bay horse that I won't hang. No matter what judge and jury say." He hooked his thumb toward Olinger. "Old Bob down yonder, he's bound and determined to fill my back with cut-up dimes on the trail to Lincoln."

The attorneys talked among each other before departing for their dinner, and the Kid picked up a piece of bread that had fallen on the floor and flicked it across the hall into Billie Wilson's cell. The counterfeiter, lying on his cot, lifted his hat.

"You hear all that?" the Kid asked.

"I'm not deaf," Wilson replied.

"Why haven't they hauled your fine self to Santa Fe?"

"I haven't asked and am in no hurry." He sat up and pulled the cot closer to the door. Grinning, Billy did the same. Wilson glanced down the hall at Olinger, then whispered. "What really happened at Lincoln that day, Billy?"

The Kid was glad someone had finally asked. Neither Albert Fountain nor John Bail had wanted to hear his story. Even Ira Leonard had not seemed interested in the Kid's version. Likely, they all figured him guilty. He wanted to talk, to tell someone, and Billie Wilson was a pal.

Chapter 27

"Billy's friendly smile always conquered us."

—George Coe

March 31-April 1, 1878
Lincoln, New Mexico Territory

It had been raining hard, and soaked to our skin we were when we rode up to Isaac Ellis's place late that afternoon. The first person I saw was my friend Will Ellis, only he didn't look particularly happy to see me, even less satisfied with the Regulators behind me: Frank MacNab, Jim French, Fred Waite, Rob Widenmann, John Middleton, and Henry Brown.

I swung down from my bay horse and offered my hand, which Will took hesitantly. "We're closing up," he said after a quick glance toward his pa's store.

"Used to be I could count on some hot food here, Will," I told him. "Used to be you'd let me dry my clothes before you run me off. Used to be . . ."

"Used to be a lot of things, Billy." Reluctantly, he let out a sigh. "Come on. I reckon Pa would like to see you, say hello."

Henry and I followed him inside while Jim French took care of the horses. The rest of the boys tried to find a spot to stay warm, except John Middleton, who walked back to the road to keep an eye on town.

Isaac Ellis gave us a much friendlier greeting. "Boys," he said, "you look like you're about to catch your death." He motioned us to the stove and told Will to fetch cornbread and coffee from the kitchen.

"There's others with 'em," Will said. "Outside."

"Well, feed them, too, son," he snapped, and Will left. As soon as the door shut, Ellis lost his smile.

"What happened to Morton and Baker, Billy?" he asked.

I shook my head sadly. "They killed McCloskey."

"George Coe says you told him you never meant to let them two get back to Lincoln alive."

"George Coe wasn't there."

"I know Alexander McSween would have no part of that, no part of murder—"

Henry stepped away from the stove. "We don't answer to McSween. We answer to John Tunstall, we answer *for* Mr. Tunstall. What them boys got, they deserved." He walked over to the wall and hefted a pickaxe. All the while, Isaac Ellis kept staring at me.

"And McCloskey?" he asked.

"William was riding alongside Morton, got careless. Morton reached over, yanked out his six-shooter, and shot William off his horse. Next thing I know, he and Baker were loping away. They fired once, and we shot back. I ain't crying over them cutthroats. Didn't think you would, either."

"But you scattered like quail. You should have brought in the bodies, told Sheriff Brady what happened. Green Wilson would have protected you."

"*Protect us?* You were at Mr. Tunstall's funeral, Mr. Ellis, while I was locked up in that damned pit." I had to stop, hold my temper. "Anyway, that's what happened. It's the honest truth."

Course, it wasn't. George Coe was right. There was no way I was going to let them two birds get back to Lincoln so they could escape from jail and light a shuck for Old Mexico, but we gave them a sporting chance. As soon as we reined up, Morton and Baker knew what was fixing to come. So did McCloskey. He whirled around and said, "You're not going to harm these men, Billy!" I was checking the loads in my Colt, didn't even look at him. Next he started pleading with Dick Brewer, but Brewer . . . he thought more of Mr.

Tunstall than I did. McCloskey found no help there, begged
Middleton to help, but John shook his head. So McCloskey
put his hand on the butt of his six-shooter.

Well, that was a damned fool thing to do, because Henry
lifted his shotgun and blew McCloskey out of the saddle.
That's when Morton and Baker spurred their horses. You
know what happened then, but that's not the story you
wanted to hear.

I don't know if Isaac Ellis believed me or not, but he
shrugged and made his way behind the counter, even offered
me a peppermint stick candy, which I accepted. I also bought
a Wide Awake Library romance.

"What brings you to town, Billy?" he asked. "It's not
safe."

"Mr. McSween's coming back," I told him. "We left him
at Chisum's ranch. I expect he won't get here till tomorrow,
what with all the rain we've had."

Henry tossed the pickaxe on the counter and asked for a
box of .44-40s.

"He knows Sheriff Brady has an alias warrant for him,
doesn't he?" Mr. Ellis asked.

I nodded. We all knew. That's why we were here.

"Where is Brady?" Brown asked.

That's when Isaac Ellis started suspicioning us. He pursed
his lips, found the box of shells for Brown's Winchester, and
finally answered that Brady was at his ranch. When I asked
for a box of shells, too, you could see the worry on his shoulders double in weight. So I grinned and told him not to brood
too much, that we would be riding out tonight. We paid our
bill, shook hands, and left. They were sitting on thorns—that
was plain as day—but I guess we could have spent the night
there. I didn't want them getting hurt, though, so we rode to
the river, waited till full dark, and eased our way to Mr. Tunstall's store.

Then we got some sleep.

We came to Lincoln to kill that son of a whore Brady.

The way Henry and I had it figured, if we got lucky, we
might send Billy Mathews, George Hindman, and Jimmy
Dolan to hell with Brady. Back at Chisum's ranch, Mr. Mc-

Sween had told Dick Brewer and me that he knew Brady would eventually try to arrest him, and he feared he would be murdered like Mr. Tunstall was. "You boys have to prevent that," he said.

That's what we were doing, at least to my way of thinking. Dick and I later got into a bit of a row over that, him saying that we had acted foolishly, had dug all of our graves.

Quién sabe?

We woke that morning wet and hungry. Henry poked a few holes in the adobe wall, and we just sat there, our backs to the wall, holding our rifles, wondering, knowing we were about to cross the Rubicon. That's Shakespeare, Billie.

Around that time, Yginio Salazar come running into the corral, and MacNab come this close to blowing that youngun's head off. Salazar's eyes were about to pop out of his head, and he threw up his hands, begged us not to kill him.

I got up, tossed my arm over his shoulder, and calmed him down. Reckon he didn't recognize any of us until he had stopped shaking. He stared at me and said, *"El Chivato . . . Billito?"*

"It's me," I reassured him and spoke to him in Spanish, asking him what brought him here so early in the morning. He said he came to feed Mr. Tunstall's dog, said he had been doing it since the poor man got murdered. *Zounds.* I guess we had all forgotten about Mr. Tunstall's bulldog, though I warrant the Reverend Ealy and his family had been looking after that cur.

Henry told me I ought to ask Yginio if he had seen Sheriff Brady, so I did. Yginio turned scared again. Can't rightly blame him. He was only fifteen years old. I gave his shoulder a good squeeze, told him everything was all right, that we were here only to protect Mr. McSween. Yginio pulled away from me and pointed down the street.

"He just rode in," he told us. "Eats breakfast at the hotel with his deputies." He said that in Spanish, and I translated for the boys.

"Ask him if Dolan's with them," Henry said again, and I did, though I didn't care much for Henry giving orders so suddenlike. We hadn't elected him captain.

Yginio said no, he had not seen Dolan lately, not since he broke his leg. That was news to us, so we made him explain what had happened. Dolan had been drunk—which didn't surprise us—and had jumped off his horse to start a fight with Harvey Morris. That was just like Jimmy Dolan. Harvey Morris had bad lungs, was about as strong as dead cholla, and never carried a gun, not even a pocketknife. But Harv worked for Mr. McSween, and since he wasn't handy, Dolan must have figured to settle his score by killing or beating up poor Harv. But it didn't happen, because the drunken oaf broke his leg. That got us all to giggling. We sure wished we could have seen that.

I told Yginio to run back home, that we would feed Mr. Tunstall's dog today.

"We ought to keep him here," Henry suggested, only he really wasn't suggesting a thing. "He can pull a trigger same as us."

Well, I had had enough of that. I sent Yginio along his way and turned to Henry. "I told you we're not involving any Mexicans in this affair."

"Why?" John Middleton asked.

"Because Brady's married to one. Mexicans are sentimental. Things might turn on us, turn on them. I won't be part of that. They're good people. It's policy. That's all."

Henry shrugged, and that was it, although once he knelt beside me, he whispered, "Sooner or later, this whole thing's gonna boil over, *El Chivato,* and everybody's gonna have to pick a side, including the Mexicans. Likely today. You know that."

Maybe so, but I didn't want Yginio having to make that choice on that day, though he joined us a month or so later, then almost got killed in July, and then got a yellow streak up his back. Haven't had much use for him since. I don't know, maybe we should have made him shoot Brady.

Well, we waited again. Seemed like hours, and by now I knew some of the boys were just about shaking. We had sent Middleton again to watch the street, told him to be careful so that the Ealys didn't see him. Henry had wanted Widenmann for that chore, but I didn't trust that German one whit—still don't, even though he was a witness for me. I wanted him where I could see him. He wasn't no traitor, nothing like that. I mean, he wouldn't run warn Sheriff Brady, but he might fall asleep, might let all of us get captured and killed. Or he might just sneak off and hide. He didn't have the sand for what we were doing. I don't even know why he rode into Lincoln with us, except maybe he wanted to prove himself.

He proved himself, all right. Proved himself to be the biggest coward that ever rode with us Regulators. Should have stayed clerking stores.

A few minutes later, Middleton come back, almost out of breath. "They're coming," he says, "down the street. Got more hardware than inside Mr. Tunstall's store."

We got up, checking our rifles and revolvers, moving to the gun holes Henry had knocked into the wall the night before.

Widenmann said he heard something, hurried to the far wall.

"Widenmann!" Henry said in a sharp whisper. "Get back here, you damned fool!"

That German had turned pale as Mexican cotton, said he heard Mr. Tunstall's dog whimpering, that it might bring Brady over to investigate, said he would feed it, and before Henry could choke out a curse, that sorry bastard had cleared the coop. When Henry whirled around and aimed his Winchester at Widenmann's ass, I laughed and told him to save his lead. He spit out tobacco juice, muttered an oath, and took his spot by the wall again.

We saw them: Jack Long first, Peppin . . . then heard Brady's voice but didn't see him.

"Hindman's with them," MacNab whispered. "He was with them that kilt Tunstall." His finger tightened on the trigger.

"Just wait," I said softly. "Don't want to send them running before we got a clear shot at all of them."

As soon as I had finished, Billy Mathews and Brady stepped into view. Brady had gall. He was carrying my Winchester, the one I had been toting back when me and Atanacio Martinez and Fred Waite had tried to arrest Dolan and

Evans for murdering Tunstall. Well, I was going to get that back.

"All—" I started, only never got to finish.

Boy, it sounded like Gettysburg, I reckon, us shooting, jacking round after round into our repeaters, firing till we couldn't see a thing because of the smoke from our weapons. It got quiet, just briefly, and I heard Brady mumble something, maybe he was saying a prayer, and when the smoke cleared, why, that son of a bitch was just sitting in the center of the street, my rifle at his side.

"The bastard's still alive!" Henry roared, and we shot him again.

My ears were pealing, but we started reloading, Henry cussing us like the devil. "You hit only two of those bastards! Damn it, Peppin and Mathews got away. This is all going to hell!"

"I winged Long," Fred Waite cried. "I know I did."

Henry spit again. "*Winged* him. We were here to kill them all! Now we're in a fix."

Peppin and Mathews had run clear back to the Cisneros home, but Long headed to the Torreón. They didn't exactly have us in a crossfire, but it wasn't the best fix we could have wished for.

Hindman was crying for water, moaning for his mama, and Ike Stockton ran out of his bucket of blood, screaming at us not to shoot, that he was going to help Hindman. He lifted him up, started dragging him away, but MacNab shook his head. "No you don't, Hindman," he said. "You don't get to live." He shot Hindman dead, and I wouldn't be surprised if old Ike didn't soil his britches, though he didn't say so when he testified yesterday.

Well, I had already headed to the corral gate, started to open it, and Middleton asked where I thought I was going.

"To get my rifle back, you fool," I said.

All these Murphy-Dolan men say I was running to get that arrest warrant for Mr. McSween off Brady's body, but there's no truth to that. Just wanted my rifle back. It was a crazy thing to do, but the way the blood was pumping through me right then, it seemed logical. Jim French run over to me, said he would help—I guess his blood was roiling, too—so I tossed him my big sombrero and told him to put it on his head.

"What for?"

"To give them something to shoot at!" I laughed, and Frenchy put on my hat, giggling, while Middleton was grabbing our horses, saying we were plumb loco. Frenchy and me ran, ran hard, shooting at the Torreón and the Cisneros house. I was shooting, anyway, cause I was a better shot than Frenchy, so I told him to get my rifle. He got there, got right over the body, then a bullet slammed into his gun holster, and he yelped out like a dog that had gotten its tail stepped on. Next thing I know, a bullet hit me in the thigh, and I was hollering, too. The both of us hobbled as fast as we could for the corral, dived in, rolled in the dust, while Middleton shut the gate.

It fell silent again.

"You finished?" Henry asked.

I tried to sit up, but I was bleeding like a pig in a slaughterhouse and dropped to the ground.

"Boys, I don't think I can ride." I kept grinning, though.

Well, being the pals that they were, they shook their heads somberly and rode off. Couldn't rightly blame them. After they left, I heard Mathews and Peppin, figured they could count and would come looking for me, so I made myself stand up. Limped over to the store, knocked on the door, and the Reverend Doctor Ealy opened it up.

"Billy," he said, shaking his head. He helped me inside, cut away my trousers, and pulled a silk neckerchief through the bullet hole. That hurt a right smart, but I didn't utter a sound—well, maybe a few grunts—and he tied it up.

"That's the best I can do for now, Billy," he said. "They'll be looking for you."

They already were. He helped me into a storeroom—Peppin and Mathews were banging on the door—and I saw the trap door. He opened it, helped me inside, closed it, and told me to wait till he came back. That's what I did, till those deputies got tired of looking. Waited there the rest of the day and half the night before Doc Ealy came back. He checked my wound, told me I was lucky.

I agreed. "Couple of inches higher, and I would be singing too high for even a tenor."

He didn't laugh. "You'd best ride," he said, "if you can."

My leg was stiff, but the bleeding had stopped, only it hurt like blazes, so he gave me a bottle of laudanum. I took a swallow, limped out the back door, and he said I could find my bay horse at Yginio Salazar's place.

Well, that's what happened. Did I kill Brady? Hell, we all did, though I don't know if I even hit the devil. I tell you one thing, though. Those sons of bitches, especially Billy Mathews, that say they saw me are lying. They thought I was at Brady's body, but it was Jim French, wearing my hat.

I know what you're thinking. About yesterday. Why did I say I'd drop my trousers to prove I wasn't hit in the thigh? Hell, Billie, that's poker. That's a bluff.

Now, I need to think about what I should say on the stand.

Chapter 28

April 9, 1881
La Mesilla, New Mexico Territory

He clenched both fists until the knuckles whitened, feeling the beginnings of an asthma attack, when William H. Bonney took the stand. Ira Leonard had been unable to deliver a note to Bonney during the noon recess. Sheriff Southwick—most likely bowing to William Rynerson or Bob Olinger—had stationed a deputy outside in front of the barred window. He should have known better, should have known that Albert Fountain and John Bail were first and foremost Masons, then lawyers. They owed their souls to the Santa Fe Ring.

"What is your name and place of residence?"

"William Bonney. My name's William Bonney." His chains jostled as he pointed out the courtroom's main doorway. "I've been living in Sheriff Southwick's calaboose since late last month."

Bristol pounded his gavel. "This is no place for jokes, Bonney."

"Well, then, I've been living in Lincoln, White Oaks, and Fort Sumner. I was living in Lincoln County, at John Tunstall's ranch, when the troubles began." He looked up and smiled at the judge. "How's that?"

Instead of Bail, Fountain was handling the direct examination. "Are you also known as Billy Kid, and Antrim?"

Bonney seemed glad of the chance to correct that point. "Yes, sir, I am. But I was never Billy *the* Kid, not that I know of. Governor Wallace started calling me that, and the newspapermen picked it up, but I was just Billy, *Billito,* the Kid. I've been called a lot of things."

Fountain shook his head and offered a rare smile. "You take things easy, don't you?"

The witness's grin easily outshone his attorney's. "What's the use of looking on the gloomy side of everything? The laugh's on me this time."

"How do you make your livelihood?"

"I haven't stolen any stock, if that's what you mean. I made my living by gambling, but that was the only way I could live. They wouldn't let me settle down. If they had, I wouldn't be here today." He rattled the chains again. He seemed to enjoy that, seemed to be enjoying himself.

"Who, Billy? Who wouldn't let you live?"

"Jimmy Dolan, Jessie Evans . . ." He turned his head and stared momentarily at Judge Bristol, running his tongue over his protruding teeth, contemplating naming the judge as one of the conspirators, but finally shrugged and faced the jury again. "Men of the House, Dolan's hoodlums, and the Santa Fe Ring."

Newcomb objected. "There is no proof that such a ring exists, Your Honor."

"Sustained."

That was no surprise. The Ring owned Warren Bristol, too.

"Was Sheriff Brady one of those men, Billy?"

"There were certain men who wouldn't let me live in the country. He was one of them."

"But he was a lawman."

"That doesn't mean much in the West, sir. Criminy, Pat Garrett was rustling cows before he became a lawman." Newcomb fired out an objection, but Bonney kept talking, hurrying to finish before Bristol unleashed his gavel on Bonney's head. "I was a lawman before he ever was. Funny how things turned out."

Bonney punctuated his statement with a smirk while Bristol admonished him. "Mister, when there is an objection, you immediately stop speaking until I have made my ruling. You talk out of turn once more, and I will hold you in contempt." He spit tobacco juice and instructed the jury to disregard the witness's statement.

Bonney added: "I don't have problems with Pat, though. He's a good fellow. But Chisum, he got me—"

Bristol's gavel pounded, and Bonney apologized. *His mouth, his cocksure attitude.* Leonard shook his head. He would never have allowed Bonney to testify for those reasons. A few moments passed before Fountain resumed the examination. "It is in your estimation, Mr. Bonney, that Sheriff Brady did not uphold the law of Lincoln County?"

"He upheld it if it suited him. If it suited Lawrence G. Murphy or Jimmy Dolan. When Mr. Tunstall opened his store, the House started losing business, and that was something Dolan could not live with. It wasn't his nature. Then Dolan got into a feud with Mr. McSween, something over some inheritance. Never really understood all of that. So Dolan got Sheriff Brady to hold Mr. Tunstall's property as part of the suit against Mr. McSween, but that wasn't right, not fair. And even before that, Brady had threatened Mr. Tunstall, threatened to kill him, and likely would have if Mr. McSween hadn't stepped between them, if there hadn't been other witnesses."

A chair squeaked as Simon Newcomb rose with another objection. "I don't see how any of this uncorroborated testimony is pertinent to the case at hand."

Fountain was prepared, though. "He opened the door, Your Honor. The prosecutor introduced Tunstall's murder."

"So he did," Bristol said. "But let's speed things up, Mr. Fountain."

"When John Tunstall was murdered—"

"Objection, there—"

Fountain didn't wait. "There are indictments, Your Honor.

Indictments handed down by a grand jury that you yourself impaneled. Mr. Tunstall was murdered—"

The gavel popped again. "Let's move on, gentlemen. Mr. Tunstall was shot and killed. There are indictments, but no one has been tried for the crime; therefore, it cannot yet be determined if he was the victim of a crime or was killed, as officers have said, resisting arrest."

When Fountain spoke, the edge in his voice surprised Leonard. Maybe he had underestimated the attorney. "After Mr. Tunstall was found with a bullet in his breast and his face beaten in with the butt of a rifle till his brains poured out, did you try to serve arrest warrants for James Dolan and Jessie Evans?"

So far, Fountain and Bonney had held up pretty good, but Leonard still felt that putting Bonney on the stand was a catastrophe.

"I did," Bonney said. "Brady knocked out the constable, hauled him off to jail with me and Fred Waite, who were assisting him as Regulators, duly appointed by Justice Wilson. He kept us in jail for days, till Mr. McSween made him release us with a court order. And he didn't give us our weapons back, either. He had no call to keep them."

"Others were killed?"

"In Lincoln County in 1878? Yes, sir, you could hardly count that high, seemed like. We feared for our lives, lived in cold camps, hid in caves while trying to round up the men who murdered Mr. Tunstall."

"You caught two of those men, didn't you?"

"Yes, sir. We rode down Morton and Baker, took them to John Chisum's ranch. We were trying to deliver them to Sheriff Brady, though I didn't think it would do much good. Prisoners were always escaping from Brady, if he wanted them to. We were in a canyon after we left the Chisum ranch. William McCloskey, he was a Regulator, had been a friend to Mr. Tunstall, he rode alongside Morton. Morton grabbed Will's six-shooter, shot him in the heart. Then he and Baker made a run for the top of the canyon. Morton fired back at us—we were chasing them by then—and we shot back."

"But you left their bodies where they fell."

Bonney nodded. "If we had delivered them dead to Brady, he would have killed us."

"Billy, why did you go to Lincoln on the day Sheriff Brady was killed?"

"To protect Mr. McSween. He was coming into town that day. We got there the night before, spent the night at the corral at Mr. Tunstall's store. We knew Brady had a warrant for Mr. McSween, and we knew if he ever served it, Mr. McSween would be planted alongside Mr. Tunstall."

"Did you kill the sheriff?"

"No, sir."

"Do you know who did?"

"No, sir."

"But you were in the corral when the Regulators started shooting."

"Yes, sir. We learned from a Mexican boy—I don't want to say his name, because that would mean his death—that Sheriff Brady and a bunch of man-killers planned on ambushing Mr. McSween when he rode into town later that day. Henry Brown started shooting when he saw them, and the others joined in."

"Where were you at this time?"

"Feeding Mr. Tunstall's bulldog."

Fountain paused, swallowed, and gave Bonney an icy stare. "Rob Widenmann said he was feeding the dog."

"He's a liar."

Leonard closed his eyes. Bonney was calling a defense witness a liar.

"And you did not run out to Brady's body?"

"No, sir. I rode out after the shooting."

"Witnesses have identified you."

"They're mistaken. They saw a fellow running in a big Mexican sombrero, but that doesn't mean it was me. By jingo, you could ask Charlie Bowdre or Big Tom that. They'd know I'm telling the truth. Charlie and Tom got killed because a bunch of assassins thought they were aiming at me."

"So you think you are innocent?"

"I know I'm innocent. Besides, I wasn't the only Regulator in Lincoln that day. I think it hard I should be the only one to suffer the extreme penalty of the law."

As Fountain returned to his chair, finished with the examination, William Rynerson stood, excusing himself as he bumped legs, made his way from his bench to the aisle, and left the courtroom. Leonard found that odd, felt tempted to follow him, but had to stay, needed to hear Simon Newcomb's cross.

"Why did you become a Regulator?" the prosecutor asked.

Bonney shrugged. "Seemed like a good idea."

"You were interested in justice?"

"I wanted to bring the men who killed Mr. Tunstall to justice, that's true."

"Perhaps you can explain this loyalty. You knew John Henry Tunstall, a foreigner, for what, six months, maybe? You worked for him. He paid you wages. Yet when he was killed, you felt a strong desire for revenge—a man you hardly knew."

Shaking his head emphatically, Bonney said, "I knew him well. He treated me kindly, gave me a chance when most folks in this territory wouldn't. He didn't deserve to die like that, and those . . . those . . . those vermin who murdered him sure didn't deserve to run about the territory like they were royalty."

Newcomb smiled. "He was . . . how is it you put it, a *pal*?"

"Yeah. He was a pal, not just to me, but to Dick Brewer, Charlie, Big Tom, Frenchy, the McSweens, even that skinflint and hard rock John Chisum."

"And they were your pals, too, especially Bowdre and O'Folliard."

"Good friends, indeed." He nodded his head with enthusiasm. "Had a lot of laughs together. I wish Pat hadn't killed them."

"You respected, admired John Tunstall?"

"Yes, sir."

Newcomb's voice rose as he lashed out his attack. "And you would have these twelve jurors believe that you had nothing to do with the murder of Sheriff Brady! You were feeding your employer's *dog*! Isn't it the truth, sir, that you orchestrated this whole act? You rode to Lincoln, knocked holes in the corral wall for your rifles, waited for Sheriff Brady to walk by so you could murder him. That's the truth of the matter, isn't it? This was an act of revenge, a willful and felonious act of premeditated murder."

Bonney remained calm. "If it was anything, sir, it was self-defense."

Newcomb stared at the jury as he spoke. "Self-defense. And Morton and Baker were killed trying to escape." His laugh lacked humor. "Isn't it true, sir, that you rushed out of the corral and ran toward the lifeless, blood-soaked body of Sheriff Brady to steal the warrants he possessed, that alias warrant you have mentioned for Alexander McSween?"

Now Bonney laughed. "What good would that have done, counselor? You should know better. You think I would risk my life for a piece of paper? Criminy, the judge here would have just wrote out another one."

Rynerson had made his way back into the courtroom. He nodded at Newcomb but didn't bother returning to his seat. Instead, after the prosecutor acknowledged Rynerson's gesture, the towering former district attorney left again. *What are they up to?* Leonard wondered.

"Your character witnesses say you are a good man, a man who looks after his friends. Do you agree with their assessment?"

"I'm not one to judge."

"But you value friendship. That's why you joined the Regulators, isn't it?"

"A man's not much if he doesn't . . ." Bonney stopped, his boyish expression vanishing, as if some memory had reached up and gripped a stranglehold over his throat. He stared blankly, finally shuddered and shook his head, his manacles shaking as he sank back in his chair. "I try to look after my pals. I tried to look after Mr. Tunstall, but Jessie Evans and the Ring murdered him. I tried to take care of Mr. McSween, but they killed him, too. And I reckon they're bound and determined to send me chasing after them." He sat up, defiant again. "Let them try."

Newcomb was in his chair before Bonney had finished.

"Any more questions?" Bristol asked.

"No, Your Honor," Newcomb said. "I cannot get a straight answer from the defendant, so I am finished with him."

A moment later, the defense rested its case.

Chapter 29

"He was a low-down, vulgar cut-throat, with probably not one redeeming quality."
—*Grant County Herald*, on Billy the Kid, July 28, 1881

April 9, 1881
La Mesilla, New Mexico Territory

After Bristol granted Newcomb's request for a five-minute recess, reporters put away their pencils and paper, replacing them with pipes, cigars, cigarettes, and matches. Smoke soon hung thick in the room, and Ira Leonard felt the need to step outside for fresh air and follow the slippery prosecuting attorney.

He spotted Newcomb in front the sheriff's office, talking to William Rynerson. Leonard considered becoming an eavesdropper but ruled that out. Even if he knew what they planned, he couldn't warn Fountain or Bonney in time. Besides, he was not the defense attorney of record. So he walked onto the plaza, which was bustling with activity on this Saturday. A pretty *señorita* sat underneath the nearest cottonwood, singing to her lover, whose head rested on her lap. Near the church, a half-dozen children played marbles, while pedestrians, ox carts, wagons, horses, burros, and mules filled the streets. He smelled fresh bread and the spicy aroma of Mexican cooking.

The world goes on.

He took a deep breath, slowly exhaled, and walked back inside, tobacco smoke irritating his eyes. Moments later,

William Rynerson and Simon Newcomb re-entered the courtroom and found their seats. The bailiff called court to order,
and Newcomb rose.

"Your Honor, the Territory would like to call a rebuttal witness."

"Who is it?" Bristol asked.

"Billie Wilson."

Albert Fountain leaped to his feet. William Bonney's
shoulders sagged.

"I must protest," Fountain said. "Billie Wilson is a convicted felon sentenced by Your Honor himself to twenty years
in the territorial penitentiary for counterfeiting, resisting arrest, and other crimes. His word is as worthless as the bogus
money he passed throughout New Mexico. Besides, he was
not in Lincoln on the day Sheriff Brady died. Anything he
says is hearsay or uncorroborated testimony—inadmissible."

Newcomb just stood there smirking, shaking his head, as
confident as he had been since the trial began. "Your Honor,"
he said softly but forcefully, "the entire defense has been witnesses lauding the defendant's character. Billie Wilson is
being called to rebut that testimony. He will not testify to anything regarding Sheriff Brady's murder."

"Then his testimony is not needed," Fountain said. "He has
nothing to offer. And his status as a convicted—"

"He will testify to the Kid's character, as I have said. I
think the jury deserves to hear what Mr. Bonney's comrade
has to say about him. This is a man who rode with him. So far,
the jury has only heard from a former Regulator the defendant
himself has called a liar, a former sweetheart, a preacher's
wife, and a woman of dubious reputation."

"Objection!" Fountain shouted.

Bristol waved his hand at the defense attorney and wiped
his mouth with the back of his hand. "I'm going to allow Mr.
Wilson to testify about the defendant's character," he said,
and Fountain sank into his chair with a groan. Bonney had not
moved. "I'm not going to let him talk about what the Kid may
or may not have told him while incarcerated. He can only
speak as to what went on while they were riding together.
Don't worry, Mr. Fountain, you will have your chance to chal-

lenge anything the witness says on cross-examination. Bring in the witness."

The pipes had been put out, the cigars flipped into the spittoons, cigarettes crushed on the floor. Reporters busily took notes as James Southwick and Bob Olinger escorted Billie Wilson down the center aisle. Unlike William Bonney, Wilson was not handcuffed. The sheriff and deputy marshal retired to the back of the courtroom while the witness was sworn in.

"Do you know the defendant?" Newcomb asked.

"I do, though I don't know what his real name is. During the time I rode with him, he called himself Billy Kid, Kid Antrim, the Kid, but usually William Bonney, or Billy for short. I called him Billy. We were sometimes called the two Billies."

"When did you first make his acquaintance?"

"It was in Colorado in the fall of '79. He had just sold some rustled livestock, and I tried to get him to change a hundred-dollar note. My note was counterfeit, of course, and he spotted it immediately. I'll say that for him. He was fast. Next thing I knew, I was staring down the barrel of his double-action revolver."

"I'm surprised he did not shoot you."

"He laughed at me, holstered his gun, and offered me a chair. The next thing I knew, I was riding back to New Mexico with him and the others."

"And who were those other men?"

"Big Tom O'Folliard and Charlie Bowdre."

"They were friends of the defendant?"

Wilson shrugged. He hadn't looked at Bonney once, keeping his eyes trained on the prosecutor. "He called them his pals."

"But they weren't?"

"Oh, they were his friends, at least they thought they were, but Billy . . ." He shot a nervous glance at Bonney, but quickly refocused on Newcomb. "Billy didn't care for anybody but himself."

"Were you at the Greathouse & Kuch ranch last year when Deputy James Carlyle was killed?"

Before Wilson could answer, Fountain had objected. "The

death of Carlyle has not once been mentioned in this trial. It cannot be introduced now in rebuttal. Besides, it has no bearing on the death of Sheriff Brady."

Bristol frowned but sustained the motion.

"Very well, but Tom O'Folliard and Charlie Bowdre have been mentioned as friends of the defendant," Newcomb said. "Mr. Bonney himself testified to this fact just minutes earlier. Are you saying the defendant was not a true friend?"

"True friends don't do what he done." He spoke in such a low whisper, Bristol made him repeat it for the jury, louder.

"What happened on the night Tom O'Folliard was killed at Fort Sumner?"

Wilson's gaze fell to his brogans. "It was the nineteenth of December last. Freezing cold it was. We had gotten a note from one of the Kid's Mexican friends, José Valdéz, that said Pat Garrett had left Fort Sumner, headed back to Roswell, so things was safe. We were playing poker when we got the letter. Bowdre's friend Tom Pickett and another Mexican brought it, said they got it from Charlie Bowdre's wife. Billy was tickled, said he had a hankering to see Paulita Maxwell, eat some of Deluvina's cooking, drink some real coffee. Then he tossed his hat in the pot, a big old sugarloaf sombrero with a green hatband, only he took off the hatband.

"'What's that?' Big Tom asked. He and Billy were the only ones left in this game, and Billy, he just grinned and said, 'I'm calling your bet, Big Tom. But I ain't about to bet my favorite hatband.' Big Tom, he sniggered and showed two pairs, can't recall what they were, and Billy said, 'You won,' and picked up the cards. Only I was standing behind him, and I saw that Billy also had two pair, but a higher two pair, kings and something. I didn't say anything, but I got suspicious. Big Tom, he worshipped Billy, felt proud to have his hat. He tossed away his Boss of the Plains and put on that sombrero. He was happy."

"Go on," Newcomb said.

"Well, Billy took the Mexican's hat, I mean the one who had brought us the letter from Missus Bowdre with Pickett. Put his green hatband around it and gave the Mexican Big Tom's hat, even though it almost swallowed his head. And we got ready and rode to town. Tom Pickett rode with us. The Mexican, though, he went home wearing Big Tom's hat. Well, Garrett was waiting for us in Fort Sumner, Garrett and his posse. As soon as we rode in, they started shooting. Poor Tom never stood no chance. They was all aiming at him, you see, because they thought him to be Billy, because of that hat.

"Somehow, all of us made it, except Big Tom. Anyway, we rode off, but Dave Rudabaugh's horse took a bullet and bled to death. He had to ride double behind Pickett. The wind blew off my hat, we were riding so fast, and I couldn't stop to get it. It was mighty cold, and my horse started faltering. The snow was coming down hard. We couldn't see a thing; at least, I couldn't. I thought I was gonna freeze to death, moaning that my head was cold, my ears frozen. I thought I would surely die. Must have gone a little mad, and Charlie, he tossed me his hat, told me to put it on and keep quiet. I did. Some time later, we made it to this stone building and took shelter there.

"Billy wouldn't let us build a fire, and I understood why, but it didn't help our nerves. Pickett said that come morning, he was riding out, wanted no part of us, and Charlie, he stuttered that he would join him. I figured it was time to leave the territory, too. Rudabaugh said he was bound for Texas, but Billy just laughed, said he wouldn't leave New Mexico. But I think he was mad we were abandoning him.

"First thing that morning, we got up, and Charlie said he was gonna feed the horses. They was all tied up outside, except Billy's bay mare. He brought her inside with us. Before he left, Billy tossed him his hat, the one he took off Pickett's Mexican friend. He was laughing, Billy was, saying that he didn't want Charlie to catch a head cold. Charlie put the hat on, stepped outside, and Garrett's posse was waiting for us again. They shot poor Charlie apart, and he fell back inside, bleeding from the mouth, bleeding from it looked like a dozen bullet holes."

Wilson wet his lips, closed his eyes.

"But he wasn't dead, was he?" Newcomb said.

"No, sir. Well, those wounds was mortal. We all could see that. By then, I knew that Billy had played Charlie for a fool, just like he had played Big Tom for one. He wasn't looking after nobody but himself. Figured if Charlie walked outside wearing a Mexican hat and got killed, well, so be it. But if he wasn't shot at, that meant that the posse hadn't caught us yet."

"What happened next?"

Wilson looked up, finding the courage to stare at Bonney, only Bonney's head was bowed, his eyes trained on his manacled feet.

"I'll never forget it," Wilson said. "We got Charlie on his feet, and I yelled out to Pat Garrett that he was shot and wanted to surrender. Then Billy, he jerked Charlie's gunbelt till the holster was on his belly, Charlie moaning all the while, and put Charlie's right hand on the butt. Billy says, 'They have murdered you, but you can get revenge. Kill some of those sons of bitches before you die.' And he shoved Bowdre out the front door."

"Pals." Newcomb shook his head and sat down. "No more questions. Thank you, Mr. Wilson."

Fountain stood, citing more objections, that the testimony of a convicted felon was inadmissible, but Bristol overruled him. Fountain immediately asked for a sidebar, but Bristol denied to hear more. "I have made my ruling, counselor," he said irritably. "Do you want to examine this witness?"

The attorney jerked around to face Wilson.

"Have you been convicted for counterfeiting?"

"Yes, sir."

"Have you been sentenced to twenty years in prison?"

"Yes, sir."

"Why should we believe anything you said?"

Leonard sighed. Fountain had run out of steam; everyone knew that.

"I have no reason to lie. Mr. Newcomb hasn't promised me a thing." Leonard doubted that, but it didn't matter. Knowing he had lost, Albert Fountain sank into his chair beside his client.

"No more questions."

Chapter 30

> *"Murder in the first degree is the greatest crime known to our laws. The legislature of this Territory has enacted a law prescribing that the punishment for murder in the first degree shall be death. This is the law: no other punishment than death can be imposed for murder in the first degree."*
>
> —Judge Warren Bristol

April 9, 1881
La Mesilla, New Mexico Territory

In his chambers, Warren Bristol poured four fingers of Tennessee whiskey into his glass, settled into his chair, and began reading the instructions to the jury Albert Fountain had requested.

1. Under the evidence, the jury must either find the defendant guilty of murder in the first degree or acquit him.

2. The jury will not be justified in finding the defendant guilty of murder in the first degree unless they are satisfied from the evidence, to the exclusion of all reasonable doubt, that the defendant actually fired the shot that caused the death of the deceased Brady, and that such a shot was fired by the defendant—with a premeditated design to effect the death of the deceased, or that the defendant was present and actually assisted in firing the fatal shot or shots that caused the death of

the deceased, and that he was in a position to render such assistance and actually present and rendered such assistance from a premeditated design to effect the death of the deceased.

And so forth.

He skipped over the third and fourth instructions, saw where John Bail had signed his name underneath Fountain's, and tossed the paper onto his desk. Bail might have put his signature on the request, but it had been written entirely by Fountain. Bristol finished his drink and thought about having another, but it wouldn't do for the presiding judge to have whiskey on his breath when he instructed the jury.

Fountain was a pretty good attorney, had fought hard, but he never should have let Bonney take the stand. Bristol had John Bail to thank for that. He opened a new plug of tobacco and bit off a sizable chaw, worked it until it was soft, then picked up a pencil and began writing his own instructions. He had two hours to finish. That's how long he had called the recess.

"Gentlemen of the jury," Bristol began, blocking out the interpreter's Spanish translation, "the defendant in this case, William Bonney, alias Kid, alias William Antrim, is charged in and by the indictment against him . . ."

He wondered if those twelve Mexicans could understand this legal babbling, wondered if even Mariano Toribio knew what he was really saying. He reminded those dumb greasers that Bonney was charged with the murder of Sheriff William Brady, that they were hearing the case here in Old Mesilla because of a change of venue from Lincoln County.

"In the matter of determining what your verdict shall be, it would be improper for you to consider anything except that evidence before you," Bristol said. "You as jurors are the exclusive judges of the weight of the evidence." *Make them feel proud.* "You are the exclusive judges of the credibility of the witnesses. It is for you to determine whether the testimony of any witness whom you have heard is to be believed or not." *Remind them that the Kid is a liar.* "You are also the exclusive judges whether the evidence is sufficiently clear and strong to satisfy your minds that the defendant is guilty." *You know damned well he's guilty, and if you don't, savvy this:*

"There is no evidence tending to show that the killing of Brady was either justifiable or excusable. As a matter of law, therefore, such killing was unlawful, and whoever committed the deed or was present and advised, aided or abetted, or consented to such killing committed the crime of murder in some one of the degrees of murder.

"There is no evidence before you showing that the killing of Brady is murder in any other degree than the first." He looked up from his papers briefly. Simon Newcomb tried to hide his smirk, Fountain frowned, Bail just sat there nodding, and the Kid picked at a fingernail with his thumbnail.

"Your verdict therefore should be either that the defendant is guilty of murder in the first degree or that he is not guilty at all under this indictment."

He explained murder and the law to the jurors. Finally, he got to the main instructions.

"In this case, in order to justify you in finding this defendant guilty of murder in the first degree under the particular circumstances as presented by the indictment and the evidence, you should be satisfied and believe from the evidence to the exclusion of every reasonable doubt of the truth of several propositions:

"First. That the defendant either inflicted one or more of the fatal wounds causing Brady's death, or that he was present at the time and place of the killing, and encouraged, incited, aided in, abetted, advised, or commanded such killing.

"Second. That such killing was without justification or excuse.

"Third. That such killing was caused by inflicting upon Brady's body a fatal gunshot wound.

"And fourth. That such fatal wound was either inflicted by the defendant from a premeditated design to effect Brady's death, or that he was present at the time and place of the killing of Brady, and from a premeditated design to effect his death, he then and there encouraged, incited, aided in, abetted, advised, or commanded such killing.

"If he was present—encouraging, inciting, aiding in, abetting, advising, or commanding this killing of Brady—he is as much guilty as though he fired the fatal shot. This is the law of the land."

He had to go on, defining "reasonable doubt" as he did in all criminal cases, but he felt confident that even a bunch of illiterate greasers would have no choice but to bring in a verdict of guilty. Albert Fountain had delivered a fine closing argument, but Simon Newcomb's rebuttal had also been solid. Bristol finished, listening to Toribio's translation and scowling at the jury. *Make them fear me, so they won't bring in the wrong verdict.*

As the bailiff led them away to deliberate, Bristol pulled out his pocket watch. He would give them ten minutes to reach a verdict.

They came back in seven.

April 11, 1881
La Mesilla, New Mexico Territory

"Hello, Billy."

The Kid opened his eyes and faked a yawn. He swung his legs over the bunk, sat up, then shook his head as if his visitor had woken him up. Hell, a body couldn't catch a wink of sleep with all the noise going on outside.

"I reckon I shouldn't have testified," he said with a grin, "eh, Ira?"

Leonard didn't smile. His hair looked even whiter than it had been before the trial began, and he held a rolled-up copy of *Newman's Semi-Weekly* in his left hand, clenching it hard. The Kid had already read the editor's assault on William H. Bonney's good name. "Where you been keeping yourself?"

"I was at the trial," Leonard said. "I tried to get inside, but they weren't letting you have any visitors; at least, they weren't letting me see you. I told you the chances were good we would lose on this level, Billy. I don't want you worrying. I can handle your appeal."

With a chuckle, the Kid stood, but instead of walking toward Leonard, he jumped, grabbing the window's iron bars, and pulled himself up to stare at the crowd outside the Corn Exchange Hotel. "I think I'm gonna stick with Mr. Fountain, Ira. He said he'd represent me on appeal if I can get him some money. I'm trying to get my bay horse back. One of those damned brigands with Garrett stole it back at Stinking Springs."

His back to Leonard, the Kid smiled when Leonard mumbled an *Oh, I see.* He expected Leonard to leave, but the attorney stayed in the hallway, talking about legal affairs until the Kid's arms tired and he dropped to the floor.

"The testimony of Billie Wilson should be grounds for appeal," Leonard was saying. "I can also argue that Judge Bristol should have stepped down. The rumor in Lincoln County back in '78 was that you wanted him dead, so he couldn't be impartial. And with his instructions, the jury had no choice but to find you guilty."

Shaking his head, the Kid told Leonard to shut up. Leonard looked up, his mouth agape, as the Kid faced him.

"Ira, I *am* guilty. Criminy, you know that. I killed Brady, and I helped kill Hindman. I'm a better sharpshooter than any of those with me, including Henry Brown. You think I missed? Every bullet I fired found its mark. It was me who ran to Brady's body, not to grab some stupid warrant, but to get my rifle back. Brady stole it from me, that spud-eating bastard. I can show you the scar in my thigh where Billy Mathews almost shot my pecker off."

Suddenly tired, he sat down. "I don't have any regrets, either. Except that I got caught, tried, and convicted when Henry and the others lit a shuck for parts unknown. Brady, Dolan, Evans . . . those men killed John Tunstall, killed a lot of good men, but that's the law for you. . . . The law of the land, at least *this* land." He pointed his chin at the empty cell behind Leonard. Billie Wilson had been shipped off to Santa Fe immediately after the trial. "Hell, I don't even blame Billie for what he did, that little *hijo de cabrón*."

He shook his head and stared at his manacled feet. "You and Albert are wasting your time. I don't think I'll make it to Lincoln. Bob Olinger is looking for a reason to kill me.

Likely, I'll be dead before we get out to Pat Coghlan's ranch."

Leonard cleared his throat. "I'll pray for you, Billy."

That prompted another laugh. "Funny how things change, Ira. It's like I said the other day. Pat Garrett was a bandit before he was a lawman, and I was a lawman before they called me a bandit. You were one of the biggest sinners I know."

"I'll be in Lincoln, Billy. I will—"

"I am what I am of choice," the Kid said firmly, and sighed. "It'll be over shortly."

Leonard fell silent. The Kid leaned back in his bunk, pulled a hat over his eyes, and listened to Leonard's footsteps growing fainter down the hall.

April 13, 1881
La Mesilla, New Mexico Territory

When Bristol asked if he had anything to say before passing sentence, the Kid just shook his head. He sat beside his attorneys, with Bob Olinger standing behind him, shotgun in hand. They must have thought him to be one bad *hombre* since he had just been found guilty of first-degree murder.

"Very well," Bristol said solemnly. "It is therefore considered by the court here that the said defendant, William Bonney, alias Kid, alias William Antrim, be taken to the County of Lincoln, in the Third Judicial District of the Territory of New Mexico, by the sheriff of Doña Ana County in said judicial district and territory and there by him delivered into the custody of the sheriff of the said County of Lincoln, and that he, the said William Bonney, alias Kid, alias William Antrim, be confined in prison in said County of Lincoln by the sheriff of such county until Friday, the thirteenth day of May, in the year of our Lord One Thousand Eight Hundred and Eighty-one. That on the day aforesaid, between the hours of nine of the clock in the forenoon and three of the clock in the afternoon, he, the said William Bonney, alias Kid, alias William Antrim, be taken from such prison to some suitable and convenient place of execution within said County of Lin-

coln, by the sheriff of said county, and that then and there on
that day and between the aforesaid hours thereof, by the sheriff of said County of Lincoln, he, the said William Bonney,
alias Kid, alias William Antrim, be hanged by the neck until
his body be dead."

The shotgun pressed against the Kid's spine. "All that
legal talk, my boy, means you're a dead man," Olinger said
in a hoarse whisper.

The Kid bit his lip to keep from smiling. They were going
to hang him on *Friday the Thirteenth*?

Part III

Chapter 31

*"Billy never talked much of the past; he was always
looking into the future."*

—Frank Coe

April 15, 1881
La Mesilla, New Mexico Territory

The fat gent from *The Mesilla News* ran up as Southwick and
Olinger escorted the Kid to a Dougherty wagon illuminated
by flickering street lamps. With a sigh, the sheriff stopped,
allowing his prisoner one final interview. Southwick had
shown some brains, telling reporters that the prisoner
wouldn't leave for Lincoln until later in the week, then had
made arrangements to sneak him out late at night.

At least one reporter, however, was smarter than the Doña
Ana County lawman.

"Why did you testify?"

"Well, I had intended at one time not to say a word in my
behalf, because people would say, 'Oh, he lied.'" He
laughed. "Reckon I was right. At least the jury thought so."

"Have you read *Newman's Semi-Weekly*? Simeon Newman has written a lot of hard stuff about you."

"He created prejudice against me during my trial and is
now trying to incite a mob to lynch me. I like your paper,
though. You're always willing to give the reader both sides."

"Thank you. Governor Wallace is still in Santa Fe, and
Governor Sheldon has not arrived yet. Do you expect a pardon?"

"Considering the active part Governor Wallace took on our side and our friendly relations, I think he ought to pardon me. Don't know that he will do it."

"What do you think of the jail here?"

The Kid wondered if the sheriff had put the reporter up to asking the question. Maybe that's why the inkspiller was here at ten o'clock. "It's the worst I ever struck," the Kid answered. It was the truth, too.

Southwick stepped in front of the reporter. "That's enough," he said harshly, and pushed the giggling Kid forward.

After helping the Kid into the ambulance, Deputy Dave Wood shoved him into the back seat. "I'm gonna chain you to the seat, Kid," Wood said in a pleasant-enough voice. "If you try anything, Bob there will blow your head off."

"You better hope I don't try a thing, Dave," the Kid said cheerily. "Because if Bob shoots me, you're liable to collect enough change for your widow to open a new bank account."

As soon as he was secured to his seat, the shackles around his wrists bolted to the wagon's floor, the Kid said, "I have to piss."

No one laughed, and the Kid shrugged. His wrists and ankles were sore, his skin practically raw, from weeks of being shackled. Dave Wood sat beside him, holding a Spencer carbine, and Bob Olinger and Billy Mathews sat across from him. Another deputy, D. M. Reede, sat in the driver's booth. Four men sat on horses in front of the wagon, including John Kinney. The Kid's good humor faded away. He didn't see one friendly face.

"I want you to know this," said Southwick, who had no plans of making the trip to Lincoln County. "If there is trouble—your fault, anybody's fault—I've ordered my deputies to shoot you first."

As soon as Southwick stepped away, the wagon lurched forward into the darkness.

April 19, 1881
Blazer's Mill, New Mexico Territory

It didn't take him long to make friends with Wood, Reede, and J. W. Bell. Olinger, Mathews, and Kinney—he knew they'd never sit down with him for a friendly game of poker, but he didn't need them. If those three assassins hadn't killed him yet, they probably wouldn't . . . maybe only because of the presence of Wood, Reede, and Bell. Especially Bell. Pat Garrett had already hired him as a Lincoln County deputy.

They let him out of the rickety old ambulance twice a day, whenever they stopped for their noon meal or to make camp. Today, they had stopped for the night at Blazer's Mill, and while Mathews, Olinger, and Kinney tended to the mules pulling the wagon, the Kid led Wood, Bell, and Reede, plus a handful of Indian and Mexican kids, and two pretty girls, to the chuck house.

"It was like this," said the Kid, his wrists and ankles still shackled. "John Middleton had seen Buckshot Roberts first, and he run in here to tell us. Dick Brewer got real serious, while Charlie Bowdre was about to boil over, I tell you. He wanted to walk outside and shoot that old reprobate dead, but Frank Coe, he decided to play the peacemaker. So we gave Frank about twenty, thirty minutes, then Charlie ran outside, the rest of us right behind him."

He stepped off the porch, kicking up dust as he walked to the edge of the building. He pointed, grinning as every eye behind him stared at a patch of earth.

"That's where Buckshot was standing when Charlie told him to throw up his hands." He clapped his hands loudly and shouted, "Bam!" One of the Mexican boys gasped, and the Kid spun around, clapping louder despite the pain shooting through his wrists, walking toward his guards, smiling as they backed up. *"Bam! Bam! Bam!"* He pushed an Indian girl aside and ran—as fast as he could with those leg irons—and jumped back on the porch.

" 'It's too hot for me!' That's what I said. Charlie and Buckshot shot each other, only Charlie wasn't hurt bad. But Buckshot, he was mortally killed, I guarantee you. A bullet smashed George Coe's hand, another slammed Middleton to the ground, and a third almost took Doc Scurlock's leg off. I tell you, it was something to see."

He heard a voice behind him and turned, taking off his hat and bowing slightly to Clara Godfroy. "Ma'am," he said respectfully, "I was just telling these boys and girls what happened that day. It's good to see you again. You look pretty as a peach."

She shook her head in disgust and told Bell, "When you're finished, supper's on. It's fifteen cents for each of you, and I won't stand no argument about peace officers eating for free." Her eyes landed on the Kid again. "I've heard that enough."

The door slammed behind her.

"Then what?" Bell asked.

The Kid replaced his hat. "You see Doc Blazer's office over yonder?" he asked a Mexican girl. She reminded him a bit of Paulita Maxwell, and he thought he might pay her a visit after he left Lincoln.

The girl looked. "*Sí.*" Everyone else looked, too. It was like he was playacting again in Silver City.

"Buckshot had crawled back there, but we figured he had Doc's old rifle. That man hadn't played out yet. Dick Brewer, he was determined to serve that warrant, though, and he ran, Henry Brown and me following him like pet dogs." He ran, grinning at the footsteps behind him, laughing at J. W. Bell's warning:

"Not so fast, Billy! Not so fast."

He didn't make it to the bridge before stopping, out of breath. After spending four months in confinement, chained up like some rabid dog, the short dash left him tuckered out. Besides, if he kept running, Bell might panic, think he was really trying to escape. Or Bob Olinger might see him and shoot him with Kinney's Sharps rifle just for spite. Instead, the Kid located the wood pile and pointed at it.

"That's where we hid," he said once his chest stopped heaving. "Buckshot had barricaded himself in. We didn't know if he was dead, but we weren't going any farther, I tell you that. So Dick Brewer, he jumps up and shoots. *Bam!*" He paused for effect. "Nothing. Maybe Buckshot was dead. We wait, seemed like an hour, and then Dick decides to chance another shot. Only as soon as he lifted his head . . ."

His hands clapped hard. The handcuffs again bit into his wrists.

"Bam! Down went Dick, his head blown off. And me and Henry decided it was time to *vámonos muchachos*." He shook his head as he walked into his audience. "Yes, sir, old Buckshot was a dying man, but he whupped us that day."

"Where you scared?" J. W. Bell asked.

"Dad-burn me if I wasn't."

The smallest boy shook his head. "*El Chivato*," he said, "I know you were very brave. You were not scared."

With a snort, he tousled the boy's hair. "Let's eat," he said and escorted his escorts to Mrs. Clara's chuck house. J. W. Bell walked beside him, so close the Kid could have reached over, snatched his pistol, and shot him dead . . . just like he said Morton had done to Will McCloskey. It was mighty tempting. He could kill the closest guards, take his chances with Olinger, Kinney, and Mathews. Hell, he was a better shot than any of those three.

"Must have been something to see," Bell said.

The Kid nodded. He'd bide his time. "It was, pal."

April 20, 1881
Santa Fe, New Mexico Territory

"Garfield." Lew Wallace shook his head in contempt. "I am beginning to wonder if he plans to abandon me." He wadded up a piece of paper and tossed it toward a trash can, although it fell at least a foot short of the target. "As if he thinks I would accept a position as *charge d'affaires* in Paraguay or Uruguay. I have had enough of these primitive assignments."

Ira Leonard picked up the paper and placed it in the can. "I have grown fond of New Mexico, General," he said, "and I think your wife loves this place."

"Susan is a romantic." Wallace smiled. "She is back in Crawfordsville now. I hope to join her soon. You, my friend, are also a romantic, but I do not think you came to the Palace to talk about my political ambition. You are here to discuss William H. Bonney." He opened the humidor and withdrew two long cigars, extending one toward Leonard.

Leonard took it in his fingers, ran it underneath his nose, savoring the aroma of Havana tobacco, and, with a sigh, tucked it into his coat pocket. "If the general has no objections, I would like to save this till after supper." It was a small lie. He had quit smoking but didn't know if Wallace would believe him, and the governor's ego had a tendency to be fragile. He didn't want to hurt his friend's feelings.

"According to my information, you are no longer Bonney's attorney." Wallace clipped and lighted his cigar.

Leonard said nothing. He was also an officer of the court, and therefore could not defend Bonney, knowing him to be guilty of killing Brady. But guilty or innocent, Bonney had rights. Billie Wilson's rebuttal testimony should not have been allowed, another judge should have heard the case. He could get Bonney a new trial, then see how the cards fell with someone else handling the defense.

"I have written a letter of introduction for you, Ira," Wallace said. "I am sorry that I was not able to appoint you a judge in this territory. Mayhap Lionel will have better luck."

"Thank you. As for Billy . . ."

Wallace shook his head and stared skyward, sending a line of blue smoke drifting toward the vigas. "I do not see how a fellow like him should expect any clemency from me."

Leonard had expected that. Wallace still felt betrayed by the Kid. He sat down, exhausted, and exhaled. "I was talking to him before departing for here," he said tiredly.

"Who?" Wallace looked up. "The Kid?"

"Yes, sir. In jail at Old Mesilla. He said something I could not forget. It was like God was speaking to me through him."

The cigar went to the ash tray on the governor's desk. Leonard had his undivided attention now. "Go on," Wallace said.

"He told me, 'I am what I am of choice.' And then he said, 'It'll be over shortly.' " Leonard's eyes held a question. "You know those words, sir?"

"I should," Wallace said softly. "I wrote them, although in my novel, the Egyptian says, 'It will be over shortly.' I detest the use of contractions." The governor's eyes brightened, and he smiled. "I fear you are reading providence into the words of a petty bandit, Ira. Jesus does not say those words in my tale of the Christ. They are spoken by Iras, the daughter of Balthasar—a full lustrum after the crucifixion."

"I know. It just struck me —"

"Perhaps Mr. Bonney read my novel during his incarceration."

Leonard arched his eyebrows, and Wallace's lips twisted into a rueful smile. "Yes, I suppose he would not." The governor picked up the cigar, sucking on it till the end flamed back to life, and let out more blue smoke. "Bonney is right, though. He could have become an honest citizen, but he preferred outlawry—by *his* choice. And it *will* be over shortly. I shall sign his death warrant as soon as it reaches my desk."

April 21, 1881
Fort Stanton, New Mexico Territory

He stepped out of the ambulance and stretched his legs, enjoying another audience—this one comprising a troop of those buffaloes in blue: colored soldiers of the Ninth Cavalry. They had fought Apaches, but they all looked scared of the notorious Kid. "Boo!" he said, and jingled the chains.

They didn't run away scared, didn't smile—in fact, they looked at him as if he were nothing but a beetle—but J. W. Bell laughed.

"Come on, Billy." Bell led the way to the post adjutant's office. Inside, a corporal offered the Kid a chair, but he declined, saying he had been sitting all the way from La Mesilla. The soldier knocked on a door, and moments later Bell disappeared inside, leaving the Kid alone with the black trooper, Kinney, Mathews, Olinger, and Reede. George Wood had remained outside to water the horses and mules.

"Reckon you boys will be sorry to be rid of me," the Kid said. The only response he got was a grunt from Kinney.

"Well, I won't miss y'all any, either. Looks like you won't get to fill my belly with all the dimes you cut up, Bob."

Olinger shifted the shotgun. "Day ain't over yet, my boy."

He gave up on any more conversation. The door opened, and Bell stepped out, followed by a tall, strapping fellow in a linen duster and wide-brimmed black hat. The Kid couldn't hide his grin.

"Juan Largo!" he shouted, and almost tripped over his leg irons. "By god, pardner, it's bully good to see you!"

Pat Garrett offered him a somber nod, then handed John Kinney a slip of yellow paper. "Here's a receipt for the prisoner," Garrett said. *Like he was buying a horse.* "See that Sheriff Southwick gets it."

"All right," Kinney said. "Good luck, Sheriff." Kinney walked outside, followed by Reede and Mathews, who spit at the Kid's feet. Olinger thumbed back one of the double-barrel's hammers.

"Ain't you going, Bob?" the Kid asked.

It was Pat Garrett who replied. "I've hired Olinger as a deputy, Little Casino. To help Deputy Bell guard you."

"How's that suit you, Kid?" Olinger said dryly.

He couldn't hold back his laughter. "Right down to the ground."

Chapter 32

"Lincoln County has never had a jail, until the last few weeks, that would hold a cripple."
  —Pat F. Garrett, *The Authentic Life of Billy, the Kid, the Noted Desperado of the Southwest,* 1882

April 27, 1881
Lincoln, New Mexico Territory

The tender lyrics of a Mexican ballad drifted with the breeze into Pat Garrett's office. Lincoln County had rented the two-story adobe building—the biggest in Lincoln—and turned it into a courthouse. Garrett found it ironic that the Kid was jailed upstairs in what had once been The House—the Murphy-Dolan store.

He signed a report, started to do some more paperwork, but couldn't concentrate because of the sad Spanish song. He rose from his desk and crossed the floor to the makeshift jail. The Kid sat there, leg irons and handcuffs locked to the floor by chains and bolts. It had to be mighty uncomfortable sitting like that, but the Kid greeted Garrett with his perpetual grin.

The song ended, and another one began. Garrett looked out the window at the street below, finding a young Mexican girl and a boy not much older standing in the shade, staring at the jail, girl singing, boy strumming a guitar, serenading the Kid again. He'd never understand their fascination with this buck-toothed, affable, but cold-blooded killer. He closed the window.

"Where's Bell?" he asked.

"His turn to feed the others," Olinger replied. "I get to look after our guest of honor this afternoon."

Garrett grunted. He knew better than to underestimate the Kid. That's why he had one man guarding him at all times, and his other deputy in charge of the five other prisoners, none of them worth a lick of salt. That's why he had the Kid chained to the floor. He pursed his lips and thought about returning to his office. Instead, he squatted by the Kid.

"You need anything?" he asked.

"You mean like a priest?"

Garrett nodded, although he had no idea what he had meant. He certainly hadn't even considered a priest. He didn't believe in God, or at least had doubts about His existence, and despite the Kid's singing in Sunday choir, he doubted if the Kid had much faith in the Almighty. "I didn't think you meant a hacksaw and a Winchester," the Kid said. "No, I'm fine, Juan Largo."

"You might ought to change your mind, my boy," Olinger said. "Your days are short."

"Oh, I don't know," the Kid replied cheerily. "There's many a slip 'twixt the cup and the lip."

Olinger snorted and slapped the Kid's head with his double-barrel. "You stupid little peckerwood, always laughin'. I hope you try somethin', hope you try to escape when I take you down for dinner, boy. See if you die laughin' . . . or cryin', like your pal John Jones."

The Kid had barely flinched when Olinger's shotgun struck his head, but now his grin reversed into a hard frown, and he craned his neck toward Olinger as far as he could, bound like he was. "What do you mean?"

"John Jones. He was a friend of yourn, wasn't he? Ma'am and Heiskell Jones's oldest boy?"

"What do you mean?"

Olinger patted the shotgun. "I gave him both loads a while back. Quite a mess, but not as messy as your carcass will be."

The Kid jerked around, his eyes burning through Garrett. "You hired this *cabrón*?"

Olinger's shotgun struck harder, and the Kid cried out in pain.

"That's enough, Bob," Garrett said.

Olinger cursed underneath his breath and walked away, sitting down in a rocking chair by the window.

"I have to leave for White Oaks," Garrett began, just to say something.

"Collecting taxes, Sheriff?" The Kid tried to look smug, but Garrett saw through that facade. He was upset, the look of death in those cold eyes, and Garrett could not forget that time in Fort Sumner when the Kid had shot Joe Grant dead. The Kid wanted to kill Bob Olinger; Garrett couldn't blame him. He didn't care much for Olinger himself, but he had a job to do. The Kid had chosen his path. Garrett had picked his. Neither could turn back now.

"No, Billy." He stood slowly. "I'll be buyin' lumber for your gallows."

April 28, 1881
Lincoln, New Mexico Territory

Ira Leonard had visited him that morning, making the Kid wonder if the lawyer had been appointed his shadow. The man never let up, even though his visit had been to inform the Kid that Governor Wallace had no plans of clemency— as if that were a surprise.

A parade of visitors had followed. Green Wilson, Sam Corbet, and a couple of Mexican teenage girls came by, Wilson just to say hello, the girls to giggle and bat their eyes. Corbet had been a clerk in John Tunstall's store. The Kid didn't know him well, and didn't know why the man, nervous and pale, had decided to pay him a visit . . . until he mentioned José Aguayo's name.

José was a friend.

"How is José?" the Kid asked. He fought the urge to look at Bell and Olinger, standing by the window, or the other prisoners near him. He had been sold down the river by his cellmates too many times in the past, but as long as Corbet and he spoke in a code, as long as the clerk didn't soil his britches and arouse suspicion, it would be all right.

"He's fine." Corbet's teeth chattered. "Digging a new . . . privy. Should be finished this afternoon."

The Kid clucked his tongue. "Glad it's not me. Tell him I said howdy."

Privy. Corbet left. He had delivered his message. Now the Kid had to wait.

Suppertime came, and Olinger replaced his shotgun in the gun rack with a Winchester. It was his day to escort the other prisoners across the street to the Wortley Hotel to eat, leaving J. W. Bell to guard the Kid.

As soon as Bell saw Olinger and the others crossing the dusty street, he made a beeline for the Kid. "Tell me, Billy, about the time you shot Joe Grant." Bell's eyes gleamed like a schoolboy's. "Pat never speaks of it, though I heard he was there. Did Chisum hire Grant to kill you? And how'd you get those bullets out of his gun?"

The Kid laughed. "Let me tell the story, will you?" He told it without embellishment, pausing for effect, laughing along with Bell, although he found it hard to tell a story dramatically with his hands bolted to the floor. When he finished, Bell slapped his thigh and shook his head.

"Kid, you beat all I ever saw. I mean, you are a mess."

"Yeah, and I'm about to mess in my britches. Can we go to the outhouse now?"

"Can't you wait? Bob'll be back with the other boys, and I can take you then before we go eat our supper. Sam's serving roast beef and mashed taters."

He sucked in his stomach, pressed his lips together, swallowed, and shook his head. "Don't think I can hold it, J. W. Unless you want to mop the floor."

With a chuckle, Bell pulled a key from his vest pocket. He unlocked the chain securing the Kid's hands and feet to the hardwood floor and stepped away, drawing his revolver and thumbing back the hammer. "Now, be slow when you stand up, Billy."

"Put that thing down, J. W. You know me better than that."

The gun did not waver. "You know me better, Billy. Pat would nail my hide to the barn if I let you get away."

He stretched, his smile widening, and held out his hand-cuffed wrists with a pleading look, but Bell shook his head slowly. "They stay on, Billy. You know the rules."

After another laugh, the Kid walked to the staircase, gripping the rail as he carefully made his way down, trying not to trip on the leg irons. Bell kept a safe distance behind him, and they went through the back door and hurried to the privy.

As the Kid opened the door, he turned to Bell again. "Reckon there's no point in me asking if you'd take these bracelets off till after I finish my business."

"That's right, Billy. Hurry up, will you? And close that door."

Inside the reeking privy, he unbuttoned his trousers and lowered them about his raw ankles, then sat on the toilet and started humming *The Bonnie Blue Flag* as he thumbed through the stack of newspapers on his right. He almost lost his breath when he found the short-barreled single-action Colt, grunted for effect, and began whistling.

"How can you whistle in there?" Bell called out.

He didn't answer. *Good old José Aguayo.* Maybe that had been his problem. He had befriended too many *gringos* in his day, and they never proved loyal—not like a Mexican. Even Mexican girls, like Paulita, had more loyalty than American hussies, like Sallie Chisum. He finished, pulled up his pants, and stuck the revolver in the waistband, covering the butt with his untucked shirt.

Outside, he found Bell waiting, .45 still drawn but no longer cocked.

The Kid looked truly happy. "Sometimes," he said, "that's better than a good lay."

Bell waved the barrel about his nose. "Christ, Billy, shut that door." Gagging, he stepped aside.

The Kid just laughed and walked back to the courthouse. He could do it now—but no, that had problems. He was still in irons, and Olinger would come quickly, armed with a rifle instead of that short-range shotgun. *Shotgun! Yeah.* He had plans for Mr. Bob Olinger. He held the door open for Bell, but the deputy stopped. "You first, Billy."

"You're too cautious, J. W. We're pals." Seeing that Bell

wouldn't take the bait, the Kid let out another laugh, stepped inside, and, Bell behind him, headed up the stairs, waiting, waiting . . . finally tripping himself on the top stair, yelping in pain as he slammed face-first to the floor.

Bell quickly holstered his gun and knelt over him.

"You all right, Billy?" he said urgently and rolled the Kid over, gasping when he spotted the Colt in the Kid's hand, crying out as the barrel smashed against his skull. Bell tumbled backward, bouncing halfway down the stairs before stopping his slide. He pulled himself up, shook his bloody head, and stared at the cocked revolver aimed at him. It took a few seconds for everything to register.

"Billy . . . ," he began.

"I don't want to shoot you, J. W." He kept his voice cordial. "Just stand up and toss me the keys to these handcuffs."

"You can't get away, Billy. Don't be a fool—"

"They can't hang me but once, J. W." The friendliness left his voice, and he waved the gun barrel slightly. "Move."

Bell stood on wobbly feet, wiped the blood off his forehead, and blinked. The Kid gestured again with the revolver.

"You wouldn't shoot me in the back, Billy," Bell said and turned around. "We're pals."

He couldn't believe the dumb bastard. "Bell!" he cried out as the deputy started down the stairs. "Damn it, J. W.!" Bell bolted down the last few steps, and the Kid fired, catching the deputy in the small of his back, smashing him against the first-story wall, knocking a calendar to the floor. Bell groaned, reached for the door, and the Kid shot again but jerked the trigger, missing as the deputy hurled himself outside.

It had all gone to hell. He cursed, shoved the Colt into his trousers again, grimacing from the heat of the barrel. He hopped to the gun case, grabbed Olinger's shotgun, struggled to make it to the open window facing the Wortley. He expected to see Bell round the corner soon but didn't. Here came Bob Olinger, though, Winchester in his hands. He had apparently left his prisoners at the hotel.

"Bob!" a voice shouted from behind the courthouse. "The Kid has killed Bell."

Olinger stopped underneath a tree, wet his lips, unsure of what to do. The Kid had no indecision, however, and a clear target. He thumbed back both hammers. Olinger must have heard the clicks, or perhaps he merely felt the Kid's presence. He looked up at the corner window.

The Kid smiled. "Hello, Bob," he said before pulling both triggers.

Ira Leonard mouthed a silent prayer as he rode into town at dusk. The bodies of Olinger and Bell lay on the courthouse porch, covered with blood and flies. Back in Missouri, a sight like this would have brought out everyone in town—kids, ladies, and preachers—and a half-dozen photographers, but in Lincoln the citizens were more respectful of the dead, and the nearest photographer hung his hat in Las Vegas. Long-faced Green Wilson, Sam Wortley, and old Godfrey Gauss stood beside the corpses. Leonard swung down from the saddle and tethered his horse to the hitching rail.

"What happened?" He already knew the answer.

"It was the Kid," Wortley replied. "He shot Bell in the back, then blew Bob apart with his own shotgun."

"How did it happen? How did he get a gun?"

Wortley shrugged. Wilson shook his head. They looked at Gauss, who sat down with a sigh. "I was out in my garden," the gardener said, "when I heard the shots. I hurried over to see what was going on, and J. W. ran into my arms. By the time I laid him on the ground, he was dead. I yelled to warn Bob, but the Kid shot him dead. Then he made me fetch him a pickaxe and bring him the keys to his handcuffs. He got the handcuffs off but could only knock the chain off one of his ankles. That took him about an hour. He also had me go saddle a horse." The old man stared up at Leonard. "He asked for your horse, Mr. Leonard, but you weren't here."

"No one did anything," Wortley said in disgust. "Everyone was too damned scared." He quickly added: "I was home, didn't hear about it until Justice Wilson came for me."

Gauss came to the defense of the citizens of Lincoln. "Sam, these people haven't forgotten what the Kid's done.

He killed Brady and Hindman less than three hundred yards from this very spot. Ain't nobody going up against the likes of him when he's just murdered two more peace officers." He looked at Leonard. "We brought him another horse, Billy Burt's blue roan. The Kid said he'd send the horse back." Gauss sighed again as he stared at the bloody bodies. "He said he was sorry to have to shoot J. W. Said he couldn't help it. Then he walked over to Olinger, kicked his boot, and said, 'You are not going to round me up again.' He smashed the shotgun in two pieces and threw 'em on Bob's body. He cussed him a mite more, then loped out of here. He was armed, well-armed, with a couple of Winchesters and several pistols."

"How long ago?"

"Two hours," Wilson answered. "Happened right about suppertime."

"Where's the sheriff?"

"We sent Sam Corbet off to White Oaks to fetch him back," Gauss said. He shook his head. "It's all started over again, ain't it, Mr. Leonard?"

He did not know how to answer.

Chapter 33

*"I wasn't the leader of any gang—I was for Billy all
the time."*

—Billy the Kid

May 7, 1881
Fort Sumner, New Mexico Territory

The fact that Billy Burt's horse had gotten loose made the
Kid laugh. No doubt, once the roan came back to town, the
good folks of Lincoln would brag that William H. Bonney
was a man of his word. The truth, however, was the mare had
been spooked by the Kid's dangling leg chain, had bucked
him off more than once because of that, and finally, near
Agua Azul, had left him tasting gravel and loped toward Lincoln.

His chains were off now. Afoot, he had drifted into the settlement of Las Tablas, where José Aguayo and a frightened
but friendly Yginio Salazar knocked off the leg irons and put
salve on the Kid's ugly, raw wrists and ankles. He ate and
slept, taught Aguayo's nine-year-old boy a new card trick,
and, four days later, walked away, carrying a Winchester carbine, pocket Remington, and .41 Thunderer. He left the other
weapons with Aguayo as payment for his hospitality and
help.

Salazar had offered him the use of his horse, but the Kid
declined. He wouldn't leave these people afoot, even Salazar,
didn't want the Mexican population to start having doubts
about *El Chivato*.

He chuckled now as he walked into Fort Sumner at night, recalling prosecutor Simon Newcomb's closing argument.

"*El Chivato,*" Newcomb had said, eyes facing the jurors but pointing a long finger at the Kid. "You know what that means, better than us white men. A friendly insult, a young he-goat, a *kid,* but there is more to that. *El Chivato* is a fighter, one who strikes quicker than a rattlesnake, even deadlier than that serpent. He is not your friend. He is not anyone's friend. He is a sneak, a betrayer. He is a vicious, cold-blooded killer who shot down two peace officers without provocation, without warning, without mercy. He must be hanged."

Hearing horses, he pulled back the Winchester's hammer and ducked behind one of the cottonwood trees the soldier boys had made the Navajo prisoners plant along the road in the early '60s. He became aware of his own heart pounding as the horses rode toward him, away from the settlement. The last time he had come to Fort Sumner to see Paulita Maxwell, Big Tom O'Folliard had gotten killed. Did Pat Garrett know him that well, know that he would come to be near her, to hide out with his friends here, rather than try for Old Mexico or even Texas?

Hearing their voices, he relaxed, although he remained deep in the darkness. The riders were *vaqueros* most likely, speaking in Spanish, laughing, smoking cigarettes as they returned to some *rancho* after having a few rounds.

He waited five minutes after they passed before continuing to the old Army post, quiet and dark with the departure of the *vaqueros.* He located Pete Maxwell's big house, kept close to the wall until he found the right window, glad to find it open. He tapped on the sill. Nothing, so he crawled inside, leaned the rifle against the wall, and saw a figure in the bed. He tiptoed closer and knelt beside her. She looked so angelic, in such a deep sleep, he didn't want to wake her. But . . . he pressed his hand over her mouth, and the eyes jerked open and fingernails dug into his arm.

"Paulita," he said urgently in Spanish, "it's me. Be quiet." He repeated this, and finally she calmed down.

"*Billito?*" she asked hesitantly when he removed his hand.

Before he could answer, she had thrown her arms around him and kissed his sunburned lips.

May 30, 1881
Santa Fe, New Mexico Territory

Lew Wallace embraced his friend and colleague warmly outside the Palace of the Governors. A Dougherty wagon was parked on the Plaza, the driver patiently waiting to take Wallace to the railroad. In a few days, he would be back home with Susan in Crawfordsville, and this backwoods blight on the universe would be but a distant memory. In a short time he would be in Istanbul, the United States minister to Turkey, where perhaps he would begin work on another religious novel, or maybe his autobiography. President Garfield had finally come through, given him a worthwhile appointment. Now that he was leaving, his popularity had trebled. Territorial newspapers had lauded him for his accomplishments, stopping the turmoil and bloodshed in Colfax and Lincoln counties, dealing with the Apache menace. Even the Ring-controlled *Santa Fe New Mexican* had praised him.

His only boil would be the legacy of Billy the Kid. Pat Garrett had telegraphed him, saying he could not fulfill the governor's death warrant because the prisoner had escaped. Wallace had put out another five-hundred-dollar reward for the delivery of the outlaw, but now that he was leaving the territory, the Kid would be Acting Governor Ritch's problem. Not his.

"I shall miss your company, your virility in our pursuit of justice," Wallace said. "I know we have had our differences, but I love you as I would a brother. I wish you well, Ira."

"Safe travels, General," Leonard said. "*Vaya con Dios.*"

"*Siempre.*" Wallace laughed. "You see, I have learned some of the culture, some of the language." He handed his valise to a Mexican orderly, who stored it in the ambulance with the rest of his luggage. "What are your plans?"

Leonard shrugged. "I have clients in Lincoln, White Oaks, and Las Vegas, but I am thinking of settling down in

Socorro. I stopped there a few times on the railroad. It's quieter than those three burgs, and I am tired."

"Our fight aged you considerably, and I am not only referring to your white hair. I pray that you have no plans of representing the Kid anymore."

Shaking his head, Leonard reached into his coat pocket and pulled out a folded letter, which he opened and handed to the departing governor.

Judge Leonard:

I finally figured out why you have been fighting for me so hard, even after Judge Bristil removed you & sentenced me to die. You figure that General Wallace's book about God helped save your soul, so now that you been born again, you're bound & determined to save me.

Well, I don't have complaints with Christians, but you're giving God all the glory for all the wrong reasons. Rev. Ealy, he is a God-fearing man, always has been, always will be, but you took the high road after you got shot at & almost choked to death on your own tongue. That isn't Christianity—it's cowardice.

Sorry to be so blunt, but I figured this will end our relationship. Enjoy heaven if you get there. Don't look for me, though. I'll be tormenting Bob Olinger down in hades.

> *Your obedient servant,*
> *W. H. Bonney*

Wallace sighed and folded the letter before returning it to Leonard. "He is a vulgar miscreant, unworthy of another thought, another second of your time. Let Sheriff Garrett handle him, Ira."

"He had a certain charm—"

"When it suited him. As God as my witness, I do not know what you see in that vile little boy, why you still fight for him."

Leonard's smile held no mirth. He pocketed the letter and shoved his hands in the mule-ear pockets of his trousers. "As the general knows too well, I was once a vile, middle-aged man, a vulgar miscreant. You saw more in me, sir. You fought for me. And you helped save me from the fires of hell."

Wallace's face warmed. "You saved yourself, Ira, with the help of our Lord Jesus Christ. What I saw in you was a brave man, a good man, a fighter for justice, a fine lawyer. You were never vulgar, never vile, never a miscreant." He offered a rare mischievous grin. "Well, never too much of a miscreant."

They shook hands again before the driver helped Wallace into the ambulance.

June 18, 1881
Fort Sumner, New Mexico Territory

Bless her heart, Paulita did not want him to go to the *baile* that night, but the Kid was in the mood to dance. He had been hiding out around Fort Sumner and Taiban for more than a month, and no one had come looking for him, asking questions, arousing suspicion. It was like Pat Garrett was scared to come to Fort Sumner, or maybe he was the Kid's friend after all.

But he figured that Garrett and the other law dogs simply believed what the Kid had told Old Godfrey Gauss before riding out of Lincoln back in April: "You won't find me this side of Ireland."

His skin had darkened underneath the blistering sun of the Staked Plains, so he could pass himself off as a Mexican. At least twice, he had done so, speaking fluent Spanish and laughing like he hadn't a care in the world when he walked into the saloon to find it occupied by strangers. He would play his role again, if needed, at the *baile* tonight.

He had promised Paulita the first four dances and Deluvina the next two. When the guitar player broke a string during the middle of his second dance with Deluvina, he escorted her to a table, then headed for the bar to fetch them some lemonade and himself a cup of coffee.

Pete Maxwell, Paulita's brother, was tending bar. He looked about as happy as a grizzly in a bear trap.

"*Billito*," Maxwell said dryly as he filled a cup with black coffee.

"Pete. I see they are keeping you busy on this night," he said in Spanish. "If you would like to dance, I will be happy to relieve you behind the bar."

Maxwell shook his head, found two clean glasses, and filled those with lemonade. As he slid them toward the Kid, he looked past him, and his eyes narrowed. He lowered his head and whispered, "A stranger, *Billito*."

"*Gracias*." He pulled his sombrero down low and sipped his coffee.

"It is not safe for you here, *Billito*," Maxwell said. "No more. You should go, ride to Texas, ride to Mexico."

"Coffee isn't as tasty as yours in Texas or Mexico, Pete."

Maxwell's eyes became slits. "It is not my coffee that you find tasty."

The Kid laughed, and he turned to English. "So that's what has you riled. Pete, we've been pals for a good long time. You should know my intentions with your sister are honorable."

Maxwell hissed something and backed away, staring at the fellow who now stood beside the Kid. He felt the stranger's eyes on him but didn't turn to face him. Instead, he took another sip of coffee, then lowered his hand below the bar, hooking his thumb in his waistband near the pocket Remington. He cursed himself for speaking in English, for joking with Pete about Paulita. He should have listened to Paulita's brother and left the minute the stranger entered the saloon.

"Kid? Is that you, Kid?"

The man gripped his shoulders, spun him around, and the Remington was in the Kid's right hand, cocked and pointed at the cowboy's belly—only the smiling stranger didn't notice. He was grinning like some drunk, fingers digging into the Kid's shoulders. He let go to let out a Rebel Yell.

"Kid Antrim! I thought for sure the Apaches had your scalp hangin' in some wickiup!"

He blinked. *Apaches do not scalp,* he thought, and started to correct this simpleton, whose face twisted into an even bigger smile. Recognition pounded him like a sledgehammer. It couldn't be, but there he stood. The Kid quickly lowered the Remington's hammer and put the pistol away.

"Tom?" he asked.

"Tom O'Keefe in the flesh, pardner. Lemme stand you to a beer."

His mind raced back to September of '77, when he had left La Mesilla with his new friend, Tom O'Keefe, when they had been jumped by Apaches on the way to Lincoln County to find work, to start a new life, to disappear in the countryside.

"I thought you were dead." The words were slow to form.

"Thought the same of you, Kid," O'Keefe said. He put a mug of beer in the Kid's hand, then hoisted his own. "By god, *amigo,* it's mighty good to see you." The glasses clinked, and O'Keefe downed most of his beer in two or three swallows. The Kid took a tentative sip, not liking the bitter taste, and set his mug on the bar.

The music had started again, and most of the patrons had moved to the dance floor. He tried to find Paulita, but she was dancing with Jesus Silva. Deluvina sat talking to Manuela Bowdre, and the Kid figured it prudent not to pester Charlie's widow, leaving him stuck with O'Keefe.

"What happened?" the Kid asked.

"You mean in the Guadalupes?" O'Keefe finished his beer. "The Apaches come down shootin' an' screamin', an' I jumped on my horse. Fired a couple of times. I yelled for you. But they was just too many of 'em. I rode, bareback, all the way to that mick's ranch. Came back lookin' for you but didn't find no trace, an' I figured you was dead, that they had carried you off to be tortured by them squaws. After that, I had seen enough of New Mexico Territory, so I drifted back to Texas. Been workin' on a ranch in Tom Green County. We drove some beeves to Fort Stanton, an' I come by here to cut the dust. Goin' to Anton Chico to see my sister." He turned suddenly sober. "Hell, Kid, I'm sorry I abandoned you like that. There was just too many to fight. I figured we was both dead."

He nodded dumbly. For almost four years, he had thought he had abandoned Tom O'Keefe to die.

"What you been doin' with yourself, Kid?"

"Guess you don't read the newspapers," he said and immediately regretted it. Maybe the story of Billy the Kid had not gotten all the way to Tom Green County, Texas.

"Nope. Don't read the newspapers, nor nothin' else. Never learnt my letters."

"I'm a newspaper correspondent," the Kid lied. "I'm going by the name Ash Upson." That little joke made his grin return, though only briefly.

Hell, he *had* abandoned Tom O'Keefe. He wondered what would have happened if he, like O'Keefe, had returned to Pat Coghlan's place in Tularosa, if he had met O'Keefe again, maybe drifted to Texas and disappeared there. No Lincoln County . . . no Buckshot Roberts . . . no William Brady . . . no Jessie Evans . . . no Tunstall, McSween, Garrett, Leonard, Dolan, Bristol, or Murphy.

He picked up the beer and drank.

Chapter 34

"Advise persons never to engage in killing."
—Billy the Kid

July 10, 1881
Roswell, New Mexico Territory

Even the peppermint candy he sucked on like a cigar failed to mask the whisky on postmaster Ash Upson's breath. Writing tablets, newspapers, and a couple of leather-bound books littered the countertop, which Upson tried to clear before Ira Leonard passed him a letter.

"How is Sheriff Garrett's novel coming along?" Leonard asked.

"It's a book, sir." Indignant, Upson stuck the candy atop his ear the way a carpenter would hold a pencil and folded his arms. "Not fiction."

"Oh." Leonard slid him a coin.

"I need an ending, of course, but the Kid's escape makes things much more interesting." Excited again, the inebriate tried to pick up the nearest paper, a Cincinnati edition, but fumbled with it because of his sticky fingers, and the guts of the *Commercial* fluttered to the floor, the front and back pages glued by peppermint. He tore it away, letting the rest of the paper fall, and, wiping his hands on his sleeve garters, found another newspaper, from Boston, and held it up with a smile. "The boy's getting publicity in the States, thanks to his escape. Now the book's bound to sell, make me and Pat rich."

Leonard waited for his change. "I'm sure J. W. Bell's family is happy for you."

The sarcasm didn't register, and Upson stamped the letter, slid Leonard his pennies, and went back to his manuscript, chewing on his thumb instead of candy. The Kid had been popular, but Leonard didn't think the excitement would last, not since a madman named Charles Guitteau had shot down President Garfield at a Washington train depot. No one would remember William H. Bonney in a week, except those living in New Mexico Territory, and few of those would buy a book about *El Chivato.*

Leaving Upson to his writing, Leonard stopped underneath the awning outside, trying to determine his next course. He was here on business, to meet with John Chisum, but his client was late. Roswell was hot, dusty, and small, practically deserted, and his options were limited. He removed his hat, ran fingers through his sweaty hair, and debated on going to the hotel, café, or finding a bench in the shade.

"Good afternoon, Ira."

He almost dropped the hat when he saw Susan McSween. He discovered his vocabulary, returned her greeting, and donned the big black Stetson. "What brings you to Roswell?" he asked.

"I'm meeting with Pitzer Chisum this evening," she said, "to discuss buying one of his bu—one of his he-cows—and some stock for . . ." She gave up on trying to practice Victorian mores. "Some heifers for breeding. And you?"

"I'm meeting with John. Legal matters."

Her smile seemed radiant. "The Chisums live by their own clock, as usual. Could I offer you a glass of tea?" Her head tilted toward the jacal that passed for a café.

It was too hot to stay inside, so they took their drinks onto the veranda, staring at the empty street, talking about nothing in particular, never bringing up their personal relationship that had ended months ago. Sue had never been one to live in the past. She was a lot like Bonney in that regard.

Leonard spotted the dust first, rising in the east. Three riders, and for a moment he thought it might be the Chisums, but the lead horseman was too tall, and when the distance had closed to fifty yards, Leonard recognized Pat Garrett. He didn't know the other two men, but Susan McSween did.

"The big one's John Poe," she said. He looked a bit like Garrett, only much heavier and a tad shorter. "The other is Kip McKinney. His new deputies. Looks like they've worn out their horses again."

He could understand why. People were seeing Bonney everywhere in the territory, and newspapers kept publishing the sightings. Back in May, Leonard had been at the *Las Vegas Daily Optic* to place an advertisement for his legal practice when a reporter brought in a dirty waif, announcing, "I've found the Kid." A couple of tramp printers, appreciating the humor, decided to better the joke. Leonard remembered the item in the paper the following day: "The printers placarded him in large letters, 'Billy, the Kid,' and turned him loose upon the community."

"Do you think they'll ever find Billy?" Sue asked.

He finished his drink. "He's likely a thousand miles from here by now . . ." *If he's smart,* he thought about adding. The lawmen left their horses at the livery stable and entered the nearest *cantina,* across the street from Diego's Café.

"A friend of mine in White Oaks said her brother saw the Kid at a dance in Fort Sumner," she said. "Said he was living with some sheepherders at Arroyo Taiban."

"I've heard he was hiding out in East Las Vegas . . . Puerto de Luna . . . Taos . . . Raton . . . Silver City . . . Golden . . . even Santa Fe . . ." He turned back to her with a smile.

Shaking her head, she looked down the road again. More dust. This had to be the Chisums.

"It's John," she said. "No sign of Pitzer."

He didn't follow her finger pointing to the approaching horseman. A short man exiting the *cantina* had commanded his attention. The fellow looked up and down the street, then slid around the adobe wall like some petty thief, disappearing down the alley.

"Pete Maxwell . . ."

Sue turned to him. "What did you say, Ira?"

Garrett and his two new deputies exited next, batwing doors banging, and walked toward the stable. The lanky sheriff stopped, turned, hollered for Poe to get fresh horses, and hurried to postmaster Ash Upson's office inside the little mercantile. By then, John Chisum had reined up at Diego's.

"Hello, Mr. Leonard," Chisum drawled. "Sorry to have kept you waitin'. Good day to you, Missus McSween. Brother Pitzer says he'll be along directly. He's feelin' poorly . . . like me."

Leonard shook hands with Chisum after the cowman dismounted. Chisum wanted to wash up, put on a clean shirt, and suggested that they discuss their legal affairs over supper. "You're welcome to join us, Missus McSween," he added. "I'm sure brother Pitzer will be here by then. Shall we accompany you to the hotel, ma'am?"

Leonard didn't want to go to the hotel. He wanted to cross the street but knew he couldn't. His obligation was to his client, John Chisum. Garrett was hurrying from the postmaster's office to the stables. *The Kid is no longer your affair,* Leonard told himself. *He told you as much in his letter.*

Bonney had been wrong, however, about Leonard's obsession, had been wrong about Leonard. He shook away an image that had haunted him for two years, tried to block out his concern about the meeting between Pat Garrett and Pete Maxwell. When they reached the one-story adobe hotel, Leonard left Chisum at the desk and escorted Sue to her room facing the courtyard.

"What's the matter?" she asked.

"Nothing," he started, but she gave him one of her dubious looks, and he sighed.

His hat came off, and he collapsed in a rocking chair on the *portal* outside her room. He had wanted to tell someone for a long time but hadn't even known how to bring this up to a priest.

"You remember when Jessie Evans and the boys tried to kill me back in Lincoln?"

"I'm not likely to forget." He felt her arms on his shoulders, the way she used to massage them. The tension slowly faded.

"I remember . . . seeing my body on the floor that night, like I was some haunt hovering about the ceiling." He waited for a cynical snicker, only none came. "It was my body, but then it wasn't. It was Billy Bonney's, a bullet in his heart, and we were no longer in the Wortley, but some other place. I was standing over his body, shaking my head, tears running down my face. Someone was screaming at Pat Garrett, but all I heard was my own voice, gripping Billy's limp, cold hand, reciting *The Lord's Prayer* but wondering why I hadn't done anything to stop this, why I couldn't have saved him." He shuddered and shook his head. "I guess that's why I worked so hard as his lawyer."

"It was a dream, Ira," she whispered. "That's all it was. Not God speaking to you, though I am glad you found Him. You'd be dead if you hadn't. You would have killed yourself drinking, would have become another Lawrence Murphy or Jimmy Dolan, a sick, mean drunkard. You did your best to help Billy, but he doesn't want anyone's help. He never did. It was just a bad dream. Forget it."

He wished he could.

July 14, 1881
Fort Sumner, New Mexico Territory

Her fingers pressed deeper into the muscles along his naked shoulders, but he seemed unresponsive. She leaned over, kissed the nape of his neck, then gave up on her massage and wrapped her arms tightly across his chest.

"Why are you so melancholy?" Paulita Maxwell asked him in Spanish. "I want my old *Billito* to return. You are too sad, *mi corazón*. You have not been happy since that cowboy talked to you at the *baile,* and months have passed since he left."

"Not quite a month," the Kid corrected her.

"It is true. Yet it feels much longer."

She eased him down onto her bed and kissed his lips gently. At last he responded, running his fingers through her hair. "I have been thinking that I should leave," he told her in English, saw she did not comprehend, and repeated it in Spanish. "Would you come with me?"

Her eyes danced. "You know I would, *mi Billito*. Where would we go?"

"Does it matter?"

"No, as long as I am with you."

After they made love, he jumped out of bed, his eyes bright, like the old *Billito* she had known and loved, but still a bit distant. He pulled on his trousers, reached for his revolver, thought better of it, and said, "I'm hungry. Are you?"

"*Sí.*" She told him her brother had butchered a calf that morning, if he felt like carving some steaks. "I will cook it for you if you bring it to me."

"I'll meet you in the kitchen," he said. He started for the door but turned around and picked up a piece of jewelry, one of her necklaces. She couldn't tell which one. He fastened it around his neck, picked up his butcher knife, blew her a kiss, and left. He had never worn one of her necklaces before, but then he was always doing things to surprise her. He had also never gone anywhere without a revolver or rifle, but at least he had the knife.

Pat Garrett reined up in the shadows and dismounted in the peach orchard, motioning for McKinney and Poe to do the same. He licked his lips as he stared at Pete Maxwell's big adobe house shining underneath the full moon. No one spoke as the sheriff surveyed the parade grounds while removing his spurs. The two deputies did the same.

"Let's go," Garrett said at last, and they hobbled their horses in the darkness and cautiously approached Maxwell's house, stopping at the picket fence, listening again.

"You fellows wait here while I go in and talk to Pete," Garrett said. Poe and McKinney stared at him curiously but said nothing. They hadn't heard what Pete Maxwell had told him in Roswell a few days ago; they didn't need to know. He opened the gate, closed it, and pulled softly on the single-action Frontier Model .44-40 holstered on his right hip.

"Christ, Pat," McKinney whispered. "It's gotta be midnight. You sure you want to barge in? Maxwell might shoot you for some thief."

"He won't," Garrett said. "You boys keep your eyes open. The Kid might be here."

McKinney snorted, shaking his head. They had been looking everywhere for the Kid, hadn't seen a hair, but they had never been to Fort Sumner. Garrett hadn't thought Little Casino would be foolish enough to stay in the territory, but he had not considered Paulita Maxwell's influence, at least not until Pete Maxwell met him in that Roswell *cantina*. Poe simply stared at the house.

"Keep to the shadows," Garrett said. "Stay in them bushes."

Garrett walked nervously to the sprawling house. He wiped his sweaty palms on his pants trousers when he stopped on the porch, then moved as quietly as he could to Maxwell's room on the southeast corner. It was a hot night, and Maxwell had left his windows and door open. Garrett was thankful for that. He took a tentative step, but the floorboard underneath his boot squeaked, and he froze, right hand gripping the Colt's handle tighter. Nothing. No sound except Maxwell's snoring. Garrett was thankful for that, too.

A door hinge squeaked, and he quickly ducked into Maxwell's bedroom, waiting for his eyes to adjust to the darkness before walking quietly to the bed. He tugged on Maxwell's arm with his left hand. "Pete?" he said. "Pedro?"

The snoring sputtered, stopped, and Maxwell opened his eyes.

"Is he here?" Garrett asked.

Maxwell swallowed. "With . . ." He couldn't finish, although he almost spit out the rest. He didn't have to say more. Garrett understood, but that raised another problem. He had no plans of charging into Paulita's bedroom, risking her life. He might be a lot of things, a man of political ambition, but he wouldn't hurt a woman if he could help it, even for a five-hundred-dollar reward, a big-selling book, and a hero's reputation.

He sighed. Maxwell sat up in the bed, started to tell him something else, but both men heard the soft footfalls outside.

Garrett drew his Colt, turning to face the door but seeing only the porch and ground illuminated by moonlight. Then he heard a voice.

"*Quién es? Quién es?*" A long pause, the question repeated. No answer came.

He knew that voice. He had heard it often enough, and he thumbed back the hammer as quietly as possible.

"*Quién es?*" More footsteps. Closer. "*Quién es?*" It was the Kid. Little Casino had spotted McKinney and Poe because of the full moon. A figure appeared in the doorway, a silhouette.

"*Pedro,*" the voice whispered, "*quiénes son estos hombres afuera?*"

Something glittered in the Kid's hand . . . if it was the Kid. Garrett couldn't be sure. He began to doubt himself. A moment earlier, he was certain this was his old friend. But now?

"*El es,*" Maxwell said.

Garrett fired. The flash blinded him, the noise deafened him, and he ducked to his left, cocking the Colt again, pulling the trigger once more. Ringing filled his ears, but he made out the whine of a ricochet, the almost simultaneous thud in the headboard—inches from Pete Maxwell's head.

Maxwell jumped from underneath his covers, bolted out of his room.

"Stop!" John Poe cried, and Garrett panicked as Maxwell screamed in his heavy Spanish accent, "*Don shoot! Don shoot!*"

Garrett took up the warning. "Don't shoot, boys!" he shouted at his deputies. "It's Pete Maxwell, for God's sake!" He ran after him, tripped, fell sprawling on the porch. He rolled over, cocking the Colt, expecting the Kid to put a bullet in his head, thinking the Kid had tripped him as he ran outside. He saw the knife on the floor, a hand beside it, its fingers curled and still.

"Pat!" McKinney's voice. "Pat, are you all right?"

The Kid hadn't tripped him. Garrett knew he had fallen over Little Casino's body.

McKinney's voice: "What the hell happened?"

He looked up, found the deputies standing over him. Poe helped him to his feet, and he motioned with the barrel toward the bedroom.

"That was the Kid," he said, barely recognizing his own voice. He cleared his throat. The ringing in his ears had stopped, but the bite of gunpowder hung heavy in the air. "I think I got him."

Poe stepped back, suddenly aghast. "Pat, the Kid wouldn't have come here. God, man, you've shot the wrong fellow."

"It was him," Garrett said. He took a step toward the doorway, but stopped, uncertain. "I'm sure it was him. I know his voice too well to be mistaken." Trying to convince himself.

He heard more footsteps, followed by the pounding of a horse's hooves.

Maxwell stood beside them, shaking in his nightshirt, which stunk of urine. Everyone stared at the knife and hand, all they could see in the darkened bedroom. Garrett faced the crowd gathering on the porch. He saw Paulita and Deluvina, the big girl holding the pretty one's hand. He couldn't be sure, but Paulita seemed to be crying. That restored his confidence, although his stomach still swayed.

"Fetch a candle," he said.

"You piss pot! You son of a bitch!"

A slap, a scream of anguish, and then a big man escorted Deluvina Maxwell out of the corner room. The girl lashed out at the deputy, cursing him—no, cursing someone behind him, someone still in the room—in Spanish before running down the porch and wrapping a young woman in her arms.

Paulita.

They disappeared, and all Ira Leonard heard was soft sobbing.

He sat in the saddle, his chest heaving, fighting for breath, knowing he was too late. *Just like in my vision.* He should have left Roswell and followed Garrett back on the tenth, but he had kept telling himself his duty was to John Chisum. Instead, he had saddled his horse a day later, after drawing up the cattle baron's last will and testament. He had ridden hard to get here. If he had left an hour earlier, if he had pushed the buckskin harder. If . . .

Muffled voices came from inside the corner room, and Leonard finally dismounted, feeling the glare of the deputy who had just thrown Deluvina out of Pete Maxwell's room, as he tethered his horse to the hitching rail and stepped up to meet John Poe's charge.

"Who are you?"

"I am William Bonney's attorney," he answered, and pushed his way past the leviathan.

Flickering candlelight filled the bedroom like a church, but it smelled of gunpowder, of sulfur and brimstone. *Like Hell must.* Or maybe it was his imagination. Pete Maxwell, Pat Garrett, and Kip McKinney stood over the body on the floor. McKinney was saying something about an inquest. Maxwell just looked sick. Poe stepped around Leonard and approached Garrett, whispered something to the sheriff, who only now noticed Leonard. Garrett stared at him briefly, dully, until recognition came.

"You're too late, counselor," Garrett said in a weak voice. "The Kid drew on me. I had no choice."

He looked around but saw no weapon. The lawmen had likely picked it up already. Outside, someone began strumming a guitar, and a ballad began in Spanish. He didn't understand the words.

Leonard removed his hat and knelt over the body. He brushed a stray lock off the corpse's forehead. Bonney's feet were bare, not even in stockings, and his trousers had been haphazardly buttoned. He wore no shirt. His eyes were closed. He looked so damned young, Leonard thought. A kid. A kid with a dark hole in his left breast, little blood. Death had likely been instant. At least there had been no suffering.

Something glittered about the dead man's throat, and Leonard reached over tentatively, fingered a gold chain, pulled it closer, felt the ornament attached and knew it was a crucifix. He fondled it gently, draped it over the hairless chest, then lifted Bonney's cold right hand, squeezing it tightly, and raised his own head as tears flowed into his beard.

Tears welled in the sheriff's eyes, too.

"Our Father," Leonard began . . .

Pat Garrett started to mouth the words with him, but quickly turned away.

Epilogue

*"It is now in order for Pat Garrett to be well
rewarded for his services in ridding the Territory of
this desperado. He is in very moderate
circumstances, but has spent many dollars in pursuit
of the 'Kid.'"*

—*Las Vegas Daily Optic,* July 18, 1881

*February 29, 1908
Alameda Arroyo, New Mexico Territory*

Pat Garrett was in his cups.

Which had typically been his state for more than twenty-five years.

The buckboard bounced across the ruts as he and young, drunk cowhand Carl Adamson made their way from Garrett's ranch toward Las Cruces to meet with Wayne Brazel. Last March, Brazel had signed a five-year agreement to lease Garrett's ranch to raise goats, which had sounded like a mighty good deal back then, only not now. In January, Deacon Jim Miller had offered to buy the whole damned spread, and Garrett needed the money. It would help his family, help get him out of debt. But first he had to get those damned goats off his property.

He was sick of smelling goats.

Adamson opened his flask, took a nip, and passed it to Garrett, who flipped the reins, shaking his head. They had already consumed Garrett's jug of liquor, and his kidneys were about to explode.

"I hear Billy the Kid was hung like a mule," Adamson said. "That's why all them ladies liked him so."

A grunt was Garrett's reply. He had grown sick of talking about Billy the Kid. His book, *An Authentic Life of Billy, the Kid, the Noted Desperado of the Southwest,* had sold poorly. Some folks blamed Ash Upson for that, but Upson had always been Garrett's friend. Garrett looked after the drunk, took care of him, bought him drinks, breakfast, until the journalist finally drank himself to death in 1894 while living on Garrett's Texas ranch.

The last time he had been in Fort Sumner, he had stopped at the Kid's grave. Someone had put up a marble monument with "Pals" carved in above the names of William H. Bonney, Tom O'Folliard, and Charles Bowdre. *Pals.* Like hell they were.

"By jingo, Pat, there's Brazel now."

His eyes focused slowly, and he almost ran over a goat that darted across the road. He pulled on the reins, slowing the buckboard as they approached the rider. It was Wayne Brazel. Garrett glanced at the Burgess folding shotgun resting between Adamson and him.

"You're supposed to have twelve hundred goats, Brazel," Garrett said, getting to the point, not waiting to discuss the matter civilly in a Las Cruces saloon. "There's a damn sight more than that. Can't travel a rod without smellin' goat shit and goat piss."

"That should suit you, you *hijo de cabrón*."

Garrett stopped the buckboard completely and reached for the shotgun. Brazel pushed back the tail of his coat and gripped a Colt .45 holstered on his right hip. Adamson gasped for breath, but the two men stopped.

The wind picked up, chilling Garrett, yet all he heard was the sound of goats. He moved his hand away from the shotgun and set the brake.

"How many goats do you have?"

"Eighteen hunnert, I warrant," Brazel said. "I'll sell 'em all to you, Garrett."

He couldn't afford to buy that many. His deal with Miller was souring again. Garrett felt the need for a drink, and he pulled off his right glove with his teeth, then asked Adamson for the flask. He took a sip, never taking his eyes off Brazel.

The only thing he had ever done right in his life had been killing the Kid, but what a price. Everything else had been a disaster. Hell, even that son of a bitch of a governor, Ritch, had haggled over paying him the five-hundred-dollar reward, although the territorial legislature and John Chisum had eventually footed the bill, and then some. Leaders of the Santa Fe Ring had chipped in, too—secretly, of course. He had used the money to buy this damned ranch, which had turned out to be nothing more than a crooked faro layout. You never could win.

He had failed as a custom's collector in El Paso, failed as a rancher, failed as a sheriff, failed as a friend to President Teddy Roosevelt, failed—especially—as a husband and father, although his wife always accepted him, even his dalliances with whores, his fondness of the bottle, his life as an agnostic.

Of course, he was still alive. Most of the men he had known back during the Lincoln County troubles were dead and gone. Doc Blazer had died maybe ten years ago. The Kid's pal, Henry Brown, had wound up as the marshal of Caldwell, Kansas, only he liked the life of an outlaw too much—like the Kid, in that regard—and tried to rob a bank in Medicine Lodge, where he was captured and gunned down by a lynch mob when he tried to escape.

Cancer took John Chisum up in Arkansas three or four years after the Kid's death, and his brothers' creditors foreclosed on the New Mexico ranch in 1891, ending that empire. Like Ash Upson, James Dolan drank himself to an early grave, and was buried in '98. Jessie Evans? He had escaped the Huntsville, Texas, prison and disappeared, but a story went that he had been gunned down over in Arizona Territory in '83. Billie Wilson had been pardoned in '85—the Ring's influence—and disappeared from New Mexico.

No one had won the Lincoln County War. Tunstall, McSween, and the Kid had been killed. Dolan had lost his business and all of his power. Garrett had lost his power and influence, too, not that he ever held much.

Judge Bristol retained his bench until the Democrats retook the White House, and he had resigned in 1885, retired to Deming, came down with the gout, and blew his brains out in 1890. Simon Newcomb had also put a Remington in his mouth in the Exchange Hotel in 1902.

Billy Mathews had died of pneumonia in Roswell almost four years ago. Juan Patrón . . . George Peppin . . . William Rynerson . . . Lew Wallace . . . Green Wilson . . . John Bail . . . they were all gone.

Garrett had taken Albert Fountain's death the hardest. The Mason who had defended the Kid in La Mesilla had tried to rid the territory of rustlers, but he and his eight-year-old son had been murdered by Oliver Lee and Jim Gililland, only no one ever found the bodies. That's what had brought Garrett back to New Mexico. He had been living in Ulvade, Texas, practically retired, when Fountain had disappeared in the spring of '96. Garrett had been brought back to solve the mystery, only he had failed at that, too. Lee and Gililland had been acquitted in 1899. Maybe he should have gone back to Texas afterward, but he still had this ranch, figured he would give New Mexico one more try. Besides, his wife wanted to be here, be closer to her relations. Maybe . . .

Even Ira Leonard was dead. That bulldog of a lawyer had hung his shingle in Socorro after the Kid's death, but his lung troubles returned, forcing him west for California. A few years later, he returned to New Mexico as Socorro's postmaster, where he died in 1889. He was only fifty-seven, never became a judge, didn't do much but preach the gospel and lick stamps, but they say the whole damned town turned out for his funeral.

Pat Garrett was pushing fifty-eight, only he felt twenty years older. He doubted if anyone would come to see him planted, except those who wanted to piss on his grave.

There were still some around, some who knew the stories but seldom spoke of them, like the Bacas, Coes, Kip McKinney, and John Poe, but they kept their distance from a man like Pat Garrett. Sallie Chisum Robert was living quietly on her ranch near Artesia with her husband and family, and Paulita Maxwell had wed shortly after the Kid's death. She still lived in Fort Sumner, guarded by that hellion, Deluvina. Had a good-looking kid, too, that looked a hell of a lot like Billy Bonney. Paulita's brother, Pete, had died at age fifty in '98. Sometimes, Garrett dreamed that Deluvina had found out it had been Pete who told Garrett where to find the Kid, and she had poisoned him. Old Pete never lived down how he ran screaming out of his bedroom the night Garrett killed the Kid. Folks in Fort Sumner had called him Don Shoot, even to his face.

Thomas B. Catron was still kicking, a rich man up in Santa Fe, probably even more powerful than he was a quarter-century ago. Susan McSween had remarried, to a lawyer named Barber, then gotten a divorce, and now lived in White Oaks, where she ran a big ranching operation. Hell, that old bitch raised cattle, made a fortune, while Garrett was stuck with goats and creditors.

"I want these goats off my land," Garrett said.

"Buy 'em all," Brazel answered. "Ain't that why we're goin' to Las Cruces?"

Garrett cursed, climbed down from the wagon, picked up the shotgun, and stepped a few paces off the road. He shifted the Burgess to his left hand, began unbuttoning his trousers with his right. "I gotta piss." He announced the obvious.

Briefly, he looked back at Adamson and Brazel, shook his head and muttered, "Well, damn you. If I don't get you off one way, I will another."

A young goat bolted from behind some rocks and yucca, and he backed away, almost spraying his trousers with urine. He blinked, shrouded by some alcoholic haze, heard the grating noise of the goats, only they no longer sounded like goats. The stinking kid, the one closest to him, lifted its head, pawed the earth, staring at him, its face turning into the boyish, grinning face of *El Chivato*.

He must be drunk, surrounded by a thousand Little Casinos. He heard the Kid's voice. "*Quién es?*" Then he heard something else, the triple-click of a revolver, and he started to turn, tried to raise the shotgun, unbutton his pants, and stop urinating all at the same time.

The bullet slammed into the back of his head, blew out a

chunk of bone, brains, and eyebrow as it exited, and he was on the ground as another slug slammed through his back and into his stomach.

Garrett tried to speak. He should have known better, should never had turned his back on a coward like Wayne Brazel. Or maybe this is what he had wanted. Maybe that was what Little Casino had wanted on a summer night almost twenty-seven years ago.

He heard Carl Adamson's voice, felt himself being rolled over. "This is hell." Adamson sounded far, far away.

His eyes fluttered, his head turned, and he saw those damned goats, a few of them, at least. The rest had scattered in a panic at the gunshots. Goats, but not goats. *El Chivato*. Little Casino. The Kid. Billy Bonney . . . laughing at him while he groaned.

Then the cold blackness swept over him.

Author's Note

Billy the Kid and the Lincoln County War have been chronicled countless times by historians and journalists, but scant attention has been paid to the 1881 trial in Mesilla that I have fictionalized in the preceding pages. The reason for that is simple: While the Kid and the range/merchants war received a lot of coverage (newspaper articles, government records, and letters) during the late 1870s and early 1880s, the actual trial was, to the utter frustration of historians and this novelist, pretty much ignored. Transcripts do not exist, or have not been located, and about the only noteworthy documents unearthed are the jury instructions requested by the defense and Judge Warren Bristol's charge to the jury. Neither Sallie nor John Chisum would have testified, and Sallie had already married William Robert by the time of the Kid's trial. Likewise, Susan McSween had remarried in 1880 and went on to become "the Cattle Queen of New Mexico." I kept them single for the sole purpose of narrative. Who really took the stand? Isaac Ellis, J. B. Mathews, Saturnino Baca, and Bonnie Baca were subpoenaed as prosecution witnesses, but no one can say with certainty if the Kid testified on his own behalf.

Still, I have tried to keep the trial as authentic as possible, substituting the Kid's letters, newspaper accounts, and testimony from Colonel Nathan Dudley's Court of Inquiry for some quotations in his testimony; however, my defense and rebuttal witnesses, and some prosecution witnesses, are pure speculation and imagination. Then again, many so-called histories about William H. Bonney, including Pat Garrett's *Authentic Life* and Walter Noble Burns's *The Saga of Billy the Kid,* are mostly pure speculation and imagination. Much of the Kid's life remains clouded by mystery, so why should his murder trial be any different?

Luckily, I am friends with two Kid historians and am thankful for their insight and help. Jon Tuska, who also happens to be my agent, is author of *Billy the Kid: His Life and Legend* (University of New Mexico Press, 1997), while Bob Boze Bell, executive editor of *True West* magazine, is author and artist of *The Illustrated Life and Times of Billy the Kid* (Tri Star-Boze Publications, 1996).

For the record, Ira Leonard became a born-again Christian between the time he first met the Kid and the Mesilla trial. There was an assassination attempt on Leonard's life in Lincoln, but who shot at him isn't known, although Jessie Evans or some other Murphy-Dolan man is a pretty good guess. Leonard might have been a womanizer—one of Isaac Ellis's sons, it's said, threatened him with a shotgun over a woman—but no one has ever linked him, personally, with Susan McSween. Her reputation, however, was often called into scandalous question—albeit by men holding grudges against her, such as Colonel Nathan Dudley—during the 1870s and 1880s, and she was rumored to have had affairs with John Chisum and Jim French.

The story of the Kid's travels with Tom O'Keefe might be the product of Garrett ghostwriter Ash Upson's imagination, although it could have some basis in fact. The chance meeting of the Kid and O'Keefe in Fort Sumner in 1881, however, is definitely the product of my imagination and not history. How well Pat Garrett knew the Kid, and where they first met, has never been verified, nor have the Kid's rumored relationships with Sallie Chisum (he did give her candy hearts) and Paulita Maxwell (she denied being his lover). Did Pete Maxwell sell out the Kid for his sister's sake? *Quién sabe?* That's also a question historians have never positively answered.

And, of course, there is always that nagging story that Garrett did *not* kill Billy Bonney at Fort Sumner, and that the Kid lived to a ripe old age as Brushy Bill Roberts. Another story that I heard in Lincoln says John Tunstall's father secretly brought Bonney to England to escape the Santa Fe

Ring's grasp. But put these stories into perspective. Jesse James, John Wilkes Booth, Bloody Bill Longley—even Adolph Hitler and JFK, if you read the tabloids, not to mention Elvis Presley—have all been rumored to have faked their deaths. It makes for good copy, but poor history. Garrett undoubtedly killed Billy the Kid that night. Ira Leonard's presence shortly thereafter comes from my imagination.

Bonney did not care for the editorial content of *Newman's Semi-Weekly,* which folded shortly after the Mesilla trial. Was it a mouthpiece for the Santa Fe Ring? I don't know. Likewise, the suicides of Warren Bristol and Simon Newcomb are not recorded by history. John Poe, however, allegedly did kill himself in Battle Creek, Michigan, in 1923.

Pat Garrett was murdered near Las Cruces in 1908, but who killed him remains a mystery. Wayne Brazel, who was grazing goats on Garrett's ranch, was acquitted in a trial, claiming self-defense (What was Garrett going to do? *Piss on him?*), but some historians believe Deacon Jim Miller pulled the trigger. Others point to Carl Adamson. Some claim a conspiracy because Garrett was getting too close to solving the Albert Fountain disappearance, although double jeopardy would have protected Oliver Lee and James Gililland. The remains of Fountain and his son, by the way, have never been found.

In addition to Bell's and Tuska's histories, many other books proved helpful in my research. They include: *Billy The Kid: The Story—The Trial,* by Randy Russell (The Crystal Press, 1994), which reproduces the meager documents pertaining to the trial; Maurice G. Fulton's *History of the Lincoln County War,* edited by Robert N. Mullin (University of Arizona Press, 1968); *Violence in Lincoln County 1869-1881,* by William A. Keleher (University of New Mexico Press, 1957); *Pat Garrett: The Story of a Western Lawman,* by Leon C. Metz (University of Oklahoma Press, 1974); *Billy the Kid: A Short and Violent Life,* by Robert M. Utley (University of Nebraska Press, 1989); *The Land of the Pueblos,* by Susan E. Wallace (John B. Alden, 1889); *Such Men as Billy the Kid: The Lincoln County War Revisited,* by Joel Jacobsen (University of Nebraska Press, 1994); *Jessie Evans:*

Lincoln County Badman, by Grady E. McCright and James H. Powell (Creative Publishing, 1983); Frederick Nolan's annotated edition of *Pat F. Garrett's The Authentic Life of Billy, The Kid* (University of Oklahoma Press, 2000) and Nolan's other seminal works—*The Lincoln War: A Documentary History* (University of Oklahoma Press, 1992) and *The West of Billy the Kid* (University of Oklahoma Press, 1998).

Dennis Hall and John Alba helped me with the Spanish, and attorneys Bonnie Bratton, Jay Goodman, and Mike Smith coached me through the law and offered courtroom scenarios. I also must thank the staff of the New Mexico State University Cooperative Extension Service's Rural Economic Development Through Tourism Project for letting me tag along on its 2002 Billy the Kid Familiarization Tour through Lincoln and De Baca counties. Thanks also go to DeAnn Kessler of the Lincoln State Monument, Scott Smith of Fort Sumner State Monument, the staffs of the New Mexico State Library and Archives in Santa Fe, and the National Archives in Washington, D.C., as well as the people of Mesilla, Lincoln, and Fort Sumner for their hospitality and help.

Johnny D. Boggs
Santa Fe, New Mexico
December 28, 2002

The Guns and Gavel Series
by
Spur Award-winning author
Johnny D. Boggs

Spark on the Prairie
The Trial of the Kiowa Chiefs

"A fine snapshot of history."
—Sandra Whiting

"Somewhere Louis L'Amour [is] giving this
young author a nod of approval."
—David Marion Wilkinson

0-451-20912-5

Also in this series:
Arm of the Bandit
0-451-20741-6

**Available wherever books are sold or
to order call 1-800-788-6262**